THE GOOD MUSLIM

- Re Camer
- Debi?!
- Sela ple
- Rybbis.

For my beautiful wife, son and daughter, whose patience,
support and loyalty have been humbling ...
living with a tortured genius all these years
cannot have been easy.

THE GOOD MUSLIM

SAS VETERAN'S GRIPPING DEBUT THRILLER

ALEX ANDERSON

BROWN
DOG
BOOKS

Published under licence by Brown Dog Books and The Self-Publishing Partnership, 7 Green Park Station, Bath BA1 1JB

www.selfpublishingpartnership.co.uk

ISBN printed book: 978-1-78545-255-0
ISBN e-book: 978-1-78545-256-7

Cover photo by Alex Anderson
Cover design by Kevin Rylands
Internal design by Andrew Easton

Printed and bound by CPI Group (UK) Ltd, Croydon, CR0 4YY

PROLOGUE

COUNTY TYRONE, ULSTER. 1987.

In the grey half-light of dawn, he felt the fury of the storm as it flailed and buffeted the scrawny tree line. Curtains of rain, driven sideways by a howling wind, lashed down at the huddled line of men. His borrowed cap and clothes were soaked, and water gathering at his collar now began to snake down his spine. Looking down he could just see ruts gouged in the mud where his rubber boots had slid away from under him as he knelt against the side of the ditch. Mush in his socks told him rain had seeped in, or the boots were leaking, probably both. Cold he had never experienced before cut into his bones, and when he commanded his fingers to move over the metal of his weapon, he saw twitches of movement but felt nothing. Maybe his frozen fingers could not be trusted when the time came.

In the distance, a faint speck of yellow light in an isolated farmstead pricked the gloom, signalling that a household was stirring to meet its day. His companions lined along the ditch all noticed it at the same time. Two men on his left pointed then began a conversation, shouting above the wind, in that bizarre mix of English and profanity. Even in ideal conditions he could barely understand them. A few days earlier, disgorged by the churning, filthy trawler and still homesick for Tripoli, he had found himself entrusted to these rough but not unkind people. One moment he was treated as an exotic guest, the next as an encumbrance, all the while subjected to a constant barrage of friendly insults.

One of the two stepped in close and clapped him on the shoulder. 'Ok, Darky, mate? We're not often this lucky with the fucking weather…should see it when it's bad.' The other man's face showed laughter and he fumbled inside his jacket pocket, extracting a bottle. He waved the others into a tight circle, each man huddled in, bringing his weapon.

'The fucker's up and about.' He jerked a thumb over his shoulder in the direction of the light. 'Remember what he is, lads, he's a fucking tout. Let's do him in and get the hell away.' Just like in the films, he watched this man take the cork out with his teeth and hold the bottle up in salute before taking a long pull. The bottle made its way around the five men, reaching him last. The men watched, nodding encouragement. One yelled, 'Sláinte, Darky! Put some lead in your pencil.'

The glass rattled his chattering teeth as he tipped and swallowed, eyes closed, rain beating off his uplifted face. Instant liquid fire tore at his throat, convulsing him. Then his eyes goggled as the breath left him, and even the wind could not drown out the explosion of laughter from his companions. The man reached out to claim the bottle back. 'Masks on, lads!' he shouted. 'Into your positions, safety catches off.'

After a minute, a tingling warmth kindled in his gut. A surge of confidence started to build and he found himself working blood back into his frozen fingers by taking one hand at a time off the Kalashnikov and stuffing it into his trouser pocket, pushing it to his crotch for warmth. He found that by doing this with a strict count of a minute per hand he was beating the cold. And by rolling his shoulders vigorously inside the oversize jacket he found he could generate warmth around his chest. Maybe, he was not sure, the wind was dropping and had lost some of its bite. The man next to him called over, 'Ease up on the rain dance, Tonto, or we'll all fucking drown.'

Headlights from the farm hit the scudding clouds and drew a sharp whistle from the lookout furthest along the tree line. Each man hefted his weapon, getting ready.

'He's leaving. Just one car,' the lookout called.

'You sure?' the man with the bottle called.

'For fuck's sake, take a look yourself.'

He was extraordinarily alert now, no sense of cold. He thumbed at the safety lever of the Kalashnikov, clacking it up then down again: no problem with his fingers, but his mouth had gone bone dry.

'At the junction...turning our way.'

Twin beams, juddering over rough ground, turned the raindrops into a shower of crystal as the car eased off the rough farm track and onto the main road.

The wool of his balaclava was itchy and he realised he was sweating. The eye and mouth holes allowed some fresh air and he licked his lips, wanting a long drink of cool water. His gut was churning now and he wondered if this was fear.

'He's past the marker. Three hundred yards and coming on fast,' the lookout shouted.

'Drop the fucker!' the leader yelled. The man at the extreme right of the line pulled a cord and a length of telegraph pole, hidden vertically in the tree line, began to move. It spun a little, as if in slow motion, then pitched forward across the narrow road, catching in the stunted tree opposite and stopping a foot above the tarmac.

Even as the car slewed to a shrieking halt, bullets were slamming into it. Cracking blasts stabbed his eardrums and long muzzle flashes seared his eyes. Spent cases from a Kalashnikov on his left hit him on the cheek and temple. He felt his own weapon bucking, its butt hammering his shoulder. The car rocked with the impact of strikes, its windshield puckering with rosettes and the side windows showering glass from exiting bullets.

Then he became aware of screaming, maybe from inside the vehicle, certainly from his companions. 'Stop! Enough! For fuck's sake, stop!' The man with the bottle earlier was now on the road, steam rising off his weapon as he stalked warily towards the car. The storm had quietened and they all watched as he craned his head at the results of the ambush. Abruptly, he jerked back, lowered his weapon and stood upright. They heard him pleading, 'Jesus, Jesus! Aah, no, Jesus! Please not this.'

One of the others strode in to look, and then turned away without a word. The wind and rain had paused, silenced by the shock. All five men, now gathered at the vehicle, could see a man sitting in the driver's seat, leaning back, hands down, blood spattered over his torso and the top half of his skull scooped off above the right ear. A mess of tissue, bone, cartilage and flesh sat like a topping above the victim's nose. Moving spasmodically in the passenger's seat was another figure, a young adult, his jacket and jeans sprayed with blood. He was still alive but badly hurt and his blood-soaked right hand dabbed, from a school satchel on his lap, towards the men, pleading, then jerked back to his face.

'For the love of Christ,' someone said. 'The wee lad…one of you…put him out of it.'

'You fucking do it,' someone else said.

'I'm out, no ammo.'

'He'll talk if he lives.'

The man with the bottle said, 'We stay here a second longer, he won't need to.'

Another voice said, 'Darky, step up, mate. Welcome to the struggle for freedom…now finish the fucking job.'

CHAPTER 1

The court building on St Georges Road increasingly reminded Hash that in Britain crime did pay and here was the proof. Sixties architects with their pretensions had robbed Cheltenham of its Georgian perfection and never been brought to book. The courthouse was an abortion of grey concrete fronted by a pair of cantilevered steps offering the choice to go up left or right. Either route, Hash had decided, led to flabby, lenient justice.

The balcony at the head of the stairs afforded a handy vantage point for people to smoke and chatter. By the time Hash arrived, a haze of smoke and nervous bravado hung in the sharp March air. Anyone watching him coming up the steps would have had no difficulty singling Hash out from the shell suits. He was clearly a member of the establishment, posh bastard, one of them…not one of us.

Ready with the pretrial briefing for his Bench, the clerk to the justices emphasised the defendant's considerable form, and the presence of his family in support at the back of the courtroom.

Once in court, Hash, in unison with the two other magistrates, one the Bench Chairman and the other a winger like himself, bowed and sat. After placing his pen alongside his folders, Hash held his left hand just above his notebook, hovering for two seconds, just long enough to see the tremble in his fingers, something more common of late. He was never sure if this was adrenaline or stress.

Standing alone in the glass-screened dock, a lanky young man struck a pose somewhere between self-consciousness and nonchalance. He looked uncomfortably smart in a suit which Hash guessed had been in mothballs since its last court appearance. What looked like a new haircut revealed scrolling tattoos on his neck. He fidgeted slightly and a hand crept up now and then to rub his raw neck. The man looked up at the Bench, and around the court before darting a conspiratorial smirk to his family team at the back of the court. His rolling eyes and 'here we are again' look drew a rash of grins from his mates. A reporter, making a hasty, late entrance, took a seat halfway down the court. When the clerk's demands for identity commenced proceedings, Hash scribbled the name and address.

The defendant's clear responses to the ritual hinted at coaching from his lawyer. Every utterance from the defendant was suffixed with 'sir'. Four consecutive words without a swear word was pushing the man to his limits and, in fairness, Hash reflected, a complete sentence with verbs, whilst standing up, had not been called for. The clerk read out the charge: 'Burglary of a dwelling whilst the occupant was present'. Hash knew from his training seminars that this act guaranteed a custodial sentence. The thug was almost certain to be behind bars by the end of the day.

An early courtroom technicality sent the Bench to the retiring room for a short recess and Hash used the toilet on the way. Washing his hands and seeing himself in the mirror, he mouthed a silent pep talk in black and white movie English: 'Cheer up, old scout! Things could be worse. Chin up, chest out!' Lines probably uttered by David Niven or Kenneth More, cheery-faced above a blood-soaked uniform, dying a valiant death somewhere on the North-West Frontier. Hash challenged the balding man with tired, brown eyes in the mirror, forcing a mask of intense concentration, head cocked, eyebrow raised, trying his best courtroom 'eye contact' stare. He flicked at a speck of dust on his blue suit and then tightened and repositioned his silk tie so that the knot sat perfectly.

The court resumed, to hear the only prosecution witness, an elderly widow, occupant of the burgled flat. When called, the old lady got straight to the point, holding out a trembling finger.

'That is the man who was in my flat.' Her voice was so faint that the clerk had to coax her to repeat. She did so then paused, breathless and shaking. Hash realised she was terrified. She took a breath, pulled herself together, looked at the defendant and held his gaze. 'He's the one who robbed my flat.'

When she sagged with the effort the Chairman offered her the chance to sit. She remained there, looking at her hands, dabbing her eyes with a handkerchief. The thug in the dock kept his eyes on her, only switching when his legal aid lawyer coughed.

'What was he doing at the time you saw him?' the prosecution service lawyer asked.

'He was holding my stuff.'

'What stuff was that?

'My personal belongings. My silver photo frames,' she whispered. 'It's the photos I want back. My late husband, my mother and father.' Her voice faltered. 'All passed away.'

'You are quite sure the man who stole your possessions is the man you can see in the dock?' the lawyer repeated.

'And he had a knife, one of them Stanley things,' she said.

Hash guessed the old girl's photos would be lying in a bin somewhere or just tossed into the mud wherever the thug had passed after ripping them out of the frames. He would have swapped the frames for drugs, got high and moved on.

A whispered conversation between the man and his lawyer ensued and Hash's mind strayed to family photographs he kept at home. The favourite black and white of his own family that hung in the kitchen was irreplaceable: it was all he had to remember them by. And after his wife had died, when the anguish had abated, he had taken a favourite snap out of the album, framed it in silver and kept it permanently at his bedside. Taken on a windy hillside, on the eve of parting, the lens had captured a wistful expression in Flora's dark eyes. Her delicate hand held back strands of long, dark hair from the wind. If anyone ever destroyed those two photographs, he would be capable of murder.

Finishing with his client, the lawyer looked up at the bench and announced that his man now wished to plead guilty. The thug in the dock shot the 'shit happens' look at his crew. The elderly victim still sat in the witness box, trembling with strain. The clerk looked up for the Bench's decision. The Chairman nodded to Hash and the other winger. 'The Bench accepts the defendant's plea.'

The counsel for the thug took his cue. 'Your Worships will be mindful of the need to obtain reports before passing sentence,' he began smoothly, 'and the matter of bail now arises.' He looked at his client, affecting a look of pride. 'In acknowledging guilt, your Worships will give credit to my client for taking responsibility for his actions. A small step but an important one, perhaps.'

Hash doodled a concentric pattern in biro around the thug's address as he listened to the lawyer advance the notion that, in actual fact, his client was the victim. Back home in Libya, Hash knew theft from a defenceless old lady would earn the perpetrator a massive battering from enthusiastic prison staff before being tossed as a plaything to the other prisoners.

'Denying bail will put my client at risk from the very influences, associations and temptations he is struggling to break away from,' the legal aid lawyer continued. 'Granting bail, if your Worships were so generously minded to approve it, with strict reporting conditions of course, may appear lenient but is a far-sighted option.' Hash looked across at the thug who was watching the magistrates, an expression of contrition on cue.

Tiring of the legal pitch, the clerk sent the Bench to the retiring room where, as the junior winger, Hash was asked to speak first.

'No bail,' he said.

The Bench Chairman said nothing, nodding to the other

winger, a woman in her sixties whom Hash knew, from previous sittings, to be a medical professional.

'Bail to be granted,' she said. The casting vote rested with the Chairman but he stalled. Without waiting, the woman offered her argument.

'He'll be put banged up with the lowlife.' Hash recalled her 'hip' persona from before. She was someone 'down' with the right jargon, as though intimately familiar with street life. 'Screws will turn a blind eye, blah blah, all the gear he wants,' she shrugged, rolling her eyes at the anarchy. 'I mean,' she was labouring it, 'come on... We all know what Gloucester Prison's like.' She added, 'He'll be a wreck when he comes out and we'll start at the bottom. Someone else will get robbed and,' she flipped two open palms in the air, 'hey-ho.'

Hash could feel his temper simmering. 'Surely, we're not here to discuss the shortcomings of Gloucester Prison,' he said. The Chairman, enjoying his temporary neutrality, said nothing. Hash continued. 'We're being asked if our friend in the dock is a bail risk. And I think he is.' He tapped his open notebook. 'He's a violent thug who robs and then waves knives at old ladies.'

'Is he going to run away?' the woman asked. 'And if he does, are we saying we can't catch him?'

'It's not just about him reporting to the police every so often,' Hash countered, 'it's what he does with his time... who else he threatens with his Stanley knife.'

The Chairman remained silent.

'Victim?' Hash asked. The woman looked puzzled by the question.

'I'm not worried about your friend, the screws and…the "gear".' Hash waggled his fingers in inverted commas and saw the woman stiffen. 'I'm worried about the old lady. What if he goes after her? Doesn't she deserve a break, especially now she's given evidence?'

'To be precise,' she said, 'he didn't go after her…just after her belongings.'

Hash shrugged back. 'He threatened her after breaking into her flat. Acting responsibly is not part of his make-up. He's a thug.'

'We give him bail and tie him up with stringent reporting conditions,' the woman said. 'He reports at midday and at eight in the evening. He must stay away from her home. If he threatens her or breaks any of the conditions, then he falls even harder.' She folded her hands on the table.

'He won't threaten her,' Hash shot back. 'He's not completely stupid. His mates will do that. I say he stays inside,' Hash said. 'We take all those 'ifs' off the table.' He looked across at the Chairman. 'It sends a signal to the community.' He held up his pen. 'You saw the reporter, taking notes.' They both waited for the Chairman to get off the fence.

When the Bench Chairman gave his decision in court it brought fist pumps from the supporters at the back of the court. Afterwards in the retiring room, formally destroying their notes and collecting their coats, the Chairman appeared at Hash's elbow.

'Hard luck, Hash. It's the system: doesn't always work the way it seems it should.' Hash wanted to curse his feebleness but his mind was on getting to school in time to pick up his son.

'We'll get him when he breaks his bail conditions,' he said, dropping his folders into his briefcase.

'Harrow man, I see,' the Chairman persisted. 'What house?'

'Sorry?'

'What house?' The man was looking at Hash's tie. 'I was at Rendalls,...suspect well before your time.' Hash realised he meant the school tie.

'This...?' He flapped at it. 'It belonged to an old uncle who knew I was coming to England. Back in Jordan everyone wears one because of the King. I was never there.'

The Chairman's head went back in surprise. 'Why do you wear it, then?' What had started as friendly, fence-mending exercise now had a sour taste.

'It was a gift.'

'You shouldn't be wearing it in court,' the Chairman continued. His smile was strained. 'No school, club or regimental ties, remember.'

Hash said, 'I'll bear that in mind,' and excused himself.

He left by the rear entrance, the usual practice of magistrates wishing to avoid recognition. Striding fast to warm up, he imagined the thug would already be celebrating in the pub with his mates and the *Echo*'s next edition would read, 'Offender robs OAP at knifepoint. Court sets him free.'

CHAPTER 2

Behind, further back on Cheltenham Racecourse's vast parking area, Hash could hear the chainsaw buzz of a tiny motor. Amazing just how far the irritating whine could reach, Hash thought. His son Jim, easily one hundred yards away, face turned to a cold, clear sky, worked the radio controls while a model Spitfire soared and swooped hundreds of feet above him. Jim, small for his fifteen years, concentrated hard on the aircraft, moving his torso slowly the way he wanted the aircraft to go, a free-dance artist transmitting his moves. Hash's heart lurched as he saw Jim's intense concentration, pursed lips and determined jut of his chin, so characteristic of the boy's mother. In the hellish times ahead, this split-second snapshot would keep Hash's hope alive.

He whistled to the boy, teasing, trying to break his concentration.

'Bandits! Ten o'clock!' he called out.

Jim, familiar with the ploy, flashed a smile, scarcely taking his eyes off the model. 'No, please…Dad.'

'Achtung! Engländer! Spitfeuer,' Hash persisted, working his stock of comic German from old black and white war films.

'Don't get your knickers in a twist, Dad!' the boy yelled back, eyes locked on the plane. 'You might wet yourself.'

But a challenge was a challenge and the Spitfire banked, its tiny motor rasping in protest at the command to swing round in search of prey. It dived, lining up on Hash and the dog. Jim guided the aircraft to fly at them for a few seconds before pulling it up and executing a roll as it powered past its targets. Hash applauded and the dog barked.

'Twenty minutes,' Hash called. He knew Jim had heard and turned away towards the vast meadow, whistling for the dog.

As he walked, he thought about the request he had received earlier at Jim's school. His son's favourite teacher had broken away from talking with another parent and waved him over: more a command than a greeting. The young teacher had been Jim's form mistress two years ago and still taught him English. Seeing Susan Pine always made Hash feel good about life.

'Got a minute, Mister Hashmi?' Her expression hinted at conspiracy. 'I was going to ask you a favour.'

'"Hash" to you, and because it's you asking...all the time in the world.'

Her giggle took him by surprise and two nearby mums looked round.

'It's the head,' she began.

'Not again...what's he done this time?'

'He wants a favour.' She plucked at his arm. 'I said you were perfect.'

The headmaster had risen swiftly from behind a wide desk

covered in paperwork. Easily fifteen years Hash's junior and dressed in an immaculate suit and crisp shirt, he looked more like a businessman than an academic. He came around the obstacle to offer a moist handshake.

'Kind of you to drop by, Mister Hashmi,' he began. 'A request. I was wondering if you could spare an hour to join our sixth form debating society, talk about your background and give them some of your life experience.'

Hash looked at Susan then back at the headmaster. 'What has Miss Pine set me up for?'

'Susan runs it,' he explained. 'They always hold a debate before the end of term. We wondered if you would be prepared to make a guest appearance.'

'What's the debate?' Hash had asked.

'Religious tolerance, essentially.' The headmaster had paused for a second, looking out of the window, as though seeking inspiration. 'I'll come up with the motion, but won't make it too heavy. The chaplain will speak, and we have a Jewish mum, but...' He held both palms out to Hash. 'We need a Muslim parent to balance it up.'

'You're the prime candidate,' Susan added.

'Aaah,' Hash said, 'maybe the only candidate. But I have to confess I'm not a perfect Muslim.' He protested, 'I've been known to drink beer, I bet on horses.' He assumed a helpless expression. 'Often at the same time.'

'Not everyone's perfect. Muslim-lite works better, for me at least.' The headmaster winced at his own wit. 'You come from Jordan, don't you?'

'Originally, of course, but I've not been back for years.'

'Where Arabs, Jews and Christians live side by side.'

'Well...' Hash canted his head, '...up to a point.'

'With a name like Hashmi...you're not connected to the royal family?'

'If you're looking for an endowment, sorry to disappoint you. We're an old family from Amman.' Hash had heard himself tell the lie so many times he almost believed it. 'A family of lawyers...always in court, just not the royal court.'

The headmaster was too well into his theme to acknowledge the wit. 'But you are actually...someone who, for our purposes has, um,' he searched for the word, 'integrated...I hope that doesn't sound patronising?' He observed Hash for signs of offence. 'And you also serve as a Justice of the Peace, if my source is correct?' Again he turned to Susan for confirmation. 'There can't be many Muslim JPs in Gloucestershire these days,' he continued. 'Aren't you the only one?'

'As far as I know,' Hash said.

'Susan and I want this debate to zoom in on Britain's religious tolerance,' the hand waving at the playing fields beyond the window, 'or lack of it.' He looked back at Hash. 'The students run it. You won't have to participate in the debate, of course. You introduce yourself, tell them about your home in Jordan, give some cultural and religious insights. Five minutes at the most.'

'What day are we talking about?' Hash asked.

'Friday next week, mid-morning, we break for Easter holidays afterwards,' Susan said.

'That actually puts me in the middle of the races, the Gold

Cup,' Hash said. Seeing the flicker of doubt on his face, Susan said, 'We're flexible, of course.'

'Actually, I'll be there myself…the school takes a box,' the headmaster said, 'apologies for the short notice, so many things to think about.' He gestured at his desk. 'Of course, if it's too much, I'll…'

'I'd be absolutely delighted,' Hash cut him off.

'That's really good of you,' Susan said as they walked back to his car.

'You sprang this surprise, so you owe me.' Hash teased. His smile brought a wary look to her face. 'You owe me,' he repeated.

'Owe you what?'

'You let me take you out for dinner afterwards.'

As he walked on the racecourse Hash found himself looking forward to the debate, pleased to have Susan as his prize. He often wondered what his chances could be with her. With her, he experienced the almost forgotten tingle of pleasure when real mutual attraction sparks. An extra, tantalising glimmer where Susan was concerned was how she had connected with Jim in a way no one else had managed before or since. Although she seemed impossibly young, in reality she and Flora would not be too far apart in age. After Flora had gone there had been other relationships, but bringing another woman deeper into their lives seemed too big a step. Hash knew he did not have the courage to look Jim in the eye and tell him another woman was moving in.

Ahead of him as he descended the grassy slope, the new dog,

Shamsa, a Weimaraner bitch, streaked ahead. He watched her muscled flanks ripple as she accelerated, her undocked tail acting as a rudder as she swerved and turned. She had settled in fast in the six months since they had taken her in. Along with what the rescue agency had coyly described as 'a strong personality', she brought exuberant affection into a lopsided and sometimes lonely household. She and Jim had bonded quickly, as though each fulfilled a need in the other. All the souls in his house were 'rescues', Hash reflected as he strolled on.

A huge sea of meadow in winter green rolled away in front of him, heading north, finally breaking against the brown shoulder of Cleeve Hill a mile distant. A church spire, slate roofs and ribbons of tree lines stood out in the middle distance. This was England and, even at its weariest after winter, Hash simply loved it. He saw beauty in this Cotswold landscape in all seasons: whether fine or filthy weather something in the scenery always pleased him. He wondered if his soul had become truly British and he silently thanked whatever God there was for bringing him here.

He glanced at his watch. Five-thirty, with evenings getting longer by a noticeable fraction. Scents of woodsmoke drifting across on the early evening chill raised the temptation of a pub meal in front of a warm fire before getting Jim back for homework. As he walked down the gentle slope, Shamsa looked for his approval to cross the footbridge and begin the next leg of the walk. He waved his arm forward and the dog leapt away.

The noises of construction, clanking and drilling floated across from the racecourse where last-minute preparations for the racing festival were hitting deadlines. Crews were probably working through the night at this stage, Hash assumed. When he had driven in, his first walk on the racecourse for a week, all the boards and signs were already up to guide cars and punters to the entrance gates.

Shamsa was barking an alert somewhere beyond the tiny footbridge and he called her name several times. Behind a sparse screen of trees, Hash recognised the friendly face of a fellow dog walker, a middle-aged woman fussing at her three whippets, leads taut as they hauled her down onto the bridge.

'they know it's dinner time,' he called across,' raising his tweed cap.'

He raised his tweed cap. The three dogs pulled towards him and he spent a moment patting them. 'Got your hands full there.'

The woman gave a smile as Shamsa trotted back to check on the hold-up.

'Friend of mine had one of these.' She pointed at the Weimaraner. 'Mad, she was...nutty as a fruit cake.'

'The friend or the dog?'

'I couldn't have one...never be able to pronounce the name,' she said.

'We've only had her for a few months. Still waiting for her to find her feet.'

She ruffled Shamsa's ears. 'Pick of the litter?'

'Not likely,' Hash said. 'We always take someone's rejects... give them another chance in life.'

'Shamsa,' the woman trilled, and the dog cocked her head. 'Strange name for a dog.'

'Arabic for sun,' Hash said. 'She's our new ray of sunshine.'

The woman's dogs pushed and shoved around Hash's legs. 'Getting crowded here.' Hash eased past her and got to the end of the bridge. As he briefly wondered about hopping over the muddy pool at the end, his eyes snagged on a detail on the bridge structure, down at boot level. He steadied himself with one hand on the rail and waved to the woman.

'This place'll be too busy for walking in a week or so,' she said, returning a friendly wave. Hash hopped over the puddle and moved on, only just aware of the woman saying goodbye. As he walked away from the little copse, urging Shamsa across the road, Hash felt a stab of anxiety. Acute, unwelcome, it was almost physical.

Shaking the disquiet from his mind, he made himself think about the race festival. From the middle of next week, thousands of happy punters would have the place floating on a sea of Guinness. One of them would be an Irish chum from the old days, dragging him into the inevitable, kamikaze drinking ritual. Pint after pint, and stories of yesteryear dredged up to be burnished with bigger and better fibs. It thrilled and scared him in equal measure because, in spite of his grandstanding in front of the headmaster and Susan, his hard-drinking days were over.

Barking up ahead made him step out after Shamsa. She could be stirring up trouble with another dog. He walked fast, crossing the road, unbolting the steel gate, and letting himself into the huge meadow. He found Shamsa excitedly working thickets along the stream. Hash guessed she had disturbed the old hare who lived there. Hash now glimpsed it streaking off, out of sight to the dog. The wily old animal had become something of a highlight of Shamsa's walk and Hash prayed it would never be caught.

With the chase long abandoned and both master and dog at the highest point on the meadow, the sound of sputtering and revving signalled through the windless air. Hash assumed Jim had landed his Spitfire and was probably burning off fuel, clearing the tubes as part of the shutdown drills. As he turned to look down at the sparse copse by the bridge, the same unbidden stab of anxiety flared.

Reaching the wicket gate before recrossing the road, Hash stopped and waited, bracing himself, sucking cold, clean air into his lungs so fast it froze his throat and sinuses. As he moved towards the little footbridge, the handrail came into focus and a jolt of pure adrenaline stopped him.

Down at ground level, wound around one of the scaffold uprights, four bands of brown tape held his gaze in a vice. A few millimetres apart, one on top of the other, they formed a collar, almost unnoticeable in the weakening daylight. But Hash had been meant to see them. The shock kept him rooted to the spot, his eyes screwed tight shut. He remained like this for a few seconds, but when he opened his eyes the tape was still there. Shamsa heard her master's long, low moan and came forward to his side.

When he could concentrate he opened his eyes and the first thing he saw was Jim in the distance, crouched over his aircraft. Hash looked back at the tape. Whoever had put it there had smeared some mud over it and let raindrops splashing off the concrete speckle the newness of brown and do the 'blend-in' job. He remembered there had been only one heavy shower four days earlier, before the dry spell had set in. He worked out he had walked the dog on the racecourse probably a week back, and as he always crossed the bridge he knew the marker was between five and six days old. He guessed that, then, someone had been on the bridge. That person had stooped down with a roll of brown tape. Person or persons? Why was he thinking singular? Maybe there was another person as lookout. The guy doing the tape job would have taken less than a minute; the other job of hiding a package would have taken a few minutes more.

Whistling to the dog, Hash knelt and scraped off the tape with his car keys. Keen to get involved, Shamsa came in, splashing muddy gruel over Hash's legs. Examining the sticky brown tape as he made his way slowly back to join Jim at the car, he saw it was electrical tape and no great forensic 'eureka' leapt at him. Rolling the tape into a ball, calling and waving to Jim, he tossed the tape away.

Jim was on his knees by the car doing his checks to the model aircraft, ready to lift it onto the back seat. He caught sight of his father's frown. Fending off Shamsa as she pushed her nose at his face, he looked up, catching his father's mood and the dark stains on his trousers.

'Walk over, already? You did actually wet yourself, then,' Jim said.

Hash forced a smile, barely registering the humour; he was realising he had made a mistake scraping off the tape. If he had left it alone he could maybe, just maybe, have gained some time.

'How about something to eat, now, before we go home?' Hash finally asked. He definitely did not want to go home. He needed distraction, a bright, fresh atmosphere.

'Something hot...maybe curry?' Jim said.

'Pub?' Hash countered.

'Too cold and draughty.'

'Pub with a roaring fire?'

'Curry?' Jim asked.

'Then I tell you what.' Hash held up a finger as though a brilliant idea had just occurred. '...How about...curry?'

'I was about to suggest that,' Jim said.

They were given a booth at the rear of the restaurant. The owner, Siddiq, carried a tray of drinks to the table: a Coke with ice and lemon went in front of Hash, and Jim got the litre bottle of Cobra.

'Personal service and on the house,' Siddiq said with an expression of irony, 'because your father is a good Muslim.'

'If he is,' Jim said, 'he's keeping it pretty quiet.'

'How about saying thanks, Jim?' Hash said. Siddiq ignored them both. 'Your father will be in the mosque with me tomorrow.' Siddiq shot a sideways glance at Hash. 'You will see. The imam likes him very much.'

'Does he?' Jim said it quietly, looking at the Coke, wanting to start.

'Maybe he will bring you.' Siddiq was smiling.

Hash reached for the beer and pushed the Coke across to Jim.

'School, exams, pressure…such fun, you know,' Jim said in measured tones. 'But if I change my mind, I'll let you know.'

Siddiq gave a short chuckle and sat down with the pair, shoving Jim along the cushioned bench.

'You play cricket?' Siddiq's ritual chaffing began. 'I think you are a bowler…spinner…or fast?'

'I play Quidditch,' Jim replied.

'Rubbish sport, for girls only,' Siddiq snorted. 'Better you play cricket, like your father.'

'If I played cricket like my father I would be too embarrassed to admit it.'

Siddiq smiled at Jim even as his eyes flitted to his squad of waiters. He ran several restaurants, from Cheltenham across to Gloucester and up to Birmingham, but this one, on Cheltenham's Bath Road, was his flagship and business headquarters. Small, fussy and always immaculately dressed in a charcoal grey suit with blue shirt, tie and cufflinks, Siddiq liked to greet his guests personally. He and Hash had been friends for a long time. Siddiq had known Flora and been one of the few at her funeral. He rose, excusing himself to attend to other customers.

'Dad,' Jim interrupted Hash's thoughts. 'If he's so smart, I mean so smartly dressed, then why does he have such a scruffy beard?' Jim sucked at his Coke and waited. 'All long and straggly, like an old badger.'

Hash knew the reason, though looking around at the rest of the clientele in the restaurant he doubted if Cheltenham's finest either knew or cared.

'It's a Muslim sign of being devout. It means he's a religious man,' Hash said.

Siddiq now swung back, past the table. 'Midday tomorrow…
the imam says don't be late.' Siddiq tapped the table and waved
one of his waiters across to take their order. After the waiter had
gone, Hash leaned forward.

'All this talk of religion reminds me. I'm giving a talk to your
sixth form next week.'

'Cool, Dad. What about?'

'Religious tolerance.'

'Ouch! Not as cool as I thought. How come you've been
asked?'

'I suspect they needed a Muslim parent and they only have
me,' Hash shrugged.

'But do you go to the mosque?'

'Not very often.'

'Do you pray in a row, on your knees, bum up in the air?' Jim
took a pull at his Coke.

'That's the traditional way Muslims pray.'

'Why am I not a Muslim, then?'

'Your mum and I agreed we would let you choose, when
you're ready. That's part of religious tolerance, by the way.'

Jim went silent while a waiter laid a dish of chutney and a
plate of poppadoms in front of them.

'Why is Siddiq so nice to you, Dad?' Jim asked when the
waiter had left.

'Mister Siddiq, to you,' Hash said. 'Because I helped him in
the old days,' Hash took a sip of beer. 'I helped him set up his
businesses when he was just starting out. And then he helped me.'

'What sort of help?'

'Buying up restaurants. He's an accountant, I'm a lawyer. That sort of business.'

'Boring stuff, then,' Jim said.

'That's nice, thank you.'

'You really a Muslim, Dad?' Jim persisted. 'You're not supposed to drink alcohol but you drink like a fish.'

'As we're being so open with each other,' Hash said, 'I drink to ease the pain.'

'What pain?' Jim was looking at him, mildly interested in this turn of the conversation.

'The pain of paying your school fees and then watching you do so badly.'

'I knew that was coming, Dad.' Jim sighed. 'Lame...but I'll let you have half-marks.'

MONDAY NIGHT

Just before ten that evening, a phone call put Hash back on the road. A tenant in one of his properties had called in with a problem. The time of night was unusual and the urgency in the stolid Portuguese's voice told Hash it was serious. The man had run the chippy for almost fifteen years and had worked it well, delivering a consistent rent. Hash could make out the words, 'trouble, bastards, and police' in a torrent of heavily accented English.

'Going out for half an hour!' Hash called up the stairs. It would take him ten minutes to get his ageing Discovery across town to the housing estate where the chippy was. There was no reply from Jim's room and he had to climb the stairs, knock on the door, and gently prise one headphone off Jim's head before he could pass on the message. He considered taking Shamsa with him then maybe getting down to the racecourse and the footbridge afterwards. But that might be rushing things. 'One thing at a time,' he said to the dog, pushing her back down in her bed.

A light drizzle covered the windscreen and the wiper blades scraped on his nerves as he drove. He left behind the red-brick terraces where he lived and passed The Suffolks heading into Tivoli, watching for some of his favourite houses. One day soon, when there were no more school fees, he and Jim would move. Not to something big and showy, just big enough, detached, probably Georgian and definitely elegant. He continued down Lansdown Road, picking up the A40, but never intending to leave town, and took the Hesters Way turnoff at the big roundabout before GCHQ.

The chippy came into sight at the end of a long approach into Princess Elizabeth Way, and Hash pulled over to dial a call. Driving on slowly as the phone was connecting, he could see two staff behind the counter, the Portuguese and his wife. Apart from no customers all seemed to be well. The two figures bustled behind the steel and glass food display and bins. He saw the man reach for his phone and heard his voice over the speaker.

'Mister Hash?'

'How are you...all ok?'

'These young bastards!' the tenant spat. 'They come in

drunk tonight, they fighting, call names, make order then no pay…bastards.'

'I'm coming now.'

'Too late now…they gone…bastards!'

'How many?'

'Three guys…always the same ones…always the same tricks.'

'I'm looking for them.' Hash accelerated past the chippy, turning the Discovery off the main road and into the nearest housing estate, slowing to a crawl when he saw people ahead. He was not hopeful. The culprits could be sitting in a car, or had disappeared into one of the hulking, sixties tenement blocks in the immediate area. He gave up after ten minutes, returning to his tenant.

'Young guys,' the Portuguese began before a burst of Portuguese from his wife at the back of the shop halted him. He listened to her then pointed to his throat and side of his neck, tracing with his finger, 'Tattoos…flowers.' The wife nodded confirmation then looked over to Hash.

'Look at the TV.' His stubby finger jabbed at the CCTV lens high up on the back wall of the shop. The three of them crowded at the small monitor and waited as the husband hit the play button. Hash watched a grainy black and white pantomime of three men, one with smudges on his neck, at which the Portuguese stabbed the screen. 'Pretty boy. Tells me he's my best friend, wants to look after my business, be my partner.'

Hash knew he was looking at the thug from the morning's court case, the man who had won bail and was back in business.

The figures jerked around on the screen as though play fighting, the tattooed ringleader turning to the Portuguese in a mock appeal for help. Hash caught a sense of escalating menace in the exchange of waving arms and the flicking of V signs. The ringleader then shed his protective persona, taking cans of drink from the fridge cabinet and tossing them to his friends, stuffing others in his pockets. At one point, another of the trio man hurled a can towards the back of the shop, off-camera. The wife unleashed a torrent of Portuguese and pointed to a stain on the wall. Her husband stabbed at the screen again. 'This when they tell me to open the till. Bastards!'

'How much?' Hash said.

The man blinked at Hash, then shrugged.

'How much did you lose tonight?' Hash repeated.

The man bobbed his head and counted on his fingers. 'One hundred sixty-six pound...then.' He pointed at the drinks fridge. 'Twenty-four pound for drinks. Maybe I lose customers, too. They don't come if they see trouble.'

'One hundred and ninety pounds, then.' Hash pulled out his wallet, counted out ten twenties, and held them out to the man.

The Portuguese shook his head. 'Not necessary, Mister Hash. Normally business is good...but tonight.'

'Yes necessary,' Hash countered. Placing the money in the man's hand, he added, 'Next time take photos...we go to the police.'

'Take photos...you joking, Mister Hash. Police bastards...' The man spat. 'Fucking useless...they do nothing.'

He found Jim downstairs slumped on the sofa, Shamsa beside

him, and a news programme on the television. Jim looked up as Hash entered. 'That dog's too lazy to bark when you're spoiling it,' Hash said, then pointed to the screen, 'What's this?' He was looking at footage of men wearing Arab headdress, riding in pickup trucks waving black ISIS flags and firing weapons into the air. The narrator was talking about the death of Muammar Gaddafi as the camera cut to scenes of the dictator's swollen and bloody face, jowls shaking as men pushed him roughly. Knowing exactly what came next, Hash seized the channel selector, switching the television off.

'Dad…' Jim protested.

'You'd have nightmares for weeks. Why on earth are you watching that stuff?'

'It was interesting.'

Hash ruffled Jim's hair. 'So, we're interested in Middle Eastern politics all of a sudden? Why is that?'

'Because they want democracy,' Jim said, 'like we have.'

'So…not because you want to stay up a bit longer?'

'Seriously, Dad,' Jim said. 'I can watch it on my phone, if I want. You can see anything on the net.'

'You need to put that rubbish out of your mind and get to bed.'

Sleep for Hash was impossible, as his churning mind refused to dump the day's events. The connection between the tattooed thug they had let walk free and the fracas in the chippy had been poetic justice. Nobody was going to feel sorry for any rich fat cat magistrate if they insisted on releasing the scum back into the wild. The extortion, maybe too early to call it by that name, might be the tip of an iceberg and would have to be confronted. Asking the tenant to photograph the thugs had been naïve. But all was kids' play compared to the tape on the footbridge. That had been like hearing a doctor deliver an ominous diagnosis… something terminal. Then…scraping off the brown tape, that had been a basic blunder, too: his mistake. Being out of practice by a few decades was no excuse for sloppiness. If he had left the tape he could have won time. Instead he had signalled to them that Hash had received and was back in the game. He wondered if Jim had already seen the gory images of Gaddafi's death, somewhere else, maybe on the internet. For the first time in many years he felt fear incubating in his gut like some necrotic parasite.

CHAPTER 3

TUES 3RD MARCH 2015. EARLY MORNING.

With a slight ground mist covering the racecourse, Hash had to slow down as he topped the hill by the vintage railway station. The promise of another fine, spring day made Hash wonder if the dry would last until the festival. He would normally have parked near the tiny vintage Victorian station with its magnolia paint where he had often taken Jim on the hissing, chuffing steam engine. As he drove past the quaint building with its fretted woodwork it always evoked childhood memories of scenes from his own father's collection of old black and white films. Scenes where Victorian dandies greeted their ladies with extravagant courtesies; or lean, gruff cowboys stood, tongue-tied at the sight of a beautiful heroine.

'Got to be a quick one,' he urged Shamsa, swinging the rear door open. 'We need to get Jim out of bed and off to school.' The dog pounded out, driven by the urgency of Hash's voice and her canine lust for information: 'pee mail', as Jim called it. He walked steadily in her wake as she tore ahead, zigzagging to the lure of fresh scents. Hash became aware of anxiety in the pit of his stomach.

Even before they reached the footbridge, his eyes were sweeping the area. He had to remind himself he wasn't on a battlefield strewn with mines, just a parking area converging on a bridge with nothing more threatening than a scruffy copse and some dog shit. He could see through most of the spindly saplings as he drew closer. The footprints in the congealed mud at the beginning of the bridge were so numerous he could not tell if any of them were fresh.

There was no new tape on the steel upright, and as he softly whistled for the dog, he could see where his key had left bright scratches on the metalwork the day before. Shamsa reappeared, hovering impatiently as Hash stood on the bridge. He took one more glance around, checking for other dog walkers or anyone else, then he peered at the bushes: nothing, nobody anywhere in sight, and he doubted that could last. Snapping off a dried twig he held it to Shamsa for a second, then threw it hard towards the railway embankment, aiming for the culvert. The dog watched his arm jerk then dived after the arcing stick. For a few seconds, he could hear splashing movement and caught a glimpse of her grey coat. She was back within less than a minute, with the stick. Hash repeated the move twice and followed her in on the third. She would have been barking like crazy if there had been anyone in there.

Hash stepped into the stream bed, feeling the water wrap its cold grip around his Hunters. A few careful strides, edging his way over slabs of stone slick with moss, brought him to the mouth of the culvert. The brickwork must have been at least a hundred years old, but the red and black bricks looked clean, almost new. He crouched down to look inside. Shamsa was beside him in the water, nose pointed at the dark tunnel. Light at the other end told Hash there was nobody in it and he felt the irony.

Standing up again, Hash drew his phone and keyed the torch, holding its beam to a small, circular aperture on the culvert wall. This was set at waist level and looked like a slot for drainage left by the Victorian builders. He shone the torch inside and looked along the shaft. Lodged about eighteen inches along its length, Hash could see a package wrapped in black plastic. He was aware of his heart thumping as he gently eased his fist inside to grip on the package. It came out smoothly, feeling light and dry to his touch.

Back home, with Shamsa fed and dozing in the warmth of the kitchen, Hash called up to Jim to make sure he was awake. Shoving the plastic-wrapped package into a sideboard drawer, he flicked on the kettle, put two slices of bread into the toaster, then paused to take stock.

His eyes fell on the old black and white family photograph, one he had had enlarged and framed, and which always he kept on the dresser shelf, almost hidden by other memorabilia. Young faces returned his gaze: his Libyan family, father, mother two sisters and an infant nephew, all with contentment in their expressions. He was there, too: a version of himself thirty years younger, leaner, with long sideburns and a look of arrogance he now remembered with a shudder.

The toaster popped and, reaching for the butter, Hash yelled upstairs to alert his son. He took a cup of tea and the toast upstairs and slid it inside Jim's door. After showering, he shaved and dressed, knowing today his style would also be conservative but elegant, appropriate for a successful businessman who could still find the time to serve his community. First, he had to attend a scheduled competence test at the Magistrates' Court and afterwards he would walk the short distance to his office on the Promenade. The whole building, one of his freeholds, was rented out to a firm of architects but with the basement office suite retained for his use. Here, Wilma his Phillipina secretary and bookkeeper held the portfolio together, collected the rents, filed the returns and paid the tradesmen. He chose the same dark blue suit, and this time eschewed a blue shirt for a blush pink with a dangerously exaggerated cutaway collar, mother-of-pearl buttons and double cuffs. Since acquiring British citizenship in 2000 he had become irresistibly attracted to British style, intrigued by the notion of elegant understatement, but fearful of either getting it wrong or being considered flashy. Pink shirts, thick ties and brown shoes were for estate agents, and though Hash considered himself a man of property, he saw himself as an investor rather than a trader. He left aside the Harrow tie, pricked by the embarrassing memory, and instead took one in woven silk that was light blue with pink spots. He completed the outfit with well-worn but highly polished black brogues. Jim was at the kitchen table checking his mobile phone when Hash came downstairs.

'Ok for my court appearance, Jim?' he asked.

The fifteen-year-old barely looked up from his phone.

'What have you been arrested for?' Jim sighed, glancing up to give him the once-over. 'Pimping again?'

Hash lunged at the boy, seizing his shoulders to throw him off his chair, but held him midway. The boy smiled.

'Eat, eat, eat!' Hash gestured at the boxes of cereal, taking the phone out of Jim's hands. The boy looked at the plate and picked up a carton, deciding.

'How about going to stay with Grandma and Grandpa for a bit?' Hash suggested. 'Now.'

'When, now?' Jim looked surprised. 'Holidays don't start until next week.'

'Now, today. How about I speak to Miss Pine and get you released early?'

'Any excuse and you're talking to Miss Pine,' Jim said. 'Isn't it working?'

'Isn't what working?'

'I told her.'

'Told her what?'

'You had a massive crush on her…but you're incredibly shy.'

'What did she say?'

'She said…' Jim poured cornflakes and reached for the milk, keeping his father in suspense. He spooned food into his mouth and chewed. 'She never does it on the first date, especially not with balding…'

'Who teaches you that stuff?' Hash cut him off. 'I hope you said no such thing.'

'Chillaaax, Dad,' Jim said. 'I made that up.'

'All of it, I hope?'

'No, just the bit about the balding middle-aged man.'

'Actually, if you must know,' Hash said, 'she's the person who has invited me to talk on religious tolerance.'

'I don't mind if you fancy Miss Pine, Dad.' Jim held his hands out, palms upward. 'But Bible-bashing to get to her is weirding me out.'

'Anyway,' Hash pressed, 'answers! How do you feel about an emergency dash to the sickest grandfather in Ireland?'

'Is it a real emergency?' Jim asked.

'Your granddad had a stroke and he's getting worse,' Hash said. 'That's a fact.'

'How about I go and stay with Uncle Sean?' Jim countered. 'He's so cool.'

Hash shook his head. 'The last time he had you drinking Guinness.'

'Uncle Sean is magic,' Jim said. 'He shows me how to shoot and fish. He's a hero.'

'He's also a certified psycho,' Hash said.

'But you like him, too?' Jim argued.

'That's different.' Hash clipped the lid on the sandwich box, placed it on the table, and gently took the phone from the boy's hand. 'Sandwiches, apple, juice, crisps and KitKat. Maybe, I'll speak to Sean,' Hash added. 'You start off with Granny and Grandpa and then, when you've put a bit of work in, maybe, just maybe,' he stressed, 'Sean will drive over and take you on trips.'

'What sort of trips?' Jim asked, picking up his phone.

'Hunting and fishing, like you said,' Hash offered. 'You'll have fun over there. You could take one of your models. One that would fit in a suitcase.'

'My little quadcopter?'

'Why not? Plenty of space to fly it when you're not helping out on the farm, earning incredible pocket money.'

'Cleaning out the pigsties,' Jim said. 'Hammering a nail through my hand could be more fun,' Jim said.

Hash put his hand over the boy's phone and repeated in a low whisper, '...Incredible pocket money.'

'Why such a rush to get rid of me?'

'I have to go away for a few days, do some stuff with some chums.'

'Fun stuff? I could come along, too.'

'Boring stuff. Accounting, numbers, meetings, long days in offices.'

'I could stay here and look after Shamsa,' Jim countered.

'You mean stay in bed all day, force-feed the dog and make her crap in the garden?'

'I'd clean the crap up.'

'Last time I only left you for two days and old Mrs Hamilton never stopped phoning me.' He mimicked the voice of their elderly neighbour. 'Your bloody dog was barking for two days.'

'Nosy old bag,' Jim said. 'She's a nosy old cow.'

'She loves you, Jim, in spite of the things she's seen, stuff that would have sent any weaker person insane.'

'What stuff?' Jim put down his phone.

'Your nappies when you were young,' Hash said.

'Dad,' Jim pleaded.

'She's a very kind lady and don't you forget it.' Hash checked his tone, not wanting to kill the mood. 'Anyway...I'll be joining you after I take care of this rotten business stuff.' Hash paused for a second, then murmured in another low whisper to Shamsa who lay on her bed in the corner of the kitchen. 'How does a new quadcopter sound?' Hash continued. 'Grandma really wants you to go and stay. She was on the phone to me this morning.'

'What was the bit about the quadcopter, Dad?'

'Aaah,' Hash smiled, 'Might we be a tiny bit interested?' Hash held out his hand. 'Deal?'

'What sort of budget are we talking here?' Jim cautiously extended a hand. 'I'm well past the toy stage, Dad. I fly with the professionals, you know.'

'Yes, of course you do,' Hash said. 'All is negotiable but totally dependent on your smiling cooperation.'

'How much, Dad?'

Hash made a fist and flicked up one, two and finally three fingers. 'Shall we say three hundred quid?'

'That gets me a Phantom 3 Professional,' Jim said. 'Top of the range, all the pros have them.'

'Deal?' Hash repeated.

Jim looked into his father's face, as if checking for the catch, then slowly shook hands. 'Deal.'

'What will you tell Miss Pine?' Jim asked. 'She's not my form teacher anymore and it's not holidays yet.'

'No, but I'll go through her to get to your form teacher.' Hash was thinking on his feet.

'Whoa.' Jim waved him away. 'Too much information...I'm eating.'

'I'll get her this afternoon, take her to one side, brief her it's urgent family stuff, something like that.'

Hash waited until Jim was well on his way, heading for the college. Then, hurrying back to the kitchen he retrieved the package, took the kitchen scissors, and cut away the plastic. He found himself in possession of three items. The first was an old model BlackBerry phone with half of its QWERTY keyboard in Arabic. There was a charger with a three-point plug. The third item was a car key. The key's plastic butt showed the Citroën chevron and the symbols for 'lock' and 'unlock'. Hash powered up the phone and seconds later it told him it was on an Etisalat UK contract. He was familiar with the Emirati network and guessed it disguised the real provenance of the phone.

When he keyed the centre button the phone demanded to be unlocked with a password, and his watch told him he was running out of time. Too many failed attempts to unlock the phone could provoke a shutdown. This task needed calm, logic and a pen and paper. Hash had half of the password in his mind already, a number etched into his consciousness decades ago, one the anxiety had brought back with it, a number so simple he would never forget. Whoever had sent the phone would have inserted that part of the code. The rest he had to crack himself.

Hash picked up the phone and slowly, as if giving the device time to follow, he typed in 12021960, his date of birth, the twelfth of February 1960. The phone told him it was an incorrect password: close, but no cigar.

He shook his head as if to dismiss the failed attempt and ask the phone for another go. There had to be a clue somewhere but, with the kitchen clock piling on the pressure, telling him he was running late, this was not the time to test the old phone's patience.

Leaving the phone on charge, he paused at the hallway mirror to make a final check on his appearance. It was neither cold nor wet enough for a coat, but the scruffy Barbour jacket was part of the uniform and slipped over his suit easily. The tweed cap with its Harrods label completed the 'county' look. Shamsa, bought off with a large rawhide chew, ignored him as he closed the door. It took him fifteen minutes at a brisk walk across the north-south grain of Cheltenham's streets, straight across the Bath Road, through Tivoli and past the first of the Ladies' College boarding houses. He used the exercise to freshen his mind, searching through the cobwebs of time, recalling lessons on codes.

LATER

Back home and calculating he had about an hour before Jim would be walking in through the door, Hash picked up the Arab BlackBerry, tuning his mind as he did so. Old model for old-school operators. Still stung by his uncomfortable encounter with the not so cute Miss Pine, he struggled to concentrate. Getting permission to extract Jim had been tougher than he thought and he now had damage to repair; the dinner date was probably 'on hold' at best.

The display on the mobile told him he now had a full battery and an SMS waiting. He saw whoever had prepared the phone had pegged the date at January 26th. He would worry about the relevance of that later, when he had unlocked the device.

'First Susan and now this...' Hash hissed, rummaging in the bin, retrieving the packaging and taking a pen and pencil to the kitchen table. Slumping into a kitchen chair, he put the device, the charger, bubble wrap and liner in front of him. He chided himself again for clearing the letter box down at the bridge too early, and signalling he was a player. He could have left the tape and still cleared the box, checked the contents and then run like hell. But he was stuck with it now. He sifted the wrapping, searching for any clues. There were none. Next, he looked at the Citroën key on the fob: nothing except the tiny brand name with the chevrons and the symbols for lock and unlock. Then a clue hit him, rewarding his freshness of mind theory. He keyed in his special number and the letters spelling Citroën, only to be rejected. He reversed the sequence and was rejected again.

Wondering if he had a limited amount of tries before the phone closed him out, a part of him wanted to deliberately fluff his lines. Maybe he could get disqualified from this particular game, or at least a bye to the next round. Maybe he would feed a message back into the letter box saying, 'phone damaged, send replacement'. Then he remembered, years ago in a lecture at Ben Gashir, the instructors casually showing photographs of an agent somewhere in Europe, sprawled on the boulevard in a pool of blood, an agent who had tried to evade a mission.... 'We'll find you,' they had said.

A glance at the kitchen clock told him four-thirty. Jim would be back in forty-five minutes. His chat with Susan had started well then gone rapidly downhill. There had been her shy smile at first and the hint of a blush. But the moment he suggested taking Jim away early she had become official and curt. She had heard out the classic play of a favourite grandparent at death's door and knew she could not refuse. But it was plain she felt insulted.

Giving the Arab BlackBerry a break and concentrating his mind on what he knew he could achieve, he dialled his mother-in-law on the landline. His next pitch met with more success. The first precious minutes were taken up listening to old Bella's aches and pains, then the old boy's problems. Hash was almost hopping with impatience when she said, in her country drawl, 'Aye. Suppose we could take wee Lord Jim for few days. It wouldn't be the end of the world.' Hash knew that was Irish for 'Send him now!' The old couple would be over the moon. Jim always cringed at the title 'Lord', a teasing compliment to his English accent.

'I'll get Sean to meet him off the plane,' he said.

'You'll do no such thing,' Bella said. 'He'll be drunk.'

'He'll be fine,' Hash comforted. 'It's too long a drive for you. Sean's on the doorstep. The plane will be arriving late, might even be delayed. I'll call him well before opening time.'

'Well…' Her doubt hung in the ether. 'Make sure you do. He's only good for drinking.'

'I've already emailed him,' Hash lied. 'He's looking forward. He'll feed him and drive him over to you.'

'Aye…Ok, then.' Her tone was heavy with scepticism.

'Relax, Bella, please. Remember,' he lied again, 'I'll be over, myself, in a few days.'

Hash spent fifteen more vital minutes booking a seat on the

Birmingham to Aldergrove easyJet, scheduled for departure at nine that evening. He sent a warning SMS to his brother-in-law while the printer chugged out a boarding pass. He tore up the stairs, taking them three at a time. Shamsa, alerted by the activity, followed him into the bedroom. Ten minutes later they were back down with a roll-on case stuffed with the basic clothing Jim would need for an extended stay on the farm. Warm clothes to travel with were laid on the bed. It would still be cold in Tyrone for weeks to come.

Sitting down again with the BlackBerry and the car key, he noticed the key blade had, in tiny, lower-case letters, the name 'valeo' stamped on it, high up near the plastic. From the depths of his memory, his law training told him this was Latin and had something to do with strength. He keyed in his code date of birth followed by the five letters on the blade. The phone almost heaved a sigh of relief and immediately pinged an SMS at him. Hash read 'BHXLS5C15'. His gut twisted at the instruction to wade deeper into the swamp. Birmingham Airport, long-stay car park five, somewhere in area C15, something, someone was waiting.

The SMS had come from a Libyan dialling code, he guessed probably from a mobile. The Etisalat contract was a feint, maybe even unintentional, and he knew it was fruitless to pursue that line for clues. The Libyan number alone was proof of who was playing and he realised that by releasing the SMS from its limbo, its sender would see delivery had been made. Again, the icy hand of fear wrenched at his innards.

The doorbell triggered excited barking from Shamsa. Hash moved from the kitchen and saw a hunched figure on the other side of the glass. Mouthing a silent curse, he fixed his best smile and opened the door.

'Mrs Hamilton, how nice: what can I do for you?' The way she looked past him so hopefully told him she was hunting Jim. When she wanted something she rarely wasted time on pleasantries.

'Jim's going away,' Hash said, 'I was just packing his suitcase.' He saw her face fall.

'But if there's anything I can do?' Hash let it hang in the air. Shamsa had come forward and she tousled the dog's ears. He was in an agony of impatience.

'Where's he going?' she said. Hash had to smile at the nosy questions. 'Granny in Ireland, I expect.' She answered her own question, sounding disappointed.

'I mean...anything,' Hash insisted.

'Just wanted some wood chopped.' She sighed. 'I'd do it myself, but...'

'No problem, I'll do it tomorrow,' Hash soothed, then as he started to close the door he caught sight of Jim approaching. Jim read the situation and tried a theatrical backtrack, mouthing an exaggerated 'No!' at his father.

Mrs Hamilton turned, seeing Jim. 'Just the man. Got some wood needs chopping. It'll only take a few minutes.' Normally, Hash would have been on the old lady's side and today was surely the right day to intervene on behalf of every old lady. But the message on the Arab BlackBerry had started the clock ticking.

'He's got a plane to catch and we're running late,' Hash said with firmness. 'And he's got to change.'

Shamsa had joined the small gathering, yelping with pleasure and trying to jump up at Jim as he squeezed past.

'Jim's got to get changed, Mrs Hamilton,' Hash repeated gently.

'Otherwise I'll be late,' Jim called from the sanctuary of the hallway.

'And he's got to be down in five minutes. Or else.'

'Sometimes think you spoil that boy,' Mrs Hamilton grumbled as she turned on the pathway. Only Mrs Hamilton was allowed to talk to Hash like that. When Flora had died, she had pitched in and she had been the first outsider in Jim's fan club. She had showered affection on Jim in her eccentric way. Hash listened to her grumbling: she was another one he would have to make it up to.

He ran into the kitchen, scooping up the Arab BlackBerry and the Citroën key. He yelled up the stairs to Jim. 'Two minutes!'

'What's the hurry, Dad?'

'One minute,' Hash called back.

He dropped the items into his Barbour pocket.

'Thirty seconds...!' he yelled, getting a muffled shout back.

He dashed into the sitting room, opened a desk drawer and picked up Jim's passport. From another drawer he took a wad of banknotes and peeled off three hundred pounds. Crossing to the printer he whipped off the boarding pass and double-checked the name and flight number.

'Now! Or the plane will leave without you!' he yelled and blew a stream of relief at hearing Jim's feet thud on the stairs.

CHAPTER 4

TUESDAY 3RD MARCH CHELTENHAM

Hash pushed at the wheel of the Discovery, then pounded it in frustration. Rush hour traffic in town was costing vital minutes and he was beginning to worry about conditions on the motorway.

'Got to get through,' he growled.

'Music, Dad,' Jim soothed, reaching forward. His finger pushed one of the numbers on the console and got a local DJ finishing off a traffic report.

'Yes…no!' Hash thumped the wheel. 'Find another channel, find BBC2.'

'Dad. If you used your sat nav, you'd see the jams.'

'If I'd renewed my subscription that would indeed be possible. Thanks all the same.' Hash forced a smile.

'How did you swing it with Miss Pine?'

'She took some persuading and I'm in her bad books.'

'But she gave permission?' Jim asked.

'She said she'd pass it on with her support. But she wasn't happy.'

'You've blown it, Dad.' Jim shook his head in commiseration.

Just as they were approaching the motorway slip road, a local station announced the northbound M5 was choked below Worcester, with standstills on the M42 between junctions three and five.

'We'll blow it again, if we're not careful,' Hash muttered, hauling the Discovery over to the right, circling on the flyover roundabout, heading back to Cheltenham.

Jim looked up from his phone. 'Dad?'

'Train,' Hash said. 'Otherwise you won't make it. You sure you're OK with the train?'

'I've only done it, like, a hundred times, Dad.' Hash was happy at the boy's confidence. 'Uncle Sean's going to meet you,' Hash said.

'Yesss.' Jim punched the air.

'Don't let him take you to a pub.'

At the railway station, Hash made Jim hold up one item after the other.

'Phone?'

'Check.'

'Passport and ticket?'

Jim held them up.

He bought the rail ticket and handed over an envelope with the money inside.

'Wow,' Jim said, 'you must really want to get rid of me.'

'Can't bloody wait,' Hash smiled. 'Three hundred,' he said, holding a finger to his lips. 'Keep it in your pocket and don't open it until you see Granny.' He slipped a twenty-pound note into Jim's back pocket. 'That's for a sandwich and a Coke on the journey. You'll be in Birmingham at seven... Don't dawdle: get the first train to the airport.'

'I take it,' Jim cocked a quizzical eyebrow, 'this is not a down payment on the quadcopter?'

Father and son looked at each other.

'One day, you'll be a good businessman,' Hash said.

'What I'm saying is' – Jim held up the envelope – 'this is just to get me through the next weeks on a muddy farm...'

'Maybe we should make it performance-related.' Hash made to snatch the money back. Jim retreated towards the ticket barrier, waving the money.

'Not the down payment...right?'

'Why don't you just wave the money around until someone mugs you?'

Jim hoisted his daysack onto his shoulder and made for the ticket barrier.

'What time do you have to check in by?' Hash asked, one last test.

'Eight o'clock, Dad.'

'Safe trip,' Hash said, pulling the boy back for a hug. 'Give your old man a hug. Catch up with you next week.'

'Ok.'

'Call me when you get there, and give my love to your gran and grandpa and don't let Uncle Sean take you drinking.' Jim waved back once more before trotting down to the platform.

When Hash returned to the Discovery, Shamsa was staring intently past him, straining for a last glimpse of Jim. She whined when he opened the door, as if in reproach. Hash had to comfort her.

Hash arranged his own phone and the Arab BlackBerry on the dashboard tray, side by side, then buckled himself in. He comforted the dog until he saw the train leave the station. Getting the lad away before things moved beyond his control had been his smartest move so far, winning himself some headspace.

Light was fading under leaden skies as he took the Discovery back onto the northbound M5, and he was struck by the irony of retrying for Birmingham Airport. This time there was no urgency, nobody to drop off or meet, no reason for speed; if anything, this was a time for caution. True, he told himself, if it had not been for the traffic jams, a combined trip might have been better. He could have seen Jim through the system, waved him off, and then moved to the next task. But no matter – the train would make sure Jim made it on time.

As the heaving rain slowed traffic to a crawl, he used the time to get through to Sean before Bella did. The man's mobile phone was off and Hash had to think for a minute. It was early, but not for Sean. The chances were his brother-in-law was in his favourite drinking den. The place, in Belfast's Republican west, had always been a hang-out for Sean in his heyday and was now the only place that tolerated him. When the phone rang the handset was lifted immediately. The silence at the other end reminded Hash of the naked suspicion still so close to the surface after the years of trouble. In the background Hash could hear accordion music and the buzz of conversation. After a few seconds a voice simply said, 'Kelly's'.

'Is Sean there?' Hash asked.

'Mate,' the voice said quietly, 'we have a thousand fucking Seans in here.'

'Just tell Sean it's Darky.'

The man at the other end muffled the receiver but Hash could just make out, 'Tell Sean there's a Darky after him!' and caught the gust of laughter before the phone went muffled again as it was being passed to another pair of hands.

'Darky...see you?' The accent was exaggerated Belfast. Hash could hear rebel music and laughter and Sean's voice, raised to cut across the babble.

'See me!' Hash said, 'what about ye?'

'Oh...the best, the very best.'

'Your mobile was off.'

'Never trust the thing,' Sean said. 'Been taking tea at the Palace, old chap?' Hash wondered how much Sean had already drunk.

'Away and fock yerself,' he mimicked, already weary of the exchange.

Sean's change of tone at the other end of the line signalled a truce. 'Sorry about the mobile,' he said. 'I was in confession.'

'Like hell,' Hash said. 'Sorry about the short notice, can you do it?'

'Why not?'

'Good man. Can you keep an eye on him?'

'Aye.'

'You're coming over next week. I need you, mate.'

'That's nice...mate.' Bitten by the sarcasm, Hash looked at

the phone. Sean had been drinking: the question was, how much so far.

'I'm serious now,' Hash said. 'I've got a problem and I need help.'

'Ok…Ok. Jim's fine with me,' Sean said.

'He still has his nightmares,' Hash said.

'Me an' him, too. Why the panic?'

'I might have a bit of a problem.'

'Who with?'

'Tell you next week.' Hash paused then added, 'I'll make it a business expense. Cover your costs.'

'This is family. I don't want your money.'

Hash felt his temper flare. 'Promise me you'll be there for Jim? And keep your mobile on.'

'No problem.'

'Then get him down to the farm?'

There was a pause on the line. Sean had never been forgiven by his parents: no hero's welcome after the years in the Brit jail at Long Kesh.

'I've told your mother and she's expecting you both.' There was still silence.

'Mate?' Hash said. 'You still there?'

'Aye, Darky. All under control.'

'This means a lot to me. Speak later when he's landed. See you next week.'

He laid the phone beside the Arab BlackBerry and exhaled long and slow. He could do without Sean on one of his downswings. The years in a Brit concentration camp had destroyed the Sean he had known all those years ago. In his thirties Sean Barr had been a handsome, swashbuckling rebel, a freedom fighter. A British court saw him in a different light, as a brutal killer who even turned his gun against children. Ten years into a life sentence, the Good Friday Agreement opened the prison doors and waved him out. But there was nowhere for Sean to go. The new era of peace cast him as yesterday's hero. Hash knew he was shunned by his parents and guessed he sought comfort in the drinking dens along the Falls and Whiterock roads, scooping beer with the other diehard Republicans still fighting their war against the Brits.

Hash also knew the real Sean, or what was left bloodied but unbowed, a loyal friend and a devoted uncle. Even by the exceptional standards of West Belfast thuggery, Sean still ranked as a hard bastard. Nobody would get near Jim on Sean's watch.

CHAPTER 5

When he pulled off the M42 at junction 6, following the sign to the airport, it was past eight o'clock and he guessed Jim would be through the system and sitting at the departure gate. It was now fully dark and raining heavily, which suited Hash. He nosed the vehicle through the barrier of the 'Drop and Go' parking area and found the nearest parking space. He put his tweed cap on, whispering to Shamsa he was only going away for a minute and for her to guard the vehicle. He did not lock the car; if anyone wanted to steal it, they would have to deal with her first.

Under the protection of his Barbour jacket, he made Long-Stay 5 car park in ten minutes. Zone C, row 15 was long, empty of people, but full of cars. He could see the disappearing outline and tail lights of a shuttle bus, splashes of rain kicking up off its roof, as it swung out of the park heading for the terminals. Most travellers had parked and gone ahead and Hash began his search knowing he was virtually unobserved by anyone on foot. A security camera operator, with a bank of screens to monitor, would simply see another shadow traipsing along rows of cars; a soaked driver returning from a long trip, tired and trying to remember where he had left his car.

Like a seedy punter, he sought out Citroëns and offered his electronic fob, pressing the 'unlock' as he approached. After five rejections, a little C3 flashed a welcome. Through the rain, Hash saw the car was red: the weak lighting made him double-check. He glanced back to make sure he was alone then looked inside to see if there were any obvious packages on the seats. None in sight, he went straight for the hatch. Opening it released a smell of old, worn upholstery and sickly air freshener. A mid-size trolley suitcase lay in the boot space. He quickly checked the front and rear of the car, including the glove compartment. There was no paper, no object to identify the car in any way, and anyway, he knew it was all about the suitcase.

Hoisting it out, judging its weight at around fifteen kilos, he looked around again, then, as the rain danced off every surface, he closed the hatch. When he hit the 'lock' button the car blinked goodbye. He crouched down and put the keys on top of the back left wheel. Stepping back, he fished out his own mobile and snapped the car, making sure he got the registration and colour.

On the way back to the car, deciding on a detour, he dashed inside the departure terminal, tugging the suitcase on its wheels. He checked the desks and the departures screen, seeing Jim's flight to Aldergrove showing as closed and no staff on duty. Passing the Marks & Spencer's concession on his way out he paused to grab sandwiches and water. Neither he nor Shamsa had eaten since midday.

The Discovery was back on the M42 fifty minutes after arriving at the airport. Hash guessed Jim's plane would be taking off, maybe even in the air. Whatever was in the suitcase, its weight making him curious, would have to wait until later and the security of home. He calculated an hour, if the traffic was good, would see him unlocking its secrets. He chewed on the food, feeding the crusts and the last entire sandwich to Shamsa.

Nose-to-tail congestion in the rain wrecked his estimate and fatigue began to drain him. Blinking his tired eyes and shaking his head failed to freshen him. The flashing of brake lights and the scraping of his windshield wipers grated on his already raw nerves.

He wondered if he should make a clean breast to the British authorities. He toyed with a plea bargain scenario. It would guarantee safety but the cost would be personal ruin and probably time in prison; maybe one of those soft 'open prisons' he had heard about in court. He could see the *Echo* reporter scribbling, 'Cheltenham Magistrate unmasked as spy in our midst'. He wound the window down, letting freezing air into the car, then shook his head vigorously trying to wake himself. He tried Jim's mobile. No luck. Jim had most probably switched off for the flight.

At the first turn-off for Cheltenham he saw it was just after ten and estimated Jim would have landed. He pictured the boy advancing, embarrassed, towards Uncle Sean who would start off gruff and then give him a rapturous bear hug before marching him to the nearest McDonald's. This would delay the long drive across Ulster to Tyrone and the border farmhouse at Clady. Bella would be waiting up, but the old boy would have been put to bed so he could be fresh in the morning. Sean would not have to confront both parents. His mother would be enough, sure to remind him he had caused the father's stroke. He would drop Jim and go straight back to the Falls Road.

As the Discovery took the Cheltenham exit, Hash tried Jim again. Again there was no reply. The boy had maybe forgotten to turn his phone back on: unusual for a teenager. He checked for signal strength on his phone; sometimes the atmospherics played with the signals. Trying Sean's number, the purring ringtone kicked in, stirring butterflies. Clicking and rustling told him Sean was on the line.

'I'm waiting on him. The sign says baggage is in the hall.'

'He'll be a few minutes yet. I'll ring back,' Hash said.

'What did Bella say?' Sean asked, apprehensive.

'Looking forward to seeing you both,' Hash lied. 'Said the old boy has his good days and bad days, and misses a man on the farm. They reckon they'll have to give the job to Jim if you don't get there soon.'

'Bollocks,' Sean snorted. 'You know she'll go mad at me.'

'Jim wants to do some shooting.'

'Not so easy in Belfast these days.'

'In the country, dickhead. I told him you're the best.'

'Showed you a thing or two...'

'Not quite how I remember it.'

'You got my bed ready...which wing am I in?'

'Thought I'd put you in the Maximum-Security wing. All sorted, new bars on the windows...hacksaw on the bedside table. Don't change your mind at the last minute.'

'Wouldn't miss the crack,' Sean said.

'Call me when Jim's with you.'

'Aye, Ok.' Sean hung up.

In contrast to his earlier mood, Sean's spirits seemed to have lifted and his speech was clear. Killing time, Hash pulled over at a pump and filled up. On his way out he rang Jim but got no answer. After another wait of five minutes, Sean rang. 'No sign of him. Still a few people off that flight coming through, though.'

'Can't understand it,' Hash said. 'He should have been through well by now.'

'Give him a ring?'

'He's not picking up. Maybe forgot to turn his phone on.'

'He's a teenager,' Hash said. 'That phone is his lifeline.'

'Two other flights have landed after his,' Sean said. 'There are folk coming through in shorts and suntans...don't think it's that hot in Brum.'

'You sure you're at Aldergrove?'

'For fuck's sake,' Sean growled. 'You sure you sent him to the right fucking country? I'm standing here for an hour and I'm not blind.'

'He took off at nine. Maybe there was a delay.'

'The plane's fucking landed, and all the passengers got off.'

'Maybe you can ask at the desk, ask for a passenger list?' Hash asked. The phone went dead.

Blinking on the dashboard caught his eye. He was holding his phone and realised the Arab BlackBerry had pulsed another SMS. He steered across into the empty car park of a retail estate and sat there, engine running. Picking up the old phone, he keyed in the unlock code, fumbling it the first time, then redoing it.

A message read, 'I am OK father.'

A wave of nausea hit Hash and he dropped the phone on the seat, opened the car door, hung out and vomited. He could feel the veins in his neck and temple throbbing as he heaved. He got out, caught his breath and leaned against the vehicle, sucking in air. Shamsa watched.

'How soon can you get here?' Hash walked a short distance from the Discovery, pulling at the bottled water, rinsing and spitting. He felt sweat on his face, with the drizzle cooling him. He was climbing back in as Sean growled,

'Well, I'm still at the airport, if that helps. He been in touch yet?'

'He's not coming.' Hash's voice was hard, unemotional. He stared down at the puke, steam rising off it. 'Has Bella called you?'

'What the fuck are you talking about?'

'Has Bella rung you?'

'No.'

'Thank fuck,' Hash said. 'If she does, tell her I pulled the plug on the trip.'

'You're a bit short on detail, mate.'

'I'll tell her he's had one of his turns.'

'I didn't realise he was bad,' Sean said.

'Much worse,' Hash said. 'How soon can you get here?'

'Has he had a turn?'

'Something's happened.'

'So you just said. What?'

'He just sent me an SMS telling me he's OK.'

'That's a result,' Sean said. 'Where is he, then?'

'That's the problem. The SMS came from his phone but it maybe wasn't him sending.'

'What the fuck are you talking about?'

'That's not the bad news,' Hash said. 'The really bad news is that the message came through to,' he took another swig of water, 'another phone, one I've just been lent.'

'Someone stole his phone, then,' Sean said.

'And then made him send a message to a stranger's phone. I told you it's complicated. That's why I need you here. How soon can you get here?'

'You've fucking lost me, mate. I see my licence guy on Friday, he signs me off to come to the mainland on Monday. Got a hospital appointment on Monday, and can't miss that. What's the fucking rush?'

'You're the only one who'll understand, the only person who'll get this fucking mess. But we have to talk face to face.'

'Jesus,' Sean breathed. 'Must be serious if you need me that badly.'

'When do you get in on Monday and how long can you stay?'

'They'll let me come for the races only. Out on Monday but back Saturday. If I come back a minute late he'll shit down my throat.'

'Unless I get you work, a contract, legitimate?'

'Could work. The arse would like that.'

Bella's voice was brimming when she picked up. She could not see Hash, sitting in the driver's seat, his mouth sour with his own vomit, bracing himself.

'Is the young lord on his way to us, his humble servants?' The slow country drawl would normally bring a smile to Hash's face. 'The wee soul must be dead beat.'

'Bad news, Bella, I'm afraid,' Hash said. She did not hear him. 'Bella?' Hash was gritting his teeth.

'Aye? We're waiting for Lord Jim. His room's ready, the one his poor mother…' Her voice went silent for a second or two. '…Wee Lord Jim, the spitting image of his mum.'

'He's not coming, Bella.' Hash screwed his eyes, waiting in the charged silence.

'Tell me you're joking…dear God…please.'

'Bella, he's not at his best.'

'Has that idiot Sean crashed the car?' Her voice was a growl.

'Nothing to do with Sean,' Hash said. 'I've just told him, too…he's been waiting at Aldergrove.'

'What's going on?'

'I think he's had a turn,' Hash said.

'A turn?'

'You know how he gets too worked up about something,' Hash said.

'What thing?'

'I don't know, Bella. Could be something at school, some pressure, growing pains, teenage worries, maybe someone said something.'

'Is he ok? Where do you have him?'

'It happened at the check-in,' Hash nodded vigorously at the empty car park. 'He just collapsed on me.' Hash shook his head in wonder, waving his free hand. 'He came to and I just brought him straight back home.'

'I'll have a word with him,' she said.

'He's fast asleep. He'll call you tomorrow.'

'Are you sure it's OK?'

'We'll both be over by the end of next week.' It was a lie he desperately wanted to believe.

'I'll speak to you both tomorrow,' she said. 'What am I going to tell the old boy sitting here?'

Immediately after putting the phone down on Bella, he dialled Jim's mobile and waited. A digitised voice told him to leave a message. He looked at the Arab BlackBerry to double-check it was Jim's number. He tried to concentrate on the sequence of events. Jim had been waved off at the station at around six in the evening. Then he would have made it from New Street to the airport in half an hour, checked in at eight, due to fly around nine. Surely he would have called if there had been a delay? But Sean had told him the flight landed on schedule and all the passengers were gone.

'For fuck's sake, Hash, get a grip,' he moaned to himself. Shamsa flinched at the anger.

Whoever was out there had read the moves. He began to seethe with self-loathing. Maybe Jim had been mugged, his money and phone taken? Maybe he had been marched to a cashpoint. If it had been thugs like the ones in the chippy, he would have been easy meat.

The first SMS had come from a Libyan number, maybe the sender was in the UK or even in Libya. His mind jumped to the suitcase sitting in the back of the Discovery. The second SMS had come through at twenty past ten, from Jim's own phone. They wanted Hash to join the dots and Jim would never use 'father' unless he was taking the mickey.

A new SMS pulsed, two words only. As he read it tears began to sting his eyes. He rocked from side to side in the driver's seat, choking back a scream of rage, jamming his knuckles against his teeth.

CHAPTER 6

TUES 3RD MARCH NIGHT.

'Dafe coming,' read the second SMS.

Hash knew Jim could not possibly have sent this one, yet it had come from the lad's own phone. Hash knew there was nobody in Jim's address book with the name Dafe. This meant someone was either dictating to Jim or simply using his device. He looked at the keyboard on the Arab BlackBerry, where the 'f' and 'v' buttons were close. He toyed with the possibility the fingers sending the message had made a typo error, straying from 'dave' to 'dafe'. The gremlin inside his head, kicking at his skull, told him to try kidding someone else. The word 'dafe' came all the way from Ben Gashir and Hash's previous life. Jim was just the messenger, Shanghai'ed to pass it on.

Hash's brain was racing. First out of the window was any notion of going to the authorities. He was on his own and somehow, he had to catch up and overtake, get an advantage. Jim's absence from school now needed to be prolonged, a better excuse needed. Hash thanked God for the school holidays. His clumsy assumptions where Susan was concerned had been a timely shock. And he would need her help again. She was probably key to keeping the school quiet. He would have to patch things up with Susan, tell her Jim was down with some virus and staying put with his grandparents. The grandparents would be fed the line that Jim was in hospital in Cheltenham, under observation for a few days; the same virus would do. Then, to spin it, out he would tell them the lad was at home, confined to bed.

Sean would need to get the full picture but only when he came over and sat face to face. Maybe Siddiq could be used, too. Hash felt a flicker of hope. He could open up, just a little, to Siddiq and trust him to keep his mouth shut. On an impulse, he keyed a return SMS to the Libyan number: 'Confirm my son OK'. He doubted he would get a reply, but it was just possible they would want to reassure him.

Hash realised the engine was idling and he was sitting in a deserted car park with a puddle of vomit at his feet. Both he and Shamsa needed to get back. He revved the engine and, keeping the driver's window down, nosed out into almost empty streets. The rain had stopped and the surroundings seemed fresher for the earlier downpour.

The 'dafe' SMS had been another order. Transliterated from Arabic into English, the word meant 'guest'. They could have sent it in Arabic but would have known that Cheltenham was the world centre of eavesdropping software. Instead, someone with a sharp brain had mashed the languages so the word would look like an innocent typo on a teenager's phone. Soon, Hash pondered, and maybe the bastard was already on the way, an unwanted guest would cross his threshold.

Twenty-seven years ago, in early December 1988, a similar cryptic instruction had brought a 'dafe' to his doorstep. In this man, a fellow Libyan a few years older than himself and permanently on edge, Hash had recognised fear and anxiety. The man had spent hours at various telephone kiosks, revealed little and moved on after four days. A week after that, Pan Am Flight 103 exploded over the Scottish town of Lockerbie. When Muammar Gaddafi's hand was detected in the catastrophe, Hash instinctively knew he and this 'dafe' had been part of it. At that moment, he had turned his back on Gaddafi and his madness, though the disgust and shame had stayed with him ever since.

Whoever was out there calling these shots was from those days, the heirs to the Gaddafi regime. But who exactly and how had they got through to him so quickly? These people were so far ahead of him now it was staggering. The guys who now had Jim were professionals and had read Hash easily. So easily they knew he should be in panic. He needed to steel his nerves and get his edge back. The bargaining chip played both ways. The first thing was to get a guarantee Jim was safe. If Hash's cooperation was what they were after, they could only get it if Hash was confident Jim was alive and unharmed.

As soon as he was home he flicked on the laptop. Jim's phone had been a two-for-one deal on his business account which allowed him to monitor Jim's usage and he had downloaded a find-my-phone app to locate the phone if it was lost or left on a bus.

Jim's iPhone had transmitted the 'OK' message at 2221 from the junction of Stratford Road and Henley Street in the Sparkbrook area of South Birmingham. Hash could see that was only a few miles from the airport and even less from New Street Station, and he wondered how they had grabbed Jim. Almost certainly, they had followed him, but where had they started watching…? From home…? On the train?

The 'dafe' message had come through at 2305, forty-four minutes later and from the junction of Grafton Road and Kyotts Lake Road, in the same area as the first. He Googled the streets and found himself zooming in amongst parades of Asian shops, restaurants and grocery stores. He wondered if Jim had been driven around in a 'holding pattern', made to send the first message, maybe rewarded with food and then made to send the second.

Hash realised he could be on those dark, wet streets in an hour and when daily routines started he could walk around them with a photo of Jim, asking people if they had seen the boy. Equally, he reasoned, whoever had the phone could be playing a game to throw him off the scent. Maybe they had moved the phone to Sparkbrook as a decoy, with Jim being held somewhere else. Hash rang Jim again but the iPhone was switched off.

If he drove there and set up, he considered, and they switched it back on and let Jim send another message, that would put him right on the spot. Maybe he would get lucky and zero in on the exact location. On the other hand, maybe they were waiting for him to try so they could teach him a lesson about who was in control. Another transmission could get him dummied into a wild goose chase, or an ambush. Hash massaged his aching temples and closed his eyes. Maybe they were waiting to see if the Arab BlackBerry would move.

Most of the people living in Sparkbrook would be Asians. Although he knew it would be smarter to be looking for Jim with a team who knew the area, staying at home and worrying was useless and when his unwanted guest arrived there would be even less freedom of movement.

WEDNESDAY.

MARCH 4TH. SPARKBROOK, BEFORE DAWN

As the first hint of light tinted the darkness, Hash was pulling into a pay-and-display car park off the Stratford Road. The approaching dawn kindled some hope he might be near enough to see and grab Jim. However slender that hope, it was better than staying in Cheltenham, worrying to death. The Arab BlackBerry remained on the kitchen table, bleeping to anyone counter-monitoring that it was left in Cheltenham.

Walking the streets between the sites of the phone emissions, Hash looked for likely places Jim might have been sitting the previous evening. He saw drab, two-storey, red-brick parades of Asian restaurants, halal produce, convenience stores all with their signs in English, Arabic and what he guessed was Sanskrit or Amharic. Windows were screened with adverts or stacked with produce ready to go back out on the pavement when the awnings were unfurled. Most restaurant windows were draped with heavy curtains. As he walked, he looked up at the first-floor windows. Maybe a young lad too terrified to sleep would spot his father.

As the working day gathered momentum Hash decided to observe from the warmth of his Discovery. By some fluke, Jim might break free if he recognised the vehicle and Shamsa would bark if she saw him. He switched on his laptop, connected to the net and kept vigil, dialling Jim's number every half-hour.

Bella rang at nine.

'How's our little lord? He any better yet?'

'Still under the weather,' Hash replied. 'Some sort of flu bug. It's been going round the school, apparently. It's put a few of the other kids out of action, so Jim's not the only one.'

'You had us all worried there,' she said. 'I thought you said it was his epilepsy. Is he up to a chat with his granny?'

'I'm out of the house. He's in bed. At least he was when I left him. But you could try his mobile.'

'I haven't got the number,' Bella said, 'but it'll wait.'

'I'll give you his number,' Hash said, 'The more people that call him, the more he'll like it. Got a pen?'

'Doesn't matter, Hash,' she said. 'I'll call him later, maybe he'll be feeling better.'

'How's the old boy?' Hash asked. He was looking out of the Discovery windscreen, not concentrating on her. Eventually her silence at the other end of the phone warned him she was expecting an answer.

'Sorry, Bella, I got distracted. His lordship just texted me. I think he wants pizza.'

'For breakfast? Tell him not to eat rubbish,' she said, 'and tell him his gran sends her love.'

Around eleven the battery on his laptop started to fade and, going to the rear door to plug in a charging cable, he saw the suitcase. In the stress of the last twelve hours he had forgotten all about it. Opening the rear door of the Discovery he pulled the case to him and checked the two outside pockets, finding nothing. He unzipped the main compartment and the cover fell back. The contents had been wrapped in a large, blue plastic shopping bag. He needed two hands to get the bag out and upended onto the boot space. Two items slid out, both similarly wrapped in blue plastic, but bound tight with strips of masking tape.

Hash extracted the first, feeling something rectangular and light, like a pack of printing paper. Easing it out, he found himself looking at a vacuum-sealed block of images of The Queen. Wads of notes, rubber-banded in quantities, each about an inch thick. The face notes had the £50 denomination. He flipped the block, end over end to look at it from all angles then, walking his fingers across the whole he came up with twenty wads. Someone wanted him to look after one hundred thousand pounds.

He dropped the block of notes back into the suitcase, threw in the second sealed object, zipped it up and slammed the vehicle door.

CHAPTER 7

MORNING.

I was thinking of calling you,' Hash said, looking at Siddiq's name on the phone.

'Now you have me,' Siddiq's voice was quiet but friendly. Hash had to concentrate to hear him. 'Where are you, my friend?' Hash looked out of the window at the drab red-brick buildings, the people on the streets all heavily clothed against the cold, grey morning.

'I'm on my way to the mosque,' Hash lied.

'You're too late, my friend,' Siddiq said.

'Not your mosque,' Hash said. 'I'm going to one in Birmingham.'

'What's wrong with our one in Cheltenham?'

'I've got a problem,' Hash said.

'And the solution is in a mosque in Birmingham?' Siddiq sounded surprised. 'I also have a problem.'

'What sort of problem?'

'But my problem is not in the mosque.' Siddiq cleared his throat and his voice dropped. 'I am bringing you someone.' He cleared his throat again. 'Someone special.'

Hash's tired mind came alive. 'Who?'

'I need you to help me.' Siddiq's tone became confidential. 'Shall we say...I have a guest who needs to be looked after.'

Hash concentrated on Siddiq's every word. 'How urgent?'

Siddiq took time to answer. 'Quite urgent, sensitive, something best talked about face to face.' He paused. 'Someone who is arriving unexpectedly.'

'A guest?' Hash repeated, reaching to turn the ignition keys.

Siddiq's voice was quieter than usual. 'A special person, sort of a guest but not a guest. If you follow me?'

'You're making it difficult, Siddiq.' Hash was wondering how Siddiq had become involved.

'That's why it's better we talk face to face.'

Hash knew Siddiq had a network of Bangladeshi relations stretching across the Midlands: restaurants, import-export and other businesses, all linked by Byzantine marriage and business alliances. 'I also have a problem,' the man had said. He now wished he was right back in Cheltenham instead of wasting time on this wild goose chase. He felt the stirrings of hope conflicting with fear. If Siddiq was involved with the 'dafe', then he was involved with Jim's disappearance.

'I am having a bit of trouble with Jim,' Hash tried.

'I'm sorry to hear that,' Siddiq said. 'I hope I can help.'

'You know Jim. Could be a teenage thing,' Hash fed it out. 'Teenager stuff.'

'Is he at home?' Siddiq asked.

'Why do you ask?' Hash said.

'Because you are driving to a mosque in Birmingham for the first time in your life.'

'He's at school,' Hash lied. 'I'm doing a charity thing up here.'

'Who with?' Siddiq asked. 'Charity begins at home.' There was an awkward silence between the two men. Siddiq broke it. 'Please come and sit with me, it'll be easier to talk.'

Hash calculated he and Siddiq went back over twenty years when a business relationship developed into a friendship. They were two foreigners in an English town and had met in a small mosque north of the High Street. In the beginning, with only a handshake as security, Hash had lent cash to the ambitious Bangladeshi and the loan had been repaid with interest. The formula had repeated itself until now, in business terms, both men were tried and trusted colleagues. Both were wealthy now: Siddiq had been successful in the restaurant business, while Hash had applied his energy to property development, acquiring a considerable portfolio of residential and commercial premises.

As he drove, he again wondered if he should just go to the police and hold his hands up. He would hide the money before he surrendered. Maybe he would leave it with Sean. Or better, with Siddiq who could at least apply interest and take a small commission. A hundred thousand working for him over the coming years would be a tidy pension pot when he was finally released from jail. The second package had not felt as regular as the block of money, and he would check it when he was behind the curtains at home. The stash of money was a hallmark of the old-school methods, pay cash for everything, leave no electronic trail. Hash knew the cash was his to grease wheels with and the Libyan auditors were the least of his worries.

The gremlin in his head came back, 'What are the chances of the British working fast enough to save Jim...answer, marginally better than nil.' Jim was everything to him. The Brits would begin a game of cat and mouse, interested in Jim as leverage; they would use him exactly as he was being used now, as a pawn, a bargaining chip. Hash shuddered at the thought of Jim, tired, worried, afraid, and maybe hurt. He cursed himself for being so slow off the mark, for not having moved faster.

At home, he lifted the suitcase onto the kitchen table, pulled out the money block and laid it to one side. The second bag, the heavier of the two was also vacuum-sealed, and he saw through the filter of blue plastic what looked like an angler's vest. Hash guessed a cheap make, maybe even second-hand, its khaki fabric stained with dirt or oil. Hash ran his fingers over the pockets feeling lumps of solid material that gave slightly to his pinching touch, as if blocks of kids' plasticine were packed into every pocket.

Taking out the vest and keeping it sealed, he made a closer inspection. Going around all the pockets, feeling the blocks in each one, he finally came to the top right pocket and felt two small, cylindrical objects. These he decided must be batteries or at least plastic tubes to hold batteries, and his fingers felt for the wires beneath the cloth and plastic skin that would surely lead to a detonator tucked into the nearest block of explosive. Holding the waistcoat up, he judged the weight at around twelve kilos, maybe eleven of which was explosive.

Enough to blow his house across Cheltenham with a bang that would be heard ten miles away in Gloucester. There would be nothing but a hole in the ground where he stood. Mrs Hamilton would die, too. Gas fires from ruptured mains would keep the emergency services at bay for some time. He flipped it over again to examine it through the plastic, looking for any other features. He guessed the bomber could set it off himself or an aerial inside the fabric could receive the detonating signal from an obliging third party.

Sitting opposite Siddiq, in one of the corner booths of his restaurant, Hash could see his friend was nervous. When he spoke it was in quiet, conspiratorial tones. 'We need to hide someone,' he said.

'We?'

'You need to hide someone,' Siddiq said. 'I'm asking you.'

'Why me?'

Siddiq looked left and right, checking there was nobody within earshot, his face taking on a shifty expression.

'If it's for you,' Hash cut in, 'I'll do it.'

Siddiq's face cleared and he sat back against the booth seat. 'Just one person,' he said. 'I know you have places.'

'But you have places, too,' Hash said. He and Siddiq sometimes compared their various properties. 'I'm sure yours are better than mine.'

Siddiq sat back against the seat, his gaze shifting to his staff.

'Can't use my places,' he said.

'How soon?'

'Very soon.'

'I've only got two places empty, just now,' Hash said. 'One in Hesters Way.' He looked at Siddiq, 'The tenants just moved out. And the other is a nice little place behind GCHQ.' He knew the word 'nice' would draw Siddiq.

'They'll need a bit of cleaning. Have you got someone to do some quick cleaning?' Hash said.

Siddiq sucked his teeth and shook his head, making the shifty, sideways glances. 'Can't use my staff,' he said. 'Too risky.'

'So, then...which one?'

Siddiq tapped a finger gently on the table. 'That place,' he said, 'The HQ place.'

'Today, tonight, tomorrow...?' Hash leaned back and held both palms in the air. 'Give me a clue.'

'Tonight, tomorrow most probably.' Siddiq canted his head one way then the other. 'Depends when I am told.' For the first time in their acquaintance Hash looked at Siddiq with suspicion. His friend of so many years, normally suave and courteous but now all of a sudden so furtive, a mixture of nerves and embarrassment.

'Let me know,' Hash said. 'I'll go and prepare the apartment this afternoon, get the place heated and aired, freshen it up.'

'What about Jim?' Siddiq looked directly at Hash. 'How can I help?'

It was Hash's turn to be evasive. Was Siddiq aware Jim had been grabbed, or was he just the messenger about the safe house for the guest? At Ben Gashir the instructors had drummed into Hash how a cell on the ground in enemy territory operated more securely the less each member knew collectively about the activities and responsibilities of the others.

'He has run away,' Hash said. Siddiq's eyebrows shot up.

'I took him to the station last night,' Hash continued, 'but he didn't go where I sent him.'

'What is wrong with the boy?' Siddiq looked genuinely shocked.

'I need to find him.' Hash patted his pocket. 'I tracked his phone location to Sparkbrook.'

'Sparkbrook!' Siddiq exclaimed. 'That's why you were driving there today.' He nodded slowly. 'You were looking for him?'

'What else could I do?'

'Go to the police?' Siddiq said.

'That would not be my first choice.'

'What would be?'

'I don't know, to be honest.' Hash shrugged. 'Maybe he'll phone when he's tired.'

'Is he sick, needing medication, a doctor?' Siddiq's questions seemed genuine and realistic.

'He has epilepsy, especially vulnerable when he's stressed. I have the medication when I get worried.' It was a lie but if Siddiq was passing on information, then it was worth inserting a medical complication.

'If he doesn't come home, you should go to the police, check the hospitals, surely?' Siddiq became animated.

'I need to know he is OK or have him communicate,' Hash said.

'And you were going to the mosque in Sparkbrook?' Siddiq's brow shot up. 'Which mosque, my friend?'

'Of course not. I was going to check the streets and cafés where the signal came from.'

'Maybe that's not a bad idea,' Siddiq said.

'It's the only idea, so far.'

'I meant the mosques,' Siddiq said. 'Going to a mosque is better than going to the police…in Sparkbrook.'

'We both know I can't go to the police.' Hash watched Siddiq's face for any hint of agreement; there was none.

'Depending on the mosque, of course,' Siddiq continued his train of thought. 'Do one thing, now,' he said. 'SMS me a good photo of him, a good one of his face.'

'Why?'

'I can pass the photo on to imams in Birmingham, to the right mosques.'

Hash scrolled through his pictures looking for the most recent snap of Jim and they agreed on one showing Jim kneeling with Shamsa, smiling his characteristic pursed smile.

'Like his mother,' Siddiq said. 'Better than you going to the police. Do you have any money?'

'I can't believe you're short of cash.'

Siddiq ignored the jibe. 'You are sure you don't want to go to the police?'

'Sure. When do you want the money and how much will it take?' Siddiq did not answer directly, just canted his head one way then the other. 'A gesture only. Come to my mosque tomorrow and we'll sit with a friend.'

'I'm in a real hurry, Siddiq.'

Siddiq held up his right hand, fingertips pinched. 'Better to listen and think. If you rush into any mosque you can make it worse.'

In the pitch-dark, with Shamsa standing guard, he checked the footbridge with his hands. There was no fresh tape and as he walked back to the Discovery even the gradual incline sapped his strength. He had been awake for twenty-eight hours.

CHAPTER 8

THURSDAY 5TH MARCH. MORNING.

A ply board sheet was propped against the window from the inside of the chippy and the Portuguese was tacking a length of plank to batten it to the window frame. His wife stood by, broom in hand. Catching Hash's eye, she slowly shook her head from side to side.

'They come again, last night,' the husband said. 'Tell me they want to be my friend, find the bastards who did this.' He smacked a fat fist into his palm. 'Bastards smash my camera. Then the window.' His wife went outside and began sweeping the pavement. The Portuguese looked at her, then at Hash. 'She very frightened now.' He turned back to Hash. 'I tell them fuck off! They come in before closing time, same story, be my friend look after me. Then...' He flicked his fingers. 'Turn crazy. Swear at me, my wife. She very frightened.' He nodded towards his wife outside. 'She wants to go back home. Retire, she says. Enough of this bloody country.'

'The same people?' Hash asked.

'Of course.' The Portuguese tapped his neck. 'Same guy...

tattoo boy with his two friends.'

'Police?' Hash asked.

'No way, Mister Hash. Police come for five minutes…also not pay for fish and chips…no come back. These guys back tomorrow and after tomorrow.' He hammered at the plank, driving a nail into the frame. 'What I do, Mister Hash?' He looked at Hash over his shoulder. 'I fix this, pay two hundred for new glass today.' He swung the hammer, 'They come back tomorrow…another new window. How many times?'

'I will speak to the police,' Hash lied.

'Every night this?' The man gestured at the ply board. 'Now my customers are frightened, too.'

'I will do something.' Hash tried to sound convincing.

A small sign above the door proclaimed the house a 'Masjid', for the Muslim community. An internal wall had been knocked through to create a prayer hall, and Hash counted twelve others, praying in two lines at the midday prayers. He saw faces from Siddiq's crew of waiters as well as young men in smart leisure clothes; probably students from the nearby language school in Rodney Road. Hash prayed silently: his lips moved but no sounds came out. He had not forgotten the words but was grateful to Siddiq, upfront and speaking clearly, for leading the way. Vague snatches of the responses triggered automatically but Hash's mind was on Jim. By now he would have spent his second night away from home, exhausted, terrified.

After prayers Siddiq held him back as the others dispersed then led him into a gloomy, unloved kitchen. A pine table shoved against the wall made room for four chairs. The only decoration on the wall was an Islamic calendar showing the Kaaba at Mecca. As Siddiq beckoned to the cheap, wooden chairs they were joined by a short, wiry man with a medium-length grey beard. Hash had seen him amongst the worshippers earlier. He was dressed in grey trousers and a brown bomber jacket zipped to the neck. He looked in his mid-forties and offered the Arabic greeting, 'Salaam-Alaikum" without a smile but with a handshake as strong as hell. The beard was the most obvious sign of his devotion, traces of henna showed, yet to be rinsed away and shaved above and below his mouth, leaving no moustache. Hash felt the man's owlish stare boring into him from behind rimless glasses.

'This gentleman is Mister Hakim, and he may be able to assist you,' was all Siddiq said, pointing at the chairs. They sat and a silence set in, prolonged and pregnant. The stranger looked at a spot on the table and Siddiq looked at Hash, the same nervous smile playing on his face. Breaking the ice, Hash pulled an envelope from his pocket, placing it on the table, choosing the spot where the man's eyes seemed focused.

'This is for the mosque,' he said. 'Five thousand pounds.' Hash had no qualms about using his newly acquired wealth.

The silence continued with neither Siddiq nor Hakim making a move to take the envelope. Finally, Siddiq eased forward on his chair, clearing his throat. 'A very generous gift, my brother.'

Hakim nodded but otherwise said nothing, then his gaze lifted from the table and focused on Hash, like a poker player. After a further moment of silence Hakim forced a hard smile. 'And?'

'My son...' Hash began but was then immediately interrupted by Hakim speaking for the first time.

'The boy who has run away from home?' He jutted his chin at Siddiq. 'He told me.' The confidence and brutality of the assumption startled Hash.

'Is he a Muslim?' Hakim continued in a quiet voice. Hash was still stunned by the first exchange and Siddiq filled the silence.

'He is the son of a good Muslim.' The other man ignored Siddiq, looking at Hash. 'I want his answer.'

'My son is not a Muslim and' – Hash paused for emphasis – 'he has not run away from home.' He was wondering if this was some sort of test, a trial with Siddiq as a witness. Maybe this tense Hakim with the owl-like gaze was behind the Libyan messages, and now sent to assess Hash's state of mind, his willingness to comply.

'But maybe he is and maybe he has,' Hakim countered. 'You say he is not.' The stress was placed on 'you'. The man allowed himself a hard smile. 'How sure are you? How do you know he is not a Muslim? How well do you know your son? Do you know what he watches on the internet?' A boxer could not have rained a more devastating flurry of punches.

Hash's mind reeled as he faced his interrogator. Siddiq was looking embarrassed, intimidated by the provocation. The envelope lay on the table, unopened.

'Maybe your son ran away,' the man said, 'and is now on his way to join the jihad.'

Hash shook his head slowly, feeling his anger building and was about to protest when Hakim spoke again. 'Maybe your son knows exactly what he is doing.' He stalled Hash with a raised hand. 'Do you know how many young people in South Birmingham have already gone to the jihad?'

'My son is not an adult,' Hash began to explain, 'he has issues.' He groped for the words.

'Issues are perfect,' Hakim interjected. 'A lot of young men with issues have gone,' Hakim answered his own question. 'Around two hundred so far. And none of the parents saw it coming.'

'My son has issues,' Hash began again, 'issues related to the loss of his mother. He still suffers from her death.' Hakim said nothing, merely watched Hash squirm.

'I put him on the train to Birmingham on Tuesday evening,' Hash said. 'I've had two messages from his phone and I traced the calls to Sparkbrook.' He told the two men about his vigil in the streets the previous day.

'And you were going there to look for him? Why didn't you go to the police, instead?'

Hash wondered why Siddiq had not briefed the man. 'Maybe I will go to the police.' Hash leaned forward. 'If nobody else can help me.'

'I told him not to,' Siddiq offered. Hakim had understood but seemed unfazed by Hash's veiled threat.

'I thought I might see him on the street,' Hash said. 'Maybe he had been mugged and released, his phone stolen, something like that.'

'Why not go to the church, instead of the mosques?' Hakim said.

'There don't seem to be many there.' Hash raised his hands. 'To be honest, I didn't know what the hell I was doing.'

'I told him the imams would think he was an undercover policeman, like those immigration cops,' Siddiq tried again. Hash had not remembered hearing that, but was grateful for his friend's intervention.

'I told him we could get the boy's photograph around our imams and friends in a few minutes,' Siddiq added.

'Maybe the boy's on his way to jihad, thanks to' – Hakim held up his fingers in inverted commas – 'an imam.'

'He's never shown any interest in Islam, or any religion,' Hash said.

'So why are you here, giving money to the mosque.' The man looked down at the envelope.

'Are you a father?' Hash asked. 'Put yourself in my position and tell me what you'd do?' Hakim nodded but did not answer.

'He could have called the police into Sparkbrook,' Siddiq said. 'Mister Hash did not want that to happen. He looked at the small man and emphasised, 'Now. It's a question of helping a friend, not letting him rush into a bad decision.'

Hakim looked at his watch then stood, preparing to leave.

'We'll be in touch,' he said, holding his hand to Siddiq.

'Tell me what to do?' Hash said.

'Insh'Allah,' the man said. 'God willing. We'll be in touch.' Hash felt the crushing handshake again. 'You're forgetting the money.' Hash pointed to the envelope.

'You gave it to the mosque,' Hakim said.

In the car park, Siddiq calmed Hash. 'Don't worry, my friend.'

'Such nonsense about Jim,' Hash said. 'Who is that man? Do you trust him?'

'You have to trust him.'

'Where does he come from?'

'He's an imam…'

'And he's from Sparkbrook,' Hash said.

'He's a very important businessman,' Siddiq added.

'He didn't seem to like me.'

'He is very cautious.'

'What happens now?' Hash asked. 'I just wait for him. What about the money?'

'You gave enough. Tomorrow is Friday and he will be seeing many people at his mosque. But…' Siddiq's voice dropped to a whisper. 'Now you have to do one thing.' They had stopped by Hash's car. Siddiq tugged Hash's arm. 'You have to get ready for my guest.'

'When's he coming?'

Siddiq gave a pained smile, as though it was an embarrassing admission. 'Very soon but I don't have the exact details.'

THURSDAY MID-AFTERNOON.

When Hash got back from the mosque there was a message flashing on the Arab BlackBerry. He picked the phone up and read, 'OK'. It had come through, with the same Libyan dialling code, at 1230, when he had been in the mosque with Siddiq. He dropped into a kitchen chair and looked at the phone, his hands trembling with relief.

'OK', Hash reflected, was short but huge; a cynical acknowledgement the bastards were pretending to feel his pain and cared enough to confirm Jim was 'OK'. The spectrum of 'OK' was vast: at one end, Jim would be comfortable, fed, rested and OK, at worst he would be battered, starved, terrified but still alive, and to the Libyan Mukhabarat that would qualify as OK. It was also an acknowledgement they needed to keep communication. Someone, some bastard from years ago, was throwing him a crumb to keep him in line. 'OK', Hash reflected, was a hundred times better than 'Not OK' or no answer at all.

He wondered if he should tell Siddiq about the Libyan connection, but all of a sudden there was something sour in their relationship. Sean, on the other hand, would need to know who they were dealing with: it would surprise him, but not throw him, as long as he still had the stomach for the game. Played correctly, kept out of sight and sober, Sean was an asset, a secret weapon. These thoughts brought Hash a surge of comfort. Deciding action was better than inertia and gloom in the kitchen, he took a wad of five thousand pounds then loaded Shamsa and his laptop into the Discovery. As before, he left the Arab BlackBerry behind and was about to close the front door when a thought popped into his brain.

From the passenger seat, Shamsa watched her master turn around and go back inside the house. Hash picked up the Arab BlackBerry, unlocked it with the code and tapped a response to the Libyan sender. 'What favourite name does Granny use?'

Heading west through Cheltenham, the anticipation of wading through motorway traffic wearied him. 'Groundhog Day,' he murmured to Shamsa. He felt he was plodding in pursuit when he should have been galloping. He revived himself with the thought that at least Sparkbrook would be well lit and the shops and restaurants bustling for some time to come. He thought of Hakim's efforts and the potential interference he, Hash could cause on the streets, especially if the man was genuine about looking for Jim. Something about the man's attitude, his confidence, arrogance even, carried a health warning, but on the other hand Siddiq had stressed the man was to be trusted.

As he was passing the housing estates near Princess Elizabeth Way, another impulse made him divert. The chippy would soon open for business. He allowed the Discovery to nose its way deeper into the estates, through the maze of roads all named after famous English poets. This reminded Hash he had the address of the tattooed thug and in a few minutes he had found the exact block. He half-expected the man and his mates to be outside, waiting for him. The building and its neighbouring blocks stood grey in the waning light while Hash sat and observed its denizens struggling to get by, living innocent lives, waiting for buses, holding their kids' hands, pushing prams or being dragged along by dogs. None of them seemed to be 'thug life'.

After an hour or so, when it was fully dark, Hash moved and parked discreetly away from the chippy, but close enough to see what was going on despite the boarded window. He ran the engine to put warmth into the cabin and banish the condensation. Fighting drowsiness, he watched it until closing time, waiting to see whether the thugs would pay a call. He watched a trickle of customers build into a strong queue and saw the Portuguese and his wife working hard to service their clients. Around ten-thirty he realised he had subconsciously aborted the Sparkbrook vigil. The conclusion came as a relief more than regret at a missed opportunity.

CHAPTER 9

After ducking the trip to Birmingham and a fruitless observation of the chippy, Hash had forced himself back home. Knowing he needed to dominate the anxiety, he had taken a hot bath and crashed. The habit of the dog walk brought him round at daybreak.

Showered and downstairs, with a mug of tea waiting, he was about to phone Siddiq when the front doorbell triggered Shamsa into a barking fit. The figure on the other side of the glass was female, but not Mrs Hamilton. Hash opened the door to a pretty face and a wide smile.

'Susan,' he said, his spirits lifting. 'Just when I thought you'd dumped me.' He held out his hand, she took it and Hash could not bring himself to let go, and gently tugged her over the threshold.

'Just thought I'd drop Jim's holiday work off.'

Hash found himself trying to remember which part of the make-believe he had spun. 'Sorry,' he began. 'Late night, didn't get back in until the early hours.'

'Life in the fast lane.'

'I wish,' said Hash. 'Chasing someone who's giving me a headache.'

'Well, I won't stay long, then,' she said.

'On the contrary, you must stay. It would cheer me up. Unless you're still in a bad mood?' He pointed towards the kitchen but she hesitated.

'I'd heard the dying granny story a hundred times. Just surprised at it coming from you.'

'Grandfather with a stroke, and he's deteriorating,' Hash said. 'We don't know how much longer he's got. Jim's an only grandchild and, would you believe it,' he shook his head in disbelief, 'he's now down with some sort of virus, confined to bed on the farm.' He flicked on the kettle and pointed to a chair, 'So a cup of coffee and a chance to put it right with you is what I need.'

Looking at her watch, she made a decision, then nodded and put the bag of textbooks on the table. Hash prepared the mugs and watched out of the corner of his eye as she laid out the books, checking the bookmarks with her notes. It made him feel happier than he could imagine and brought emotion to the surface, so much so that he had to look away. She was someone who cared about his son, was going out of her way to help him.

Hash placed a steaming cup by the books. 'I'll take them over with me,' he chuckled, 'Jim will be so pleased.'

'How is he?'

'Exhausted. He's been down with this virus, so his grandmother tells me. She's talking about quarantine.'

'Really? Poor boy.'

Susan's reaction pleased Hash, as though her scepticism had evaporated. He prised open a tin and held the contents out. 'Biscuit?' She took one. Shamsa came forward and nudged her thigh, hinting. She stroked the dog and talked to it softly.

Pointing at the books, he sat down and started to go through the assignments. Feeling her closeness and smelling her scent was a balm. Jim had once declared her, 'the best teacher, ever'. Her small, delicate forefinger traced across the open books and down the shortlist. Hash could barely concentrate. He desperately wanted to ask her if the dinner date was beyond salvation. As he was contemplating the move he heard the Arab BlackBerry ping a waiting SMS.

'Do you need to get that?' she asked.

'It can wait,' Hash lied.

'So, what does a boy like Jim get out of a farm in Ireland?' Susan asked when the assignment checklist was done. She sat back and picked up the mug in both hands.

'A complete contrast from computers in Cheltenham,' Hash said. 'Fresh air, farm animals, a torrent of pocket money, of course.' He paused. 'A chance to sweet-talk his grandparents into splashing out on his current obsession.' Hash scrolled through a stream of photographs on his phone and tapped on one of Jim and his Spitfire. 'His craze for the last three years, non-stop ever since I gave him a kit for Christmas.' Hash flicked through a stream of photographs showing Jim with an array of models.

'Boys and their toys,' Susan commented.

'He's an ace at his club, better than most of the adults,' Hash said. 'Wins prizes, does aerobatic displays, you name it.' Hash sipped from his mug. 'It's good to see him so focused, anything to get him out of his room and away from the memories of…'

He pointed up to the dresser where a photograph of Flora stood beside the old family portrait.

'Does he still miss her?'

'Of course, and it breaks my heart. He thinks he's been cheated,' Hash said. 'He used to ask me what he did wrong, that his mum went away.' Hash sipped his coffee again. 'It takes him down very deep, every so often.'

She nodded. 'I've seen that at school.' There was silence between them, but Susan quickly broke it, saying softly, 'But at least you can be proud, he's such a talented kid.'

'Thanks to you, in particular,' Hash said. 'Maybe I should be taking him to Jordan more often, instead. Introduce him to the language and all his aunts, uncles and cousins.' Hash gestured to the old black and white group photo.

'Why don't you? Expensive tickets, no doubt.'

'Oh, it's not the cost.' Hash shrugged. 'It's that other thing,' he said, 'the Jordanian mother and her matchmaking.'

'Sounds interesting.'

'They wouldn't rest until I was married off. I'm still a catch, you realise. This place, my bank balance, the chance of a British passport, my good looks.'

'Your modesty.'

'Indeed.' Hash offered the biscuits. 'Who'll be taking Susan Pine down the aisle?' When she smiled he added, 'My father will make your father an offer of twenty camels.'

'Look, Hash.' Her eyebrow arched and she examined her biscuit. 'I only came round to drop off some assignments.'

'Tell your father we'll raise it to twenty-five and he'll get free camel's milk for the rest of his life.'

'He'll probably just stick with the twenty camels.'

She got up and took her cup to the sink. 'So...back to reality.' She looked over her shoulder, smiling at Hash. 'There might be one more assignment, and if there is, when I'm back on Sunday morning. I'll drop it by.'

As Hash opened the door she hesitated on the step.

'Stay there,' Hash said. 'I need all the neighbours to see you.'

'Looking forward to the debating society?'

'Very much, especially afterwards.'

'Me, too.' She gave a shy wave as she left.

'Be sure to tell your father.' Hash pointed at his mobile.

She put her hands over her ears as she walked back down the path.

Rushing back inside, he seized the Arab BlackBerry. The SMS, from the Libyan number, 'Dafe coming', sent a depth charge of adrenaline through him. When it subsided the anxiety level stayed up a notch. He switched on the computer, waited and then rang Jim's iPhone. As before, there was no answer and the locating app offered nothing.

Maybe, if the guest was moving, then Jim was on the move, too. Maybe he had been set free by the five thousand pounds.

Hash sat, elbows on the table, eyes closed and thumbs kneading his temples, trying to revive his concentration. He ran the scenarios again. Maybe Jim was not moving and they still had to keep him communicating. So far, the 'OK' was the only straw he had been allowed to grasp. Siddiq and the hard, little bastard at

the mosque could, of course, both be in the game. And Siddiq…
what did twenty years of friendship and business count for? But
maybe, Hash argued against himself now, maybe they also had
something on Siddiq and his friend was doing his best. Maybe
Siddiq had gone out on a limb, taken a risk involving Hakim,
the bearded little fucker who had accused him of alienating
his child. He looked at his watch. He could make the midday
prayers if he hurried.

Shamsa came up to him and laid her muzzle on his knee.
He stroked her ears just as Susan had done. Hash cudgelled his
mind back on track. Maybe the 'dafe' would unlock the mystery.
Then, with an almost physical thump in his gut he remembered
the suicide vest, sitting in its plastic skin. He cursed out loud and
the dog flinched. The bloody vest and the money simply drove a
coach and horses through any 'happy ever after' scenario.

The landline interrupted his thoughts with a call from the
clerk to the justices reminding him he was on standby for any
court sitting the coming Saturday morning.

When he got to the mosque, prayers were already over with
a trickle of worshippers leaving the building. Siddiq was the last
to leave and when he caught up with his friend he was surprised
to see him looking irritated. Siddiq tapped his watch and said.
'Now, soon.' Hash's own patience, strained by fatigue and lack
of sleep, was equally short. 'Now? How soon?' Then he added,
'Where and how many?'

'Is the place ready?' Siddiq asked.

'Of course. Where's Jim?' Hash parried. Siddiq shrugged but
gave no answer.

'What news from your friend Hakim? The one I gave all the money to?'

Siddiq shrugged again. 'He will do his best for you, Insh'Allah.' Siddiq offered a half-smile, his expression back somewhere between conspiratorial and embarrassed. 'Is the place OK?'

'It's been ready for years. Everything's in place.' Siddiq seemed relieved and patted his shoulder. 'Good job, my friend.'

Walking back up Naunton Crescent, Hash could see old Mrs Hamilton standing outside her door, looking left and right. She saw him a few seconds later and was waiting when he drew level.

'Hell of a noise,' she said, 'again.'

She left it hanging but Hash was not in the mood for guessing games. He could hear Shamsa barking on the other side of the door and he let her out. The dog rushed past and let rip with a series of barks.

'Hell of a noise,' the old lady repeated, pointing at the dog, 'Her, the madam.'

Hash said, 'Sorry for that, Mrs Hamilton. What's the problem?'

'Your dog…' She always used the possessive when she was in a bad mood: your son, your car, now it was 'your dog'. '… Made so much racket I thought you were being burgled. Had to come out.'

'Everything seems fine,' Hash said.

'Twenty minutes ago it wasn't,' she said, arms folded, looking from Shamsa to Hash. 'I had to come out. But your visitors had given up.'

'What visitors?' Hash asked.

She looked at him reluctantly, groping for the words. 'You know, those types.' Her wink was almost comical. 'In a car,' she said. 'Went the wrong way up the one-way road, then parked and one of them knocked on your door.'

'A red car?'

'Think it was,' she said. 'Anyway...madam here...' Shamsa had returned from her patrol and was standing looking up at Hash. 'Madam here started barking and wouldn't stop.' She reached over the low wall and patted Shamsa. 'Did not like those two nasty men, did you?'

'Two men in a red car,' Hash said.

Mrs Hamilton considered the question for a few seconds then gave a quick nod. 'Dogs know, you know.'

'Know what?' Hash wanted to make her say it.

'They can smell it.'

'Curry?' he said.

She shot a startled look at him. 'No, you silly sausage! They can smell fear.' She unfolded and refolded her arms.

Inside and away from Mrs Hamilton, Hash flicked on the computer out of habit. Whatever Siddiq was planning was gaining momentum, and his nerves were contagious. There was no message on the Arab BlackBerry and Hash called Jim's iPhone on his own mobile then walked into the front room, checking the view from the bay windows. Jim's ringtone purring in his ear came as a shattering surprise. He was aware of his heart thudding as he waited for someone, maybe Jim, to answer. Instead, it went to message and Hash hesitated, almost paralysed, before saying, 'Jim, this is Dad. If you get this message contact anyone, the police are looking for you, ask anyone for help, and come home.'

He switched his phone off and went to his laptop, keyed the locating app and waited. The process took a few seconds before the screen showed a bookmark sprouting out of the West Midlands. His scalp began to crawl when he saw it was sitting on Cheltenham. Zooming in further, he pinpointed Jim's phone to a car park off the Bath Road.

Jim's phone was two streets away. He could drive there in less than a minute, catch sight of him or call him again. Maybe Siddiq and Hakim had done something after all. Maybe Jim was actually on his way home with them.

A change in light in the hallway flickered a shadow of movement and Hash caught it from where he was sitting in the kitchen. Shamsa must have picked up sounds inaudible to the human ear and she started a low growl. Ignoring it, Hash dialled Jim's phone again, leaning over to soothe the dog. Again the dialling tone sounded in his ear as he was patting and stroking Shamsa. But she shook him off, rising from her bed, and stood staring intently at the hallway. Sensing alarm, Hash rose, phone in hand and peered into the hallway. There was a figure on the other side of the frosted glass. The ringtone was stronger and it seemed to have a familiar echo. Hash could see a figure through the glass, and now realised he was listening to Jim's personal ringtone coming from the other side of the door.

CHAPTER 10

The figure on the other side of the glass shifted. He was tall and moved awkwardly as if searching for something in a pocket. The echoing ringtone stopped in the same instant as the purring on Hash's handset. Hash saw the twist of the figure's head turning to look down at something in his hand. Shamsa was barking short, rapid barks of alarm. At the same instant, the shape behind the glass bent, reached forward and knocked on the door.

Hash hung onto the dog's collar and opened the door. Standing in front of him was a tall, lean Asian, with a dark, strong but unkempt beard. He was wearing a baseball cap, a cheap, thin jacket and jeans, and in his left hand he carried a sports bag. He stood in silence, as though Hash would know what to do. He did not even hold out his hand or smile. He gave the Arabic greeting, 'Salaam-Alaikum.'

'Alaikum as'salaam,' Hash replied, extending his hand. Hash felt the strong grip from a calloused hand, the hand of a labourer.

'Kayf hallak?' Hash spoke in Arabic, asking how he was. The man responded with the universal Muslim gesture, touching his right hand to his heart, and gave the traditional Arabic reply, 'Alhamdulillah,' Thanks be to God.

'Can I help you?' Hash continued in Arabic. At this point the man's face showed a blank self-consciousness, and Hash realised Arabic was not the man's native language but he must have had some Koran Arabic. He tried the question again, in English, and saw a flash of puzzled frustration in the brown eyes.

The man fished in his pocket and held out an iPhone which Hash instantly recognised as Jim's by its cover. He looked past the man's shoulders on either side, hoping Jim was behind him and the nightmare was over. He caught sight of Mrs Hamilton, watching from her window.

The stranger looked anxiously down at Shamsa who was still growling, then peered past Hash into the hallway. 'Dafe,' he said, his right thumb tapping his chest. 'Dafe.'

Realising the man was on public display, Hash beckoned him into the house and the guest moved with clumsy haste. He kicked off his cheap, scuffed shoes as he squeezed past and Hash caught the whiff of airline cabins, the fusion of sweat, overcooked food and recycled air. He stooped to pick up the shoes and dropped them inside. The man stood waiting in the hallway, his face a mixture of wonder at the house, his eyes flicking down to where the dog had retreated, growling.

Hash hauled Shamsa into the kitchen and out into the little rear conservatory, quietened her and left her there. He took the holdall, noticing its lightness, and dropped it by the stairs, pointing the guest into the sitting room. The man went in but remained standing until Hash motioned for him to sit. 'Tea, chai?' Hash asked. The man's head bobbed at the universal word.

In the kitchen, Hash flicked on the kettle. The man was no Libyan whom he could talk to, discuss the target with, or pump for information on Jim. With his lean, rangy frame and rough hands he had the look of a peasant, probably a Pakistani, recruited straight out of some poor village north of Peshawar. Maybe he had been the surplus mouth in some sprawling tangle of relatives, singled out and sent to a madrassa to be groomed for martyrdom.

It struck Hash that, all along, he had never believed either he or Jim was destined to wear the vest. He did not know why he had taken that for granted. It was as though, with his background and training, he was always in the next tier up, one of those who 'facilitate' and never one of the expendable pawns. A bizarre sense of cautious relief began to warm through him as a piece of the jigsaw dropped into place. He was going to assist the newcomer in his task and would need to be alive to do it.

Hash carried the tray to the sitting room and laid it on the coffee table. The man had hardly moved, still upright and uncomfortable in an easy chair; maybe he would have felt better sitting cross-legged on the carpet. Hash held the sugar bowl to the guest's mug of tea and counted in two spoonfuls of sugar. The rough, bearded face cracked enough to show some gratitude. He took the mug, muttering in Urdu some words of prayer or thanks, and blew on the surface, tasted, then reached for more sugar. Helping himself to two more spoonfuls, spilling some grains onto the tray, he stirred, sipped and blew again, smacking his lips.

Shamsa's barking had started again and Hash knew he had to calm the dog down. He did not need the constant intrusions from his nosy neighbour. There was only one way and that was to get the two accustomed to each other. He got up and brought Shamsa into the sitting room. The guest reacted instantly, standing and backing away behind the chair, holding out his free hand, unleashing a torrent of Urdu. The body language was clear enough…too much too soon. Changing tack, Hash led Shamsa back into the kitchen and looped her lead to the kitchen table and clipped it to her collar. He left her growling a low rumble of suspicion.

With hand signals, he told the man he was safe and got him seated again. Calming down, he sat and drank his tea, alternately blowing then slurping noisily. He made no attempt to explain himself. Hash observed him, assuming he had been brainwashed, indoctrinated, crammed for his mission, then inserted before he could forget the details. He guessed the airport was probably Birmingham, where he had been collected and then dropped off…and Hash, whom he had been briefed about but whose name he probably did not know, would handle everything after that. His host would take care of him, set him up and send him on his way. The memory of his Lockerbie guest flashed in Hash's mind.

Hash asked him in Arabic if he needed to wash his hands. He cocked his head, giving a quizzical look, but said nothing. Final confirmation, as if Hash needed it, that his guest was no Arab. When Hash made washing motions with his hands this brought a nod. They went to the hallway and were about to ascend when Hash stopped and pointed to a large photograph of Jim. It had been taken a year or so earlier and showed Jim out in the open with one of his model aeroplanes. Hash pulled out the iPhone and went through a mime routine, connecting the phone to the boy. The guest stood, looking from the photo to Hash and back. He was getting the connection, but his face showed no sympathy; he shrugged his shoulders once and then again when Hash persisted.

He led the man upstairs and showed him the spare room and bathroom. He went back down the stairs and waited until the sound of taps could be heard before looking at the holdall. It was a cheap rip-off of the Manchester City brand with cargo pockets at either end. Quickly, Hash went through it, first finding a folded prayer rug and a small Koran. Underneath was a pack of safety razors and a few packs of cheap underwear branded with Urdu manufacturing labels. He found a small packet of safety pins and a roll of what looked like electrical tape. On hearing the cranking of the flush handle from upstairs, he returned the contents and zipped the pockets just as the stairs began creaking. When he appeared in the kitchen doorway, Hash made a gesture at the cooker, holding pinched fingers to his mouth and said, 'Food?'

The man nodded again but had an unspoken question on his lips. His sleeves were rolled up and he had taken his shoes and socks off in preparation for prayer. His hairy arms were wet, and droplets of water glistened on his dark beard. He bent to his own sports bag and took out the prayer rug and Koran, holding them up to Hash.

Hash took the man back into the living room and pointed at a spot on the carpet, then drew an imaginary line from that spot, following it through the wall, into the distance, south-east across Leckhampton Hill out to the Channel, across Europe and all the way to Mecca. Visibly content, the man began to lay the prayer rug down following the direction Hash had indicated.

From the kitchen, the landline interrupted them. Siddiq's greeting was perfunctory and conspiratorial. 'Are you ready?'

'He's here,' Hash whispered the words.

'The special guest has arrived,' Siddiq said.

'I know that,' Hash said. 'He's in my front room, praying.'

'You have to come and meet me, now.' Siddiq's voice was urgent. 'Now.'

'And leave him here?' Hash thought that maybe this was when Siddiq was going to produce Jim, work the reward magic now the main deal was done. Maybe the silent Asian had kept his word? Maybe Jim's delivery had simply been brokered on Hash housing the character off the plane and holding him for a few days.

'Meet me at the railway station,' Siddiq commanded.

When the prayers had ended the guest returned to the kitchen, an expression of calm relief on his hard face. Holding the small Koran out to Hash, he began to say something in explanation. He opened it at the flyleaf and tapped a large finger over a biro scrawl which read in Arabic, 'Friday 13th March 1500'. The kettle was coming to the boil as he read and reread the message.

Hash knew the man was not an Arab, so this could not be his guest's handwriting. He saw the man pointing to it and making a thumbs-up, waiting for Hash to acknowledge. Next Friday, at three in the afternoon, something would happen, should happen, had to happen, and Hash, Jim and his suicidal guest were linked to it.

Hash put his finger on the words and nodded to the man, returning the thumbs-up, seeing relief his eyes. It was as if a pre-rehearsed checklist was being followed; first Jim's phone, now the written message, which the man himself probably could not even read but which his host would be sure to understand. Hash mimed to the man, pointing to him to stay put and he would bring food in half an hour. Hash took the dog with him, to be on the safe side.

Siddiq's Mercedes was sitting in the station car park and Hash walked across to it. Dusk was beginning to fall and the first spots of rain hit his face as he covered the short distance. The window came down smoothly to reveal Siddiq's face, grinning from ear to ear.

'Get in, my friend.'

As soon as he was inside, Siddiq told Hash, 'Any minute now.' He was fidgeting with anticipation, like a mischievous schoolboy. 'You have the place ready? You are ready?' He pointed down to the tracks where a train had just pulled in, doors now easing open and people disembarking. Seeing the excitement in his friend's face made Hash wonder if he was in an elaborate set-up and Jim was coming up the steps from the platform, at exactly the place he had last seen him.

'Now,' Siddiq said, pointing. Hash followed his gaze and saw a melee of people, all ages and genders, surging up from the platform, then clustering under the awning of the station entrance, staying out of the pattering rain. Some were looking for relatives, one or two lighting a cigarette, and others taking a moment to decide between bus and taxi. There was no sign of Jim yet.

Siddiq's finger pointed excitedly at the throng. 'Can you see? Can you see?' Smiling more manically than ever, he looked at Hash and winked. Hash looked at the thickening cluster of people, all keeping under the narrow roof that fronted the station building. 'Get out and make a surprise for your guest,' Siddiq told Hash.

Half of the people under the awning were on their mobile phones and some of them were women. Siddiq was beside himself, 'Make a surprise!' he urged. Hash reached for the door lever. He could still not see Jim in the crowd under the awning. He thought Jim would be as keen to see him and would hardly be hanging back. He looked around the edges of the building to see if the lad had sneaked out from another exit.

Unable to contain himself, Siddiq got out of the car and waved Hash out. He whispered a name and threw a shy, furtive wave to someone in the crowd. 'Hello, my darling,' he whispered again. Hash got out of the car in time to see a blonde woman break away from the knot of people and stride towards them. She was tall and slim, and as she got closer Hash could see she was beautiful. Siddiq pointed towards her and for a second Hash looked behind her, as if Jim was there. Next, Siddiq and the woman ran to each other. She was a head taller than Siddiq and as she wrapped her arms around him, crushing his head against her denim bosom, Hash caught Siddiq's expression of rapture.

After they had embraced, kissed and embraced again, Siddiq introduced them.

'This is my best friend, Hash,' he said. She held out a firm hand and looked away from Siddiq to Hash. 'Hash,' she tried the name, serious and self-consciously, 'my name is Anna. Pleased to meet you.' Her vowels were East European and he guessed she was early thirties, a woman who kept in shape. Her eyes, strikingly blue and alert, lingered on Hash for a second.

Anxious to get out of the rain, Siddiq said, 'Mister Hash has an apartment for us to use. We can go there now.'

Hash led the way out of the station, watching Siddiq's Mercedes in his rear-view mirror and wondering how he had got things so wrong. Twice today he had been expecting to see Jim, and twice his hopes had been dashed. He had completely misread Siddiq's 'guest' story. Anna was Siddiq's secret guest and Hash had been roped in to set them up in a love nest. He had missed the clues when Siddiq had blanked at the mention of some other guest. Now he knew why Siddiq the married man had been so jumpy and nervous all this time, keeping his girlfriend a secret. Siddiq had taken advantage of Hash, knowing about the properties and relying on his friend's discretion and generosity.

On the other hand, and like a true friend, Siddiq had willingly piled in when Jim's predicament had been introduced. In fairness, Hash had to concede, Siddiq had not asked too many probing questions before harnessing the unpleasant Hakim. He had to conclude Siddiq was probably oblivious to the whole set-up, the suicide vest, the money and the newly arrived 'dafe'.

The love nest he had inadvertently set up for his friend was a further complication. Hash had acquired the maisonette in the late-eighties, just after he had been transferred from Ulster to Cheltenham. The purchase price paid in laundered Libyan cash, fed in through the chip shop and a laundrette, had clinched the deal. Over the years it had mellowed from a new development into a pleasant middle-class environment. The good schools nearby attracted excellent tenants. For most of the past twenty-five years the place had been let, providing Hash with the lucrative and legitimate formula his property portfolio was founded on.

But the investment had been made for a totally different purpose. As with all property investment, Hash applied the mantra, 'location, location, location'. The maisonette's master bedroom upstairs overlooked the rear of Cheltenham's Government Communications Headquarters, GCHQ, Europe's biggest electronic spying station. The garage that came with the sale sat at the back in a row of garages which butted up against the twelve-foot perimeter fence. In the old days when he was playing it for real in the Gaddafi team, Hash prided himself he had chosen and secured the perfect launch pad for a physical penetration of the huge complex. Over the years, as Gaddafi's momentum had stalled, only brambles and ivy had made any progress at getting through.

Giving the two lovebirds a tour, he found himself looking out of that window, across the complex now lit with harsh white light. He knew the perimeter would have acquired more sophisticated protection than the men and dogs of the late-eighties. Now that seemingly vacant space would be seeded with sensors, watched day and night with cameras, both thermal and infrared. In spite of the advance of technology, Hash took an almost perverted professional pride in knowing he could still do his part in getting someone across the fence and all its defences, inside a few minutes.

Siddiq wanted him gone, he could see that. Anna had gone back upstairs and the two men stood at the front door, Siddiq toying with the bunch of keys.

'Are you sure it's ok?'

'What about Jim?' Hash cut in. 'Any news?'

Siddiq shrugged. 'I will call that man.' He looked at Hash. 'If Jim is in Birmingham, then that man will find him.' He looked back upstairs. He smiled a guilty smile at Hash.

'You have to give it time, my friend.'

CHAPTER 11

SATURDAY. MIDDAY 7TH MARCH.

The guest seemed happy in his room. His early morning prayer routine had disturbed the dog and her growling objections had dragged Hash downstairs to get between them. Fetching her a treat from the store in the rear porch he fussed her, thanking her, telling her to keep on top of things while he slipped out and made for the Magistrates' Court and his sitting. Afterwards, he stopped by at Siddiq's restaurant on the Bath Road.

Siddiq waved him to his booth, smiling his conspirator's smile, eyes twinkling. Hash took the seat, refused the offer of beer, asking for coffee instead.

'How is Anna?'

'Quiet, my friend, quiet.' Siddiq's head dropped into his shoulders and a forefinger hit his lips, his smile broader than ever.

'Fantastic,' he whispered. 'Oh my God, fantastic.' Amused at the ecstasy on his face, Hash said, 'You look exhausted, been at it all night? Who actually knows about her?'

'Nobody.' Siddiq waved a hand around the room. 'That's why I asked you. I trust you, my old friend.'

'How long is she staying?'

'Forever,' Siddiq said. He paused to gauge Hash's reaction then gave an uncharacteristic giggle. 'Just joking, my friend. Maybe a few months.'

'Difficult to keep these things quiet,' Hash said. 'A beautiful girl, locked up on her own in a strange neighbourhood, with a big Mercedes parked outside every night.' He watched Siddiq's face take it in. 'Just joking, my friend,' he said, '...sort of.'

Hash ordered chicken biryani for two, with all the naan and dhal he thought his guest could tackle.

Siddiq asked, 'What is the news of Jim?'

'I was about to ask you.'

'None from my side,' Siddiq said.

'When we sat in the mosque,' Hash said, 'with your friend Hakim. Does he really have connections?'

'What connections?'

'To the jihad types.'

'He hates them,' Siddiq said. 'He hates them; just like we do. That's why I trusted him for you.'

'He is really against the bad guys?' Hash toyed with the thought of handing his new guest over to the man. 'I'm glad someone is.'

'He is your best friend, better than me, for this business.' Siddiq waited until the coffee was placed in front of Hash and the waiter was out of earshot.

'Who is he working for?' Hash asked.

Siddiq put both his elbows on the table and clasped his hands as if in prayer. 'He is a business colleague. He runs the biggest taxi fleet in the south of Birmingham. Actually,' Siddiq put on wry expression, 'he's a Pakistani and as a rule I don't have much time for them, but...' He canted his head from side to side. 'He's a very good Muslim, very straight.'

'He didn't seem to have much sympathy for me.'

'Maybe he thinks you're not a good Muslim. And he's very careful. He has enemies, people who hate him.'

'The jihadis?' Hash said.

Siddiq nodded. 'That's why he was hard with you. You are not the only father looking for a runaway. Believe me, my friend.' Siddiq leaned forward. 'All the mosques are different; some imams speak for Daesh, some for Al Qaeda, but only a few speak out against these rubbish people.'

'And he's one of the few?' Hash said. Siddiq gave an emphatic nod. 'Correct.'

'Does he need more money?' Hash asked.

'Maybe Hakim knows you're not telling the whole story,' Siddiq said. 'I know you are hiding some information, so maybe it can't be that difficult to see.' Siddiq looked him. 'You can trust me.' Hash had imagined Siddiq's hand in the loss of Jim: who else in Cheltenham was that close and knew his routine? He had imagined Anna the girlfriend as the 'dafe', and the unpleasant imam as a go-between. Maybe his mind was working so slowly he was missing other obvious connections. Maybe this was a further charade, a litmus test of Hash's discretion, protecting the guest sitting in his kitchen.

'A business deal went wrong and some people are angry with me,' Hash said. 'Very angry. So they took Jim.' Siddiq's intake of breath stopped him. 'I've got some money together.' Hash held a hand up, 'I've got what they want.'

'Why Birmingham?' Siddiq asked.

'Because that's where Jim's phone was transmitting from, twice in the last few days.' Hash stared at his coffee. 'Birmingham was the only clue I had.'

'Any Bangladeshis involved and I will know soon,' Siddiq muttered. 'Pakistanis, more difficult, more time, but that's why you're lucky to have Hakim.'

Returning with the takeaway, Hash began to prioritise. He would keep the communication with the kidnappers, try to crank it up and hope for them to drop any clues. His only hope of finding Jim was through them. Cooperate for as long as it took to shake solid information off the branch. If Hakim the Pakistani imam proved as good as Siddiq said, with all his eyes and ears in South Birmingham, he would throw the bomber's money in that direction. And when Sean was finally acclimatised they would work up a plan for when the vital clue appeared.

Hash had realised Sean was the ace up the sleeve as long as he could keep him off the radar and off the bottle. Whoever had set this all up had been watching him, following his entire life, but could not know of Sean. Maybe it would be asking too much of Sean to partner up. Sean was fighting his own demons: ten years in a Brit prison camp and then rejection by his own mother and father would destroy anybody. Hash would die to save Jim, but nobody else would go that far. The best he could hope for was Sean to watch his back while he did the fighting.

He knew, with the Friday deadline, he should take the bomber on a series of recces of GCHQ, and the weekend was a good time to start. This would involve a look at the maisonette and the garage. Siddiq and Anna might see the bomber but that was a risk he would have to take. Hash doubted anyone outside the house would notice.

Years earlier, Hash had assumed he would be pivotal in any attack on GCHQ. All he needed was advance warning to ready the space and dig up the weapons for the assault team. In those days, he saw GCHQ as a justifiable target, a concentration of enemy combatants. In the years that followed between 1990 and 2011 Hash had loved, married, raised a son, and then lost his love to cancer. The military campaign in Ulster had unravelled and Gaddafi's crusades turned into lethal farce. The Brits held out the hand of friendship and he had found himself amongst good people. Today, he saw the futility of hitting such a target. The only tiny shred of justification, particularly as the centre had been hardened by progressive security upgrades, was that an attack would guarantee international headlines, but few people, if any, would get hurt.

Hash had watched the 2011 Libyan uprising on television and waited to be activated, expecting Gaddafi, the old desert scorpion, to have a sting in his tail. But the regime had collapsed faster than anyone could have predicted and Hash's masters in the Mukhabarat never pressed the button. Gaddafi's fearful, shocked and bloodied face, then the pictures of his corpse in the Libyan dust, fed the hope the networks had gone, his controllers scattered forever.

Like a freed slave, Hash had begun to hope. His false life as a nationalised UK citizen with a successful business had become a reality. The electrician's tape and the snatching of Jim told him he had been badly mistaken.

CHAPTER 12

Mrs Hamilton's curtain twitched as he went past and he caught a glimpse of her shaking her head slowly, wearing her disapproving face. He wondered what he had now done to deserve the 'deeply disappointed' look. The prayer rug was still folded and lying on the sofa. There was no sign of the guest. Hash called a greeting up the stairs. When he opened the food cartons in the kitchen he knew he would smell the food. Shamsa in the kitchen, lying on her bed, did not get up and he wondered why she had not been at the door to say hello when she heard his key in the lock. She stood up at last and came to him, pushing her muzzle into his hands. He saw she was limping, and guessed she must have done some damage out on the walk. Squatting down to cuddle her, he found a cut on her foreleg. A centimetre of tear showed pink flesh where the skin had broken. She began to lick it as Hash tried to examine the wound.

When he had gone to court he had left the man in his room, probably reading his Koran. It seemed as though the guest intended to spend much of the time in prayer and reflect on the

121

imminence of his afterlife. The cup in the sink and the warm kettle told Hash that he ventured down and made himself tea. He called upstairs again and began to lay the table. Hash wondered if the man was on some sort of fasting ritual. He called up the stairs again and got a mumbled response. While waiting he went to the garage and brought the suitcase into the kitchen.

The man ate with his fingers, slowly at first, intrigued but wary of the strange flavours. Any notion of fasting vanished as the pace quickened. He tore strips of naan and dipped them into the dishes, his lips smacking with relish. Hash unzipped the case. When the man had finished, Hash cleared away the plates and cartons then hoisted the suicide vest onto the table.

The guest did not recoil in wonder or horror. It was as though confronting a suicide vest was perfectly natural, like meeting an old friend. He looked at the vest and motioned for scissors. Hash brought them and watched as the man cut away the plastic. The smell of almonds, sweet and cloying, filled the room. Hash opened the back-door and windows to flush the toxins away. Shamsa kept to her bed, licking her wound.

The man glanced at Hash's movements, then stood up and slipped the waistcoat over his head, pushing his arms through. Standing, arms akimbo, he turned, slightly left then right, as though he was in a Savile Row fitting room, waiting for his tailor's unctuous approval. Hash could see the canvas fabric straining, its various pockets packed with flat brick shapes. There were at least three packs in the rear adding to the four in the front: he felt his initial guess of twelve kilos of explosive was still good. If the man actually got inside the GCHQ buildings and cracked it all off, there would be mayhem.

The bomber wriggled and shrugged in the vest, testing its fit. Hash could see loops and cords at the rear, as though the wearer should be laced into his vest, like a corset and then unable to undo himself. A short, coiled length of blue and black wires sprouting free from the right armpit indicated an initiation system. Hooking his right thumb into the coil, the man jerked the wire out of the lining a little way. The would-be martyr seemed rehearsed and perfectly calm, trying on a garment that would soon blow him to pieces. His fingers probed into the right breast pocket, where Hash had felt the two cylinders, then pulled out a piece of folded paper, unfolded it, gave it a cursory glance, and then held it to Hash. It was the same biro scrawl and the same message in Arabic: 'Friday 13th March 1500. Send confirmation.'

Accepting the obvious, that the precision of the timing was significant, Hash wondered if there were other, maybe hundreds of vests positioned around the UK timed to go off at three the following Friday. Or was his man part of a sequence where one at a time they would detonate every hour, a Mexican wave of mayhem.

He decided to explain the need for a reconnaissance. Pointing to himself and then to the man, he said in English and again in Arabic, 'We are going for a drive.' He pointed two fingers at his eyes, 'Look…Target…'

He got a half-nod of comprehension. He tapped his watch on the number and held up five fingers,

'This evening.' He pointed to five o'clock on the kitchen

clock. The bomber nodded and started to take off the vest, allowing Hash to help.

The drive took them west through town, out to the edge of Cheltenham. As the huge, doughnut-shaped complex came into sight on their right-hand side, Hash said, 'Target,' and smacked his fist into his open palm. 'Boom!'

He could see the bomber was making the connection between the ground view and the vest. With daylight ebbing fast, Hash turned off the main road and onto a smaller road and looped north to get behind the complex.

He had taken the same route with Siddiq and Anna. He drove slowly, letting his guest see the layers of fences that protected the complex. He did not want to point or make it too obvious that a target reconnaissance was in progress and his companion seemed to be following the process without too much difficulty. Again Hash felt a bizarre pride at being able to talk through the options he had hatched so many years earlier.

Parking up not far from the maisonette, where they had a view of the row of garages butting up against the main fence, and using words and mime Hash went through the options. The 'Under' option had begun with his idea for a tunnel from the garages that backed onto the fence. He mimed digging but then drew a hand across his throat a couple of times. 'Abandoned,' he told his passenger, adding, 'Ground sensors.' Hash shook his head. 'Not good.' There was the barest flicker of comprehension on his companion's face.

'Through?' Hash posed another rhetorical question. 'Ramming!' He ducked his head, bracing and making a motion with the steering wheel as though flooring the accelerator. He punched his fist into the palm of his hand again to mime the effect.

'Hire a JCB, probably put you in the bucket and ram the fence!' He looked quizzically at the martyr. 'Or, using the front bucket to crush and bridge as many secondary fences as possible, allow you to scramble over the JCB superstructure.' He added a 'Maybe?' and looked at the man for any reaction. There was some comprehension but it was equally clear Hash was not really getting through.

'Over…My preferred option.' Hash felt unable to contain his enthusiasm. He repeated, 'Over,' miming a diving movement with both hands.

'Ladders, six.' He held up six fingers.

'We put them against the first fence then haul up the second, and so on.'

He could have expanded how in his earlier reports to the Mukhabarat he had recommended a combination of 'Through' and 'Over', depending on how many men they were sending. Now that this was a one-man hit with a clearly stated deadline Hash knew it was better to just concentrate on one method.

'Over…using ladders…from there,' he confirmed, pointing to the row of garages.

Hash had seen Siddiq's Mercedes parked outside the house and knew he would not be thanked for disturbing him on the nest. Prayer time and business would draw Siddiq out before too long. They would wait.

Waiting in the car with dusk coming down fast, his companion stirred and reached for the door handle. Hash hit the central locking and shot a questioning look at him. The man held up his hands, palm to palm, in the prayer position. Hash noticed there was a swollen cut on the man's right wrist, a raw graze and the inflamed red spot of a puncture mark. Hash shook his head. 'Not here.' He pointed around the genteel estate. 'Too many people watching.'

A flash of irritation crossed the man's features, unused at Hash's stern tone. He nodded vigorously and tugged at the door handle which would not give.

'Maghreb.' He gave the Arabic for evening prayer.

'Okay,' Hash soothed, 'but not here…inside.'

He called Siddiq to warn him they were coming in. His call found his friend in his HQ restaurant.

'Where's Anna?'

'In the house.'

'Please call her and say I need to check the boiler, now. It won't take long.'

'Now? You said everything was Ok.'

'Better for safety. It's been some time since tenants were there.'

'Okay,' Siddiq sounded doubtful. 'I will tell her.'

When Anna opened the door, she was wearing tight denim jeans and a tight red tee shirt. A slice of bare, toned midriff drew Hash's gaze from the straining shirt. Her blonde hair, no longer constrained by the ponytail, framed her face, giving a playfully dishevelled effect.

'Did Siddiq call?' Hash asked.

'I know.' Her tone was one of languid ennui. 'The boiler, all of a sudden.' She offered her hand, 'Come in.' Her amused gaze made Hash feel like a schoolboy. Arms folded, she stepped back to let them pass.

'Won't take too long. I need to check upstairs.' Hash felt uncomfortable at his lame pretext. 'I have my plumber.' He jerked a thumb over his shoulder at the Pakistani who had held back, mesmerised by Anna.

'Plumber, really?' She peered at the bomber, a sardonic expression on her face. 'Where's his tools?'

'In the car if we need them. Just looking at the thermostat and the boiler controls.'

'Whatever.' She walked lazily into the kitchen, reaching for a packet of cigarettes.

'Smoke?'

Her accent was definitely East European, perhaps not Polish, more likely further east, somewhere in the Balkans or Hungary. Hash caught her perfume as they stepped across the threshold. He had seen her offering her hand to the guest, who looked at it, but didn't take it.

'Coffee, beer? It's all here.' She lit a cigarette.

'We need to go upstairs, maybe into the attic, then into the garage.'

'Doesn't bother me,' she said, 'as long as the water stays as hot as it was before you guys arrived to fix it.'

'Just a safety check,' Hash said. 'A landlord thing.'

The bomber stood blocking the kitchen doorway, staring at Anna, and Hash had to gently push him to the side to get past. The man's gaze stayed on Anna all the time and quite suddenly her expression changed to irritation. As though her hackles were rising, she stared back at the man with unblinking, hardening eyes, exhaling a gentle stream of cigarette smoke. The bomber broke eye contact first, but Anna kept her gaze locked on the man, grinding him with hostility as Hash pulled him away.

From the vantage point in the upstairs bedroom, Hash pointed out across to the lights of GCHQ, ticking off in a whisper the fences, their heights, their layers, touching his watch to convey how little time the man would have once he had triggered that first alarm. The man's face showed comprehension but no glimmer of worry, certainly none of anxiety. He looked back at Hash, then at the double bed where Anna's clothes lay scattered, his eyes lingering on the female garments. Hash let the bath run, feeling the water heat up almost immediately.

They found Anna in the kitchen, tapping out an SMS. 'That was quick,' she said without looking up.

'Thermostats are both fine,' Hash said. He moved past her and opened a cupboard. The bomber, back in the doorway resumed his staring. Hash looked at the boiler's display and closed the door.

'Your friend,' Anna said, putting down her phone. 'I don't like the way he's staring at me.' She looked at Hash coolly. 'Unless he wants his ass kicked, don't bring him back, ever.'

In the garage, Hash pointed to a stack of six ladders, making the bomber lift one up to confirm its lightness. 'Easy,' Hash said, pointing to the ceiling of the garage. 'On top.' He jabbed a thumb upwards. 'You can carry one in each arm. Then I follow. I put one across and you run across.' He knew the man would never get the English and resorted to the mime signals. By the distraction on his face he had the feeling the only thing on the man's mind was Anna's underwear scattered on the bed. He stopped the briefing and mimed Anna's shape, cupping huge, imaginary breasts. For the first time, the man gave a broad smile, and his head bobbed up and down.

'Later.' Hash pointed at his watch. 'Waiting for you.' He pointed upwards, 'In Paradise, insh'Allah.'

'Insh'Allah.' The man grinned.

On their way back they stopped off at Siddiq's main restaurant on the Bath Road. Hash decided Siddiq should glimpse his guest. If Siddiq was uninvolved, maybe he could harvest some clues that would lead back to Jim.

On being told the owner was absent Hash decided to take a booth and wait. When the menus arrived, Hash called one of the waiters over and eventually, trying different dialects, they prised out of the bomber what he wanted to eat. Watching his now healthy appetite and thinking of Anna's curves, Hash wondered if he could offer the man some real temptation. It just might draw him off the straight and narrow path of jihad and shake down a vital clue about Jim.

As soon as they got back to the house, Hash had the bomber sit down and together they browsed the net. Starting at the chaste end of the spectrum they looked first at Pakistani brides. The bomber's face lit up as they scrolled through a parade of impossibly beautiful and demure Asian brides decked in opulent wedding outfits. Each one gazed longingly at the camera, appealing for a suitor.

The bomber was hooked and when Hash took the search to women with less and less clothing, the man went silent with lust. Hash allowed the trawl to run for a few minutes then abruptly closed the lid. The man looked up, astonished to have the supply cut. Hash took a photograph of Jim off the wall and held it in front of him. They both looked at the photograph, Hash repeating the name and asking in English and Arabic and Urdu, 'Where is my son?'

The man shrugged, even shaking his head. There was no doubt he understood the problem and Hash's question. His face even showed a trace of sympathy. Hash pulled notes from his wallet and laid them on the table, repeating the questions. He mimed Anna's voluptuous shape and when the man smiled, he lifted the bomber's hand and placed it on the money. The man jerked his hand away, a flash of irritation chasing the moment of levity off his face. When the man shook his wrist and began massaging it gently, Hash realised he had touched the man's injury.

CHAPTER 13

SUNDAY. 8TH MARCH, MORNING.

Before taking Shamsa on her morning walk, Hash picked up the Arab BlackBerry to check it for messages. Finding none, he gave in to the pressure and typed a message back to the Libyan number. It read, 'Instruction confirmed Friday. Confirm name used by Grandmother'.

On the walk Hash noticed Shamsa's limp had not improved with a night's rest. She was not her usual self, her tail drooped and her head hung as she just went through the motions of her morning run. She still covered the ground but kept looking back at Hash, keeping him in sight. He caught up with her and when he knelt to look at the injured paw she whined softly. The gash was deeper than he thought and tendons were visible.

He let her go and walked on. Even with the few showers they had experienced the going during the festival was said to be firm. The racecourse was bustling with crews who had been working round the clock to finish off the tented hospitality areas. Where he was walking had now been transformed into a massive, zoned parking area. It was a useless dog walk for now, but the letter box had to be checked.

He plucked Sean's number out on his phone. 'Tell me?' The Irishman's mock exasperation cheered Hash.

'You still on?'

'Is the Pope Catholic?' Hash could hear Sean's lighter clicking as he lit up.

'Smoking's bad for you,' Hash said.

'You're bad for me,' Sean said. 'Any news of the lad?'

'I'm still waiting.' He could not tell him about the martyr and the deadline of the 13th. Hash was standing at the footbridge and saw there was no new tape: no mail.

'He's still in the Brum area?' Sean asked.

Hash turned back, heading for his vehicle. 'It was where the last phone signal came from.'

'So that's a plus?' Sean said.

'All I've got. Can you get down from Brum on your own?'

'No chauffeur?'

'I'll leave the keys, the address and some cash in the chippy.'

'Usual old place?' Hash wondered fleetingly if there was a pun involved.

'Same couple run it. They know you're coming.' He added, 'Put all your food and drink on tick and I'll cover it.'

'Am I not dossing in the usual place?'

'It's taken. You're in a flat.'

Sean was silent at the other end.

'Better keep you off the radar for the moment. But it's near the chippy,' Hash said, 'Take a taxi from the station.'

'A new apartment?' Sean asked, hopefully.

'No palace but it's got everything you want. Just call me when you're in town.'

The smell of frying eventually brought the man to the kitchen doorway, triggering a rumbling growl from Shamsa. Hash saw the pair looking at each other with deep dislike. The dog stood up, hackles raised and her muzzle a rictus of menace. She did not stop growling until Hash cuffed her. Entering the kitchen, avoiding eye contact, the bomber accepted a handshake, sat down and began pushing omelette into his mouth. Hash observed him discreetly as he moved around the kitchen. He refilled the man's tea and received a curt nod of thanks.

Moments later, lifting his eyes from the near-empty plate, with crumbs in his beard, the martyr looked at Hash with an expression of mischief and a widening smile. Cupping his large hands to his chest then fluttering them downwards, he mimed female curves.

Hash looked at him in disbelief.

'You're serious?'

The bomber, grinning now, looked on as Hash considered the proposition. The internet browsing and the red-blooded reaction showed the bomber wanted sex. This was almost certainly breaking the rules his guest would have had drummed into him, but Hash saw that if sex could drive a wedge between the bomber and controllers, then Hash was going to pimp for him.

'This big?' Hash's hands described exaggerated bosoms. For the first time both men laughed. The bomber guffawed with delight and repeated the pantomime.

'How many?' Hash held up his fingers, counting off. The

bomber pushed back on his chair, laughing again, waving a protesting single finger: one would be enough, thanks.

'Insh'Allah,' Hash told him then tapped at his watch. 'Be patient.' He went out to the rear porch and, rummaging in his coat, extracted a wad of fifties and returned in time to catch Shamsa standing on her bed, again growling at the bomber. He scolded her and gave her a harder cuff and a firm shove back down. He waved the notes to the bomber, earning another smile and vigorous nodding.

'Wait,' Hash said, pointing to his watch, 'I'll come back soon.'

Eventually, he ran Siddiq to earth in a wholesale shop at the lower end of the High Street. Hash peeled off two hundred pounds in fifties. 'Get one of your contacts to organise it,' he urged, 'quickly. This guy's panting and drooling right now.'

'I'll do my best,' Siddiq said. 'You realise this is not my area.'

'Don't tell me you're embarrassed,' Hash said. 'One of your lads will surely know a number to call. They're not all religious like you.'

'The big Pakistani, the one my waiters saw...who is he?' Siddiq asked.

'He's part of the problem,' Hash said. 'And I've got to keep him happy.'

'Keeping him happy might cause trouble for my side.'

'Just remember who's keeping you out of trouble with your wife,' Hash said.

'Anna told me about him,' Siddiq said.

'What did she say?'

'She said he was a thug. My men say he's Pashtun...not much difference.'

'He's the enforcer, as far as I can see,' Hash lied. 'No English. Maybe Hakim should see him? He spends the whole time praying or reading the Koran. He and Hakim might be buddies.'

'A good Muslim.' Siddiq smiled. Hash could not decide if his friend was being ironic.

At that moment, Hash's mobile rang. Hash looked at it, seeing Susan Pine on the display. 'Hello, Susan.' Hash waved Siddiq an apology and took the call. Instantly he knew there was something very wrong. The voice at the other was muffled but there was fear and panic in it.

It was as though the phone had been switched on by accident and through the rustle and brushing of fabric he was listening to a woman's cries for help. She was pleading, 'No! No!' and he could hear the deep chords of a man's voice raised in anger. With rising horror Hash knew Susan was in a physical struggle with someone and he called her name again.

Siddiq watched the alarm spreading on his friend's face. She was calling his name, 'Hash...help.' The next sounds were muffled gasps from her and growls of anger from the man. The barking of a dog in the background told him where Susan was.

'Susan...I'm on my way.' The line went dead as he stood up, looking at Siddiq. 'My God,' he whispered, 'she's being attacked.' He left Siddiq gazing open-mouthed as he strode for his car. He dialled Susan again and the phone answered long enough for him to hear a few seconds of sobbing gasps before it switched off. 'Susan, Susan…speak to me…!' Hash yelled into the dead phone.

Once he had started the drive back, he redialled and to his relief she picked up straight away. 'Susan? You OK?'

The voice at the other end was hers, but it was barely audible. She was crying, breathless sobs.

'Where are you? I'm coming right now…just tell me where you are?'

He waited, straining to catch any noise.

'I'm OK…' The voice was weak, muffled by her crying.

'Where are you…what's happening…tell me where you are?'

He was nearing the college where she had a staff flat. 'Are you at your place?' He prayed she had not been lifted by the kidnappers.

Susan's voice came over better, still out of breath and full of fear, but the traffic noise told him she was on a street, maybe walking too fast, hopefully to safety. She said something he could not make out, then the line went dead again.

Hash turned in the direction of Susan's flat in the hope she was coming back. He caught sight of her ahead of him, half-running, half-walking along the quiet cul-de-sac. He drove behind her until the murmur of his engine alerted her. Her face when it turned to him was red as though she had been crying. She saw him, recognised him, but did not stop moving. He had to overtake her and get out, to block her. She walked into his arms, sagging, and he held her in silence for a few seconds. She was now crying freely.

'What's wrong...what happened?' Hash asked.

Susan steadied herself, swallowing and as she tilted her face up to try to talk she started crying again. He saw her face was red from emotion, no swelling from any blow, but her mascara had run and her hair was a mess.

'Let's get you inside,' Hash whispered. 'Which number are you?' He had never been into her tiny flat and he shook her shoulders gently to get a response.

'Are you hurt?' She tried to speak but no words came out.

'I thought you were away for the weekend,' Hash coaxed. She swallowed hard to catch her breathing.

'I just came to drop off some work for Jim.' She managed to get the words out before stopping for more breath. She pushed a hand into her pocket and brought out a key then pointed it at one of the doors in the row. She disengaged from Hash. He tried to hold her arm but she pushed him away.

'That man...the one in your house...' She got the first words out but then stopped. Blinking and rubbing her eyes, she stared at Hash and tried again. 'That man...he...'

'He what...what did he do to you?'

Hash felt a lurch in his gut. The bomber had seen him leave on a mission, with money. The websites the previous evening had started it, wound him up and then left him waiting. On cue, Susan had knocked at the door to drop off Jim's work assignment and landed on his plate.

She had unlocked her door and was entering, without looking back at Hash. He dashed forward, just getting a hand to the door before it closed. He felt her pushing from the other side. 'Susan…are you alright…talk to me…tell me what happened.' He heard her sobbing again, pushing at the door.

'Susan…you're safe…is there anything you want me to do?' He pulled out his phone. 'I'll call the police…tell me what to do.' He held the door against her pressure.

'Leave me alone,' she said from the other side.

'Shall I call the police? Did he harm you…do you need a doctor?'

'I'm OK.' Her voice sounded weak and tired.

'Shall I call the police?'

'Don't. I'm OK.'

Hash cursed himself inwardly for wanting that answer. 'Are you sure?' he asked, bracing.

'I'm OK. Just leave me alone.'

'Please let me come back and check on you.'

She pushed the door and Hash heard locks rattle.

CHAPTER 14

When he parked up outside his own house his mouth was dry with apprehension. The instant the door opened, a menacing silence flowed around him. Hash instinctively knew some catastrophe had just happened. Shamsa should have been bounding towards him. Unusually, the kitchen door was closed and she would have been frustrated, barking welcome and reproach. Instead there was silence. He looked into the sitting room: it was empty; no sign of his guest, but the Koran was on the coffee table. The photos and other decorations were undisturbed: no sign of a struggle.

He pushed open the kitchen door and saw a bald man sitting at the table, looking back at him with fury in his eyes. On the table in front of him lay a pair of bloodied scissors. Also on the table there were locks of hair, hacked from his head. There were more tufts on the floor, which was spattered with drops of blood. As Hash's mind struggled to process the information, the man looking at him, anger flashing in his eyes, held up his right forearm and pointed at it with his left hand. He was growling in his language, jabbing a finger at his forearm.

Still trying to make sense of the bomber's transformation and the anger, Hash caught scratching from behind the rear porch and knew it was Shamsa trying to come in from the garden. The man stayed seated, his words incomprehensible but the menace unmistakeable, growling, glaring, pointing at his injured forearm as Hash crossed to open the door. He had to push the door hard against a dead weight lying against the other side. He felt it give and heard Shamsa yelp in pain.

Easing the door open, he saw her lying half on the step and half on the grass, breathing feebly, trying to raise her head. Hash knelt down beside her and immediately saw a pool of blood had seeped from underneath her onto the step. Her tail thumped weakly as she recognised his voice.

Hash took her head and gently raised it, talking to her in whispers, stroking her, and when he reached behind the dog's head his fingers felt warm and slick. He held her head up long enough to see punctures on her neck and chest. The area that the blood had soaked into was a yard wide, and even if she had been moving around Hash guessed she had lost too much. He knew these were stab wounds and it could only have been the bomber, now sitting, seething in the kitchen. Maybe she had been defending herself…maybe she had stepped in to defend Susan?

Hash cursed himself for what was going through his mind. Shamsa needed to be on the vet's operating table at this minute, but that could never happen. Shamsa would have to bleed out and die, right in front of him. She was going to please her master one last time by dying without fuss. Through his shock Hash could feel his anger begin boiling like lava. He sat up against the porch wall and took the dog's head on his lap, stroking her flank.

She struggled for a few seconds and he soothed her. Her lips and muzzle contracted and her pink tongue showed contentment at recognising Hash through her pain. Her breath came in a choked cough and Hash felt the sting of his tears rolling down his cheeks, seeing them drop onto the dog's coat. He bent his face down to hers and kissed her eyes, unable to stop his sobs.

The dog's eyes stayed closed and gradually her breathing slowed. For a few seconds her rear legs kicked in powerful spasms as though she was accelerating across the meadow after the old hare. Then she was still and Hash knew she was past pain. Whispering a goodbye from him and Jim, he thanked her for her huge heart, the unconditional love, for making their team unforgettable. Bitter tears flowed as he remembered cuffing her for her defiance of the bomber, for not soothing her distress at the station when Jim had left without saying goodbye. Hash stayed sitting for a few minutes, holding her head and closed his eyes, trying to blank out the mess.

The bomber appeared in the doorway and, looking down, tapped Hash hard on the shoulder, grunting and pointing at his right forearm. Hash saw more puncture marks on the skin and wrist where he had been bitten, and realised the man must also be in shock and pain. But the man's expression of impatient contempt goaded him. Hash jerked a thumb, motioning him to wait in the kitchen, out of sight.

Hash stayed sitting on the back step for some minutes longer. Even though he knew Shamsa was dead he stroked her face, especially her muzzle where she liked to be tickled. He heard the man moving around in the kitchen. The bastard had probably been purifying, preparing for his approaching moment of martyrdom. The appearance of Susan, so soon after the charade with women's curves and, of course, her open nature, would have led him on. Hash guessed the man had made his move and then the fight had started, with Shamsa hurling herself into Susan's defence.

Hash knew that none of that was the problem anymore. The real problems were all queuing in front. Susan was within her rights to call the police now or later, and to go to a doctor. He hated himself for wanting her shame and embarrassment to work in his favour. Shamsa could be explained away as a sudden fit; and even old Mrs Hamilton could be persuaded the dog had had a fit of some sort. The old girl knew about Hash and his 'rescues'. Everyone would be told the vet had said there was no alternative but to have her put down. He looked down at the dog's peaceful face and stroked her again. Blood drying on his hand made him realise he had been sitting in it. He willed himself into action and, pushing Shamsa gently to one side, he stood up.

Ignoring the bomber who was still sitting in the kitchen in an almost trance-like state, Hash grabbed the cushion dog bed and went back outside, unzipping the outer cover as he went. He dropped the sac of filling to one side, then lifted Shamsa into the outer. Carrying her in both arms to the garage, he laid her down gently and returned for the sac. Returning to the kitchen, still ignoring the bomber, he filled a bucket with hot water. Ten minutes of scrubbing the step, frantically working bleach over the bloodstains, removed all traces.

Back in the kitchen, seeing the man rocking in pain, he signed he wanted to help. Gently taking the injured right forearm, Hash saw what Shamsa had done. There was a two-inch tear deep in the muscle of the forearm and the area was caked with blood as well as swollen. There were other punctures and bruising on both fists, some from what must have been an earlier injury. Hash remembered the man's soreness the previous day and also Shamsa's wound. He now knew the dog and the bomber had clashed earlier.

The man needed a tetanus shot and stitches, and he whimpered as Hash felt the flesh around the bites. 'You are a stupid bastard,' he said softly, looking at the bomber. His gentle tone could not disguise his venom but Hash was beyond caring. 'You are a stupid, stupid bastard,' he repeated, 'and if you weren't going to kill yourself, I'd fucking do it myself.' The man could see enough in Hash's eyes for translation to be irrelevant. Both men glared at each other. 'What other surprises have you got planned, you stupid, stupid cunt?'

The bomber gave way, grey with pain and anxiety, and Hash's gaze swept round the kitchen. There was a safety razor in the sink, tufts of hair, too. On the floor around the sink there were more tufts, partially covering the bloodstained kitchen scissors. The man had been taking most of his hair off with the scissors before using a razor to finish the scalp. The specks of blood on the floor had to have been Shamsa's.

He gently laid the man's arm to one side and went upstairs to look at his medical cabinet. Back downstairs, he washed out the basin, clearing the hair and washing the last of Shamsa's blood off his arms. Then, filling it again with warm water, adding drops of Dettol, he tested the temperature.

Turning away from the sink to place bandages on the table, he heard the ping of an SMS message. He saw the bomber holding the Arab BlackBerry in his hands, attempting to type into it. In a spike of fury, Hash stepped over and tore the phone from the bomber's hands, making the man yelp in pain. Hash could see there was a message waiting. Conscious of the bomber's smouldering eyes following his every move, he slipped the phone into his pocket. Louder, insistent cursing from the injured man prevented him from comprehending the message and he slipped the phone into his pocket, motioning the man to the sink.

As the bomber stood there, Hash held the damaged forearm in the warm water, the man shifted from foot to foot in obvious pain. He directed a low torrent of hate in his native tongue, stabbing a free finger at Hash. Hash could feel his own anger rising, wanting to grasp the finger, twist it back until it broke.

Briefly calm, the man jabbed the same finger at his wounds. Hash guessed he would be talking about medical attention. As he looked at the badly shaven head and the shabby clothes, he knew he could never take the man out in public now except on the final run to GCHQ and oblivion next Friday. The thought of five more days together left him cold with fear; they would not last. Maybe Siddiq was capable of producing a medic who could treat the man and not ask questions.

The bomber started to talk again, pointing at the wounds,

gesturing to where Shamsa's bed had been. Hash looked across and saw that more spots of blood had escaped his notice. Shamsa's or the bombers? As he was looking, a fist punched him on the shoulder. Adrenaline surged as he recoiled, seeing rage in the man's face. It was a hard punch and it shocked him and told him, wounded or not, in a physical struggle with this man he would lose. He stepped away from the man and held up both hands yielding, soothing.

Hash kept both hands raised in submission to the bomber who was standing opposite, sending a stream of hissed curses. He hushed him, reaching for the bomber's injured arm. He mimed wrapping the arm, injecting, to signify treatment. 'Later…later.' He lowered his hands, palms downwards, 'Calm down, calm down.'

The bomber's contempt only intensified and he drew his good fist back, poised ready to throw another punch. Hash turned his shoulder to the blow in case it came and repeated the calming gesture. Both men glared at each other. Hash could feel himself beginning to hyperventilate, adrenaline pumping a mixture of panic and explosive anger.

The bomber, his fist still raised, spat on the ground, unleashed another stream of venom and spat again, this time directly at Hash. Ignoring the gobbet of spit on his chest, Hash stepped back and deliberately walked over to the kettle and switched it on. Then he motioned to the man to sit, explaining with motions he intended to bind up the wounded arm. These acts of submission seemed to have an effect and the bomber dropped his fist, the disgust still showing in his eyes. He turned abruptly and went upstairs.

As Hash moved back to the sink, a wave of tiredness and emotion hit him. He wished he could talk to Flora, or Sean, but he had nobody. Susan had been hurt, maybe badly, maybe raped. Shamsa was lying dead in the garage, her body stiffening. Nothing he learned at Ben Gashir had prepared him for this. Hissing from the water pipes upstairs told him the man had stepped back from the brink of meltdown and was washing, preparing for prayer.

Remembering the SMS he fished the phone from his pocket and read the message, 'Lord Jim sends regards.' Someone at the Libyan end was on his side, or at least playing the game for the time being. Proof that Jim was alive burst like a dam of relief and he struggled to contain his emotions in the chaos around him.

Hash took a broom and began to sweep clumps of hair into a pile then scooped them into the bin. A few minutes later, footsteps on the stairs told him the bomber was coming down. The man went straight into the sitting room and Hash heard murmuring as the praying started. Hash would leave him to it. He took a cloth and bent down to get the blood spots off the floor. The sight of Shamsa's blood brought the prickle of tears to his tired eyes. She had stood her ground and paid the price. Hash knew the dog had shamed him by doing what she knew was right.

Going into the rear porch for a mop, he passed the table where Shamsa's worldly belongings were kept: brush, tins of food, a box of biscuits and a coiled lead. This lead was made of a thick leather loop and a metre of strong chain. Shamsa had developed the trick of carrying it to Hash to remind him a walk was overdue. From nowhere, an instinct made Hash pick up the lead..

As snatches of mumbled prayer reached him from the sitting room, Hash found himself twisting the leather hard around his right fist. His left hand took the end of the chain and pulled it taut. Like a guiding hand on his shoulder, the same instinct moved him quietly through the kitchen to the sitting room doorway. He sneaked a look at the man sitting on his ankles, eyes closed, his head turning slowly to the left then to the right, following the ritual of prayer. If he was aware of Hash he did not care.

Hash saw there was neutral daylight from outside and, even though the curtains were open, nobody could see in. Wrapping the chain end in his left hand, he edged noiselessly into the room. As the bomber bowed forward again, touching his head to the carpet, Hash poised, mouth dry, heart thudding, and then braced. A moment later the man sat back up, hands resting on his thighs.

Hash darted forward, looped the chain over the man's head, rammed his right knee between his shoulder blades and hauled back. The bomber's body bucked, hands flying to the chain around his neck, and for a moment the conflicting momentum suspended both men. Then the bomber writhed, rolling forward and, feeling the man's brute strength, Hash had to go with him, knowing all he had to do was keep his knee between those shoulder blades and his body weight on the chain.

Hash's weight took them down sideways onto the carpet as the man writhed and kicked back with his feet, his big hands scrabbling to free his throat. The two men lay sideways as the bomber's legs thrashed, knocking over the coffee table. Hash, breathing through clenched teeth, kept his arms hauling back. He could hear his victim gagging but his own pent-up rage fuelled the pressure on the man's throat.

The bomber tried reaching back, first clawing for Hash's arms, then scrabbling for the leg of the coffee table, but his wounded right arm must have been too weak to heft it, and instead of smashing it onto Hash, the hand lost its grip. Then slowly the man began to weaken, animal choking sounds rasping from his crushed windpipe. Hash hauled back harder, arms aching, aware of his own breath coming in hisses, pushing his knee even harder, knowing he had just to hold the position and do nothing else. The man's hands reached back for Hash, but the fluttering fingers told him their strength was beginning to ebb.

Convulsive spasms started to shake the bomber's frame, as they had with the dog, and when they subsided Hash still held on for two more minutes. Finally, with heart hammering, he let the chain go slack and the man's head lolled onto the carpet. Cautiously, still lying alongside, Hash flexed his wrists and fingers, seeing the white skin where the chain had cut the blood flow. He held his hands out and watched his fingers fluttering with shock and adrenaline.

Dragging himself upright, Hash went to the bay window and drew the curtains. Looking down at the lifeless bomber, at the face with its half-open eyes, Hash despaired at Jim returning from this mess, and he wanted to kick the inert form in front of him. How could his controllers at Ben Gashir, such sticklers for perfection, choose this brainless peasant to serve their purpose? As he was about to drag himself upstairs for a blanket he noticed that the Koran, knocked off the coffee table during the struggle, was now lying open on the carpet, and two slips of coloured paper were lying beside it.

Righting the coffee table and stooping to pick up the Koran, Hash collected and examined the two pieces of paper. He found himself looking at a pair of tickets printed with horses and holograms. They showed a 'Friday Only' admission to next week's racing festival. Hash remembered paying good money for the tickets as part of the holiday deal with Sean, and was now baffled at his own stupidity at not getting the 'Any Day' ticket. The bomber in his hours of solitude in the house, like a thieving magpie attracted to shiny objects, must have spotted the tickets where they were kept in a cut crystal vase on the mantelpiece.

Hash stepped across to return them to the vase and saw there were already tickets there. Extracting them all, he looked at each and found he did have enough tickets for 'Any Day', but in addition he had acquired a pair for Friday 13th March, Gold Cup Day.

Even in his shock and exhaustion he now began to understand why the martyr had not shown any interest in GCHQ, and had been indifferent during the recce and to all of Hash's briefings. No wonder he had shown no fear at the challenge of breaching a site defended like the electronic equivalent of a mediaeval fortress. Hash had assumed the man was exceptionally stupid. But now he understood. The bomber, presumably following the rehearsed procedures drummed into him somewhere in Pakistan, was about to present the two tickets to Hash, signalling the next item on the operational checklist. Friday the 13th at three in the afternoon, the man in the Semtex vest was going to be at the racecourse, right in amongst thousands of happy punters, just before the start of the Gold Cup.

The rush of surprise was cut short by the doorbell. Still holding the tickets in his hand, he went to the door frame and peered into the hallway. At the front door, a man's shape moved on the other side and blue phosphorescence silhouetted him on the frosted glass. Trying to choke back panic, he closed the sitting room door. Forcing himself to breathe deeply, he put on his best smile and went to the front door. He opened it to see a young police officer, still talking into his microphone, with his eyes fixed on Hash. The policeman finished his message and a disembodied voice crackled back an acknowledgement over the radio.

'Mister Hashmi…I believe?'

'Correct, Officer. What can I do for you?' Hash's eyes took in the periphery. Sure enough, Mrs Hamilton was on station behind her window. Some neighbours across the street had been lured to their doorways.

'Everything alright?' the officer asked.

'No, it's not,' Hash replied, 'I was in the middle of praying.' The policeman shifted slightly, looking past Hash into the hallway. 'A member of the public has reported a disturbance.'

'Aah yes, That would be my next-door neighbour,' Hash sighed, pointing across to her window. Mrs Hamilton's face fell as the officer's gaze swung round to her.

'No, it wasn't, actually, sir. Another member of the public,' he continued, 'has complained about noise.'

'My dear neighbours,' Hash said, 'Who I have known for fifteen years… they usually come to me first.'

'Maybe you weren't in, sir. Have you been away this morning, then?' The policeman had hooked his thumb into his uniform waistcoat.

'I was in court,' Hash lied. The policeman's eyebrow shot up. 'Catching up on some paperwork after yesterday's sitting,' Hash explained. 'And while I was away I believe my son's teacher paid a call.' The policeman made a show of pulling out his notebook. 'A dog barking incessantly,' he read, 'in some distress…does that sound right to you?'

'We have a new dog, a rescue, and she's very nervous… excitable, especially if I'm not here when someone knocks. She's still settling in.'

The policeman's walkie-talkie hissed with another transmission and Hash saw the car's light system blip two flashes. The policeman on his doorstep turned to check his colleague in the driver's seat. This man gave a distinct shake of the head, drawing a finger across his throat. 'So, you're one of our magistrates,' the policeman said. Hash was not sure there was approval in the statement.

'Is that good or bad?' Hash ventured.

'I'm sure it's good, sir.' The policeman's smile held a ray of hope. Hash needed the neighbours to see the body language.

'We always take rescue dogs and they always take time to settle.' Hash then nodded across to Mrs Hamilton's door. 'I will apologise to my neighbours.'

The police officer, distracted by the summons from his colleague, seemed to be losing interest. 'So, all is well, is it, sir?'

'My son's teacher was dropping off some holiday work and that probably set the dog off. She called me in fact,' Hash said, 'and I came as quick as I could, Officer.'

'No harm done as far as I'm concerned, sir.' The policeman began stepping back from the front door.

'I was about to pray, but...come in and see for yourself,' Hash swept his arm towards the kitchen.

The police officer hovered, but another transmission killed his interest. Stepping further back, and looking up at the door to confirm the number, he said, 'Not today...busy as hell. We'll leave it at that, then.' He cracked another smile, 'So, sir...I'll see you in court, then.'

CHAPTER 15

Easing into a kitchen chair, Hash pulled out the Arab BlackBerry and reread the simple message. His eyes stayed on the words, willing them tell him more than just the message Jim was alive.

Glancing up at the photographs on the dresser, he imagined what Flora would be saying: she would be urging him to gather his wits, summon the strength and 'get the fuck on with it'. Bella and the old boy across in Tyrone would be even less polite. His father might play it differently, cooler, more erudite, maybe borrowing from one of the old films: 'You play till the final whistle, old boy.'

Dismissing his fatigue, he heaved himself to his feet. Though he was hungry, tired and badly needed someone to talk to, he could not stop. There was a body in his living room and he did not know how to deal with it yet. A glance at the clock told him at least there was a solution for Shamsa.

It was dark, dry and clear as Hash headed out onto the Evesham Road, continuing past the racecourse. He would have preferred it to be raining as he reached the municipal tip at Stoke Orchard, but his timing was perfect, just ten minutes before it closed. He knew the staff were impatient, poised to close the gates, offices locked and their own cars running to heat up, champing at the bit to go home. None of them would be hovering at the big skips. Arrive a few minutes before closing time, Hash smiled, and you could dump a nuclear warhead and maybe have an impatient employee assist you lifting it into the skip.

Pulling up at the big container marked 'non-recyclable', he got out, confirmed he was completely alone, no other headlights signalling the approach of another visitor, and no member of staff in a 'hi-vis' vest in sight. He tugged at the canvas dog bed, feeling Shamsa's weight inside, and swung her gently onto the edge of the container. He whispered a last goodbye, putting his forehead to her body through the fabric, smelling her familiar, sweet body odour. Then he pushed her down the sloping metal plate and let her slide into the maw of the huge container. The body thumped onto the steel floor.

Hash dialled Susan and waited. He had parked a few doors away from her flat, but saw no lights in any of the windows. After six rings the voice message came on and he said, 'Susan? It's me, Hash. I hope you're OK, feeling better? I would be so relieved to see you, even just for a second. If there's anything I can do, please, please talk to me.' He gave up and turned for home, knowing he might get a chance to see her next morning at school. He was not looking forward to begging her to hold off reporting the nightmare to the police, if she had not already done so. He hated himself for hoping Susan was one of those girls too ashamed to report the attack.

'Your girlfriend was here,' Mrs Hamilton said, taking Hash by surprise as he slid his key into the lock.

'Mrs Hamilton,' he said, 'do you ever rest?' He was torn between irritation and admiration. She stepped forward from her porch and Hash faced her over the low wall. She had her arms folded across her chest as she looked up and down the street. 'Bloody goings-on here,' she sighed, 'like Peyton Place. Mystery visitors, the police, your women...' She stopped in midstream. 'When Jim's away, eh?' She wagged a thin, crooked finger in admonishment.

'I can only apologise,' Hash began, wondering if she had been drinking. 'Unexpected trouble with a guest, a friend of a friend, someone I was doing a favour for. He's gone now, thank God.' He sensed she was enjoying being in on the drama. 'Then Jim's teacher came to deliver coursework...'

'How is Jim? Enjoying the country life?'

'Very much so,' Hash said, 'although it's not how he puts it when he can be bothered to ring. His granny and grandpa love having him.'

'Anyway,' Mrs Hamilton sniffed, 'that girlfriend of yours was here.'

'What girlfriend? Jim's schoolteacher came by this morning. She's...'

'Blonde, ponytail, five foot you know what,' the old lady smirked.

'You've lost me. Susan's dark-haired,' Hash said, trying to keep up. 'I've just been to see her, but she's not at home. Was she here?'

'She could have been dark-haired once.' Mrs Hamilton was enjoying herself. 'Bottle blonde probably. Not what I would have called your type.'

'You know Shamsa's ill? The vet stuck her in hospital. I'm really worried she'll not pull through.' At this, the old lady's smile faded and her hand shot to her mouth.

'What's the matter with her?'

'Some congenital condition.' Hash tried to make it complicated and plausible. Mrs Hamilton still looked shocked. 'Took her in to the emergency place at the racecourse and they sent her down to the pet hospital in Bristol.'

'Poor girl,' the old lady said. 'Does Jim know?'

'I can't tell him until I know for sure.'

'Maybe better he doesn't know,' she said. 'He loves that dog.'

A wave of fatigue hit Hash and he turned to face his door, knowing what was on the other side.

'It's been a long day, Mrs Hamilton,' he said. 'I'd invite you in for a nightcap but I'd be asleep on the table in seconds.'

Hash stepped around the body and went to the curtains, making sure they were shut. He left the sitting room lights off, allowing only the kitchen light to slowly filter away the gloom in the sitting room. His eyes quickly became used to the half-darkness and he looked at the body. It lay on its side, covered in the blanket he had brought down earlier. He guessed he would be shifting twelve to thirteen stone of dead weight.

Hash went through his tiny garden to the garage, opening the rear door. Fumbling in the dark, he gathered duct tape and cord.

He lashed the man's heels together, looping the cord several times to have a strong handle to grip when he was pulling the body. Tugging two black bin liners over the man's shoulders he taped the whole head at the throat: he did not want any body fluids leaking. Finally, with the heels lashed, the arms roped to the side of the body and the head swaddled, Bent over and walking backwards, Hash did a walking rehearsal of the route he would be dragging the body. Satisfied there was nothing to snag or tear at the corpse en route and only the briefest exposure to neighbourly eyes as he was crossing the lawn, he braced himself.

Grasping the looped ankles, he swung the body round on the floor and began hauling, relieved that it travelled smoothly on the polished surface of the kitchen floor. Pausing at the rear porch to check, he stepped out onto the lawn and tugged hard to get momentum. The man's head smacked onto the concrete slab when it dropped off the back step. Within a few seconds he was heaving the body into the garage, lining it up along one of the walls.

Standing in the shower, relishing needles of red-hot water as they drilled down onto his head and shoulders, working soap onto his aching frame to break down the layers of strain, Hash tried to close his mind to the chaos and shock of the day. He knew if he let his mind run wild, then valuable sleep would be impossible.

What he had done to the bomber had opened a Pandora's box. As he towelled he began to wonder if the bomber had any pre-agreed procedures to follow in the days prior to the attack, a checklist of tasks which, if left unfulfilled, would start alarm bells ringing somewhere. He had to halt the runaway train of thought, recognising the churning would rob him of rest. He swallowed two sleeping pills, smelling their sharp herbal aroma, and lay on his bed, hoping they would work fast.

MONDAY 9TH MARCH.

The next SMS pinged him awake at nine in the morning. He ignored it, lying in bed trying to orientate himself after his drugged sleep. The herbal hangover made him feel dull and slow. He squinted at the phone, hoping the message was from Susan. It was not and the anxiety started. What was she doing? What was she thinking? Had she gone to the police? Had the doctors examined her and leaned on her to report the attack? The SMS was from Siddiq. As he was about to read it, a dog barked from somewhere behind his house, maybe in the lane that ran parallel and behind the road at the front. Maybe someone was taking their dog for a walk and it had smelled the cadaver in his garage? Hash wondered how long before the martyr, lying stiff and cold out in the garage, would attract rats. The weather was chilly enough, especially from the evening through to mid-morning, and he reckoned he had a few days in hand. Until Friday afternoon, in fact. After three pm on that day, when there was no massive detonation at the racecourse, someone somewhere, with their hands around Jim's throat, would need an explanation.

Siddiq wanted to meet at the mosque. Hash left home,

showered, shaved and wanting to look his best. He walked to the school office, passing Susan's flat on the way. He messaged her while he was walking but there was no response, and when he got near her digs he loitered, pretending to look at his phone, but there was no sign he could read: curtains drawn, no milk bottles, either full or empty, and he moved on. From the secretary, on the pretext of needing details for the debate, he learned that Susan was off sick and would be away for a few days.

Bella called as he was back on the Bath Road. He felt good knowing she would be easy to soothe. 'He's allowed up and about but no visitors. No pizza either. They're serious about that,' he lied.

'Poor wee Lordy,' she crooned. 'I'd feed him a good dinner of bacon and spuds.'

'His absolute favourite,' Hash lied again.

'And you're full of shite, Mister Magistrate,' she said. Hash heard her laughing at the other end and asked about the old boy. 'Aah, that old boy's always the same.' She started with the 'some days he's good' routine and Hash lost concentration, calculating he could make it to the mosque in fifteen minutes.

At prayers he saw Hakim, small and wiry, like a bearded elf, going through his devotions with agility and an expression of serene calm. Hash was glad he had remembered to bring money. Afterwards, mindful of showing the man respect, he was deferential in his approach. Again he felt the crushing handshake and was subjected to a wordless scrutiny: the serenity replaced by suspicion.

'Salaams Haji,' Hash started, 'how is your family, your health?' The man nodded, accepting the courtesies.

'Any news?'

'Alhamdulillah, no news.'

Unsure whether the man was following the ritual of an Arab greeting or really had no information, he pressed. 'About my son...any news?'

Hakim's neutral expression did not change. 'Alhamdulillah, no news.'

'But you are looking?' Hash wanted to punch the man. 'Do you need more money?'

'Insh'Allah,' Hakim said quietly.

'So...how much?' Hash asked. Hakim shook his head and with a look of irritation countered, 'Insh'Allah...I am looking.'

'Always,' the interruption came from Siddiq, 'always about money. But not today.' The Bangladeshi had crept up behind Hash and was enjoying the surprise. 'Today is not the day to be bothering the Haji. He is a very busy man.'

'But he is looking...?' Hash felt like a serf grovelling before his masters. 'And I have more money.'

'Hakim will bring you good news, soon.' Siddiq took Hash's elbow, attempting to steer him away.

'Come, my friend, someone is waiting.' Siddiq waved towards his car. 'Follow me.'

'Are you sure? I thought we had business here,' Hash said.

'Someone is waiting.'

When Siddiq opened the front door and ushered Hash inside he could tell that the maisonette had been given the female touch. The smell of dust on tired carpets and curtains had gone. Flowers in twin vases now decorated the sitting room. Anna and another woman were smoking in the rear garden, and Anna smiled and waved as she caught sight of Siddiq coming to the French window. Recognising Hash an instant later, she continued the greeting although her smile changed, becoming a little guarded. Hash could see her talking quickly to her companion, exhaling a stream of cigarette smoke as she passed information. The other woman, similar in height, was a clone of Anna: athletic, slim, blonde with a ponytail.

'You could be twins,' Hash said as he shook hands. The other girl, introduced as Daniela, seemed uncertain at the English and the laughter.

'But which is the younger one?' Siddiq made a pantomime wink, putting an arm around Anna's waist. 'Mine or yours?' Anna, holding her cigarette at arm's length as Siddiq pulled her to him, allowed herself to be pawed. 'Come on, darling,' Siddiq whispered hoarsely, 'Don't be shy. Hash is my best friend.'

Daniela smiled at Hash, half in embarrassment at Siddiq's clumsy antics, half in an appeal to kill the farce. Hash supposed he was getting a daytime look at the present Siddiq had sent last night. He thought about the arrangement he and Siddiq had brokered for the martyr, and could not help wondering what would have happened to this girl. The scenario jerked his mind to Susan and the pain she had been put through because of the bizarre arrangement. She had still not responded to his messages.

'Coffee?' Anna had broken away from Siddiq and was at the sink, dousing her cigarette at the tap, pointing at the kettle. Daniela was still in the garden, tapping at her phone.

'Or something stronger?' Siddiq said. 'Champagne? Brandy?'

'Coffee, thanks,' Hash said. 'This place is looking good, Anna: first time it's been so fresh in years.' She shrugged off the compliment, 'Thanks, it didn't take long.'

'How long do you plan on staying?'

'Why do you want to know?'

'I can't decide how much rent to charge my wealthy friend. So...stay as long as you like.'

'Sorry to hear about your son.' Hash was taken aback that she knew about Jim. How much had Siddiq told her? 'You've got to hope he'll come back soon,' she continued as water rushed in the kettle. Siddiq, sitting down, was sending a message on his phone, oblivious to the exchange. 'What else did he tell you?' Hash said.

The kettle began to boil. Anna at the sink, face turned away, picking mugs from the drying rack replied slowly, 'He says the boy's lovely, he could do very well at school and he misses his mother.' Siddiq's phone rang and he heaved himself upright, a scowl darkening his cheerful features. Unleashing a torrent of Bengali, he moved out of the kitchen. Anna's eyes followed him then looked at Hash, her eyes rolling heavenwards. 'Always on the phone. Business, always business.'

'What did he say about my son?'

Anna considered for a few seconds. 'He's going through that teenager phase, you know.'

'Do you have kids?' Hash asked her. She shook her head. 'I've been unlucky, let's just say I had some bad luck where kids were concerned. But for your son Jim,' she said, 'if he's in Birmingham, Siddiq will find him. So, everything's going to be fine.' She put a hand on Hash's arm. 'Siddiq knows people. He can fix things. Trust me.' She held up the coffee jar, tapping a spoon against it. 'Black white, strong or weak?'

Daniela re-entered the kitchen looking shyly at Anna and Hash.

'Where's that plumber of yours, the talkative guy?' Anna asked.

'He's gone,' Hash said. 'At least for the next few days. What's the problem?' Anna had opened the fridge door, reaching in to free a container of milk.

'I don't know what it is,' she murmured into the cabinet. 'Maybe I need my thermostats looked at.'

'I can do that easily, or we'll get him across to you,' Hash said.

'It was just a joke,' she said, holding the spoon over the open coffee jar, 'but maybe I'll call you instead.'

Siddiq burst into the kitchen, his good spirits revived. 'So... let's go for lunch, a nice, long lunch...what do you say?' Anna put the coffee jar down. 'I'm making coffee now, darling. Do you want me to stop?'

Siddiq reached for her waist. 'They can have the coffee.' He jutted his chin at Daniela and Hash. 'We're going for lunch.'

When they had left, Daniela stirred her coffee for a while and when the silence became too awkward she pretended to be busy with her phone.

'Did he send you to my house last night?' She stopped texting and looked across at him.

'No.'

'Are you sure?'

'Yeah. I was in Solihull, on a gig.'

'Gig?'

'You know…a gig, dancing.'

'Why do you do it?'

She considered the question while examining her phone. 'Pays the bills. Meet interesting people.'

'How do you know Anna?'

'I don't. Just met her.'

'Where are you from?' At his persistence Daniela lapsed into a sing-song routine. 'So…my name's Daniela, I'm from Lithuania and I'm studying to be a lawyer.' In afterthought she added, 'I'm paying my own student fees.'

'Who's paying you now?'

She looked surprised. 'Now? That is you."

'Who told you where I live?'

'Don't worry,' she trilled. 'I'm discreet. Some clients are very shy. Okay by me.'

'And you never met Anna?'

She gave a bright smile and held up both hands, palms upwards. 'Anna who?'

'When you've finished your coffee,' Hash said, 'I'll take you to the station.'

CHAPTER 16

Sean stood in the garage, taking his first look at the blanketed form. 'Jesus,' he whispered, digging in his coat pocket, 'Now I know it's for real.' He lifted a foot to the dead man's shoulder and rocked the body. The knees had stiffened at a bent angle and the body would not roll over. 'How did you do it?' Sean kept his foot on the body while he pulled out a packet of cigarettes.

'Choked him with the dog lead,' Hash said. 'He was praying when I jumped on his back.'

'So much for the power of prayer.' Sean tugged out a cigarette. 'Best get him into a sleeping bag.' He lit up, looked through the garage door, then blew a steady stream of smoke across the chill. 'He'll not stink for a good few days.' He tapped the corpse with his foot.

'How do we get rid of him?' Hash asked, adding, 'I put the dog in the council tip.'

'You're joking?'

'About the dog.'

'No,' Sean said, 'about tossing this guy on the skip. Do you know what we really need?'

'Anything, tell me.'

'A fucking drink. Something strong, something to help me think.'

In the kitchen, Sean sat smoking while Hash rummaged. He put a bottle and two glasses on the kitchen table, 'Something special…we were going to celebrate your trip.'

'We still are, Darky…aah, Crested Ten,' Sean murmured, looking at the label. Hash poured two generous measures.

'To Jim,' Hash raised his glass.

'To Jim,' Sean echoed quietly. 'And God help any bastard who gets in my way.'

The two men savoured the liquid in silence until Sean.

'What about this Susan girl of yours? Is it serious?' Sean said.

Hash shook his head, 'Romantically, or after what happened? The sight of me could trigger anything. Maybe she'll go to the police, maybe her parents will push her.' He held up his palms. 'Maybe she'll do nothing at all.'

'And this guy Hakim,' Sean asked. 'What's the score with him? He one of the good guys?'

'He runs a radio cab business in the Birmingham area, all Asian drivers, and he's an imam, you know, some sort of religious elder.' Hash swallowed from his glass. 'He tried to tell me Jim had run away to join ISIS, like one of those mad youngsters.'

Sean said nothing for a few seconds, lost in thought. Then he pointed at the vest that Hash had carried from the garage. 'What do we do on Friday after nothing goes bang at three o'clock?'

'I'm just hacking each day. I haven't got that far yet,' Hash said.

THURSDAY 12TH MARCH.

They had agreed that their only contact for the time being would be in the Guinness Village at the races. The crush of punters jostling for their pints was good enough cover. Tuesday's meeting, two days back, allowed Hash to tell Sean, his voice raised above the hubbub of music and racing commentary that there had been nothing from Hakim or Siddiq and nothing from Susan. Sean hinted that he was working on someone who might move the package. Wednesday afternoon's meeting brought in the price from Sean's contact with the exchange set for the following evening in the trade stand parking area. This was where lorries and vans, quartered for the week, would be busy unloading fresh stock and moving out waste.

With Sean directing, Hash reversed the Discovery up to the back of a horse box with Cork plates, and in the rear mirror he glimpsed Sean shaking hands with another man he guessed was the driver. There were no introductions as he got out and within seconds the martyr, zipped into a sleeping bag, was carried into one of the stalls inside. In a wordless exchange, Hash handed over two thick wads of notes to a tough, thickset man in a heavy tweed coat that smelled of beer and straw. He looked at the money, thumbing the corner of the wadded notes. 'Ten thousand, is it?' he said in a thick Southern Irish accent. 'You sure, now…cos you've left me no time or light to count it.' He looked up from the notes in his hand, an eyebrow raised. 'Give me more warning next time. I can give a discount for groups, bring a bigger lorry.' Sean and the man burst into laughter and clasped each other in a bear hug. Hash was ignored. Then the man climbed into the cab and fired the engine.

They watched the lorry reverse out, making a cautious turn on the uneven ground. 'I don't think our friend's going to feel the bumps.' Sean shrugged. 'Good riddance. One moment you're the farmyard cockerel, next minute you're a feather duster.' The driver settled in his cab and flicked a salute at the two men before slipping the clutch. Sean patted Hash on the back. 'One down, how many more to go?'

Hash was watching the horse box. 'What'll they do with him? Tip him over the side of the ferry?'

Sean pulled out a packet of rolling tobacco. 'My guess… he'll hit the food chain, somewhere in the arse end of Cork.' Hash took few seconds to work it out, then dismissed it with a shudder. 'I heard from Susan,' he said.

'Good or bad?'

'Good, I think. This afternoon. She's asking me about the lecture.'

'What lecture?'

'I'd forgotten,' Hash said, 'I agreed to be in this school debate tomorrow. It's her big deal and she asked me as a big favour, I was going to take her out to dinner afterwards.'

'Maybe your dinner date is back on.' Sean stopped pushing tobacco onto the skin and nudged Hash with his shoulder. 'How did she sound?'

'She sent an SMS so I didn't speak to her. But at least she's communicating.'

'If she's sending you an SMS about a school debate, then her mind's not on that bastard.' Sean jutted his chin at the departing lorry. 'When's this debate?'

'Tomorrow afternoon.'

'Gold Cup Day…bad timing, you'll miss the crack.' Sean licked the roll-up and held it up for examination. 'Maybe better not to be here tomorrow afternoon.' Sean lit up, took the first drag, and blew a stream of smoke in the direction of the grandstand where there was still a residual buzz of activity, punters making their way to their cars, some carrying drinks with them into the car park, some hanging onto each other for support.

'Lucky, bastards,' he breathed, 'enjoying themselves. They'd be gobsmacked if they knew two old gunslingers from the IRA were watching their backs.' The smell of sweet tobacco hit Hash's nostrils. 'I could do with one of those,' he murmured. Sean ignored him.

'Remember some of the crazy ideas in the old days,' Sean plucked at a shred of tobacco stuck to his lip, 'They thought about nailing this place, you know.'

'Must have been after my time.'

'Before your time, Darky,' Sean corrected, pointing over at the tented hospitality suites. 'The idea was ditched because of the backlash after the Mountbatten thing in '79. I heard about it in the Kesh...we had lectures, and stuff like that.' He smiled at Hash. 'The top brass wanted to take the old girl out. But then some of the big names, hands with experience, said no fucking way.' He spat on the ground and wiped his mouth. 'They said the Gold Cup was sort of a truce, off-limits, out of bounds. Know why?' Hash shook his head. 'The old Queen Mum,' Sean continued. 'The old doll used to walk around half-cut, shaking hands with Paddy. And Paddy bloody worshipped her. There would have been mayhem if one hair on her head had been touched.'

'And the ordinary folk, tomorrow, at three o'clock?' Hash nodded at the grandstand. 'Is it over? Do we warn them?'

'A phone call?' Sean suggested. 'The old anonymous tip-off?'

'They've probably had twenty of those already, just today,' Hash said. 'From pissed punters who've lost their money.' Sean flicked his butt and watched the glowing tip shoot into the darkness. 'How about we dump the suicide vest where the Brits will find it, make it easy for them? That would freak them out, the place would be crawling.'

Hash swung his door open and motioned to Sean to climb in on his side. Buckling himself in, about to switch the engine on, Hash said, 'It's about priorities, about Jim and the bastards holding him.' He shook the steering wheel, 'Those good people out there aren't my priority.'

'We're running short on time, mate.'

'I've got to keep the Libyan end on my side.'

'Well, you know the bastards,' Sean said, 'how their minds

work.' He laughed at a sudden thought. 'But then you're one of them, so you bloody well should. Me?' He threw a flurry of punches. 'I'm just the technical guy.'

At the pub, when Sean had gone outside for a smoke, Hash tried Susan's number and was surprised when she picked up after just a few rings. 'Susan,' he said softly, 'how are you…is this a bad moment to call?' Her voice had a tremble in it when she said, 'No, I'm fine, you know, getting on with things. How are you?'

'Frantic with worry about you, Susan.' He hunched his shoulders and jammed the phone to his ear to keep out the pub buzz. Sean came back, saw the concentration and then went to the bar. When he returned with two fresh pints Hash was off the phone and had pushed back in his seat.

'She still love you?'

Hash blew out his cheeks. 'If only…' he exhaled. 'The bastard grabbed her and threw her around until the dog stepped in. She reckons she got out because of Shamsa.'

'Is she going to the police?'

'I told her she should and if she'd let me I would. Told her the guy was being tracked by my contacts and I'd be wringing his neck.'

'Well,' Sean raised his pint, 'at least you didn't lie on that score.'

'I told her about the dog being put down.' He contemplated his pint for a second then sipped. 'I don't need her going to the cops…that's the last thing.'

'Maybe she's too embarrassed,' Sean said. 'You read about

these things.'

'She wants me to do the debate. That takes me away from the races.'

FRIDAY 13TH MARCH. MORNING.

When Sean eventually answered his phone, his voice sounded slurred and thick with sleep. Hash interrupted his protests, urging him, 'Something warm that'll keep the rain off, your passport and maybe a small overnight bag.'

'That's all I brought in the first effing place,' Sean groaned. 'Jesus…I might be losing my touch. But there were three and I'd had a few scoops.'

Distracted by an image emerging from his printer, Hash was not listening. When the sheet of A4 was released, he laid it out on the desk, his eyes running over it, comparing it with three identical printouts, two for him and two for Sean. He silenced Sean's words over the phone, saying, 'I'm driving past you in two minutes, be ready.'

At the pick-up point, Sean's face showed haggard and pale, the effects of a drinking session all too plain. As he climbed in he started to explain. 'I had a few more after you dropped me off, then I went for a fish supper…then these boyos actually did appear…I didn't think you were serious.'

Hash thrust the four sheets of paper at him and jerked a thumb behind him, 'Thermos on the back seat.'

Sean's wariness gave way to curiosity as he looked at the pictures. A moment later he looked up, catching Hash's grim smile. 'That's Jim. Bloody hell. How…when?'

'Siddiq,' Hash said, 'eight o'clock this morning. It came through from Hakim and his boys.' He reached across and tapped the paper in Sean's hand. The sheet showed a grainy, coloured image of a scene in a park with a cluster of figures: one of them was a young lad in his teens, holding a toy helicopter.

'Must have been taken from a car, the driver was passing and thought he should snap it.'

'Top man. Fucking brilliant,' Sean said. 'But this wasn't taken this morning, was it?'

'Must have been yesterday afternoon before the light went… maybe before, even.'

'Where the hell is this place?'

'Sparkbrook.'

'How do you know?'

'Siddiq…when he was telling me not to go there.'

'Which is why we're going there.'

Hash looked at Sean. 'Siddiq doesn't really get how serious this is.'

'You sure? Maybe he's smarter than he looks.'

Hash went silent, driving fast, hustling the cars in front and within minutes the Discovery was running down the ramp north onto the M5. He relaxed enough to jerk his thumb at the basket with the thermos and mugs on the back seat. Sean reached back and brought it forward. He poured a cup for each of them. 'Jesus, that's good,' Sean groaned after the first sip, 'I needed that. My bloody head hurts.'

Hash took his mug carefully, keeping his eye on the motorway.

'So…tell me. What happened?'

'They came in just before the place closed. The old Portuguese lad went white as a sheet and I recognised the guy with the tattoos on his neck.'

'Go on.' Hash was beginning to smile.

'I was waiting for my order, really peckish, like most gentlemen after a few gargles. And I don't mind other hungry people…it's when they get cheeky with it.' He sipped again. 'And that's when things got interesting.'

Hash had accelerated hard to overtake a lorry and there was silence while Sean concentrated keeping the liquid in his cup. When the lorry dropped behind them Hash glanced across. 'And…?'

'I gave them a lesson in good manners.'

'All of them? What about the manager? Was he involved?'

'He seemed happy to let me do the talking.'

'So, no cops?'

'Not that I know of, but you never know. Afterwards, maybe.'

Hash sipped from his cup. 'We've got enough to cope with without them.' A motorway sign flashed past, Tewkesbury next turnoff, Worcester coming up, and Birmingham still some thirty miles off.

Sean buzzed the window down and sucked in cold air. 'What's the plan now, Darky?

'Get there,' Hash said, 'park up, get out on foot. Hope to see them if they take him to play with his helicopter. We get close, and…'

'Nail them.' Sean made a hammering motion with his free

hand.

'…Grab Jim and run.'

'Run where? Back to the car, run to the cops?'

'When you see we're out of the bastards' reach, then you run like hell,' Hash said. 'I'll get a chunk of money across to you. Probably leave it with Bella for you to collect.' He winked at Sean.

'That would be just bloody all I need. I'm in enough shit with them as it is, without going to them to get money off them.'

'Yeah, but this is about Jim and by then they'll know you pulled the situation round for their grandson.'

'Won't make a blind bit of difference to them.' Sean massaged his temples with both hands. 'They disowned me, ever since that…' He stopped, looked at Hash, seeing his nod of recognition, then out of the window. 'You know what I'm talking about. They turned their backs on me, ages ago. Ten years in the Kesh and not one visit from my mother or father.'

'Yes, but this is different,' Hash insisted. 'This is huge. You're making up for that stuff and I'll bloody well tell them what you've done.'

'What I've done…' Sean repeated quietly, 'that would be premature.' He looked at the sheets on his lap. 'Jim's still skinny but taller. His three friends look like minders.'

'Good you had a warm-up bout, then.'

Sean laughed. 'And here's me thinking that chippy thing was a coincidence. You set me up nicely, didn't you? Why the helicopter?'

'Quadcopter, drone or something. He's crazy about the

things.'

'They gave him one to keep him busy?' Sean said. They're being nice to him?'

'Very considerate,' Hash said. 'Maybe it's Jim's. I think he packed it for his time on the farm with the old folks.'

Sean continued to study the photograph of Jim. 'How are we going to get close without Jim seeing one of us and waving, giving the game away?'

'I don't know, yet.'

'Maybe these guys have got guns. Any updates from Siddiq?' Sean asked. 'You know…like, when the photo was taken, who took it?'

'I don't think we'll be doing too many interviews. Siddiq told me not to do anything, remember? Just confirm the photos are Jim. He says Hakim wants to get a clearer picture.'

'Was he serious?'

'Hakim is the serious type.'

'Maybe Hakim wants you to confirm, then he grabs Jim and ransoms him back to you, he knows you're good for cash.'

'I hear what you're thinking but it doesn't fit with Hakim or Siddiq somehow.'

'They've been clever enough already.'

'Doesn't sound like their style.'

'Well, you're the boss,' Sean sighed, 'You see the good in people. I come from the real world, mate.'

By the time they had followed the M42 round the southern edge of Birmingham and hit the Stratford road it was nine-forty-five with the rush hour past its peak. The radio was interrupted by a weather and traffic bulletin with the announcer saying roads into Cheltenham were getting busy and wishing the punters a good day at the Gold Cup. Hash thumped the wheel and cursed. 'That bloody debate!'

'What'll you tell her?'

'They'll just have to carry on without me. But that's twice I've really dropped her in it. It was a chance to see how she was, sort things out with her. She'll feel I've let her down.'

'You have,' Sean said. 'It's what girls are used to. You're a bloke.'

'Yes, but Susan's different.' He couldn't help smiling as Sean sobbed. 'But Susan's different!'

'She is.'

'Where do you need to be? Sean asked. 'With Susan and a bunch of schoolkids, or up here trying to get Jim back?' Hash made no answer.

'Priorities, or so you were lecturing me. Then bloody well SMS her so we can both concentrate.'

After a silence in the vehicle, broken only by Hash's grunts of frustration at the succession of traffic lights, Sean looked at his watch. 'Ten o'clock and maybe they'll be up for breakfast or in the park after breakfast.' When Hash made no comment, Sean asked, 'So how do you know the location?'

'I had to believe Siddiq, then I took it off Google,' Hash said. 'The two calls were made from around here the night Jim was taken, and when I did my own stake-out I got a look at the area. There's only one nice big park just a half-mile south of those streets. It's on the left as we're coming up now, with this low, red-brick wall running parallel with the pavement. You can see that in the picture.' Sean examined the picture. 'So I Googled the whole Sparkbrook area this morning and…' He raised both hands off the steering wheel in prayer. 'This is my best shot.'

As the parade of shops on the left of the road gave way to open, pleasant green tranquillity, they went silent, looking both at people on the pavement and deeper into the park. Mature trees, some planted in clumps, others on their own, and some colonies of shrubbery broke the scene and the clarity of the view. People were in the parkland in groups, all ages, some walking purposefully to work, others dawdling. Hash's driving pace provoked a horn blast from behind.

'Better we park up somewhere close,' Sean said, still concentrating on the view. 'I see an interesting bunch way out on the left.'

'We park, split and go for a walk, you to the top, me sticking around this end. What do you think?' Hash looked at Sean and got a nod of agreement.

After they separated, Hash walked north along Stratford Road a short distance, past a Shell filling station, keeping to the right side of the road where the shops continued. He heard his phone ping with a message. His heart sank as he read Susan's excited. 'All set? Come to the office for a coffee first.' He stopped in the doorway of a boarded-up shop with a bailiff's letter pasted to the door. She picked up immediately, her voice breathless.

'So…you ready for this? It's so good of you to do it. I don't know about you but I'm really nervous and the kids are…'

'I can't make it, Susan.' Hash shut his eyes, wincing as the blow landed. 'I've got a terrible situation.'

'What's happened?'

'I can't make it.'

'You mean you're not coming to the debate?'

'I'm so sorry, Susan, really. I would have told you earlier but this has only just come up in the last hour or so. A friend of mine…'

'You won't be doing the debate?' Her voice trembled. 'Oh no, Hash, please tell me you're joking, please.'

'I wish I could, Susan but this…'

'Why didn't you tell me?' She sounded incredulous. 'Are you nervous about it? Everyone's nervous. There's, nothing to worry about.'

'Definitely not that, Susan,' Hash had his eyes closed, trying to concentrate against the hum of traffic. 'I've got an emergency, a friend of mine.'

'Where are you?' Hash thought about lying and decided he was doing enough already. 'Birmingham. I'm taking this friend to hospital.

'Oh, I see.' He sensed the resignation and mounting anger in her tone.

'Believe me, Susan. There's nowhere I'd rather be than at the debate with you. It's just.' He opened his eyes and looked across the park. 'It's not in my hands.' There was silence at the other end of the line. 'Can you believe me?'

'Another bloody excuse. A dying grandmother,' she said, her voice acid. 'How many's that so far? I've lost count.'

'No, Susan. How can I make this up to you? I'm really, really sorry.'

'You could have told me earlier, for a start. Now I've only got an hour or so before the debate. How am I going to find someone to replace you?' Hash could not think of anything to say and the silence on the line almost hurt him physically.

'Sorry won't do,' she said, slipping into her clipped, schoolmistress voice. 'Fine. I'll tell the headmaster and he can decide what to do.'

'Susan…'

'Never mind,' she snapped, 'it's done, can't be undone. Have a great day at the races.' The phone went dead, leaving Hash looking at it.

Looking over the flow of traffic, and into the park he made a conscious effort to chase Susan from his mind. This moment was for Jim and the gift Siddiq had given passed on. He SMS'ed Sean and got figure zero, nothing to report. If they were successful maybe Sean would not even return, just fade away, staying under the police radar, reporting back to his probation officer as expected. He and Jim would give him time to get away before handing themselves in to the authorities.

He watched a police car drive slowly past, its two occupants in their yellow vests, looking bored at being stuck in the slow-moving traffic. He wondered at how quickly the officers would react if they glimpsed Sean and himself struggling with a group of men in broad daylight. He wondered if the two police officers carried weapons and how long the paramedics would take to get onsite if a life-or-death struggle kicked off. Would they even up the numbers or maybe just stand off and call for backup. Especially if the minders pulled out weapons. Maybe the minders were martyrs, too, with no fear of dying, happy to take some kufar with them.

At half past eleven, Sean called, his voice electric with tension. 'Get the fuck over here,' he said, 'quickly but slowly!'

'Where?'

'Come into the park, way over! Use the trees to creep down towards me. You'll see what I see.' Hash was across the road and over the knee-high wall in seconds. He slowed down as soon as he was on the grass. Stopping himself from peering and exposing his anxious face, he cut across the park, walking slowly, head down with his phone clamped to his ear. He thought he could hear a model engine whirring, not as loud as the Spitfire but an engine nevertheless. He reached a tree and peered to his left and right, seeing nothing in his immediate view, then headed towards two trees a hundred and fifty yards away. Sean rang again. 'Hurry the fuck up! Something's happening. They're telling him to land the thing.'

'Stay on the line,' Hash said, his mouth dry, 'stay talking. Can you see me?'

'Not yet.'

'They're at the top end and he's just brought the thing to earth and they're all standing looking at it. One of them's on the phone, arms waving like crazy.'

'How's Jim?'

'Start walking, stop fucking talking,' Sean hissed. 'I'm two-fifty, maybe three hundred yards away. I can't do it myself.' Hash had begun to stride quickly, his face still to the ground, taking an occasional squinted glance ahead of him. Finally, he caught sight of three men and a youth standing together. The distance was two hundred yards and they were a tight group at the side of a road lined with parked cars. One of the men was opening a car door and pointing inside. He recognised Jim's diminutive shape, shoulders hunched, dumbly obedient in front the men. He was holding a quadcopter.

He wanted to yell at Jim, but the distance was against him. Even just one of those men could intercept him and the group was beginning to move.

'Doors open, one's just got in the driving seat, now Jim and the other. I think someone's onto me, Fuck...'

Hash saw Jim disappear into the car and the door close.

'Bloody hell,' Sean groaned.

We're too fucking late...' Sean's voice trailed off. 'Black car, moving now. I'm crossing the road in front of them.'

'Can you stop them?'

Hash caught a glimpse of Sean on the kerb, letting cars pass. He saw a flow of cars, one of them maybe a black saloon swinging into the northbound flow on Stratford Road. He watched it go and within seconds it was swallowed up, fading into the mass of vehicles.

Sean was strangely elated when they both met at the Discovery. 'Jesus!' He held up his thumb and forefinger. 'This close...

Your man drove bloody past me, nearly knocked me over.' Hash heard him out. 'But he looked OK to me.' Sean patted Hash on the back. 'He looked OK, fit, a bit underfed but OK.'

'I can't believe it…close but,' Hash smacked a fist into his palm, 'not bloody close enough.'

'Did you get a photo of them?'

Sean had just stuck a cigarette between his lips and stopped in the act of lighting up and clicked his fingers. 'I wish I had thought of that.' He held the lighter to the tip and Hash watched the glow. 'No bloody photos,' he said, coughing as he exhaled, 'but would a video be OK?' He dragged on the cigarette a few times then dropped the cigarette, crushing it underfoot. 'Want to see?'

The camera view wobbled, unsteady with Sean's rapid movement, but the lens zoomed in on a black BMW saloon approaching the camera. There was traffic noise in the background and through the front windscreen Hash saw two men, suited, both dark-haired, smooth faces showing concern and purpose. 'Arabs,' Hash said as the camera showed the car's side windows sweeping past. In the rear seat, looking down at the quadcopter on his lap, sat Jim. The camera saw the BMW disappearing, its rear plates immediately blocked by the vehicles following.

'Jim!' Hash put his hands to his eyes, trying to hold back emotion. Sean had to pause the video and wait for a few minutes. 'Dammit,' Hash whispered, 'so bloody close.'

'Closer than we were yesterday,' Sean growled, 'We didn't get clocked by them, so there's still tomorrow.'

'Play it again,' Hash said.

On the fourth rerun Hash told Sean to freeze the video. 'Try to zoom in on that,' Hash tapped the screen. 'The stuff behind the windscreen.'

'They've had a meal,' Sean muttered. 'Chicken Hut. A newspaper, what language?'

'Arabic,' Hash said. 'Zoom in on that sign.'

'A big letter M,' Sean said, 'like one of those passes you get on the ferry to hang on your mirror.'

'Members 'Enclosure,' Hash said.

'Don't follow.'

'Members' enclosure at the races.' He looked at his watch. 'One o'clock now. They're going to the races.'

'Taking Jim to the races?' Sean canted his head left then right, 'Can only be the Gold Cup, then. They're going to hand him over, leave him there after the big bang.'

'And when there isn't a big bang? What do they do with Jim?'

'Have you not told Libya?' Sean asked.

'Didn't bring that phone,' Hash said. 'It stays at home in case someone's tracking it.' He held up his watch. 'An hour to get to Cheltenham: the roads will be clear now that most of the punters are already there.'

'One of them was talking on the phone,' Sean said as they nosed back down the Stratford Road. 'Maybe taking a message.'

'But Jim looked good, didn't he?'

'Considering what he's going through,' Sean said, 'he looks in good shape. Someone's got to be looking after him. Bloody hell.' He slapped his thigh. 'I could have reached out and ripped open the door.'

At two-thirty after dropping Sean off at the racecourse Hash was sending an SMS to the Libyan number: 'Dafe disappeared. Took all funds. Left equipment. Advise.' At two-fifty-five he was walking through the turnstile on the western entrance to the Prestbury Park Racecourse and watching the huge screen showing horses and jockeys leaving the ring across to his right. Hash wondered where the bomber had been told to position himself: perhaps in amongst the crush of people overlooking the ring. But that crowd was thinning fast, already following the horses down to the track. The screen flicked to the starting gate where the first of the jockeys were circling their mounts. Hash tried to imagine what sort of a figure the tall, gaunt bomber would have cut in amongst the racegoers. Maybe he would have gone into the crowded stands, or maybe up the stairs to meet his Arab contacts for one last briefing. He knew there was a good chance Jim was around somewhere and if he could just catch a glimpse there would be no hanging back. The big race started, to deafening approval from the grandstand. It ran for several minutes as Hash tried to ignore it and concentrate on the crowds, trying to spot anyone out of place, anyone not caught up in the excitement. Within minutes it was over, racegoers beginning to celebrate, hugging and cheering, heading for the booths to cash in their winnings. Hash's eyes raked the crowd for any sight of the three Arabs and Jim.

The vibration of an SMS against his thigh distracted him. Still scanning the crowd, he took out the phone, expecting Sean to report in. When he glanced down it was the clerk to the justices confirming the bail hearing for the following morning.

The three o'clock deadline had passed without any detonation from some standby martyr out in the crowd, and Hash wondered if his message had been sufficient to tip the mission off course and enough to keep Jim alive. Maybe he could have exaggerated the man's disappearance, saying how he, Hash, had been ready to do the job but had been very badly let down by the martyr who had been getting flaky and then lost his nerve, how he had been talking non-stop about women, failing to pray regularly, plus a host of other sins. On balance, he decided keeping it short and sharp was better: the other ideas could be shaded in later.

Standing not far from him was the headmaster, dressed in a well-fitting Prince of Wales check, tweed suit, a pair of suede brogues, and just raising a pair of expensive-looking binoculars. With a jolt of sadness, he knew the man had recognised him and was ignoring him. Susan would surely be informed. Hash raised his hand to catch his attention and offer his apologies, but the man was already walking away.

Swallowing the blow, he moved down the gentle slope, crossing the lane from the paddock, and headed through the throngs of punters towards the tented village where all the bars and boutiques clustered. He heard his ringtone and saw Siddiq's name on the screen.

'Where are you, my friend? At the racecourse?'

'Of course.'

'All day?'

'Since this morning.' Hash heard discussion at the other end, as though Siddiq was conferring with somebody else.

'Not in Birmingham?'

Hash sensed the suspicion. 'No.'

A muffled exchange took place at the other end before Siddiq came back with, 'Mister Hakim says you are a liar.'

'What do you mean?'

'Mister Hakim says he saw you, has a photograph of you. I am looking at it now. You are in Birmingham. I will send it to you.'

'I was in Birmingham, but that was much earlier.'

'Mister Hakim says you have made a big mistake. You are a stupid man who does not care about his son.'

'I can explain this,' Hash began but was cut off by Siddiq delivering the rest of the message, '...and your son will die because of your stupidity.'

With the last race of the day over, light fading and the grandstands beginning to empty, Hash linked up with Sean in the car park on the west side. Sean listened to Hash's update in silence, rolling a cigarette up, leaning against the vehicle. When Hash had finished, the Irishman added more disappointment. 'You lose me tomorrow, Darky. The licence business, remember?'

'Do you think Jim was going to be handed over here after the bang?' Hash asked. 'He could have been dumped here and made his way home easily enough.'

Sean lit the cigarette, inhaled and examined it before exhaling a stream of blue smoke. 'Some hope. Do you think they're going to buy your story about the guy running away?' Together they watched the emptying racecourse. Then Sean said, 'Maybe they'll try again, save Jim for another go.'

CHAPTER 17

CHELTENHAM. SATURDAY 14TH MARCH

Hash was joined by the same magistrates as before. Maybe the clerk intended to rub in the folly of their previous decision. The Chairman who had noticed his Harrow faux pas gave a weak smile as Hash entered the retiring room, a greeting without conviction. The female medical professional, sour-faced champion of the beleaguered, said nothing, trying to look busy. They waited in silence until the clerk called them into court.

A policeman stood in the dock handcuffed to the defendant as the three magistrates took their seats. Before them sat the same legal aid counsel and at the back the same reporter from the *Gloucestershire Echo*. Hash was struck by a sense of déjà vu.

The man in the dock had a heavily bruised face, both eyes swollen, and lips still crusted with blood. His neck was in a brace, and his right arm, in plaster, was held by a white sling. His left arm hung free but with a large dressing over the whole hand. He tried to direct a fingertip to one of his clogged nostrils and the struggle showed evidence of severe pain. Only when the clerk kicked off with the formal identification exchange did Hash realise the name and address corresponded to the tattooed thug. The man lisped inaudibly through fat lips and the answers had to be repeated. He swayed, whether coached to do so by his counsel, or for real, and it drew an intake of breath from the female winger.

Citing the defendant's failure to comply with bail reporting conditions, the clerk gave the floor to the legal aid counsel who rose, attempting a show of regret. 'My client will not contest the fact he missed his reporting obligations. As your Worships can clearly see, he has suffered a brutal assault which occurred before his curfew on Thursday evening. The police have agreed to share CCTV evidence of the attack on my client. If it pleases your Worships...' He pointed to a television screen in the well of the court and within seconds a silent, black and white recording flickered into life and Hash found himself looking at a scene inside his own chippy. There was the wide window with a central door, the familiar drinks fridge with a table next to it at which a solitary customer sat, baseball-hatted and crouched over a newspaper. In the foreground, the round-shouldered Portuguese stirred the serving bins. Hash watched the chippy door being pushed open hard, startling the seated man as three men walked up to the counter. One of the trio made his way to the drinks fridge and immediately started tossing drinks to his friends, at the same time stuffing some bottles into his pockets. With the gesticulations and obscene hand signs, there was no need for a soundtrack.

'My client' – the counsel paused the video, pointing at the

tattooed ringleader on the screen then across to the man in the dock – 'readily concedes his behaviour and that of his friends was unacceptable and is happy to compensate the proprietor in full.' He pressed the play button and the screen jolted into movement with the Portuguese appearing to remonstrate with the leader. The solitary customer in the baseball cap stood up and moved to the counter to receive his serving, and in doing so he elbowed past the men. As he turned, one of them smacked a hand underneath the wrapped chips sending the food into the air then swung a punch at the customer. 'Again, your Worships, my client fully agrees this was deplorable behaviour.' The next seconds of tape showed the three thugs crowding around the man, jabbing at him, one of them flipping the man's hat off. Hash saw Sean step back, arms akimbo, then carefully take his reading glasses off, putting them into a pocket. The Portuguese was waving his hands at the door, ordering them all to leave. In that brief instant Sean landed a punch on the tattooed man's face, sending him reeling against the drinks fridge. The court audience gasped at the speed and saw Sean step across and reach down for the man's throat. The victim, unable to break the one-handed grip, found himself being dragged through the doorway and out of the camera's reach. His two companions, drinks in hand, looked at each other and then went out after them. The camera now showed only the Portuguese proprietor, hands on his head, flinching repeatedly as, one after the other, punched rag doll figures reeled and jerked back against the steamed-up window of the chippy.

'My client,' the counsel began, as he signalled the orderly

to switch off the screen, 'failed to meet his bail conditions because he was in the General Hospital overnight, a matter put beyond his control due to the nature of his injuries, injuries so severe that at one point the surgeons feared for his life. The wounds are consistent with grievous bodily harm and I have informed the police and asked them' – he held up a USB stick – 'to find the person who carried out this assault.' He paused, gripping his lapels. 'My client stands ready to atone for his mistakes but in respect of bail, your Worships, my argument remains that he is not a risk…' Hash watched the reporter scribbling, a hint of a grin on his face. The female winger looked on, stony-faced.

Siddiq gestured to a booth at the far end of the dining room and followed him a few seconds later. He eased onto the seat, sighing as he held his hand out in greeting.

'Are you OK?' Hash asked. 'Something wrong?'

Siddiq looked tired and distracted. He focused on Hash and repeated, 'Very sad.'

'Look,' Hash began, 'I cannot thank Hakim enough. He gave me a chance to take Jim back and I could not waste that chance.' Siddiq leaned his head forward onto his hands and began to massage his temples. When he stopped he opened tired eyes and looked at Hash. 'Mister Hakim is very angry with me for bringing you and your trouble to him.'

'Does he still have Jim? How can I make the situation right with Hakim?'

'Look at this picture.' Siddiq pulled out his phone and

191

flipped a finger across the screen, selecting the image and offering it to Hash. It showed him in the doorway on Stratford Road when he had made the call to Susan. He saw a picture of himself standing, eyes closed, the pain on his face with his phone jammed to his ear.

'Hakim took this photo.'

Hash pushed back against the seat, handing the phone back. 'Where is Hakim now? Can I speak with him?'

'He is too busy for you. He is too busy for me.'

'I can give the mosque more money.' Hash reached inside his jacket. 'How much?'

'He told me he saw your son with other people, and your son was happy, playing games. He said your son has new friends.' Hash thought of the video, the two Arabs behind the windscreen and the executive car.

'What sort of friends? Boys his own age...Girls?'

'He did not say.'

'Then let me see photos of these friends and more photos of Jim being happy with them.' Siddiq shrugged his shoulders. 'Who knows what is true?' He snapped his fingers at one of his staff.

'Do you trust Hakim? Is he really helping me? Or is he holding Jim, trying to get money from me?' Siddiq rubbed at his tired eyes again as Hash continued. 'I don't think he's right about Jim and his new friends.'

Siddiq interrupted him. 'Mister Hakim says he found Jim, like you requested. He told you to keep away until he finished.' He silenced Hash who was about to interrupt. 'Because you do not understand the Asian community in this part and Hakim is the expert…nobody better than him.'

'That's why I…'

Siddiq silenced him as a waiter brought coffee and set it down. 'He told me he sent his drivers to look and they found your son with the people from the bad mosque.' He held up an admonishing finger to Hash. 'Bad people ruling this area. No police interest. British police do not protect.'

'Tell Hakim I was there to do good. I have a video of these so-called friends. Tell him,' Hash tapped his chest, 'tell him I insist on apologising in person, face to face, father to father. I will tell him I know Jim is with very bad people who are not his friends. Promise to do this for me.' He watched Siddiq digest the message and return a weak smile. After more thought then an almost imperceptible dip of his head, Siddiq signalled he would pass on the message.

'I don't know,' Siddiq answered, 'I will ask. Maybe the answer is yes, maybe no. I will ask.' Siddiq sat back, exhausted.

'There's something wrong with you. Are you okay?'

'No, not okay.' Siddiq toyed with his phone, pushing it around the table surface.

'How's Anna? Is she not keeping you busy enough?'

'She's gone.' Siddiq's face crumpled as though he was about to cry. Hash struggled to suppress a smile. 'Gone? Gone for a rest, to recover?'

'Gone away, to somewhere else.'

'When?'

'Last night.' Siddiq pushed at the phone, looking at it as

though expecting Anna to call. 'Yesterday she came back from all day shopping. She was very angry, called me names...my God, so angry, such terrible names, I did not know this Anna before.'

'Is she coming back?'

'So angry,' Siddiq continued, rubbing his eyes. 'She wanted to marry me. When I told her impossible' – he flicked both hands open – 'bang, explosion, terrible. Shouting, throwing things, hitting me.'

'Any damage?'

'Thank God no, I am alright.'

'To my property, I meant. Doors, windows, the bed, what else did she break?'

Siddiq smiled lamely at the teasing. 'I loved her, so much. I thought she loved me.'

'I think you loved her body.'

'She liked you,' Siddiq said. 'She said you were an English gentleman, not an Arab, but like Johnny English.'

Hash shot Siddiq a sardonic look. 'How quickly you recover, my good friend.' Siddiq smiled weakly. 'Maybe she will come back. There'll be another out there, so many sexy women just waiting for a rich, handsome, young Bangladeshi tycoon.'

Settling in for the drive to Birmingham Airport, Sean clipped himself in. 'I can't believe they let the bastard walk,' he said.

'Believe me,' Hash said, 'the guy could barely stand. You're famous. Wonder if we should put it on YouTube.' He chuckled. 'And you're front page in the *Echo*. Punch-up in chippy...thug gets battered.'

'Nice one.'

'A really grainy photo, luckily,' Hash added.

'I saw the camera up on the wall,' Sean said. 'That's why I dragged him out. Funny thing with me and surveillance cameras.' He tapped out a cigarette. 'Mind if I burn one?' Hash did not object. 'Years on the streets, setting stuff up,' Sean continued, 'then years in the Kesh...fucking cameras everywhere in that place.' He lit up. 'I'm probably on at least three street cameras outside but the light was bad and then the distance factor, and I had my cap back on.'

'The chippy man says you've got free fish and chips for life,' Hash said. 'He told the police they're looking for a Polish builder who comes from Gloucester. Good job there was no soundtrack.'

'Every cloud...' Sean murmured. Maybe it's better I'm off the streets for a bit?'

'We were so close yesterday. Good to keep our powder dry,' Hash agreed. 'We'll crack it next time. Can't tell you how much shit I'm having to eat with that guy Hakim, calling me a liar and an idiot.'

'Do you think he's involved, knows the whole thing, playing both sides?'

'You videoed two Arabs, maybe three,' Hash said. 'Arabs are Arabs and Asians...'

'Are Asians.' Sean finished the sentence. 'So what?'

'They don't like each other too much. If we saw Arabs with Jim then they will be run by other Arabs. Maybe they're on the Asian turf under sufferance, some sort of arrangement.'

'And you think Hakim is the Asian arrangement?'

Hash looked over at his companion. 'He's an obvious place to start. He seems to be a big noise and he'll have his area and his reputation, and his competition. But then, maybe he's a genuine good guy and trying to tell me to keep out of his way.'

'That's what you want to believe?'

'He seems to be more concerned with doing the job I asked him to do.' He thumped the wheel as a thought struck him. 'Before I forget. Siddiq's been dumped by his blonde nymphomaniac.'

'Jesus.' Sean was smiling. 'When?'

'Friday...Yesterday. When he told her he wasn't going to marry her.'

'Take it you congratulated him on his luck.'

'He was heartbroken,' Hash said. 'As though the world had crashed down on him.' He looked across and was surprised to Sean's eyes closed, pain on his face.

'You OK? Want me to stop.' Sean waved the offer away. 'Just a twinge,' he said. 'Get them from time to time.'

'Where?'

'In the chest.' He thumped himself gently. 'Have to bump-start the lungs these days, you know.'

'Maybe you overdid it in the chippy,' Hash said.

'I've had a few tests,' Sean said.

'What tests?'

'I had a whole battery of checks before I came over,' Sean said, 'things stuck up me, down me. Stuff sucked out, pumped in and swallowed a ton of shit for them to X-ray.'

He held up his packet of cigarettes, 'Started smoking Gallaher's Plain when I could steal them from the old boy. Been puffing ever since. You don't need the brains of an archbishop to work it out.'

'Is it bad?'

'That's what they'll be telling me when I go to see them, if I can be bothered.'

'What do you mean?'

'Maybe I don't want to know.' Sean took another drink. 'Just carry on in my own sweet way, and take my punishment when it's due.' He looked evenly at Hash. 'Prioritise…that's what you like to say.'

'Your health comes first.'

'Jim comes first,' Sean said. 'I had my chances long ago and I screwed it all up.'

'Yes, but if you need treatment you've got to get it,' Hash said.

'Let's change the subject. What news from our friends in Libya?'

'Silent as the bloody grave. I can practically hear their minds ticking. Like I said, I told them their candidate disappeared. I'm standing by for the next order.'

'What do you think they'll do?'

'Fuck knows. They'll have a big, long think, no immediate panic reaction. That gives us time.' He looked at Sean. 'Get yourself sorted out and come back.'

'What happens if Hakim sees Jim again?'

'Maybe we get him to take us in.'

'What if they're armed, these Arabs?' Sean asked.

'They will be…and I've got a plan.'

SUNDAY. 15TH MARCH.

Hakim watched the video in silence. Hash let the scene play one time, then on the second froze the screen, tapping on Jim's face. 'Sayyid Hakim,' Hash was careful to be respectful, 'that is my son,' he said. 'I cannot thank you enough for getting me this close to rescuing him. Surely you cannot be angry that I tried.' Hakim made no response, his eyes on Jim's face.

'I took your photo and made the connection to this part of Birmingham. It was easy. Maybe if your drivers let me go with them next time,' Hash pleaded, 'maybe I stay closer than Cheltenham and they collect me as soon as they see Jim.'

Hakim shook his head, still saying nothing. Irritated by the stubborn silence, Hash continued. 'What is the harm? If your men had got through to me as soon as the photo was confirmed, then maybe we could have succeeded.'

'Succeeded?' Hakim spoke at last, his beard quivering with suppressed anger. 'You are a fool and you do not understand what success is. Success for you is when you take your son home after he ran away. This is not success for me.'

'I don't understand,' Hash began but Hakim's fist came down on the table.

'This is clear…you do not understand,' he spat. 'You Arab people, all the same. Lazy, stupid, throwing big money around, giving orders.' His finger trembled as it pointed at Hash. 'You want us to clean up your mess. You bring it to our area, to poison our happy community. We have schools, mosques, business, clinics and then,' he stabbed in Hash's direction, 'we get the Arabs, like a cancer to our system. These people say it is jihad, say it in the mosques, but these people are not Muslims and do not know true jihad.' He looked at Siddiq for agreement.

'Then, when trouble starts, where are the Arabs?' Hakim said. 'They run away,' he answered his own question. 'They run away and they leave their shit behind. Tell me, Sayyid Hashmi,' Hakim mocked, 'where you come from, in Saudi or the Emirates, did you have Pakistani slaves to clean up your shit?'

'I come from Jordan, from Amman,' Hash answered. Siddiq watched the exchange. 'My family is not wealthy. I never went to Saudi or the Emirates. You can ask him how I made my money, how I do business.' He gestured to his friend. 'He speaks for me, knows I work hard and knows I am not a bad man.' Hash held his hands up to Hakim. 'I hate these clowns in Daesh, Al Qaeda. I would kill them myself if I could.'

'You think you can ask my help, with your money' – Hakim snapped his fingers – 'just like that. Bring your problem, make it my problem. When you're gone and it is still my problem, then what will you do for me?'

'Tell me what you want me to do, Sayyid Hakim, tell me and I'll do my best.'

'I gave you my orders to stay away and let me do the job, but you pushed in when I had only a little information. Your action could have killed your son. We saw you easily when you came here yesterday.' He pointed the same finger at Hash. 'My drivers, they have a photo of you as well as your son. You want to know why?' Hash waited. 'Because I told them you will do something stupid, frighten the Arabs and make them do something stupid.'

'I was doing what any father would do,' he protested.

'By getting in the way, you are making more problems for my men.' Hakim's voice was losing its bite. 'My men have the face of your son, they found them, they found the mosque and now they want to get the location where he is staying.' Hakim eased back on his chair. 'This takes time and patience and they are busy men, self-employed.' He tapped the table. 'Losing taxi customers by doing this task...'

'I will pay extra,' Hash cut in.

'I will come to you when I have the full picture. Then I will hand it over to you so you can pretend you did it all.'

'I don't follow,' Hash said.

'You can tell the police how you,' he stabbed again, 'and only you, found your son. I do not need police, immigration or other Arabs looking for me.'

'That is why I went there yesterday,' Hash interrupted again, 'to do the job and get my son away, not to cause you trouble.'

'You are an Arab, with money, who wants everything quickly...you are trouble. You can kill your son if you wish, but don't involve me anymore.' Hakim resumed his sphinx-like persona. 'Show me the video again.'

Hash played the clip once more and Hakim made him repeat it. 'Not enough information,' he concluded.

'What is missing?'

'In the video,' Hakim spoke with some patience, 'how many men with your camera?'

'Three men, Arabs, and my son. It is a BMW and they are going to the Racing Festival. They have eaten from Chicken Hut and my son has a toy helicopter on his lap.'

'Where is the third man?'

'He is in the back seat, beside my son.'

'No, he is not. He is driving the red car behind the BMW.' In the silence that followed Hash felt colour rising in his face. He ran the video again and watched the BMW sweep past followed by two cars. He and Sean had only noticed them because they obscured the BMW plates. The one immediately behind the BMW was red and had a rounded shape. 'This is a red Citroën and they use it to bring Jim to the park.' Hash was still trying to grasp the implications when Hakim added, 'So, Mister Hashmi, my next question. Who is beside your son if the third Arab is driving this little car?' He folded both his hands on the table and waited. Hash groped for an answer but came up with a helpless shrug.

'There is a lady sitting beside your son, making sure he does not try to jump out.'

'A woman?'

'Yes, a woman.' Hakim had dropped the ironic courtesy. 'Your son is being looked after by three men and occasionally a woman. There is a mosque where they sometimes go with your son, but not with the woman. But so far, the house they keep the boy in is the missing part of the jigsaw.'

'I had no idea...' Hash shrugged.

'A strange woman,' Hakim continued, 'but she's the one who's in charge. The others, including your son, are all afraid of her. Mister Hashmi, have you ever seen Arabs afraid of a woman?' A flicker of a smile played on Hakim's face for a moment. 'I think you can agree with me, now, that if you had not been so lucky on this occasion then things could have gone worse for your son?'

Hash was lost for words so Hakim continued. 'We agreed to do this for you, as one Muslim to another, one father to another, to use your words. Then I asked to be left alone. You broke your word. So now, what am I to do?'

'Please do not stop,' Hash replied. 'This cannot succeed without you and your men.' It was a consolation for Hash that Sean's presence had not been mentioned: he was still off the radar. 'But the woman, who is she? Have you got a photograph of her?'

Hakim's finger was instantly in the air, admonishing. 'Any interference and we cancel what we are doing for you.'

'But a description at least,' Hash pleaded, 'for me to work on.'

'All times she came in a burqa with full niqab and from that not even we can get a clue. But one exception was this day. And she came dressed in Western clothing.'

CHAPTER 18

Frequent power cuts had made regular electricity and air conditioning a dream for most of Tripoli's inhabitants. With the remorseless temperature rises of late-March and the humidity keeping pace, only the offshore breezes kept total misery at bay. Plasma Hotel on the Omar al Mukhtar road was an oasis, struggling to maintain pre-Revolution standards of luxury. Its generators fuelled by corporate patrons, it owed its survival to the need for a central, neutral location where players from all factions could meet with discretion and without the risk of being murdered.

Two men, one an elderly, white-haired, elegant man of some seventy-five years, together with his younger aide, had arrived early to prepare for such a meeting. The pair, each wearing smart suits, inspected the rooms they had hired, enjoying the cool air before the aide took off his jacket and got to work, searching with practised ease, checking for hidden eavesdropping devices. As members of Libyan Intelligence, the Mukhabarat, it was a task both men had performed many times earlier in their careers. The elder had remarked, when they planned the meeting, 'There's fashionably late, Arab late and finally, there's Daesh insultingly late.' When the search was over, they sat on the overstuffed sofa, and called room service for refreshments.

'Have we got this under control?' the older man asked as they settled in to wait.

'We've given him a 'laissez-passer' and an armed escort,' the aide responded, 'to bring him in and get him out of the city, afterwards and back to Daesh lines.'

'I meant the agenda,' the older man said. His aide extracted a notebook, opened it and squinted at his jottings. He looked from the pages to his boss. 'Last communiqué was two days ago. Plus, a full report brought out by the letter box team,' he listed. 'We have his side of the story. The martyr lost his nerve, ran away with the money, left the bombs behind. Given the sort of people we're dealing with' – he tapped the side of his head – 'cuckoo, brainless…could be true enough.'

'The man had a change of heart, wanted to live…couldn't have been that stupid. Do we believe our man?'

His aide shrugged imperceptibly. 'Our man sensed a problem when the Daesh player started showing signs of stress, maybe questioning his motivation after seeing life in England. The guy started demanding things he shouldn't have: drink, women.'

The elder dismissed the rationale. 'Damage control… details?'

THE GOOD MUSLIM

'Our man has put out feelers on his own networks. If we're lucky, the runaway will surface on the underground asylum radar. He's using Asian contacts to intercept him. Otherwise our contact says the police will get to him soon.'

'Why did they send someone like that?' the old man asked, looking at his watch.

'Meanwhile our man's good to go again.' The aide continued. 'Asking us what to do, now the school holiday's coming to an end.'

'Aah, the boy,' the older gentleman said, 'Lord Jim. Was that from Kipling...or Conrad?' he thought aloud in English.

'It's what his grandparents call him,' the aide said.

'How is that young man?'

'The team keep him healthy and busy but of course he asks for his father.'

'How do they keep a fifteen-year-old occupied?'

'He has a hobby, toy aircraft. Apparently, he prefers them instead of friends.'

The older man considered this. 'Good. Is he a clever boy?'

'It seems so.'

'The whole damned operation should have been over by now, of course,' the older man said. 'He could have been back with his father.' The doorbell went and his aide got up to open the door and took the small tray from the waiter. When he carried it back to his boss, the old man said, 'Why the hell did they change the target at the last minute...? Complete madness.'

'Amateurs. Our team said it came as no surprise to the Daesh woman, on the day,' the aide said, twisting the cap on a plastic bottle and pouring two glasses of cold water. 'She must have had a prearranged schedule with her bomber. They both knew what was going on. Our asset in Cheltenham reports the man showed no interest in GCHQ from the start.'

'I can understand them, up to a point,' the old man said quietly.

'Yes, and it's how operations fall apart,' the aide said. 'It can only work with a professional team, not when you start throwing amateurs into the mix.'

'As we see,' the old man agreed. 'But now we find ourselves in limbo.' The old man took the glass and then shook his head as if trying to order unruly thought-processes. 'We're stuck. We can't go back or go forward, until our ISIS clients…' He pointed at the door as if expecting their guest to enter. 'Our Daesh friends decide what they want us to do next.'

'We're good to go at the UK end…no compromise yet.'

'Why have they put a woman on the ground?' the old man asked. 'Given their attitude to women, it's unusual, isn't it?'

The aide shrugged again. 'Ask him when he gets here. It could be they want some appearance of a family. Our team say she's a really tough bitch, a psycho, not much of a mother figure.'

'Where are they now?'

'Safe house in the Midlands…under our control…our side of the house.'

'Just keep the boy safe and keep the father's hopes alive. So many problems in our country.' He waved a thin hand out across the rooftops of Tripoli. 'It all comes to one thing…family.'

After half an hour and barely into a game of Italian football. The reception clerk rang to say their guest was on his way up. The aide immediately ordered fruit and tea then went to the door and held it open to watch. When the lift opened to release its only passenger, a short, slim man emerged. He was dressed in jeans and scuffed brown leather shoes. Over a plain white shirt he wore a waistcoat, one of the multi-pocketed variety favoured by aid workers and journalists. The man, in his mid-thirties, a few years younger than the aide, had a shaved head and the long, unkempt beard of a zealot. Above his brow, a central smudge of darkened skin showed bruising from too frequently resting his forehead on the ground whilst praying. He was conducting an animated phone conversation as he advanced towards the aide and pointedly ignored his greetings. Instead, and without eye contact, he offered a limp hand to both men. He sat where directed, still talking and took out a set of amber prayer beads, flicking them through his fingers. When he finally put the phone down, the older man began the polite, soothing ritual that precedes every Arab meeting: enquiries about health, family and news. He addressed the visitor as 'Sayyid Director'.

The ISIS man, still looking at his phone, irritably cut him off. 'Just tell me what happened.'

The abruptness of tone made the old man flinch, already tense despite his outward sangfroid, he stiffened with anger. His aide fidgeted, uncomfortable at the immediate increase in tension. The visitor compounded the breach of etiquette with: 'We supplied our agents, you promised to deliver them to the target but nothing happened and my side' – he held up his phone – 'needs an explanation.' He sat back, playing with the beads, watching the two men opposite. 'A lot of promises, and now nothing.' He cupped his free hand to his ear. 'An explanation…please?'

'You will get it, of course,' the older man said, 'but you're not going to like it.' He maintained his mask of politeness. 'The first thing you can say is that we…' He tapped his striped tie, then pointed to his aide. 'We were working on one target for you, but you switched, at the last moment, without telling us.' The guest said nothing, waiting. The older man continued. 'We were under the impression we were working with professionals.' He held the guest's gaze, the sarcasm evident in his words, 'But that was of course naïve of us. Your side,' he jabbed a finger at the man's phone, 'doesn't know much about the complexity of the game, which is why you came to us in the first place.' The guest, no longer thumbing his beads, listened as the old man continued. 'We offered you a glimpse of our network and a demonstration, as goodwill in the deal. But how were we to know the first person you would send in would be an idiot… perhaps you don't have anyone better.' The aide hid a smile at his boss's sarcasm, noting the Daesh man's discomfort. 'A man who,' the older man continued, glancing at his aide for confirmation, 'who's now snatched the money and gone missing in the West of Britain. Of all the problems we envisaged.' The old man shook his head slowly. 'This one, we did not see coming.'

The guest raised a hand, stalling the speaker and took up his phone, concentrating on an incoming message. After a few seconds examining the display he put the phone on the table and looked up at the old man, waiting.

'All your man had to do was sit back, enjoy the ride then complete his final task,' the latter continued. 'Instead, he appears to get a taste for alcohol and discovers that sex with kufar women is much better than goats.' The older man pointed at the guest's phone again. 'Changing the target at the last moment and without telling your partners is an appalling breach of all the rules. Only amateurs do it. He leaned back in his seat. 'That's the explanation…under normal circumstances we would need an explanation and an apology.'

The guest was smiling, pleased at having riled his adversaries. 'Who told you all that?' He looked at his prayer beads as he spoke. 'The bullshit about our man running away.'

'Our man on the ground.'

'Maybe your man on the ground is a liar,' the guest countered, 'trying to cover his own lazy backside.'

'Our man has a pedigree of excellence. I've known him for years, directed his first operations in Ireland and I transferred him to the UK to build the file on the GCHQ target, the one we'd agreed to hand to you on a plate. But…' He held his hand out. 'I recognise your point, which is why, as you know, we keep his son as a guarantee.'

'The runaway will have his family punished, too,' the Daesh man offered. 'If it's true, they will forfeit their blood payment.'

'Hardly the same,' the aide said. 'The son is a guarantee of compliance, not a punishment, unless things go wrong.'

'They did go wrong.'

'Because you switched the target. No fault on our side,' the aide said.

'Enough, gentlemen, please,' the older interrupted. 'Can we get back to the proposal…two sides making a deal for the provision of services.' He pointed at the guest's phone. 'Forgive me, but I have to ask…am I speaking to the right person, here?'

'You're speaking to the Director of European Operations,' the guest answered coldly, 'and I am the right person.'

'Then you knew all along,' the aide insisted. 'We agreed on a high-profile target for the demonstration of our capability. Wasn't GCHQ good enough?'

'Maybe your choice of target was too easy,' the Daesh man said.

'It could only look easy to amateurs,' the aide said.

The guest shrugged off the counterpunch, looking from one man to the other. 'Our privilege,' he said simply. 'We changed the target at the last minute because you Mukhabarat players are singing from yesterday's song sheet. Our choice would have been more sensational, more dead kufar in the newspapers. Even if we had told you, what real difference would it have made to your man…? He's just the taxi driver.'

'Maybe so,' the aide conceded, 'but if you had only told us. Last-minute switches…' He shook his head. 'Without us knowing, with no authenticating procedures in place.' He paused. 'Our agents do not switch targets, just like that.' He snapped his fingers. 'That's not how it works.'

'That is how it works if we're doing business,' the Daesh man said.

'Are we still doing business together?' the older man asked.

'Have you got another client out there, somewhere?'

'Your side needs to understand, we're now running two operations for you and the meter's ticking. Your martyr is running around the West Midlands with too much money. He doesn't speak English so he's almost certainly dependent on third parties by now, food, shelter…the essentials, and that's before he splashes out on prostitutes.' The older man paused, holding his glass out for more water. 'We have to get our man on his track fast and shut him down before the others get to him.'

'The others?'

'The kufar, the enemy,' the aide said, his tone ironic. 'Unfortunately for all of us, they are not amateurs…the British police, immigration authorities, MI5, MI6, and then there's the asylum industry in that particular area.'

'How long will it take you to find him?'

'We need to give our man time, he's suggesting tapping into his Asian contacts. He'll need money to make that work.'

'Money that's been stolen from the mission,' the aide said.

'What'll you do if you find him?' the ISIS Director asked.

'When we find him,' the old man considered. 'And tell your bosses to be patient, he'll disappear. But he'll spend his last hours wishing he had stuck to the plan.' Distracted by his phone taking another incoming message, the Director picked it up and read the text, running the beads through his fingers at the same time.

The doorbell brought the aide to his feet to allow a waiter in with more refreshments. Plates of sliced fruit were placed on the coffee table; the waiter set small glass tumblers in front of each man and began to pour sweet, red tea from a silver jug. There was silence until he had finished and left. The guest looked at his watch, murmured a blessing on the food and picked slices off the plate. The older man took a sip of tea, enjoying its flavour, then sipped again.

The fruit and tea seemed to diminish the adversarial atmosphere. Speaking in more congenial tones, the older man resumed. 'That target had been prepared for years. Weapons were in place and it would have been a guaranteed success in terms of Daesh ability to strike deeply and surgically. It would have impressed the world. But...' He held his tea glass up. 'You're the client and if you want a different target, better you tell us and we work on it together.' He sipped and put down his empty glass. 'Tell your side that we see all the arrangements as still in place, we're still in business with you. We have the system, the agent, the support, all of it still in position, uncompromised. All of it belongs to you afterwards, of course. We hand it over intact. That's still the deal on the table.'

The guest digested the words, saying nothing, playing with his beads. The older man made his final pitch. 'Either we stick to GCHQ and go again, or we go for a target we all agree on.' He held up a finger. 'One you will really like. Either way, as a gesture of our continued goodwill, we will send one of our martyrs on this new mission, one we choose, who will do the job, play to the final whistle, so to speak.'

The Daesh man's eyes became more alert, switching from one suited man to the other. 'All of which sounds good and means you want more money.'

The old man replied evenly, 'You switched from a military target to a mass attack at a famous venue. Cheltenham

Racecourse. I see the thinking.' His hands balanced the options. 'Government infrastructure, their cyber hub versus mass civilian deaths and a very soft target, members of the establishment present, the British royalty?' The Daesh man thumbed his beads. 'How much?'

'We want double,' the old man said. 'One target, done properly, taking out a member of the royal family as well as hundreds of kufar, is worth double. If your team,' his tone softened, 'had done their homework on Cheltenham they would have known their chances of a senior royal being at Cheltenham were minimal and their chance of getting a martyr right alongside were zero. They could have pulled off an attack of sorts, but that would have been our last chance. If only you had consulted us.' He leaned forward in his chair. 'We know the systems in England. Double the money gets you a member of the royal family.'

'Who? The Queen?'

'Insh'Allah. We don't know, yet. We don't see the invitation lists. If you agree, then we will choose the time and the place. Your side fits in with the plan. We'll only get one clear shot.'

'Gaddafi's men,' the guest said softly to himself.

'We were all Gaddafi's men,' the aide said, 'even most of you Daesh men.'

'And now you're all businessmen.' The guest twisted his prayer beads.

'I'm not ashamed,' the old man said. 'We set up these networks to combat Libya's enemies. It took years, cost tens of millions, we lost good people and still' – he tapped the table –

'we've got good people in place. The Americans, the Russians and the British haven't brought us down. Gaddafi's gone...' his voice slowed, 'and they're your enemies now, aren't they? We're still in the game and we can run the biggest attack the world has ever seen, just for you, my friend. Don't tell me you're not interested.'

'I budgeted five million dollars as it is,' the guest said.

'Ten is small change to your bankers in the Caliphate. Look at what you're getting. You want us to pull this off for you, you want it to shock the world and make history?' The Daesh man said nothing.

'Your silence tells me you're interested,' the older man coaxed.

'We need to insure it.'

'That sounds like a condition,' the aide said.

'Conditions,' the guest said. 'You want my support and this,' he pointed at his phone, 'is a European operation. Here's how it'll work. You'll insert your martyr, but my team leader takes over, and because I'm not happy with the lies from Cheltenham, the boy comes under my direct control.'

'It will slow things down,' the aide objected.

'It's the only deal on the table,' the Daesh man said.

'And the target?' the older man asked. 'Can we at least agree on that?'

'As you propose, we target British royalty at a public event to ensure mass casualties.' The two Mukhabarat men waited.

'And I will want to check your martyr,' the guest said, standing up, signalling the meeting was over. 'My team leader will need to induct him. Send him across to us in Sirte: I'll have my personal escort ensure he gets through. We'll put him through our system.'

'Your system?' the aide asked.

'Briefing on the target environment, but not the actual target. We'll run him through our acclimatisation phase.'

'Acclimatisation,' the aide sputtered.

'And the last donkey actually passed all that?' The older man said.

'When I've transferred the funds, you'll probably see it my way,' the Daesh man offered.

'And we'll need to see whoever you're sending in as commander,' the aide fought back. 'Check his cover, get him to fit in, make sure he's not a classmate of our missing friend.'

'You'll find she has all the papers and cover she needs,' the Director said.

SATURDAY 4TH APRIL
TRIPOLI OUTSKIRTS.

The instructors called a group of exhausted men to form a three-sided square with the open side against the camp headquarters hut. In Arabic, they bellowed at the men to start jogging on the spot. The men chanted as they jogged, hands thrust forward, arms outstretched, knees pumping to the barked cadence of the chief instructor, himself soaked in perspiration. Poised directly above like an executioner's sword, the sun burned exposed, perspiring and bruised flesh. Tortured lungs could only breathe in dust and hot air and, knowing the hour of midday prayer was near, the longing, shared by all the men, was to hear the static crackling from the mosque loudspeakers. Midday prayers meant shade, water and relief. Abruptly, suspiciously early, the chief instructor brought the drill to an end.

He walked down the first rank, selecting one man by tapping him on the shoulder and jerking a thumb behind him towards the square of bleached sand. Then he moved along the next rank, staring but without selecting anyone. He turned up the third rank and made another selection, so that as he reached the end of the line he had two men standing in the centre of the sandy square, facing each other. Another barked order saw the two men taking up a stance, ready for unarmed combat. The chief instructor now faced towards the headquarters Portakabin where a tired air-conditioner hummed and clattered, pumping frigid air at the two Mukhabarat men. They watched through windows speckled with dust and fly spots, as the spectacle unfolded. The white-haired man, supported by a walking stick, stood, his elegance undisturbed by the heat and dust. He was smoking and observing the scene with thoughtful interest. His aide, wearing his suit with less comfort, looked at the two men and compared them with notes in a folder. The chief instructor nodded at the window, assuming authority to proceed.

Turning to his charges, the chief called the name, 'Bousaif!' Neither of the two moved but a third man, in the second rank, stiffened to attention. The use of a name was unusual to these men as it hinted at respect, a commodity sparingly bestowed in the Special Forces camp. At best, all were collectively known as 'brothers' and addressed each other as 'my brother'. The only difference was the chief instructor who was simply 'chief'. The man answering to Bousaif, medium-height, stocky with broad shoulders and a shaven head, now stepped forward. The chief ordered the men to fight, two to one, against Bousaif. The ranks burst into roars of support as the teamed pair, exchanging glances, stalked warily towards Bousaif, their boots scuffing up sand as they moved.

Bousaif waited, crouched in a posture both defensive and confident. He rolled his shoulders to get comfortably loose; his hands, held like a boxer's, opened and closed, ready to grapple. His legs were bent and braced apart. His crouch made him appear much shorter than either of his adversaries who now separated, circling to take him from two sides. Bousaif waited for a few seconds before retreating quickly towards the nearest rank of cheering men, using them as a wall to keep his assailants from getting directly behind.

As one of the pair came close, Bousaif immediately went for him, barrelling him and turning him into the line, tumbling him in the confusion and landing, knees first on him, flinging sand and grit in his face and jabbing punches at his eyes and throat as the man sought to protect himself. Bousaif jerked upright onto his feet then drove two kicks into the man's ribs. If the two Mukhabarat men heard the howl of pain they showed no sympathy. Spinning away from the prostrate figure, sensing the man's companion had to be inches away, he lashed out with a sweeping punch, just missing his man. The ranks roared and cheered the instinct as Bousaif skipped into the centre of the square and waited. The first man stayed down, shaking his face clear of sand, hands holding damaged ribs.

His teammate took his eyes off long enough to glance across and realise there was no help. Bousaif crabbed towards the man, reaching out to snag him in a powerful hold. His opponent now found himself retreating into a wall of yelling onlookers who thrust him back towards his opponent. There was a blur of movement as the two men closed and an audible snap as Bousaif's forehead made contact with the man's face. With gasps from the onlookers the man folded. Bousaif stood over him, poised to deliver the killer kicks, frozen by a command.

In some semblance of an honour the chief walked over and took Bousaif's right hand, raising it to the onlookers in the Portakabin, to the cheers of the onlookers. At that moment, the loudspeaker on the roof began to crackle with the call to prayer. Returning Bousaif to his place in the nameless ranks, the chief barked the orders, releasing the men to their devotions.

Entering the Portakabin he greeted the two men and stood to attention. 'Bousaif,' he announced, 'awaits your orders.'

'Tell him he grows his hair and shaves his beard, from now on,' the aide said.

'English?' the older man asked.

'His papers say he has good English and French.' The aide looked at the folder. 'We'll get that tested, sir.' His boss nodded, still pensive, smoke rising from his cigarette.

'Where has he served?'

Glancing at the folder to check, the aide started. 'Cut his teeth in Algeria, moved on to counter-intelligence in Europe...'

'Where exactly?'

'Rome first, then Vienna. He ran with a surveillance team in Southern Europe, keeping an eye on our problems.'

'Aah,' the older man murmured, irony in his tone, 'enemies of our beloved homeland.' He jabbed his walking stick at the distance outside the window. 'Most recent operation?'

'Iraq, with a team in Basra, operating against the Shia.'

Satisfied, the older man switched tack. 'That will please our Daesh friends. What was his degree?'

'Political Science at Tripoli.'

The older man thought for a few seconds before pointing to the now empty parade ground. 'How religious?'

'He's a good Muslim.'

The old man considered for a while, then said, 'Let him clean up, have him ready. We'll send someone for him.'

MONDAY 6TH APRIL. EVENING.

After the Maghreb prayers, the summons came and Bousaif appeared before the chief.

'Salaams, Bousaif. How are you? Well, insh'Allah.'

Bousaif responded with a cautious, 'Well, thanks be to God. How can I help you?' The chief pulled a packet of cigarettes from his pocket and offered one to Bousaif who refused with a smile. 'Go and get ready. You leave in five minutes.' 'Do not tell any of your companions.' Within three minutes and before the chief had finished his cigarette, Bousaif had returned, carrying a sports bag. The instructor took it and, still smoking, trailed his free hand through the modest contents, then burrowed into the bag. His expression changed from boredom to interest as he extracted a small, plastic photograph album. He held it up and then steadied it on the table, to flick through each of the pages, looking at each image, smiling when he recognised the man standing in front of him. He puzzled briefly at one image, an old black and white of a family group. 'My family,' Bousaif explained. The chief grunted, dropped the album into the sports bag and handed it back to Bousaif. Then he ordered him to follow, pushing the door with his foot and flicking the glowing butt into the dark.

He set off across the sandy square with Bousaif in tow. They walked in silence out towards the brightly lit chain link fence that led to the double gate which serviced all entry and exit. An armed guard, on command from the chief, keyed the padlock, swung one of the heavy gates back and watched the chief lead Bousaif out. A Mercedes saloon waiting in the darkness came to life as the driver switched on the engine and, with only sidelights on, it purred across the compacted sand towards them, halting in front of the two men. The driver emerged, greeting the chief quietly, with a smile and an embrace, before looking to Bousaif and advancing to give the same greeting. He introduced himself as 'Manager' as he took Bousaif's bag and pointed him to the passenger's seat. The chief tapped Bousaif on the shoulder as he was about to duck into the car. Turning, he was surprised to find himself embraced by the chief. 'May God go with you, my brother.'

Settling into his seat, enjoying the new world of luxury, the smell of leather and hiss of air conditioning, hearing locks click as the driver engaged the gear and the vehicle began to roll, Bousaif squirmed in his seat for a last look at his compound. He saw the chief walking back, silhouetted by the harsh fence lights, the sports bag slung on his shoulder.

Within minutes of the Mercedes pulling clear of the camp and setting course for the lights of Tripoli. Bousaif saw they had picked up an escort. He turned in his seat and caught the silhouette of two crewed pickup trucks with machine guns mounted, following behind, driving without lights. The Manager beside him chuckled quietly, reassuring his passenger that all was well.

Hours later, with dawn breaking, Bousaif woke because the swaying and jerking of the vehicle had stopped and a conversation was taking place outside. Taking in his surroundings, he realised he was at the perimeter checkpoint of a military base. Ghardabiya Airbase proclaimed itself from a bullet-pocked wall. Ghardabiya meant Sirte and Daesh territory to Bousaif.

Bousaif saw the familiar airport infrastructure: a terminal building, control tower and hangars, but all damaged by war. Walls splashed by rockets and stitched by machine gun fire, plate glass missing from windows and vehicle wreckage of all sorts, both military and civilian, scattered around. The Mercedes crunched across the debris and nosed between cargo sheds then out along clear tarmac, passing hulks on the tarmac, jets and helicopters, casualties of the fighting. One aircraft, a twin-engined affair in civilian livery, its propellers turning, was in the process of taxiing from the runway to a berth amongst its derelict companions.

The Manager finally drew up at the crash-rescue station, a single-storey blockhouse with three fire tenders lined up on parade where a handful of crew members manned the engines. A figure appeared in the doorway of the fire station, greeted the Manager with a wordless thumbs-up, and pointed round the side. The Mercedes followed this guidance to the rear of the fire station, halting in front of a cluster of Portakabins. Leaving the car, both men walked stiffness out of their legs. The Manager led his charge into the small complex and began a tour, pointing out dining room, classroom and briefing room before opening a door and bidding him enter his own room. He pointed at fresh clothes on the comfortable bed and sandals underneath, telling Bousaif to change and drop his old clothes in the basket, 'For burning.' Gesturing to the shower, he invited him to join the team in the garden for breakfast, after he had washed and prayed. When the Manager had gone, Bousaif sat on the bed, amazed at its softness and fresh smell. The room was like a hotel. He lifted the clothes off the bed and saw he now had tracksuit bottoms and a Chelsea football shirt.

After a long shower, Bousaif emerged from his room, self-conscious in the Chelsea strip. He had been so used to being marched in a squad that the feeling of having to find one's way was strange. Noise of conversation led him to the rear of the complex where a small oasis had been coaxed from the sandy soil. Bougainvillea walled the square with mixtures of pink and white blossom. Four well-trimmed date palms marked the corners, and tied off them at about fifteen feet hung a canopy of camouflage netting. Strung diagonally across the square under the netting was a garland of light bulbs on a cable. Strangely, these were still lit as though left on overnight after a party. An electric mosquito killer with three purple-lit bars hung off one corner of the net, snapping and crackling as occasional insects committed suicide. At one corner, there was a brick barbecue stand accompanied by a bar, complete with beer pumps and bar stools. At a wooden trestle table sat four strangers who stopped in mid-conversation to look at Bousaif.

The Manager, standing behind the bar preparing a tray of food looked up with a broad smile and pointed to the trestle tables as three men and a woman stood in greeting. The woman was dressed in the traditional black burqa, her hands covered by long, black gloves, and a niqab over her face which left only her eyes visible. Two of the men wore the football strip and tracksuit uniform, and the third was dressed in European clothes.

After long weeks of grinding rigour in the Special Forces camp, Bousaif was unused to civilised company, the presence of a woman and being treated with politeness. He heard his name announced by the Manager, who indicated the group, saying, 'We all speak English from now on. This is the Director.' The man in European clothes nodded. He was slim, with a thin, straggly beard in contrast to his expensive open-necked shirt. The limp hand he offered was decorated with a Rolex and smelled of cologne as he held it out to Bousaif. He sat down immediately after the handshake and fished out his phone and prayer beads. 'Director of European Operations, he's our boss,' the Manager added. The man barely glanced up, already checking his messages.

'These two gentlemen, ManCity and Gunner,' the Manager pronounced the nicknames slowly in English. 'Both of them will instruct you in the ways of the British while you are here.' The two men wearing the football shirts presented themselves, hands outstretched. ManCity was slightly built, with Asian looks, and the Gunner had a mix of Caucasian and African in him. They both watched Bousaif with wary eyes. Bousaif guessed they were in their mid-twenties, much younger than him. The Gunner said, 'Alright, mate,' as he shook hands.

'Umm Ali,' the Manager indicated the woman, 'is your team commander for the mission. She's just back from England, especially to meet you.' The woman had sat straight away and remained seated, not bothering to offer a handshake but dipping her head in acknowledgement. Bousaif found himself under scrutiny from all of them. The woman's pale blue eyes, framed by the black material, stayed on Bousaif for some time before appearing to lose interest and flicking across to the Manager. As though commanded, the Manager went back behind the bar and brought a tray of bread, honey and boiled eggs. He laid these on the table and went into the kitchen for the tea and coffee flasks. The Gunner offered a cigarette, Bousaif declined.

'At least he doesn't smoke, like you two,' the Director said, looking up from his phone. His voice was thin and the tone petulant. He waved manicured hands fanning smoke away.

Bousaif sat as directed and waited.

'Where did you learn your English?' the Director asked.

'The basics from school, some at university,' Bousaif said. The Director seemed unimpressed. Umm Ali said nothing. The Gunner chipped in nervously, 'Not a problem, mate. A little's good enough to work with.' He glanced at ManCity for support. 'As long as you've got grammar, innit…Happy days. We'll work the vocabulary in the next four weeks.' Bousaif made the obvious deduction about the length of his stay in this slice of Paradise. As though keen not to be left out, ManCity added, 'We're here to prepare you to move around in England and we'll build on whatever English you've got.' He pointed at the Gunner. 'We've both lived in England. In fact.' He seemed encouraged by the thought. 'In case you didn't get it already, we're British.'

'We were British,' the Gunner corrected. 'We volunteered for the jihad, did our bit on the front line, but we've got important skills, see? So we now help with the acclimatisation programme.'

'What they mean is,' the Director interrupted, 'they will school you on everyday British talk, habits, politics, likes and dislikes.' He wrapped the beads around his index finger. 'They will talk about everyday things you will not know about. And you will specifically concentrate on horse racing. The emphasis is on blending into a given scenario.'

'Not standing out or drawing attention because you're a stranger,' ManCity repeated, sternly. 'Could give yourself…the whole mission away.'

'When you're new in Britain it's easy to make mistakes and get noticed, innit,' Gunner nervously butted in, not wanting to miss the chance to impress the Director. 'The kufar can get right nosy if you don't watch your step, especially the women.'

'Before we deploy you,' the Director nodded to the woman, 'she will approve or disapprove you and you'll be moved into Britain for the mission.'

'When do I learn my mission?' Bousaif asked.

'When I'm ready to tell you about it.' Umm Ali spoke for the first time. Her voice was flat, her accent from somewhere in Europe.

Studying Bousaif with an intensity that made him uncomfortable, she spoke again. 'The last Shaheed scheduled for this mission disappeared just after we moved him into the English safe house.'

'We think he got demotivated.' The Gunner sounded defensive. 'With us, here in the camp,' he gestured around the enclosure, 'he was strong, committed, you know what I mean. But he must have weakened when he saw the temptations of kufar life in England.'

'That's what we mean about vulnerability,' ManCity said. 'He lost the plot.'

'See what I mean about kufar women?' Gunner tried some levity.

'He was badly handled on the ground,' the Director observed, looking up from his phone. 'He was struggling to acclimatise and he could not communicate.'

'He was a thick as shit idiot and whoever passed him fit for his mission was an ass,' Umm Ali said. ManCity and the Gunner squirmed in their seats. Umm Ali continued. 'And you,' she stabbed a gloved finger at the Director who was pointedly looking back down at his phone, 'gave him more money than his entire village had ever seen in their lives.' Her accent was hard for Bousaif to place, maybe Bosnian, definitely a Muslim but not an Arab. She jerked a thumb over her shoulder. 'So, he did what any self-respecting Afghan would do…obeyed his natural instincts, grabbed the money and disappeared.'

'His village won't be seeing the martyr's bounty,' the Gunner said.

'Sayyid Bousaif,' the Director silenced them, 'The mission will go again, with you as Shaheed and against a significant British target. We will succeed.'

'Insh'Allah,' Bousaif said, 'if God wills.'

'You know what Shaheed means?' the Director asked.

'Of course,' Bousaif said.

'It means you don't need a return ticket when you leave here, mate,' ManCity said.

'Lucky bastard.' The Gunner tried more levity.

'Which brings us back to our Afghan friend,' Umm Ali said. 'He's on the run somewhere in England, he knows the target. Who's running that problem?'

'He knew the mission,' the Director corrected, 'it's changed now.'

'He's still a problem for me,' Umm Ali said.

'They're looking for him,' the Director sighed, 'we've been through this. It can't hold us up.'

'Who exactly is looking?'

'The Mukhabarat. Their guys, the one who's been in England

for years. His controllers say he's got all his contacts on high alert, out looking. A good chance of catching him on the underground asylum network.'

'And we believe that?' Umm Ali snorted.

'We've got his son as a guarantee,' the Director said.

'I'm taking him over, then,' she said, 'just to be sure of things.'

The Manager returned with a tray. The food generated some lighter conversation but Bousaif stayed on the sidelines, content to enjoy the pleasure of an unhurried meal. He listened to the others, the nervous chatter of the two football-shirted instructors and tried not to watch Umm Ali as she pushed food under her veil.

'Are you guys sponsored, or something?' She asked, 'Etihad, Emirates? I knew Daesh had some heavy-hitting backers, but not this big.' For the first time, the Director smiled.

'What's next?' she asked. 'The Caliphate hosts the World Cup?'

'When do you go again?' the Director asked. 'I'm not sure how much more of this I can take.' ManCity and the Gunner both pretended to enjoy the joking.

'I've only just flown in. Can I finish breakfast first?' Umm Ali asked.

'Haven't you got kufar throats to slit, somewhere?' the Director asked.

CHAPTER 19

14TH APRIL. TUESDAY. CHELTENHAM.

'Hello, Hash.' The gentle greeting made him spin round and he found himself looking at Susan.

'Susan…how are you? Fantastic to see you looking so well.'

'I missed Jim amongst the known suspects in class. What've you done with him?' Her voice was devoid of her usual cheerfulness.

'Ouch…' Hash said. 'It's been a really strange holiday. How long have you got?' Hash said. He pointed across the street to a corner café. 'Time for a coffee?'

'Just broken out, heading for the shops, getting some essentials in,' she said. 'I can't stop too long. Tell me about Jim, though.'

'Remember I told you about Jordanian families,' Hash began.

'Is he better – has he recovered from that ghastly virus?'

'He's fine,' Hash soothed. 'He spent more time than he bargained for in Ireland. His granny kept him hostage until he fattened up.' Susan's expression did not change, and the way she watched his performance began to make him uncomfortable. He knew it was the look she gave to students who were lying.

'He's in Jordan,' he said, as if it were a confession. He made a shrug. 'The Jordanian granny. She had to get involved when she heard Jim was sick. These two old girls,' he laughed. 'They've hardly ever met but they're so jealous...'

'He's at school there,' Susan said. 'The secretary said you'd taken him out of college.' Realising she had done some checking, Hash put on a serious expression. 'Family money involved, in the long term, Jim's inheritance,' he explained. 'My hands are tied, to a great extent. But he's at an amazing place, pretty international with most of the curriculum in English.' Susan seemed impressed. 'It wasn't an easy decision,' Hash explained. 'I forfeited the school fees here.' He pointed towards the Cotswold stone buildings along the Bath Road.

'How long for? How will he cope?' Susan asked. 'Will they 'get' Jim, over there?'

'Susan, bless you for asking,' Hash said. 'He's got a thousand cousins in the same place. It's swarming with Hashmi and Al Hashem,' he said. 'Nobody will pick on him. And if they do,' he smacked a fist lightly into his palm, 'they call in the Jordanian granny.'

'Ouch indeed,' Susan said.

'Even the Israelis are scared of her. Are you OK, Susan?' Hash took his chance to change tack. 'I was so damned worried about you. That nightmare, you had a terrible experience and it was all my fault and when you disappeared. I felt so terrible. Please can you talk about it, tell me what happened, or,' he held his hands out, 'is it still too awful to think about?'

'I'm putting it in the "too difficult" tray, at the moment. Did you go to the police?' she asked.

'Of course I did.' Hash wondered if her lie-detecting sensor was reading him. 'But I wasn't sure what to say about you. You were in shock and then you were difficult to get hold of. It didn't seem right to do things over the phone. And then of course,' he grimaced and shook his head, 'there was the debating society. One screw-up after another. You must think I am a complete disaster zone.'

'Will the police be following up, is what I meant,' she interrupted. 'I'm not sure how much intrusion I can handle.'

'I understand,' Hash said. 'I'll make that point when it comes round. They're still looking for that guy, by the way.'

'We made the best of the debate, in the end. You definitely had more fun at the races. I hope you won?'

'I didn't win, Susan,' Hash said. 'In fact, I fear I lost a precious friend.'

She looked away then at her watch. 'I've got to get my bits and pieces and make it back before the bell goes.'

'I'm so sorry, Susan. Shall I give Jim your regards?'

She softened. 'Tell him he owes me the course work I sent.'

TEN DAYS LATER. SATURDAY 24TH APRIL.

'They've got me under the doctor,' Sean rasped, hamming up a Belfast twang. 'Got me on all kinds of pills. Pills for this, pills for that...my poor kidneys are running on ball-bearings.'

'Are you drinking?'

'Can you believe I haven't had a scoop for days?'

'Your kidneys can't believe it. When can you come over?'

'Are the Constabulary still after me, or has the trail gone cold?'

'Cold as the grave.'

'Anything from Jim?' Anything from that wee Lord?'

'Nothing bad, if you know what I mean,' Hash considered. 'He's still out of my reach. They let him pass a message now and then. It's crazy. As though things have steadied but they're not finished.' Hash could hear the clicking of a cigarette lighter as Sean lit up. 'Our friend disappearing and not leaving a forwarding address…they should be concerned…any questions from them?'

'None. And he was the only player as far as I can see,' Hash added. 'Nothing went bang anywhere else that day or since.' On the other end of the line Sean's coughing made Hash hold the phone away from his ear. 'I can smell them down the phone.'

'Gallaher's,' Sean spluttered, 'used to be free on the National Health, over here. So it's all on hold, by the sound of it. What's the word with your mates?'

'The taxi guy's on hold. He's gone on the Hajj.'

'The what?'

'It's a pilgrimage they all have to do, once in their life. I think this guy's been a few times: he can afford it.'

'Sounds a bundle of laughs. When's he back?'

'Could be a week or three. And then we have to see if we're all still friends after the last time.'

'What about your mate whose girl dumped him?'

'He's on standby to put in a good word for me. How's Bella and the old boy?'

'Just the same,' Sean said. 'Bitter as hell. Must be what keeps them going.'

'Did you go and see them, tell them about Jim and everything?' There was silence at the other end, as though Sean was deciding what to answer. Eventually he said, 'They couldn't really take it in. They say we're both mad but they especially blame me.'

'But did you actually go and see them, sit with them and tell them it's about the old days, the same rules?'

'I did but they can barely speak to me. The mention of the 'old days' was enough to set them off. The old fella's pretty much out of it, but he starts to shake and tremble and then he cries. She says he understands everything but can't speak properly anymore. She says the shame is killing them.'

'Poor old Bella,' Hash sighed. 'Poor old girl.'

'Poor old girl, is she? The shame's killing me,' Sean said.

'Are you serious?'

'Can't shrug it off like I used to. In the Kesh, we were all too bloody pleased with ourselves. All of us patting one another on the back, saying what fine fellows we were. But when I got out, it started in on me like a ratchet. And now, there's no day when I don't think of it.'

'I remember it as if it was yesterday,' Hash said.

'And there isn't a night anymore,' Sean continued, 'when it doesn't flare up at me. The old girls say I'll burn in Hell.'

'Did you ever tell them the real story?'

'Would that change anything…they'd probably hate you as well. Fucking keep up with me, Darky, mate. Besides, it came out in the papers, didn't it?'

'And do they know you're sick?'

'I wouldn't give her the satisfaction. She'd fold her arms and tell me, serves you right and you're no son of mine. I don't need that at this moment.'

'You need to be here. We can do this together,' Hash said.

'Can you do the chemo for me, that would be a great help.'

**THIRTEEN DAYS LATER. THURSDAY 7TH MAY
CHELTENHAM RACECOURSE.**

Without Jim and the dog, and because the letter box system was still live, Hash had taken up jogging as his new reason for regularly being on the racecourse. The ground rule was never to compromise another team by disturbing them at the letter box. The first rule of survival, drummed in at Ben Gashir with ample graphic examples of failure, was to maintain the integrity of the cell system: nobody must know about the other, no names, no sightings, no details. Any clumsy or inadvertent overlap of cars or persons at the letter box was, deemed a penetration and carried a death sentence, enforced by the compromised team itself. Darkness belonged to these faceless postmasters and daylight belonged to Hash.

On this blustery morning Hash sat waiting, switching up the blower to keep the windows from misting up, wondering how he was going to explain Shamsa's death to Jim. He had considered various scenarios, perhaps an accident, or maybe a shock, terminal illness, before realising that if he was having the conversation with Jim, then it could only mean the nightmare was over. He fed a minute of heat into the cabin, to seal warmth inside, then stepped out and closed the door behind him.

As he trotted across the wet grass, down the imperceptible slope heading for the footbridge, he noted today he was sharing the whole area with four cars, two well across to the right, near the riding school for the disabled, and two closer to his route. He soon passed alongside the first, a Renault car-van hybrid, a dog lovers' palace, fitted with a pet partition for two dogs.

The other car on his immediate route was a BMW hatchback in a shade of expensive metallic blue. It was the sort of blue that came with an exotic name and would sparkle in the sunshine, but still looked dull to Hash in the grey light. He noticed the windows were steamed up and the engine running, with wispy exhaust trailing, as though whoever was inside was still inside, on the phone or keeping warm. He covered the ground quickly and was at the bridge and over it, taking care to miss the mud and to note there was no tape to indicate an incoming message. He cut out across the meadow, wondering if the old hare was still around, and felt the bite of the incline as he leaned forward, pumping just that bit harder to keep the speed constant. He had to admit he was enjoying the process and wondered why he had never turned to jogging before.

As with the days of Shamsa he followed the same route and headed out to the foot of Cleeve Hill before turning back. He ran slowly: jogging was not sprinting, he told himself. He could try sprinting later. Two hundred metres off the footbridge he heard shrill yelping and barking. He slowed to a walk as the barking increased and a puppy, a Weimaraner, burst into view, running with a lead trailing from its collar.

It saw him at the same time and veered towards him, running hard, hurling itself at his knees. The tail wagging told Hash the pup was enjoying its day. Behind, calling to the pup, followed the owner. She looked flustered and called the dog's name in a wail of frustration. Hash caught the lead and then knelt, one knee in the muddy grass to pet the animal. He couldn't stop himself from gathering it up and hugging it. The owner reached him, relief written on her face. Hash could a see pretty, fresh face with blue eyes, strands of blonde hair escaping from a grey wool bonnet.

'Hope you don't mind,' Hash said. 'He started it, he wanted to say hello.'

'Thank God.' The woman's accent was foreign. 'This dog is driving me mad, always running away from me. I am always chasing.' She did not try to take the dog away from Hash, almost happy to let him pet the dog, 'It runs too much,' she said.

'He's beautiful. How old?'

'This dog.' She thought about it. 'I think four, five months. It's not my dog, my boss's dog. His name is Bruno.'

'And what's the dog's name?' Hash asked.

The woman blinked. 'No. The dog's name is Bruno.' Then,

catching Hash's smile, she laughed. 'English bastard.'

'Sorry?' Hash said.

'My boss...English bastard.' She smiled back at Hash's surprise.

'That was good,' he said. 'I wasn't expecting that.'

'I used to have one,' Hash said, stroking Bruno's muzzle and tickling his ribs. The pup loved it, squirming, nipping Hash's fingers.

'You used to have bastard English boss or ugly little dog?'

'No. I used to have one of these.' It was Hashmi's turn to laugh.

'You had one of these ugly dogs,' she said, happy to spend time. She looked up as a light drizzle started. 'First dog, now English weather.'

'My lovely, beautiful dog,' Hash said. 'This Bruno is going to be big and beautiful.'

'I was joking,' she said. Hash looked up at her. Her delicate fingers tucked the wisps of hair inside her bonnet then dug in a pocket. He saw her red nails flick at a packet of cigarettes as she lit up. She exhaled a stream of smoke, sighing with pleasure. 'Where is your dog?' She looked around her.

'She's gone. I don't have her anymore.' Hash could feel salt stinging his eyes and he concentrated on giving Bruno another stroking. The woman did not say anything, sensing the emotion. She waited. Finally, Hash stood up and held Bruno's lead out to her.

'You miss him?' she asked. Hash could not answer her. 'I miss her,' he managed.

'But now you share Bruno?' she said brightly. 'I come here sometimes.' She pointed at the car park. 'He sends me.'

'He's waiting in the car and you do the dog walking in the rain?' Hash smiled. 'Good arrangement.'

'I take his car,' she said, 'when I am working. I come lunchtime, mainly. Today is extra punishment.' She indicated her mud-spattered trainers and jeans. She took Bruno's lead and tugged it gently, making Bruno yelp in protest. Hash wanted to take the dog back and show her how easy it was to train the pup.

'I come here nearly every lunchtime to jog,' he could not believe he was lying.

'Next time. You see my BMW, you jog with Bruno and I sit in my car?'

'That's win-win for me.'

'How much you charge?'

'For Bruno, hmm, that's difficult.' Hash reached down to pat the pup. 'Special rate for Bruno.' He paused, watching her expression. 'Is free.' She digested this while finishing her cigarette and flicking it away.

'This is great,' she replied. 'That's my car.' She pointed through the trees at the BMW. 'When you see it here, then Bruno is waiting.'

Hash held out his hand. 'I'm Tariq Hashmi. Everyone calls me Hash.'

'Eva,' she said. 'Lucky to meet you.'

'I'm the lucky one, now I've met you and Bruno,' he said. They walked to her car and he watched Bruno leap inside, his muddy paws leaving tracks on the leather.

'Oww!' Eva wailed. 'Shit! Look at the mess…my boss's car.'

He waved at the BMW as it pulled away and turned towards the exit. Her hand shot out, a fresh cigarette between the fingers, and waved back. Back in his vehicle, he was smiling so wide he had to check his mirror.

LIBYA.

SIRTE. 20TH MAY 2015

The Director and Umm Ali's unannounced arrival in the early evening, brought unease to the small camp. Like students caught idling, both the Gunner and ManCity went overboard in their welcome. The coolness of the Director's response and the pointed silence from Umm Ali only increased the tension. Bousaif kept silent. Only the Manager seemed unfazed. Tapping his watch, like a schoolmaster bringing a class to heel, he called them for Maghreb prayers.

Seated opposite him, after prayers, Umm Ali acknowledged Bousaif's growth of black hair. He and heard the word 'good' through her veil.

'Passport,' the Director demanded. Bousaif handed over a worn Lebanese passport. 'Easy stuff first,' the Director continued, opening the pages. 'Date and place of birth?'

Bousaif gave his real date of birth, 5th May 1985, and his birthplace as Tripoli, which was literally true, but Tripoli in Lebanon. 'Religion, education, profession and recent travel?' the Director continued.

'Christian, political science at CNAM in my home city,'

Bousaif responded. 'Joined the family stonemasonry business when I left university. Internships with Greek and Italian partners. I've been to Cyprus recently. I had a girlfriend there.'

'Why Christian?' the Director asked. Bousaif hesitated.

'One less kufar when you press the tit...innit.' Nobody laughed. The Director held the passport to Umm Ali who shook her head dismissively. A clattering of trays and pots sounded from the kitchen where the Manager was busy. In the pleasant warmth of the evening only the random crack and snap from the insect killer broke the silence.

'Continue,' the Director said, putting the passport down and picking up his prayer beads.

'I've got a Schengen visa that allows me to visit and stay in UK for a Technical English course at a language school, in Cheltenham. I'm stopping over in Germany, in Munich, for football games.'

'Why is he hanging around in Munich?' the Director interrupted.

'I'll call him in when I'm ready,' Umm Ali said.

'When?'

'I'll know when I know,' she said. 'Until then he's better off hanging around in Europe, not small-town UK.'

'Yes, but I have other teams running operations in Europe,' the Director said. 'Maybe Munich. What if he gets caught in a backlash.'

'So...' Umm Ali opened her gloved hands, 'tell me which cities he can hang around in, then.'

'I've got tickets for games in Berlin and Paris.'

'How do you communicate with her?' the Director asked.

'I transmit on ManCity's Facebook, and I receive on Gunner's Facebook.'

'When you get to Britain, what do you say to the immigration people?'

'Show them the invitation letter from the language school.' The Director turned his head to Umm Ali. 'Your turn.'

'Horse racing,' she stated. 'Have these two clowns briefed you well on horse racing in Britain?.' Bousaif gave her a rundown on Britain's forthcoming racing events where the royal family might be expected to attend. He explained the instructors had steered him through the venues, with the help of various websites. Umm Ali said nothing

'Your holiday had to end sometime.' The Director broke the silence. 'It appears Bousaif is ready.' The man studied Bousaif. 'You've had time to adjust, mentally prepare for the mission. Are you are ready to take it through to the end?

Bousaif shook his head. 'Insh'Allah I am ready to do this.

'Martyr's speech?'

'Already already filmed it, Sayyid Director,' ManCity said.

'What about the martyr's bounty?' Umm Ali asked.

'One million US dollars to his father,' the Director answered. The Gunner and ManCity sat back, exchanging glances. 'I'd blow myself up twice for that sort of money,' the Gunner breathed.

'Epsom or Ascot?' The Director looked at the woman. Bousaif realised he was listening to the locations of his targets for the first time, and wondered why the Director was discussing them in front of the two instructors, a clear breach of security. The mistake had not seemed to alarm Umm Ali.

'One or the other…depends,' she said.

'On what?'

'On the boy, how soon we can get him competent with the new drone we've given him.'

'When will that be?'

'The Epsom Derby is the first big opportunity and runs from the fifth and sixth of June. Ascot runs seventeenth to twentieth June.'

'But there's more chance of the royal family being at Ascot,' the Director said.

'We'll know nearer the time.'

The Director grew uncharacteristically animated. 'Bousaif… your mission will be the biggest attack ever in the history of jihad…of the world. We'll have the boy filming it with his flying camera.'

'What do I do with the boy and the father?' Umm Ali asked.

'We return the kid to his dad and everyone goes home,' the Director said.

'You're not serious?'

'What do you think?'

ManCity and the Gunner looked down at their empty plates.

'Sayyid Bousaif is leaving very soon,' Umm Ali broke the silence, pointing to the two British instructors, 'You two, Posh and Becks, you need to say goodbye now.' The Gunner and ManCity rose and came around to Bousaif's side of the table. Bousaif stood up and they hugged in turn. 'God go with you,' each man said. 'I wish it was me instead of you, my brother,' the Gunner said. ManCity said nothing.

Just as they turned away, Umm Ali, who had been observing the two men as they moved off, called them back, waving them to resume their seats.

'Just got one last little issue,' she began. 'The last mission went wrong because...' She considered. 'Probably a number of things. And we're still trying to find the other guy you two trained.' Her voice had a coldness to it. 'We need to be sure Bousaif hasn't picked up a virus here.' She pointed a gloved finger, first at ManCity, then to the Gunner, from one to the other, like a metronome.

'Bousaif needs to tell me which of you two gave him a message for someone in Britain.' Both instructors went pale. The Gunner tried to speak but her hand silenced him. 'The question is for Bousaif.' The Director hung back on the bench. The Manager, leaning forward with a fresh tray, put it down and stepped back. Bousaif felt sweat pricking his face.

'Which one?' Umm Ali repeated. The metronome stopped as her hand dipped into her bag and came out with a pistol in it, a small-calibre automatic with a silencer. The Director recoiled at the sight of the black metal. Bousaif realised she was still talking to him, pointing the weapon at his chest.

'Which one?' Umm Ali's voice was low and grating. Bousaif watched as she picked up the pistol, handling it with slick movements, slipping out the magazine and thumbing the bullets, testing the spring.

'I'm not a patient person, Bousaif,' she said ramming the magazine back in and racking the slide, driving a bullet into the chamber.

'They both did,' Bousaif said.

'Aaah,' she sighed, 'now that's an interesting call.' She handed the weapon to him. When he grasped it, she guided the barrel to point at the two men opposite him. 'I think you know what's required.'

CHAPTER 20

CHELTENHAM. THURSDAY 28TH MAY.
MIDDAY

Hash could barely concentrate in court, worrying that the case might drag past the midday break and deny him a glimpse of Eva whom he had not seen for days. Standing in the dock, a defendant tried to look confident. Over the years, and as his own taste in fashion had refined, Hash had become aware of the difference between 'flashy' and 'elegant'. The fleshy middle-aged and balding man now standing before the Bench wore a black suit with a thick pinstripe and a pink shirt with a broad, pale yellow, silk tie. As he raised his hand to straighten his tie, a gold bracelet hung at his fat wrist. Instinctively Hash knew he would be finding this man guilty.

When the clerk had put the charge of fraud, the defendant pleaded 'not guilty' and the floor was given to the defending counsel. A picture of a hard-working independent financial adviser soon emerged, of an experienced, savvy hunter in the jungle of investment whose clients stood ready to attest to his skills.

Just as the clerk to the justices was getting restive, the

point was made that the defendants' clients had all been exhaustively briefed about investments going down as well as up, and had all signed a disclaimer absolving their man in the case of such downswings. The counsel compared the number of those complaints with the apparently vast number of those who did not, adding that the losers were managing their lives competently in all other respects.

In the retiring room, during the break, the chairwoman, a friendly retired schoolteacher, poured coffee for Hash, murmuring, 'I can see how this will go.'

'Let me guess,' Hash said. 'They knew what they were doing, they got their fingers burned for being just a bit too greedy.'

'So…tough luck,' the woman said. The other winger, a businessman, chipped in from his seat at the table. 'These people spend their lives building up savings, great big pots of cash. The banks don't pay anything these days so our chum in the dock always finds someone who'll listen to him.'

'They listen,' the chairwoman said. 'They think he'll see them right and then they sign up.'

'Maybe there was a cooling-off period?' Hash said.

'Undoubtedly,' the other member of the trio said, 'but don't underestimate greed, theirs or his. He's smart, probably has some waffle to get past that and his massive upfront commission.'

'What's the worst he could get for this?' Hash asked.

'We can slap him on the wrist and let him go,' the chairwoman said, 'tell him we're watching…don't do it again.'

'But he's stolen their savings.'

'They've given him money, he's taken his fees. Whether he gets a slapped wrist or a fine, they'll never get their money back,' the other winger said.

The clerk saved Hash's rendezvous by steering the decision to adjourn and let the Crown Court take the strain. As he trod the rear steps, his phone came to life with an hour-old SMS from Eva: 'am late r u still there'. 'On my way,' he replied. In the car park, heading for the Promenade and a taxi home, he caught sight of the bailed conman and a young woman embracing. Hash's first thought that the girl may be a daughter changed when he saw their hungry passion. The defence lawyer was also making his way to the pair and, when the conman noticed him, expressions of relief and celebration were exchanged between all three. Then the conman, making a show of it, handed keys to the girl and pointed to his car and waved her away. Hash watched her get into a silver Audi estate. The rear window had a 'Help for Heroes' sticker on the left edge and a 'Keep Calm Carry on Hunting' sticker on the right. Feeling his phone vibrate he pulled it out and saw Eva's message. 'Cannot make it now. Sorry.'

When he had last seen Eva, she had been gorgeous, flirty and hopeless at controlling the pup, begging Hash to help. Bruno had made the most of it, dashing in giddy circles at the sight of Hash, demanding to play and even jealous of the attention he was giving Eva. Hash's mind was increasingly filled with ideas of Eva, himself and Jim. He wondered if Eva was the sort of person who could accept the boy and grow to like him.

'Good news, my friend, you will be so happy.' Siddiq's voice, full of childlike excitement, made Hash instantly wary. 'Don't tell me.'

'Yes…Anna's come back?'

'When?'

'Very soon, it is so wonderful,' Siddiq gushed. 'She's coming from London. She can't wait to be with me again. She misses me too much.'

'Why do you do it?'

'What do you mean, my friend?'

'Why not save yourself the headaches and get a nice, gentle English Rose as a girlfriend?'

'European women,' Siddiq swooned, 'real ladies. So sophisticated, cultured. Anna has a big job, her own money, her own property.'

'I'm happy for you.'

'Is the place still OK?

'I've had to replace the bed…it was smashed.'

'No, my friend, impossible…' Siddiq went silent. Hash put him out of his misery. 'Of course, everything's okay, it's all yours.'

'Good, good, 'Siddiq sounded relieved. 'Are you in Cheltenham?'

'Yes, why?'

'Not in the mosque in Birmingham?'

'I'm on the racecourse.' Siddiq's high spirits were beginning to grate. 'Why?'

'Sayyid Hakim is back.'

'Then I'm happy for you both,' Hash said. 'I'd be happier if someone had good news for me and Jim.'

'He wants to speak with you.'

'Has he got anything for me?'

'Insh'Allah. He is a busy man, so why would he be wasting time?'

'He could phone. When does he want to meet?'

'Tomorrow at the mosque. Be ready.'

At ten o'clock, after lingering until sunset, Hash was unlocking the maisonette front door. Flicking on the porch and hall lights he walked through the downstairs rooms and into the kitchen. The place still smelled of Anna's scent and she had left it tidier than he could have managed. He went back out to the Discovery and brought in a bunch of red roses and a bottle of champagne. He stood in the master bedroom, looking out across to the brightly lit expanse of GCHQ. As he surveyed the old target he knew it was too much of a coincidence that Anna was back in the game and that Hakim, either a nemesis or an ally, wanted to see him. Down below, the row of garages stood peacefully, deserted by their owners. His eyes swept up and down, double-checking and, deciding it was now dark enough.

Parking by the garage he stepped out and eased up the over and under door, stepped in and closed it behind him. He flicked the light switch and to his left, now bathed in the glare of the strip light, lay the stack of six aluminium ladders. He checked the door was completely down, sealing him in, then started to shift the ladders, one by one to the far side. When he had moved them all he kicked at the length of carpet they had lain on for years. The corner flap began to lift and he reached down with both hands and pulled, slowly shifting the whole strip of carpet to expose a sheet of thick plywood a foot across and three feet long lying flush to the cement floor. The wood had a loop of plastic cord at one corner and Hash hooked a finger into it and began to lift. It came up easily to reveal an even layer of fine gravel. Kneeling by the exposed trench he scooped away handfuls of gravel, still dry after all these years.

A car engine purring outside made him stop and listen. He realised he was sweating and his heart thumping. Doors opening, voices, adult mixed with children, sounded like a family back home, parking up for the night. Sniffing and scratching at the garage door told him he had been detected by their pet. A woman called to the animal, her voice tired and irritated, demanding 'Fenton' come to heel. The sniffing escalated to a growl with paws scrabbling at the door. The owner became angry and Hash heard the tussle as the recalcitrant animal was put on a leash and dragged away. Hash waited until their garage door had slammed and their footsteps receded, then dug through the thin layer until he felt the canvas bag. He recalled the modus operandi back then: the assault team could not waste time digging up a deep cache, or loading magazines while sitting comfortably in the garage. A steady, quiet approach would have been a luxury so, to be on the safe side, Hash had planned for the police coming hard on their heels, maybe tipped off, probably armed. His team would have hit the garage at the gallop, one pair pulling out the ladders with the other pair hauling up the kitbag and sharing out the weapons. He imagined the two men going over would have been ready to cross the fence, weapons loaded, within less than a minute. The remaining pair would have kept the police at bay, drawing fire, throwing the grenades, making it as noisy as possible, buying time for the two comrades to get across the first fences and start shooting their way into the complex.

Testing the weight of the contents and guessing at fifteen kilos, he heaved it upright, hearing metallic clunks as the contents settled and adjusted. Hash got his left arm to the bundle, swinging it onto his shoulder. Waiting for a few seconds to settle his nerves and ears, he flicked off the light and hoisted the garage door up.

FRIDAY 29TH MAY
MORNING

Hakim was seated in the mosque kitchen as Hash was shown in. The crushing handshake and the silent, cynical appraisal instantly made Hash more irritated than apprehensive.

'Salaam-Alaikum, Sayyid Hakim. How is your family, how was the Hajj?'

'Umra Haj,' Hakim corrected sharply. Maybe one day you will take your son.'

'Insh'Allah,' Hash said, 'with your help, everything is possible.' Siddiq, his face beaming with pleasure, placed cups of coffee before them. 'Thank you, my friend.' He gave Hash a shy wink.

'You look exhausted, my friend. I hope you found everything

in order, the flowers, the…'

'My guest was so pleased with that.' Siddiq cut him off in case he was planning to mention champagne in front of Hakim.

'How is your guest? Tired after a long journey?'

'Of course, now resting.'

'Have a look at these,' Hakim interrupted, 'and tell me what you see.' He pulled his phone from a pocket and flicked through images until he found what he was looking for.

'He is happy and you still haven't heard from him?' The question came as an assumption.

'I have not heard from him and I do not believe he is happy, at all,' Hash said.

'Have a look at this one.' Hash was looking at Jim's bruised, face. The photo had been taken from a low angle and a table edge obscured most of it. But it was clearly the same long-haired Jim, injured, frightened and shocked, staring at a plate of food.

'He's been in an accident?' Hash said.

'He's been beaten.' Hakim let the information sink in. 'This was taken at a restaurant two days ago.'

'Where? Why are they beating him,' Hash gasped. 'Why?'

'They are training him. When he does good, he gets taken good food. When he does bad, he gets punished…maybe no food.'

'Animals,' Siddiq growled.

'Training…for what?' Hash said, 'I'll kill the bastards…'

'Arab bastards,' Hakim corrected.

'So you believe me now. You believe these people are holding my son and he has not gone to the jihad.'

'I believe some of what you say.' Hakim nodded. 'I'm never sure.'

'You mean I'm still a liar to you?' Hash sat back in his chair and looked at Hakim. 'What do I have to do to convince you my son is a prisoner of these people and I just want him back? You've found him, you can see they're harming him.' Hash held out his hands. 'So why don't you help me get him back?'

'You want me to hand this all over to the British police.' Hakim held the phone up to Hash. 'Would you prefer that?' Hash did not answer. 'I thought not. I am helping you, because...' Hakim pointed at Siddiq. 'I have been asked, and as a Muslim, it is my duty. Maybe also now I see the danger these people bring.'

'Who are they?' Hash asked.

'Mister Hashmi,' Hakim said, 'don't play games with me. You know these people, maybe better than me. You must have upset them very much.'

'I have told Siddiq about the business disaster but swear I do not,' Hash emphasised the words, 'repeat, not know who these people are. But I will kill them and go to prison if that's what it takes to get my son away from them.'

'I know this type of Arab well,' Hakim said, 'from the jihad in Afghanistan against the Russians...when I was a boy like your son and first saw wealthy Arabs playing at jihad. These men do not care about the Holy Koran. They are not good Muslims, they are rubbish.'

'Sayyid Hakim,' Hash tried again, 'why are they training my son?'

'In the beginning it looked like play, to keep him occupied.

Now they make him practise often, when the weather is good and even when it is windy.'

'Did your people see them beating him?'

'No, but they see them shouting at him, pushing him, especially when the woman in the burqa is there.'

'The woman from before, in March?'

'Probably the same.' Hakim nodded. 'We see her now and then.'

Hash sat forward. 'I thank you from the bottom of my heart, but can't you just let me get close and then take over?'

'What do you mean, take over?' Hakim's irritation surfaced. 'You have not been listening to me. You cannot possibly take over what I do. Your son and maybe yourself stay alive because I do not let you take over.' He tapped the image of Jim's bruised face looking from the screen. 'This could have been a dead boy.'

Siddiq cut in. 'Hakim is trying to find out who in the area is supporting these people, who is hiding them, which imams are giving help.'

'I cannot let you blunder about and leave a mess I can't clean up,' Hakim said. 'I will be living here long after you've gone home with your son.'

'Does your team know where they are keeping Jim?' Hash said.

'They did in the beginning but not now.'

'So, they change their location?' Hash said.

'Wouldn't you?'

'How do I know? I'm not one of these bastards,' Hash said. Hakim's face broke into a sardonic smile. 'Of course you're not.'

CHAPTER 21

Hash looked at the Arab BlackBerry as soon as he woke from a night of fitful sleep. There was no answer to his SMS about Jim. He had asked for a picture of Jim with an up-to-date newspaper. He knew it was a difficult request, one which would have them debating whether to engage in mind games with a desperate father. He looked at his drawn face in the mirror and splashed water on it, trying to revive vitality.

He shrugged off the anxiety, forcing his mind to the bright spot in his day and concentrating on shaving carefully. This was the closest thing to a date in years, even ranking ahead of the promise of a dinner with Susan. His watch told him he had the whole morning to prepare, and he decided he would dazzle Eva with a picnic basket, show her how the British did such things. He could get to the fantastic little deli in Tivoli that baked its own bread, then maybe to Waitrose before the Saturday rush started. He would prepare smoked salmon, and ham sandwiches with a bottle of chilled white wine and one of champagne.

Mrs Hamilton was waiting for his door to open, sensing his

anxiety to be about his business. 'Going somewhere nice on this beautiful day?' she asked from her doorway. She caught sight of the wicker hamper Hash held delicately in front of him as he walked down the path to his car. 'Fortnum & Mason.' Her voice had a mischievous edge. 'Can mean only one thing…'

'Good morning, Mrs Hamilton,' Hash cut her off. 'I called you so many times but you were engaged, so I had to go with my second choice.'

'Oh yes, Hash,' she said, 'my diary's chock-a-block these days. Where you taking her?'

'I don't know yet.'

'Which one is it this time?' She hovered on the threshold. 'The dark one from the school or that blonde with the ponytail? Never saw you do all this stuff for Flora.' She closed the door, leaving Hash stung by the last remark.

The sight of the BMW down in the parking zone soothed his frustration and he took a few seconds to check his appearance before pulling alongside. Eva emerged, first a foot in trainers, then an elegant denim-clad leg. Hash could hear her shouting at the pup in the back seat barking at the sight of Hash. She stood up, stretched slowly then treated him to a radiant smile while reaching for him. 'Say hello to the lady first,' she said, presenting herself for his approval. Figure-hugging jeans complemented by an expensive black leather bomber jacket, her hair worn up in a chignon, she twirled and fixed her blue eyes on him, enjoying the effect. 'Lady first, dog second in my country.' Speechless, he leaned forward and drew her to him, kissing her on both cheeks.

He held her to him for a few, delicious seconds, drinking in her scent. 'Well,' Eva breathed, 'that was nice…now what?' Hash let her go to defend himself against Bruno's welcoming assault. Crouching down, ruffling the dog's ears, he suggested, 'Crickley Hill, ten minutes away … a surprise! Follow me in your car. I'll take this guy … he can jump all over my seats.'

'No walking,' she pointed down at her pristine trainers. 'You and the dog but not me.'

The spread on the tailgate drew her approval as Hash unpacked his hamper and laid out the food and wine. He heard himself lying about the vintage as he poured for both and offered a toast. Pointing west to the outline of Offa's Dyke he described the beauty of the area and the Hay Festival and how he should be taking her there for another surprise visit. 'A picnic like this and you can take me anywhere,' she purred. Just then her phone rang and, as she examined it, Hash was surprised to see her expression change from blissful enjoyment to anger. She spoke quickly in what Hash guessed was a Slavic language, hissing words into the phone, stabbing with her finger, spilling wine from her glass.

'My boss,' she said, simply when she had finished. 'Bastard.'

''You speak to your boss like that? Remind me not to upset you.' Hash said. By then the storm had passed, her face had softened, the phone returned to her jeans pocket and her glass thrust out for a refill. 'Only when he doesn't do what I tell him to do,' she said.

CHAPTER 22

The SMS from waiting on the Arab phone simply asked, 'Ready?'
Then Siddiq had disturbed him as he was heading for the garden
shed to retrieve the kitbag from its hiding place. 'Come for
lunch, my friend,' he insisted. 'Anna talking too much about
you.' Hash agreed, wondering what designs Anna had in mind.
Continuing his task, he soon had the kitbag on the kitchen table.

Years ago, in the bloom of revolutionary ardour, he had
requested what he needed to support a team getting over the
GCHQ fence. Now, as he opened the bag he was struck by the
naivety of those times and the stark simplicity of his list. He
pulled out two folding butt AK47s each with a fully charged
magazine. He next took out a bundle of grease-smelling cloth
and unwrapped two Tokarev pistols each also with its full
magazine. A second bundle revealed two British Army, old style
'36' Mills grenades. He checked the pins and set them aside
carefully. Finally, wrapped in two blue police tabards with their
checked motif, he remembered he had asked for two sets of car

number plates. Surveying it all neatly arranged on the kitchen table he was pleased with his thought processes back in the day. He had the makings of a fighting approach or withdrawal using stashed, stolen cars. Although there wasn't enough ammunition for a prolonged firefight there would have been a hell of a noise and some real damage when they were inside the wire. He emptied the magazines of the rifles and pistols counting the bullets into a plastic tub, knowing Sean would expect some measure of maintenance and preparation, then doused the whole lot with an aerosol of WD40.

Wiping oil off his hands he decided to ring Sean. He could not tell him about the weapons. As with the dead bomber, he would see them in the garage.

'What's it like with you?' Hash picked up the strain in Sean's voice. There was no challenging banter, no attempt to wind him up.

'Great summer over here,' Hash said.

'Pissing with rain over here, as usual…what's new?'

'I'm in dock,' Sean said, choking off a cough. 'Inpatient treatment tomorrow.'

'How long for?' Hash asked.

'No… I'm fine, thanks, actually…good of you to inquire…'

'That's more like it, mate.'

'Oh shit,' Sean said. 'It's mate, is it?'

'And I preferred it when you were a cantankerous bastard,' Hash said. 'We've got another visitor coming. It feels like a rerun of the last one.

'Or another racecourse,' Sean said.

'The next big one is Epsom, the Derby, next weekend.'

'I can't make it that soon,' Sean said. 'Like I said, chemo leaves me wrecked for a few days, weak as a kitten and then they sit me down and read the tea leaves.'

'Shit,' Hash said.

'Shit…about my lung cancer or about me not coming across?'

'Both.' Hash was quiet for a few seconds then said, 'They've been hitting him. I saw the photo. Hakim's boys got one.'

'You sure it wasn't his boys who did it?'

'He seemed angry about it.'

'Christ.' Sean's voice was hoarse. 'Don't twist my arm. I'll come if I can, when I'm fit enough.'

'Can I do anything for you?' Hash asked. 'Do you need a cash injection?'

'About the only injections that don't hurt,' Sean said. 'No thanks…don't know what I'd do with the stuff anyhow.'

Anna delayed standing up before she greeted Hash. He remembered their last encounter, her languid appraisal and how dangerously attractive she could make herself. Now, she kissed him full on the lips then held him at arm's length looking at him. She was calculating and manipulative for all her sexiness and Siddiq looked on with a mixture of jealousy and hurt.

She nailed Hash with the one question he least wanted to hear. 'How's your son? Is he in contact, is everything alright?' He looked at her then across to Siddiq, irritated, unsure what he had told her. 'He's as fine as can be expected,' he began. 'After the troubles were behind us, we found a place for him in Jordan, at a good international school.'

'Troubles? I thought it was just adolescent problems. Did you go to the police, what did they do? Useless, I expect.'

'Adolescent problems are always trouble,' Hash managed before she interrupted, her expression somewhere between pity and resignation at his incompetence. 'What did I you tell you, darling?' She dragged Siddiq into the crossfire. 'No mother to guide him, that's what I told you...you poor thing, Hash.' She pointed to Siddiq, 'He was worried sick, so was I.' Hash heard himself saying how touched he was by everyone's concern.

'So who's looking after him?' Anna persisted.

Hash dismissed further questions with a flourish of his hand. 'More importantly...how are you, Anna? Good to see you.' He looked at Siddiq who was beaming with pleasure, 'How long this time? You were here one minute, gone the next...we missed you.'

'It depends on him.' She shot a coy look at Siddiq. 'He's the boss. He wears the trousers.'

'Sometimes I think you wear the trousers and Siddiq wears the skirt.'

'Aah,' she smiled, 'you are a good judge of character but why do you say 'sometimes' and not just 'all the time'? I keep him jealous, too.'

'Jealous?' Hash was beginning to chuckle.

'Jealous...good for him.' She blew a kiss at Siddiq then winked at Hash. 'Men...' She sighed, pleased with her performance. 'How is your plumber friend?

'Him…he's gone, ages ago.'

'Trying to make it in stand-up? I could see he had talent.'

'Drinks, everyone,' Siddiq interrupted from the kitchen. 'Enough business. Time to relax.'

'Hash, my friend,' Siddiq held the bottle of champagne for him to open and went for three glasses. Hash eased off the cork as he reappeared. 'Hash knows about horse racing, darling,' he said to Anna. 'He goes all the time to the races. Maybe he knows.'

'Knows what?' Hash was concentrating on pouring a glass. 'What do you need to know?'

'When is the next big race in Cheltenham?' Anna asked.

'Months away.'

'That's no good, darling,' Anna pouted. 'I want to go in summertime, wear my best outfit, get dressed up like the rich people do.'

'There's the Derby at Epsom. It's famous,' Hash said, pouring the third glass. 'The Queen always goes.'

'The Queen…really?' Anna looked hard at Siddiq. 'Did you hear, darling…? The Queen!'

Hash said, 'It wouldn't be the Derby without The Queen.' Holding up his glass, he toasted, 'The Queen!' Siddiq and Anna both murmured, 'The Queen,' and they all sipped in appreciative silence.

'So, will I see The Queen if I go to Epsom, darling?'

'See her from a distance or close up?' Hash asked. 'You have to be in The Queen's Stand to rub shoulders with royalty. That's where the royal action is, but you can still see her with binoculars from outside.'

'That's no good.' Anna made another show of pouting at Siddiq. 'I want to be beside The Queen, rubbing shoulders with royalty, darling.'

'Hash will arrange tickets, for this place.' Siddiq looked at his friend with a mixture of confidence and hope. 'He knows this procedure.'

'Which day?' Hash said. 'There are two days, Friday and Saturday. The Friday is for all the beautiful ladies to show off their outfits.'

'That's a good day for you, darling,' Siddiq said. 'You will be the most beautiful...'

'Whichever day The Queen is coming on,' Anna cut in.

'They don't necessarily say which day she's coming on,' Hash teased.

'Can you find out?' Anna said.

'Maybe see which days her horses are running,' Hash offered. 'She presents the prize after the big race, the Derby.'

'Darling...' Anna purred at Siddiq, reaching over to stroke his arm. 'What do you think, darling? I want to have fun this time, go out, see places, not just stay hidden here waiting for you to visit.'

'Anything for you, darling.' Siddiq drew her hand to his lips. 'Of course, darling.'

'Maybe Hash will take me if you don't want to go?'

Siddiq followed Hash out to his car after lunch.

'You can arrange this thing, my friend?' There was a look of doubt on Siddiq's face as though he knew he had been overselling

Hash's abilities.

'You've left me only a few days,' Hash said, 'And you want the most expensive tickets. It's better you go on the last two days, to be sure to see The Queen.'

'But you can do it, can't you? She can get crazy when she doesn't get what she wants. I have to keep her happy.'

'What is Hakim doing for me?' Hash said. 'I need to hear from him and then the tickets for Friday and Saturday will happen.'

Siddiq took the ultimatum calmly. 'Hakim has more sympathy,' he observed. 'This is different from before.'

'Because he saw Jim was being beaten?' Hash said.

'There's a connection.' Siddiq nodded. 'A long time ago,' Siddiq waved to where his Mercedes stood, 'before all the business, Hakim was a mujahid fighting Al Qaeda on the border. The Taliban took his brother prisoner then shot him.'

'Ouch,' Hash said softly.

'The point is,' Siddiq said, 'that was not the Taliban way. They should have ransomed the brother like they normally did. You know…the practice of hostage taking, it has rules, part commercial and part family thing. This time there were Arabs with the Taliban…Al Qaeda disregarded the rules. Afterwards, Hakim found out they had given the orders.' He looked at Hash. 'This brother was the same age as your son.'

MONDAY 1ST JUNE
CHELTENHAM

Eva had phoned early in the morning to say her employer had

unforeseen travel commitments imminent, involving her, but preferably not the dog. He had asked her to arrange kennels, but she had suggested her friend as dog sitter. The boss was happy to pay a fee. Hash waived the fee on condition she delivered the dog, in person.

'This is win-win.' She smiled, pausing in the doorway as Bruno barrelled past. She held out her hands to Hash and as they hugged he smelled scent in her hair. He felt happy, intoxicated and let his hands slip to her waist. The pup came back to check on the delay. 'Maybe you keep the damned dog forever,' Eva said. 'Maybe Jim will like him.' Intrigued by the smells of Shamsa and eager to investigate the nooks and crannies of a new house, the pup galloped through the rooms, then upstairs, coming down seconds later to claim Shamsa's bed in the kitchen.

'Your wife.' Eva looked up at the photo on the dresser shelf. 'You never told me she was so beautiful. And your son...a good-looking boy.'

'She is still beautiful,' he said.

'Does he miss her?" She pointed at a picture of Jim posing with his Spitfire.

'Sometimes,' Hash said. 'We both do.'

'So why did you send him away to Jordan?'

'Cheltenham can get pretty small and there was some family money in the pot. It was a chance to meet my folks and his cousins, and learn some Arabic. I'll bring him back for sixth form and university.'

'I'm glad Bruno is in this loving house.'

'I'll keep him as long as your boss wants.' Eva seemed

fascinated by every detail in the house. She looked around, peering at every object in the room. 'This is a man's world,' she said. 'No sign of a woman here,' she murmured when Hash came in with her glass.

'It was hard to have too much of Flora around at first,' Hash said. 'Then, when Jim was growing up, we got used to doing things our way.'

'Sad,' Eva said. 'How long has your wife been dead?'

'She passed away twelve years ago.'

'Since then, no girlfriend?'

'Too difficult,' Hash answered. 'I didn't want any other person in this space. I wanted to prove I could do everything, be mother and father. Maybe it was easier because Jim was a boy and needed a man's influence.'

'No grandmother, no grandfather closer than Jordan?'

'There's a grandmother in Ireland. She's great.' Hash smiled at the thought of Bella and her passion for Jim.

'So sad,' Eva said softly.

'Then, when Jim started school, I realised he had learning issues.'

'What sort of issues?'

'He didn't like too many people around, very shy, wouldn't speak.' Hash counted them off on his fingers. 'More interested in machinery than making friends.'

Bruno's barking came from above and they both stood, Hash moving towards the staircase. 'He must have found something. Want to see upstairs?' he offered, pointing the way. As he followed her up his eyes took in her lithe movement and the contours of her athletic body. When he showed her Jim's room, she brushed by him and he caught the scent of her hair and perfume again. At the entrance to his room they found themselves looking into each other's eyes and he felt his heart thumping. She moved her face closer and they embraced. His lips brushed her cheek and neck, then found her lips. Their first kiss was a long, intense release. He felt Eva's passion in her restless tongue. His hands ran slowly up and down her back, enjoying, not rushing as the kisses became shorter, more challenging. He was pulling her towards him and she was not resisting, her body yielding to his. She allowed him to lay her on the bed and then her hands began to search for him. She smiled up at him, encouraging the abandon. His hands went to her waist and found the button of her jeans. When he undid the button, she gave a little gasp as he gently pulled on the zip. She gasped again as his hands slid inside the fabric and touched her skin. She pushed against him and pushed her lips against his. He could feel her hands tugging at him.

Afterwards, she and Hash lay silent, spent but satisfied in the afterglow.

'I think you might be the best thing that's happened to me,' he whispered finally.

'Happened or happening?' Eva raised herself on one elbow and stroked Hash's cheek. 'It's only just begun, it's not over and you're looking so sad?'

'I'm not sad, I'm very happy I met you.' He trailed his finger along her arm, from her shoulder to her fingertips. 'You've rescued me.'

'From what?'

'A bad time in my life,' he murmured. 'Problems, with the boy, no proper mother. But,' he sat up, 'I don't want to scare you off.'

'Anytime but now.' He leaned over and kissed her.

'When can we meet again?'

'As often as you like,' Hash said, running his fingers through her hair.

'When will you come again?' he asked again.

'Soon.' She put a finger to his lips and pressed softly. 'Soon.'

Hash did not want her to stay. He had enjoyed the sweet release from his torment and the chance to forget the nightmare. But if he cared about Eva he would need to make sure she was out of harm's reach. His mind threw up Susan's shocked features and he felt himself shudder. Maybe there would be violence and he needed Eva safely out of the way. Before she left they shared one last, long kiss.

The doorbell rang at around nine-thirty in the evening and this time it was Bruno, not Shamsa who gave tongue at the silhouette on the other side of the glass. The bulk of a man behind the glass told Hash it was the visitor he was dreading. Bruno's sharp yapping, as if warning him there was real danger present, made him think about his armoury. There was one Kalashnikov and a pistol stashed in a daysack bag under the stairs, and the matching pair, also hidden, in the back porch. But he had not loaded magazines and cursed himself inwardly, knowing what

Sean would have said. The man on the other fidgeted, sensing he was being observed.

Hash opened the door to find himself looking at a much younger man, a few inches shorter but broader with a strong, open face. There was a wary, alert expression on the face which softened as Hash offered his hand and gave the traditional, 'Salaam-Alaikum'. The new arrival kept step with the ritual greetings, his accent telling Hash he was an ethnic Arab from North Africa, Palestinian or an Egyptian, maybe a Tunisian or even a Libyan. He stood back and ushered the man past into the main hallway. Bruno remained cautiously out of range in the kitchen as Hash took the man's bag, noticing it had a Manchester City logo. He took him straight upstairs to his room and pointed the direction of Mecca before telling him to come back down for refreshments when he was ready.

In the kitchen, the two men began assessing each other. Hash had nothing to lose by introducing himself, and his guest readily gave his name as Bousaif.

'Tea, coffee? And you must be hungry,' Hash said, flicking on the kettle. The visitor became distracted by the pup, holding out his hand to make friends, tempting Bruno forward. Hash took fresh mint leaves from the fridge and held them up, 'Mint tea is easy or English tea…I could try Turkish coffee?' Bousaif smiled at being spoiled.

'How about food? We can get a takeaway or I can cook. Maybe they warned you about that. If the kufar don't get you, Tariq's cooking will.' This forced a smile from Bousaif. He dropped a pair of takeaway flyers onto the table. Bousaif showed no difficulty with the English menus.

'Pizza,' Bousaif decided. Hash wanted to ask him, there and then, about Jim, about what the hell was going on. Instead he dropped the mint leaves into a cafetiere and poured hot water over them. Pushing a sugar bowl towards his guest and placing the jug and two glasses on the table, he gestured, 'Welcome.' The young man nodded his appreciation.

'Make your choice.' Hash tapped the menu. 'I call, then they deliver. Just like back home in Tripoli.' Hash smiled at Bousaif.

'You come from Tripoli?' Bousaif asked.

'Born and bred.'

'Me, too.' Bousaif stirred his tea, pressing at the mint leaves. Then he pointed at the menu, indicating. 'Margherita.' Hash took the menu. 'Good choice. I'll join you.' He dialled the takeaway and placed the order. 'Thirty minutes,' he said to Bousaif. 'Feel free to pray whenever you need.' Bousaif held up his glass and took another sip, enjoying the tea.

'It's Epsom, definitely,' Hash told Sean. 'They've sacked the first plan, by the sound of it. This guy's not interested. He just pulled out his ticket for The Queen's Stand on Derby Day.'

'When's that?' Sean said.

'This Saturday, the big race is at four-thirty. He doesn't even want to do a recce.'

'He'll be going for HM, then. Maybe I should get something on at the bookies while the odds are good,' Sean said.

'He can't hope to get her, but just being close and getting

fifty dead and a hundred injured will do,' Hash said.

'It'll be horrific,' Sean said.

'That's what they're going for.'

'The sick bastards,' Sean said. 'Four and a half days to go. What do you do now?'

'Help him,' Hash said, 'or else. Can you get over?' Hash could hear him swallowing and spitting.

'I need you, mate.'

'Whenever you call me "mate", I know you've got plans which involve getting me killed. It's all part of your unique charm, Darky.'

'Come on,' Hash said, 'you know what I mean.'

'It's no-go. You'll have to do it by yourself. Maybe Siddiq and your other mate will step up.'

'Shit,' Hash muttered.

'How's Jim?'

'They've beaten him. I saw the photo, black eyes and one side of his face all swollen.'

'The bastards...' There was coughing from the other end, a long, sustained bout.

'They're preparing Jim for something'.

CHAPTER 23

TUESDAY 2ND JUNE

At breakfast, in contrast to the mute Pakistani, Bousaif, with his occasional question and alert eyes, was a chatterbox. The man kept his Koran and prayer beads to hand; Hash and Bruno had been awakened by the murmur of prayer in the early morning, but he had kept to his room until called down. He immediately went to the sitting room and began channel-hopping until he found a football game. Hash had never had time for football and regretted not being able to talk of clubs, players and recent matches. It might have been a way to breach the man's defences, but contriving a sudden clumsy interest was worse. Bruno's irreverent curiosity proved more successful. The pup had stolen one of Bousaif's trainers when the man had been at prayer the previous evening, and far from angering the Muslim it had seemed to charm him. They found each other interesting enough to want to play occasional games, and after breakfast Bousaif had ventured into the garden, lobbing a ball for the pup to fetch.

Inside, Bousaif, like Eva, lingered over the photo gallery in the hallway and on the kitchen dresser. Hash saw how he peered at the Libyan family photo, a smile playing on his face. 'My family,' Hash ventured. 'Tripoli, in the eighties...before you were born.'

'I was born by then, of course,' Bousaif protested mildly. Hash pointed out his father, mother, sisters and nephew. Bousaif took in each name and seemed to get pleasure from the connection to his home city. 'I haven't been home in years,' Hash said. 'When I was deployed they never told me it would be forever. Someone at Ben Gashir said to look forward, never back...now I know what he meant.'

'Allah Kareem,' Bousaif murmured. 'God is good. They could have sent you to Africa.'

'You were at Ben Gashir?' Hash probed. Bousaif looked away from the photograph and met Hash's inquiry with a shake of his head, leaving Hash wondering if that was a denial, or he just did not answer those questions. Hash felt a flash of irritation at being fobbed off so casually. He pointed at the photograph of Jim holding his Spitfire. 'My son, fifteen years old...do you know where he is?' As Bousaif offered the same lazy head-shaking, Hash snapped, 'And the bastards beat him!' Bousaif's eyes hardened. Hash's mobile phone ring broke the impasse.

'I can visit today,' Eva trilled. 'See Bruno, make sure he is OK.'

'That would be great,' Hash started, 'but he is OK and he's out with me all day, looking at two buildings I might be buying. I'm involved in hospitality and all that stuff.' He heard her sigh.

'How about we meet on the racecourse if there's still time?' he offered.

'Boring!' she said. 'Not enough fun.' Hash could imagine her sulking pout. 'Are you pushing me away, Mister Hash?'

'Of course not,' he said, his voice softening. 'I really, really want to see you, to hug you

'You get what you want and now you're not interested.'

'Of course not, Eva. And I want lots more. Do you believe me?'

'Well...' She sounded unconvinced.

'Then come today...spend the day going round two building sites. You'll look gorgeous in one of those yellow vests.'

'This is a shit invitation. You have to marry me before I do these things.'

'How about tonight? I pick you up and we go out to dinner?'

'Then go back to your place?'

Hash thought of her and Bousaif meeting each other in the house. It was getting crowded. 'Could work,' Hash said.

'Nice,' Eva said. 'Very nice...I'll call you later.'

Hash looked at Bousaif. 'Sorry...my girlfriend. I don't want her to come here while you are in the house...safer for everyone.' Bousaif nodded but said nothing. 'If she appears then we tell her you are a student, just staying in Cheltenham, looking for more permanent accommodation.'

'A language student,' Bousaif said, 'studying English in Cheltenham.'

'I know the school, actually,' Hash said, 'in Rodney Road, always full of Omanis and Emiratis. We see them in the mosque.'

He paused, struck by a thought. 'Do you want to come to the mosque? It's small and friendly…good people there.'

Bousaif shook his head. 'Better to stay away from it. Friendly people ask questions, want to offer hospitality…better to stay away.'

'I get upset when I think about my son,' Hash tried again, standing up and fetching a framed portrait of Jim and his first model aircraft. 'He's very young and he will be frightened.' He sat down, pulling his chair round to Bousaif's side. 'He will be sixteen next birthday but he hardly remembers his mother.'

'He looks a good boy. You should be proud.'

'I'm going to kill them, maybe get killed as well, but they will pay with their lives,' Hash said quietly, his eyes still on the photograph. 'I'll kill anyone who tries to get in my way.' Bousaif looked at him evenly. 'I hear what you say. But you don't frighten me, my brother I have my mission.'

THURSDAY 4TH JUNE

Finally meeting Eva on the racecourse lifted his spirits. 'At last,' he exclaimed. 'I thought this would never happen.' He hugged her tightly, enjoying the feel of her body, pliant but strong. He breathed in her scent and planted gentle kisses on her neck, feeling her wriggle with pleasure. She pushed him out at arm's length and complained at his shabby treatment. 'I missed my Hash,' she said. 'First you get me excited then you disappear, keep me waiting.' Bruno had dashed down the hedgerow in pursuit of rabbits. They watched him go then looked at each other again.

'I can read your mind, Mister Hash,' she said. 'You want we make love in this public place with everyone watching? OK...I take my clothes off!' Then she waved a finger under Hash's nose. 'No, you're the gentleman.' She began tugging at Hash's belt. 'I change my mind...you take your clothes off first.' Hash had to stop her digging her hand inside his belt. 'Maybe you're hiding another girlfriend at your house.' She giggled. 'Maybe Mister Hash is playing games with poor Eva, hmmm?'

'Nonsense, Eva,' Hash whispered, holding her wrist, 'there's no one else. I've got too much going on at the moment. I just can't...'

'Eva can get very jealous,' she persisted.

'I can't,' Hash pleaded.

'Can't what? Tell Miss Eva, darling.' She twisted and probed with her fingers. 'Tell miss Eva what the problem is.' A middle-aged couple walking past smiled at the two lovers. Eva giggled softly. 'Always better to be indoors.' Then she pushed him away gently. 'You're lucky because I am busy tonight,' she said, 'otherwise I will come round and kick that other girl out of my house.'

'There is no other girl,' Hash said.

'So how about Saturday? I have the weekend free. My boss is happy with you.'

At the mention of her boss, Hash looked for Bruno. The pup had disappeared. 'Let's go and look for him,' he said, taking her arm.

As they walked she leaned against him. 'So, this son of yours...Jim,' she began slowly, thoughtfully, 'who only calls when he needs money. When did you last speak to him?' The question caught Hash off guard. 'Ages ago.'

'And did you tell him you loved him?' Hash didn't answer.

'Did he tell you he loved you?'

Hash thought about the answers. 'He asked for money. Boys and their dads don't talk about emotions very often.'

'They think only girls use words like "I love you, Dad",' Eva teased. 'If I had to tell Jim something from his father, what would it be?'. 'Come on,' she pressed, 'you have to say it.'

'I would tell him I loved him,' Hash said quietly.

They found Bruno investigating the bramble thickets lining the railway embankment and splashing happily in the stream. Eva pulled out her phone, looked at it and hissed a quiet curse. 'My damn boss.' She held the device up to Hash. 'He needs me for a meeting.'

'Now?'

'Not now, half an hour ago!' she grimaced. 'Always tells me too late.' She looked to the noise of splashing and told Hash, 'You enjoy Bruno and let me go back.' She pulled him to her and planted a long kiss on his lips then turned, making for her car.

The photograph waiting for him had come through while he had been walking Bruno. The blinking light on the Arab BlackBerry was the first thing he noticed as he entered the kitchen. Picking up the device, he opened the file and saw Jim, wearing a baseball cap, staring at the camera holding up an Arab-language newspaper. Hash immediately emailed the image to his own phone and within minutes had it on his computer, zooming in on every detail. The newspaper was the *Sharq al Awsat* printed in the UK and only a few days old. Jim was holding the paper in a way that only his middle fingers were visible, pointing upwards. the peak of the cap, pulled low, kept the boy's face in shadow but Hash could still see blue and yellow tinges around his eye and cheekbone. His anger flared as he saw how haggard he looked. After a long time spent examining Jim's neutral, forced expression, he knew he would only get more and more distressed. He would get grim satisfaction showing the image to Hakim later. The image was at least a gesture wrought from the Mukhabarat, to keep hope alive.

EPSOM

SATURDAY 6TH JUNE

MORNING

Before leaving he had watched Bousaif, standing in the kitchen coolly checking the suicide vest, even asking for his help to test the fit. He seemed as comfortable as his Pakistani predecessor. Then, with the journey underway, the man who was hours away from detonating twelve kilograms of explosives and creating international mayhem, sat calmly watching the English countryside slip past. Hash had reminded him that they must leave early to be sure of getting a closer parking place, one where Bousaif could see the 'Queen's Stand' and make his way. Hash wound the window down for fresh air and to flush out the smell from the vest. Somewhere down the eastbound M4, Bousaif had broken his silence to ask for Hash to wait until the explosion and only leave afterwards. Hash had considered the simple last request, searching his father's repertoire, reflecting how the old man would have dealt with a last wish from a doomed lunatic. His reply in cut-glass English, 'Of course, my dear boy, why ever not?' was met with a half-smile from Bousaif who sensed the irony but was content simply that his wish was understood.

'Now I have a request,' Hash said, 'My son, Jim...have a look at his picture, it's a good one.' Hash juggled the wheel and his mobile, finding the shot of Jim. He held it across for Bousaif to see. 'This boy...my son!' he began. 'Did not deserve to be involved, did not deserve to be beaten. The people who did this are pigs and have no values. Are the people who did this good Muslims?' Bousaif looked at the image and slowly shook his head. Hash pressed the advantage. 'Now that the mission is running and there is no turning back...can you as a brother Libyan, who believes in family, at least help me?'

Bousaif switched his gaze back to the landscape. 'What can I do?'

'Do you know where he is now, how I can get to him?'

Bousaif looked at Hash, shrugging 'You will see him, insh'Allah.'

'When, my brother?'

'If you are a true Muslim and he is, too, then you will meet him.'

Hash shook his head. 'He is a boy. I worry about him now,

about his health, his mind. Do you have any information on him?'

Bousaif considered for a moment, then slowly shook his head. 'None.'

'Can you understand? Is it right, that a child is held hostage?' Are you a father yourself?'

Bousaif had hoisted the drawbridge of silence. His eyes staying on the passing countryside. Hash gave up.

When they reached the racecourse, signs took them to the public parking where they got as close as they could to the grandstand. Following the attendants' directions they parked at the end of a row of already empty cars. Hash eased his seat into a reclining position, motioning Bousaif to do the same, then pulled a plastic shopping bag forward from the rear seat and placed bottles of water, fruit and biscuits on the dashboard. Bousaif had explained they would wait there all day, until he knew it was time.

Hash knew the Derby, scheduled to run at around four-thirty, was more than six hours away, time he would be spending trapped with Bousaif and with his hands off his mobile phone. After being among the first to arrive, Hash and Bousaif watched the car park fill up. Racegoers in their fine clothes extracted themselves from their vehicles, preened and set off for the members' enclosures. Others less expensively dressed walked eagerly to the gates. Hash had not expected a funfair to be operating on the other side of the fence, obscuring the last hundred or so metres of the racetrack. He was surprised to see the rides in full swing even this early. The smell of frying onions wafted over on the gentle breeze and around midday some groups came back and made a picnic around the boots of their estate cars. Hash watched how they laid out their wooden tables, placed champagne in an ice bucket, and put on the show of a sumptuous banquet under the bluest of skies. These were good people, the British at leisure. He could not resist turning to Bousaif, who was also watching them, and commenting, 'Filthy kufar.' Again if Bousaif felt the irony he did not show it. Instead, hoisting Bruno onto his lap, he soothed the pup then closed his eyes.

Hash must also have dozed, waking intermittently as the background noises, the rise and fall of cheering and tannoyed announcements, charted progress towards the big race. At three-thirty Hash finally pointed to the clock on the dashboard. Bousaif sat up and, rubbing his face with his hands, whispered a short prayer to himself. He got out of the vehicle and went to the rear door. Hash appeared beside him and pulled the door open. Inside, still in the roll-on suitcase, was the vest. Quickly, and with Hash keeping watch across the sea of cars, Bousaif pulled the waistcoat out of the case and laid it on the tailgate. Looking around, Hash checked they were completely alone, unobserved. Bousaif's fingers flicked across the garment, more thoroughly now than he had done in the kitchen a few hours earlier, pulling back Velcro tabs, satisfying himself once more that all was where it should be. Hash watched him pay particular attention to the power pack, an old-school but foolproof combination of a pair of connected cylindrical alkaline batteries. Hash sensed the man's hesitation as he contemplated the two inanimate objects which would send the lethal charge of electricity to the detonator. He reached into the breast pocket of the waistcoat and pulled out a roll of black wire which he uncoiled. Hash could see it ended in a plastic syringe. Looking at it, he could see a crude plastic collar keeping the plunger top from closing flush with the cylinder. Red electrical tape, a single strand, easy to tear off, kept it from moving. Hash knew this was the safety catch, and when Bousaif was ready he would just rip off the tape, flick away the collar and press the plunger home.

Bousaif let the lead dangle as he lifted up the waistcoat. Then he put it on, adjusting his arms, shaking the waistcoat with his torso. He felt for the straps that would tighten it to his body. Bousaif held the swinging lead and then pointed at the Barbour jacket they had bought earlier in the week. The sun had gone well past its highest point, but the day was still warm enough for Bousaif to look overdressed. They had agreed the risk was minimal as most people would be jostling for position to watch the big race, and overdressed foreigners at Epsom were not unusual. Bousaif gently pulled on the coat, holding the lead in his right hand and threading that arm first through the sleeve. Once it was through, he let the plunger swing free and pulled on the rest of the jacket. In the distance loudspeakers at the racecourse were beginning to charge the atmosphere, drumming up excitement. The commentator kept up a stream of race statistics, listing facts, figures, the runners and the odds. He looked at Bousaif putting on a tweed cap. There was sweat on the man's face and Hash momentarily imagined clubbing the man down, killing him just as he had killed the Pakistani before Cheltenham. Bousaif presented himself for inspection, as if seeking Hash's approval. Both men shook hands.

'May God forgive you,' Hash said.

'May God return your son, my brother,' Bousaif said before turning and walking towards the gate that would let him in. Hash calculated he would be entering as the race started, when there would be nobody in the queue and the assistant on the turnstile would practically pull him through so he himself could concentrate on the race. Standing on the rear bumper to watch his man, he let Bousaif get two hundred yards and across the road, then began to follow. There was just the chance the Libyan group would gather for a last-minute brief before Bousaif made his final approach. Hash moved cautiously, preparing to duck behind a car if he saw Bousaif. Up ahead he saw a sign for the Lonsdale Enclosure and caught the movement of a punter stumbling. A woman, maybe tipsy or trying to walk too fast in a dress that was too tight. There was something about her that seemed familiar. In her haste to get to the enclosure she hauled at the shoulder of her companion, a man, elegantly dressed, who obligingly put his arm around her waist. Her wide, pink hat had slipped and she took it off as she was moving, shook her hair and looked around as if embarrassed at her performance. Hash knew he was looking at Anna. In a split second the woman had turned away, hat replaced, and was allowing her companion to steer her to the ticket barrier. Within seconds she and her escort were through the turnstile and disappearing, walking away in animated conversation. Hash crossed the road to keep them in sight, wondering if his eyes had deceived him: it had been a long day and he wanted to believe there was a chance of Jim being close. Anna's presence fuelled his suspicions to the extent he momentarily considered buying a ticket from a tout and following her in. Then he realised the move could get him trapped in any security clampdown. Instead, he headed back to his vehicle.

As he walked he called Siddiq.

'Are you at Epsom?'

'Sorry, my friend,' Siddiq said. 'Anna had a last-minute business appointment. Something in London. So we did not go.'

'Did she take the tickets I sent you? What was all the fuss about Epsom and The Queen? I've spent a fortune on your tickets.'

'No, she left this morning. She was angry with me…Oh God…these European women.' Then he started talking about Hakim.

'Not good news,' Siddiq said. 'Hakim's team followed them out of Birmingham but lost them somewhere. Maybe the drivers can tell us later.'

'Later is no good.'

'He's looking for you.'

'Give him my number, I'm away from home but I need to hear anything, anything at all from Hakim.' Hash rang off. Mindful of Bruno in the vehicle, he strode for the Discovery. He would not be hanging around too long. In the background, the voice on the loudspeaker was now tense and frantic with a non-stop flow. Hash looked at his watch: four-twenty-five. Jim and his minders were off the map, last seen heading south out Birmingham, maybe linking with Anna. Maybe Hakim's men had sighted the woman in western dress and would report in soon. This was why she was lying to Siddiq.

The 2015 Derby started to a massive, surging release of tension. A tumult of cheering welled out from the stands and over the tannoy. Hash felt his mouth go dry: this was a short and furious race. He was bracing himself, wondering if Bousaif was elbowing his way to the front of the rails, maybe looking back up at the stand to glimpse the British Queen and then clambering over the rails to get closer? Hash knew he would not get close, but twelve kilos of high explosive would vaporise anyone in the vortex and blow out a storm of shattered debris. The carnage would be indescribable and hundreds of cameras would capture it: then replay it forever, first the curious, figure scrambling over the barriers, then a pulse of shock wave, then the flash and that massive, final thundercrack detonation. Hash's dryness turned to nausea and he reached for a bottle of water to sluice out his throat. He heard the excitement as the race commentator yelled into the microphone, reeling off a stream of names and numbers in a hysterical crescendo. Hash felt his shoulders hunching, ready to flinch. Suddenly he felt the earth trembling beneath his feet and a rumbling, rushing sound from across the road to his left. The drumming of hooves pounding the turf seemed like an approaching avalanche hidden by the row of tents, and he imagined the tornado of colour and straining flanks thundering past heading for the roaring, packed grandstand. The commentator, now shrieking with excitement, babbled the names of the leaders and in one last climactic gasp the name of the winner. Hash just managed to catch the name of the Golden Horn before an explosion crashed over everything.

CHAPTER 24

It was an explosion of jubilation, a primal roar of celebration and it lasted for a full five seconds before dying away to let the commentator take up again. Hash did not catch the second and third places. For a moment he wondered if the bomb could have detonated only to be drowned out by the crowd. But he would have felt the shock and seen the smoke. Bousaif had stayed his hand and was choosing a better moment. Hash imagined him burrowing through the crowd working towards the paddock, getting to the rail to set up for The Queen at the prize-giving ceremony. There was still buzzing excitement in the commentator's voice as he repeated facts, timings and names. Hash imagined him keeping an eye on the prize-giving dais, an attendant beside him talking to royal officials, monitoring The Queen's progress, getting the timing right. He guessed Bousaif was in position. The red tape would have been torn away and the thumb and index finger twisting at the plastic collar on the plunger. He wondered if he would yell

'Allahu Akbar' as he closed the plunger in his fist.

His phone rang. It was Sean. 'Any news?'

'Could happen at any moment,' Hash said. 'The bastard's out there, still going for it…out of our hands.'

Sean said, 'I can come over soon.'

Hash was not listening, his eyes were trying to process new information to his tired mind.

'Are you listening?' Sean's voice was positive, cheerful even.

'Are you listening, Darky? Say something.'

Hash tore his eyes away from what was coming and concentrated on the phone, 'Can't talk. SMS me.' He closed the call and stood up. Bousaif, walking fast, threading through the rows of parked cars, was steaming towards the Discovery. He saw Hash and circled his finger in the air, signalling, 'Let's get moving.' Hash jumped in, switching on the engine. Bousaif kept heading towards the car but did not turn into the lane where the Discovery was parked. Instead he walked past, jerking his head to Hash, urging him to catch him on the move. Hash reversed the vehicle onto the exit route, passing alongside Bousaif who wrenched the door open and jumped in. Hash could see he was pouring with sweat and breathing hard. He sat, staring ahead, his eyes wide with shock and fear. Bruno immediately leapt for his friend.'

'What happened?'

'Nothing.'

'Don't let that bloody dog set anything off!…' Hash pointed at Bousaif's right arm, held stiffly across his body, 'Is it still live?' Hash could see by the sweat and the way Bousaif held himself that something was badly wrong. He guessed the crude red tape safety collar was lying on the ground somewhere near The Queen's Stand, which meant a vest full of primed explosive waiting for a voluntary or accidental command from Bousaif's clenched, dripping fist.

'Batteries dead?' Hash asked. 'Do you want me to fix it?' He got no answer. Hash started to get animated, 'If it's live, either you fix it, or you let me fix it.' There was still no reaction from Bousaif who sat staring ahead. Hash leaned across and crashed his open palm on the dashboard making Bousaif jump at the impact. 'Let me fix it…now!' Hash yelled. The Discovery seemed to have pulled itself into a lay-by.

'OK,' Bousaif whispered, melting with fatigue. Hash could see he was shaking. 'Hold your arm to me, don't do anything else, keep your fingers off the syringe.'

TRIPOLI. 7TH JUNE.
PLASMA HOTEL.

'You go first.' The older man pushed back in his seat, indicating with a flourish of his hand that the ISIS Director of European Operations had the floor. The meeting in the same suite with the same players had the same simmering acrimony. Refreshments ferried in earlier lay untouched, but the aide poured tea into long glasses. Outside in the street the temperature stood at forty-five degrees centigrade with eighty percent humidity. In the room, the ageing air conditioning system attempted to cool the anger and mutual suspicion.

'You explain…' the Director began only to be immediately silenced by the same hand raised in caution.

'No,' the older man said quietly, 'we followed instructions. Better you explain!'

'Our plan was frustrated at the last moment by a technicality,' the Director stated. 'Your man did not read the situation in advance.'

'Men in his position live a precarious life and do not have the luxury of always reading situations in advance. We should have been looking at a huge success.' He pointed to the CNN newsreader on the TV screen. 'Look…nothing to celebrate.'

'We're doing damage control… again,' the aide added. 'Our man does not think Bousaif was compromised or followed.'

'We gave you our best man at this end and tied him up with our man in the UK,' the older man said. 'The rest was up to your team commander.'

'It appears there was a problem with access to the particular area of the racecourse,' the aide said. 'We're hearing the operator could not get in because he wasn't wearing the correct dress.'

The older man looked out of the window, pointing east to Sirte. 'What do you actually do, over there in Ghardabiya? Surely your acclimatisation training is better than this?'

'We were using British brothers who know the British customs.'

'Then they should have known the correct dress codes.'

The Director was stung. 'We also had a technical problem and we're still checking on it.' He picked up his tea glass and drank, then settled back into his seat. 'The boy.'

The older man contemplated the ISIS man. 'Don't tell me… the boy ran away.'

'He lost control of the drone with the camera.'

'Lost it completely? So…we supply another.'

'He got it to a thousand feet, we had it steady and really clear video on the camera. Then he lost control.'

'What happened?'

The Director said, 'The winds at that height were different, too strong and just took the machine away with them.'

'You need a more powerful machine,' the old man said. 'How did you clean it up?'

'The machine has a default setting which commands it to drop and hover at about four feet. Luckily we got to it first.'

'So, it was nothing to do with the dress code,' the aide said.

'A combination, and bad luck,' the Daesh Director said.

The older man mimed applause. 'From our side, the mission still intact.' He watched for the visitor's reaction. 'Do you agree?'

'The plan is still good,' the Director said.

'We have a fallback option, of course,' the aide confirmed gently. 'The next big horse racing event is Ascot.' He checked the date on his watch. 'Only ten days away.'

'What about the boy?' the old man asked. 'You need to keep him positive. He needs to want to keep doing all this.'

'We will handle it our way,' the Director said.

'You need to assist me, here. What do we pass on to the father?'

'The ISIS Director fingered his prayer beads for a few seconds. 'Leave it as it stands. You've got the father working to save his son,' he said, 'we're doing the reverse...the boy's been told he's doing all this to save his father.'

CHAPTER 25

CHELTENHAM 9TH JUNE.

When Sean emerged at Arrivals, Hash was shocked to see his friend had lost some of the bulk in his frame. Instead of the easy, athletic prowl he seemed to trudge wearily as though his overnight case weighed a ton.

'Mind if I burn one?' Sean asked as he clipped on his seat belt.

'If you must,' Hash said.

Sean patted his scalp. His hair had thinned drastically. 'What do you think of my new look?'

Hash comforted him. 'I can get you a wig.'

'An Afro?' Sean lit up and inhaled, relishing the hit. He breathed out a slow stream of smoke. Hash broke his concentration on the motorway to buzz down the window, flushing out the fumes. 'Don't give me that Holy Joe shit,' Sean said. 'Been cooped up at no-smoking since I hit Aldergrove four hours ago...how would you possibly know how good this tastes?'

'Our new friend bottled it at Epsom,' Hash said. 'He seemed fine on the journey, all martyr-like and resolute. I got him vested up and pointed in the right direction.' Sean's wracking cough stopped him. He watched Sean pitch forward, veins bulging in his neck as he fought for breath. When the spasm had passed he wiped a fleck of spittle from his lips and looked across. 'That,' he croaked, 'would have killed a Prod.'

'I saw Anna there, too.'

'Siddiq's bunny boiler?'

'But she was without Siddiq. He told me she was in London at a meeting. She's got to be involved.'

'What happened?'

'Nothing. The big race, nothing, then the prize-giving, still nothing. The next thing I see is our man galloping back,' Hash pointed at Sean's seat. 'I get him on-board. He's in a trance, white as a sheet.'

What was his problem?'

'He got held up at the turnstile, some attendant pointed at his trainers. Etiquette...dress code.'

'Living to fight another day.'

'Hakim's come up with an address,' Hash said. 'Brilliant effort.'

'Or another set-up.'

'I'm getting Hakim on-board, bit by bit,' Hash said. 'He was in the mujahideen, fighting Al Qaeda, at Tora Bora...remember, after 911?'

I remember.

'His little brother was executed on the orders of some Arab fighters.' Sean wound the window down and jettisoned the cigarette butt. 'That's why he doesn't like Arabs.'

'So, it's not just you, then.' Sean grinned.

'Jim and the kid brother were the same age.'

'He saw how Jim was standing up to the pain, taking it on the chin.'

'I'll show you a photo.' Hash reached for his mobile, juggling it and the steering wheel to scroll through his pictures. 'Here.' He passed the phone across to Sean who examined it, a scowl spreading across his face. 'The bastards,' he whispered.

In the flat, after climbing the stairs, Hash saw Sean moving more slowly than usual. He looked pale and tired. 'Something to please you, in that cupboard…take a look.' Hash pointed to the drinks cabinet. 'It's vintage, one I've been saving for a very special occasion. Got to be at least thirty years old.' Sean did as commanded, walking over, opening the door and stooping to look in. 'My absolute favourite,' he exclaimed, pleasure on his face. 'You remembered, you old devil.'

'Take it out,' Hash said. 'You know you want to.'

'Really…can I?'

Hashed waved him on. 'Knock yourself out.'

Sean ducked down to the cabinet and carefully drew out the Kalashnikov, holding it at arm's length, turning it over, admiring it. 'Brand new,' he whispered.

'There's something extra,' Hash said, 'deeper in, at the back.'

'More? Sean was incredulous. 'A magazine? You sly dog. Nothing looks better on a Kalashnikov than a loaded magazine.'

'Look, deeper in,' Hash said. Sean bent down again, looking, then stood up. 'Would you bloody well stop!' He gasped in mock delight, reaching in to retrieve a sleek, black Tokarev. Holding it up to the light, turning the weapon in his hand, slipping out the magazine, racking the mechanism. 'I'm assuming you do actually have the ammo.'

'Limited but enough.'

Sean fitted the magazine, held the pistol to his forehead and squeezed the trigger, blinking at the metallic click, 'Ouch…that could have hurt!'

'Please,' Hash said. 'No party tricks…maybe save that for later.'

Indoors, after Hash's quiet but insistent call, Bousaif emerged from his room and came downstairs. He looked drawn: creases on his face told Hash he had been sleeping. He was pale, as though his Libyan summer tan was wearing off. Hash guessed the trauma of near death at Epsom was taking its toll. Bruno, alert and eager for attention, left Hash and greeted Bousaif, nipping at his outstretched hand. 'Are you OK?' Hash asked.

'I am tired,' Bousaif said. 'I was sleeping. Someone came looking for you.'

'Who?'

'A woman came.' Bousaif slumped on a kitchen chair, looking at the kettle. 'Asking for you. She said she is your friend, Eva… some name like that.'

'What did she want?'

Bousaif shrugged it off as though it was trivial, 'To say hello, talk with you.' He tickled Bruno's neck. 'Nothing special. She says this is her dog.' Bousaif put on a puzzled look. 'I told her this is your dog. She wanted to take Bruno but the dog would not go.'

'It's her boss's dog,' Hash corrected. 'The deal is I look after Bruno because she doesn't like dogs.' They both looked at Bruno enjoying the attention from Bousaif. 'What did you tell her?'

Bousaif began a sing-song, 'I am a language student, you are my host. I'm waiting to get my course paid, then I start soon.'

'Did you tell her where you come from?'

'Are you crazy?'

'Yes, darling, I missed you. Eva was upset so she came to your house because she misses her Hash.'

He had stepped into the garden to make the call. 'But you're OK, not angry with me?'

'Not angry but upset, because I can't see you.'

'Of course you can see me, I can meet you now, anywhere but in my house.'

'Why? I been to your house. You have a student there, we talked. He's a very nice boy. He likes staying with you.'

'I can come and see you now,' Hash repeated. 'Tell me where you are.'

'No good, darling. Too late, even for Eva,' she said. 'I am busy with my boss, anyway.'

'How about tomorrow? I can come to your place.'

'The student will be here.'

'All day? Send him away.'

'It's difficult with him, he doesn't go out, sits inside watching TV. Then he asks to practise his English. I have to give him lessons.'

'Sometimes I think you're pushing Eva away,' she teased. 'Hash…it's not fair.'

CHAPTER 26

At the morning rendezvous, Sean's face was pale and he was in pain. He eased himself into the Discovery carefully, the smell of tobacco hung about him, but no trace of alcohol. He spent the first seconds coughing into a handkerchief, then he cleared his throat. 'Where did they go?' he said.

'Hakim's saying they upped and left Sparkbrook in the evening. They went separately, Jim and the woman in the red Citroën and the two men in the BMW. But they linked up at some garage on the A34 and went on down the M40 as a pair. He thinks they've gone to ground in Earls Court.'

'Sean said, 'That's not near Ascot.'

'But it's on the right side of London...same distance from Brum to Cheltenham Races.'

'We need another vehicle, Running around in your old Discovery won't do.'

'I'm working on it,' Hash said. 'Hakim's waiting to see me at the mosque,' Hash said. 'Want to come?'

'You have to be circumcised to go into one of those things, don't you?' Sean said. 'I'll pass.'

'I've got a task for you, mate.'

'That word again...'

'I'll drop you off with this little bugger.' He jerked a thumb at Bruno in the back. 'Take him for a nice walk but keep your phone camera handy. I'll tell you what you're waiting for. But it's obvious.'

Sean watched Hash enjoying a private joke. 'I assume this is all really necessary?'

'I don't think you'll be disappointed.'

After leaving Sean standing looking doubtful, attached to Bruno, Hash pulled out of the car park on Birdlip Hill and made his way back down Leckhampton Hill into town. He had called Wilma, his long-suffering secretary, telling her she was in charge while he went to London for a short business trip.

Hakim smiled for the first time Hash could remember. Siddiq hovered, about to say something, but Hakim sent him to bring tea.

When the door had closed, Hakim gestured to a chair and they sat. 'They are in Earls Court,' he began. 'And don't ask me for the address, yet.'

'If you lose them I've got no hope of finding Jim in London.'

'Go on,' Hakim said.

'I think you know who these people are,' Hash continued. 'They're an Al Qaeda cell and they're planning a mass attack at one of these horse racing meetings, and soon. I think it's Ascot.

We stopped them attacking Cheltenham. Then they went for Epsom but called it off at the last moment.' Hash saw Hakim flinch.

'Who is we?'

'I'll come to that,' Hash tried to dodge the question. 'Ascot is world-famous and only days away, and The Queen will attend. These bastards are using my son…they need him for some…'

'They need you,' Hakim emphasised, jabbing a finger at him. 'These people are using you! Yes, they have your son. But first, it is you. Who are you? Why are they using you?'

'I am no friend of Al Qaeda's, Daesh, the Brotherhood, or any of those lunatics,' Hash said. 'And you have to believe me.' Hash wished Siddiq was at hand to support him. 'I have a past life, one I am ashamed of. I thought I had escaped from it, left it in a room and closed the door, just as you did in the mujahideen. But I did not close that door properly.' He matched Hakim's gaze. 'And now the past has slipped out to follow me and call in a debt. They,' he pointed out of the window, 'the men and the woman you have found with my son, are the devils from that room. I despise and I hate them, but they have my son.'

'They are Arabs, for sure.' It was the first time Hash recalled Hakim agreeing with him. 'Maybe Al Qaeda, maybe Daesh.' Hakim flipped a hand back and forth. 'We are not sure yet. We have seen where they get their support, which mosques, which imams.' He fixed his eyes on Hash. 'If you are an outcast from their organisation then I cannot help you anymore.'

'I am an Arab and I'm proud of that. I am not the best Muslim, but I'm better than the scum who have my son.' Hash spoke urgently, 'What I know about Al Qaeda fills me with shame that they share my religion.' Hakim looked at him in frosty silence. 'Give me your word,' he said.

'I swear it.' Hash held his hand to Hakim. There was a further silence as Hakim considered the value of Hash's word. Then he reached across and shook hands with him.

'Look at this picture.' Hash unfolded a sheet of A4 and laid it in front of Hakim and Siddiq. They leaned forward to look at Jim holding the newspaper.

'The boy's fingers…' Hakim was chuckling for the first time. 'He's showing defiance, this boy…this young man.' They looked round to congratulate but Hash had turned away, his shoulders heaving. They waited.

'May God help him to stay strong,' Siddiq said.

'May God give the father some of his son's courage,' Hakim added.

'Let me know when I can go in and rescue my son. Soon, before they change addresses.' Hash pounded his fist into his palm. 'I will go in and stop them, or I will die in the attempt. You can help me save my son and hundreds of innocent people.'

'You will do this all by yourself? You have nobody to help you?'

'If I must, Sayyid Hakim. How can I best explain it?' Hash looked at them. 'I said the door was not properly closed and maybe, because I am desperate now, I have to slip back into that room myself.'

'Is that why you offered me a weapon?'

'Yes.'

Hakim eased back in the chair. 'My promise to your son is this. I will do as you ask. As soon as I have the address and, only' – he held up his hand – 'when I am ready, all my men out of the way, I will pass it to you. But...' Again he held up his finger. 'I will not take the weapon you are offering and I did not even hear this offer. 'And if' – he pointed at Hash's chest – 'Insh'Allah you are successful and you rescue your son then we will meet again and we will be happy together.' He looked harder at Hash. 'But no killing! This country took me in when I was poor. The British gave me the hand of friendship when I had no friends. They taught me to play straight bat. So, my friend...I tell you now, if anyone is killed, then I will go to the police.'

AFTERNOON

Sean was grinning from ear to ear when Hash rolled to a halt. He took a last drag on his cigarette and flicked the butt away as the window buzzed down. 'You were right about the views,' Sean said. He waved out across towards Gloucester and May Hill. 'Gorgeous sights!'

'And the wildlife?' Hash asked. 'As exciting as I promised?' Hash got out to hoist Bruno on-board and hold the door for Sean. Getting comfortable, Sean breathed out. 'I'm amazed at the birdlife up here...must be something in the air.'

'The place is famous for nesting couples, usually more active at night: you were lucky to get them in daytime.'

'Whatever...' Sean said. 'The UN should declare it a World

Heritage Site.'

'Did you see the tits?'

'Bruno was traumatised by what he saw,' Sean said.

'Let me see, then,' Hash said.

'Hang on, you old pervert.' Sean pulled out his phone. 'Shit,' he whispered, looking at the phone, shaking it. 'The bloody thing's died on me.' He looked up at Hash. 'Can you bloody well believe that?'

'Pull the other one,' Hash laughed.

'Are you sitting comfortably?' Sean said. 'Then we'll begin.' The screen steadied as a view of the woodland and parking area came into focus. The lens zoomed in on a silver Audi estate with the familiar Help for Heroes and Carry on Hunting stickers in the rear window. He saw the conman climb out from the driver's seat and the pretty girlfriend from the car park emerge from the other side. They embraced against the back of the vehicle, enjoying minutes of kissing. 'My God, you're the pervert, to have got that close,' Hash said.

'By the time they got started, you could have marched a brass band past and they wouldn't have noticed.'

Back in Sean's flat they started packing the weapons and Sean's few belongings. 'The problem with that woman,' Sean observed as Hash picked up his phone, 'is that she's too tough for your mate.' He looked into his small suitcase, tossing in items of clothing, 'Do we actually know who she is, where she comes from?' Hash was looking at his phone, concentrating on an SMS. 'Stupid old girl,' he said.

'Harsh, mate, she's good-looking.' Sean picked up his glass of whiskey and breathed in the scent of the liquid. 'She's anything but stupid.'

'I meant this old girl.' Hash tapped the phone. 'She wants me to do her sitting for her on the 12th.' Hash looked up, muttering, 'Stupid cow but I'll have to do it for her...got no choice.' He stopped when he saw Sean grinning down at him. 'I can't believe you, Darky.'

'What?'

'Fucking magistrate, you...your boy at a private school, the pink shirts and posh suits, the signet ring...what happened to wee Darky, off that fucking boat, shitting himself, frozen?'

'Still the same Darky,' Hash said.

'You've done well, fair play to you.'

'Have I? Hash said. 'I thought I'd outrun them, outlived Gaddafi and his madness.'

'How the hell did they keep such close tabs on you...all these years?'

'The team running my letter box,' Hash sipped his whiskey. 'The only logical answer. They've shadowed my life, our life. Kept me supplied, kept the line open to Tripoli.' Compromise the box and they kill me or Jim...or Flora if she'd been alive. He snapped his fingers. 'Then they brought me out of hibernation.' He was lost in his own train of thought. 'They would have known Jim from the racecourse and his models, the dogs, our whole life.' He looked at Sean and drained his tumbler. 'Another one?' He poured generously without waiting for an answer. 'Jim gets snatched. All of a sudden my devout friend has a man-eater on his hands, running him ragged.' He sighed. 'Bomber, woman in burqa…' His arm swept across the gleaming Kalashnikovs. 'And now this stuff…I'm back to square one. Play the game or die.'

'She sounds like a psycho,' Sean said, 'the type who owns you just because you happened to shag her once. She knew about Jim, didn't she?'

'Siddiq told her.'

'She appeared out of the blue. Dumped your mate after the Gold Cup, then reappears at the Derby. Are you joining the dots?'

'I am, but Siddiq brought Hakim.'

'How do you know for sure?'

'I don't,' Hash conceded.

'Is she the one in the red car and in the burqa?'

'That makes her the one who hit Jim,' Hash said.

'And that makes it personal.' Sean picked up one of the AK-47s and took off the magazine. He checked the rounds, pressing them down on the magazine. 'This spring's good after all these years.'

'Insh'Allah,' Hash said.

'I'm still good after all these years.' Sean winked at Hash, lifting his glass. 'Sláinte, Darky.' Then he fitted the magazine back on and wrapped the first weapon in a towel. He held up the Tokarev, looking at it. 'Ugly, isn't it?' He wrapped the pistol then picked up the first grenade and tried to unscrew the base plug, grunting at the effort. 'Must be gummed tight after all the time underground. Got a pair of pliers?' Hash fetched the pliers and watched as Sean wrestled the base plugs off and laid out the innards of the two grenades, 'if they work at all: it's pull, throw and get the head down, two seconds, maybe three.' He started to reassemble them. 'Look.' He held up the pliers. 'I'll pinch the end of the pins so they pull easier…give them a dab of oil, too.'

'Your time in the Kesh wasn't wasted.'

'Always happy to do your dirty work, Hash…you know me.' He slid the grenades into the Jameson whiskey tube. Hash heard them clunk on top of each other. 'Although, give credit where credit is due, you did actually kill that Paki all by yourself…no wait.' 'Susan and the dog tired him out. You just finished him off.'

'So, how are Bella and the old boy? Did you go and see them?'

'I bloody knew that was coming next,' Sean slumped in the kitchen chair and took out his cigarettes.

'How did it go?'

'Not very well. They don't want to see me, there's nothing more to say, nothing we can do.'

'They know you're ill, don't they?'

'You told them, not me.' Sean took out a cigarette and lit up, exhaling, his eyes following the stream of blue smoke. 'A judgement from God, were her words. The old boy didn't get it at first. Then he did his usual, started to cry and she tells me I've put him under the stress. All my fault. So, then I leave and drive all the way back to Belfast. I was only there for fifteen minutes but I got a cup of tea.'

'Christ…' Hash whispered, 'I'm so sorry for you.'

'Don't be, I know how my mother feels. When I look at myself in the morning I hate myself, too.'

'I'm sorry, Sean.'

'What's it say about sympathy?' Sean smiled at Hash. 'You'll find it in the dictionary…somewhere between shit and syphilis.'

'You told them you're doing this for Jim, their only grandson, didn't you? I told you to.'

'Can't remember if I did or not.' Sean drew on his cigarette.

'Bullshit,' Hash said. 'I wanted them to know.'

'Yeah, I think you told them that, too. Thanks for trying. Look, Darky.' Sean put his glass down and leaned towards his friend. 'The thing about our game.' He stabbed a nicotine-stained finger at the wrapped up AK-47. 'You can join but you can never leave.' He eased back. 'You've done well, Darky. You're the only one I know who got away with his mind in one piece, in the nick of time.'

'I didn't get away. Maybe I've had better luck than you, Sean,' Hash said. 'I had a better deal…until now.'

'I never regretted joining,' Sean said, 'and in the same circumstances I'd do it all over again, but…' He looked out of the window. 'When you get blood on your hands it never quite washes off, does it?'

'We were in a war,' Hash said.

'Innocent blood.' Sean continued staring at Hash for a few seconds, then stubbed his cigarette out.

'We're doing this for innocent Jim,' Hash said, 'your nephew, your sister Flora's son, their grandson,' he added gently. 'So that you can do the most that's humanly possible to set things right.' Sean sat, elbows on the table, head in hands. Hash saw a tremor in the hands, his knuckles whitening as they kneaded his eyebrows and forehead.

'You've got this chance,' Hash said softly. 'We pull it off

and we can walk away our heads held high. If we fail, at least we did more than most people would have even dared,' Hash said. 'That's what you're bringing to this whole thing, Sean,' he added. 'I couldn't do this without you. People like you don't come along every day. You're here for a purpose.'

EVENING

'There he goes, 'Sean said, 'just got in … starting her up.'

'Jump in … let's go.'

Sean led Bruno across the grass to where Hash had the Discovery idling and hoisted the pup into the cargo area. They let the silver Audi move into the light evening traffic, then tracked it, following the telltale stickers in the rear window.

'Not steering for town,' Hash muttered. They had rehearsed the moves in their minds but both were tense as they played it for real. Hash kept the Audi in sight for a few hundred yards then began closing on it. He was not sure how soon the driver would turn off in the direction of a client or his girlfriend, and he knew he had to force the pace. By the time they had reached the traffic lights at the junction with the High Street, Hash was directly behind the silver car. It headed across the junction at College Road only to be held up by a pedestrian crossing with the lights on red.

'Now,' Sean urged.

Hash slipped the clutch on the Discovery and it lurched forward to hit the rear of the Audi. It was a perfectly judged bump, hard enough to shock, but without any damage. Both men saw the driver's bald head bouncing back then shaking in anger and disbelief.

'You've really pissed him off,' Sean said. He slipped out of the passenger seat and made for the Audi. Hash pulled out and slowly overtook the car, coming to a stop a few parking spaces ahead. The drivers queuing behind began to filter past, gawping as they went, the first ones smiling and the remainder interested only in getting past. To keep other witnesses away, Sean went to the man's window and waved passers-by on. 'I saw it,' he told the driver. 'I saw it all, no problems, mate.'

'You should have,' the bald driver said, 'you were in the fucking car. Is the other guy blind or something? And he's not supposed to drive off...that's leaving the scene of an accident.'

'You're right, mate,' Sean said, 'blind as a bat. Wasn't paying attention, his fault. He says he's coming over as soon as he parks.'

'Tossers!' the man hissed. 'You've been drinking, haven't you?'

'Just a few, mate. It'll be alright,' Sean said. 'Are you OK, mate? No cuts and bruises?'

'Probably got whiplash,' the man said, rubbing his neck 'That was a hell of a bump.'

'Not much damage,' Sean said, 'just a wee bump, not even a scratch.'

As the man got out to inspect his rear bumper, Hash caught up with him.

'Sorry, my friend, all my fault,' he began. 'You stopped a bit too soon, that bloody pedestrian crossing.' He smacked his forehead with his hand. 'Damn, I wasn't quick enough.' The man looked up from the bumper inspection: he hardly focused on Hash's face, his irritation driving him. 'That's a body job for sure...could be an insurance write-off.'

'No problem, my friend. My fault, blame me. I'll pay. Just let me have your bank account and I'll transfer the money.'

The man rubbed his neck and turned his head slowly from side to side as though doing an exercise. 'Doesn't quite work like that,' he said, his eyes coming to rest on Hash for the first time. Sean was behind, waving on the traffic. 'In this country we take insurance details.'

'I understand.' Hash gave a wide smile. 'I am about to travel, emigrate, in fact and the paper trail may never get to me. Better I settle with you now, in cash.'

'You've been drinking or you're not insured,' the man interrupted.

'I am but it's better we settle in cash.'

'Or both,' the man's eyes narrowed as he continued to rub his neck. 'You're definitely not insured,' he said. 'Fuck...' he exclaimed. 'So, tell me why don't I just call the police?'

'Can we settle it now?' Hash 's smile was more fixed and his voice took on a pleading tone.

'So, no insurance and you're a bit shy of the police.'

'How much?' Hash said.

'It's my living, that car.' He pointed at the bumper. 'Don't know what you do for a living, mate, but I work from that.'

'Whatever is reasonable,' Hash said. 'I can pay cash.'

'You people,' the man said. 'Money solves everything, doesn't it? You just throw money at it.'

'Cash,' Hash said, 'but I'll have to get it first.'

The man adopted a sardonic expression. 'No...I don't suppose you've got two thousand in cash on you?'

'I can get it, no problem. But we'll have to go and get it together.'

'Now?'

'Yes now.'

'You're not insured and...' The man paused. 'You're in a hurry because you don't want the police involved.'

'I don't want the police involved,' Hash said. 'Do we have a deal?'

The man looked at him, then back at his bumper. Hash leaned forward and said, 'Let's get to a few cashpoints and work it out. I need to finish this before it is too late.'

'Too late?'

'The cash deal means right now, my friend, right now. Here and now, please,' Hash said. 'My friend will jump in with you and you just follow me up to the Bath Road car park, where the banks are.' The man looked at Sean and then back to Hash who was gesturing the way ahead. 'Okay,' he said.

Five minutes later they had parked in the big car park behind the parade of shops. The man had been persuaded to transfer to Hash's Discovery for the negotiation and sat in the passenger's seat. Sean sat behind, silent. The bald man had ratcheted the price up to three thousand pounds and had been visibly happy when Hash caved in.

'I'll get more money from the bank machines,' Hash said, opening the door. 'Give me ten minutes.'

In the Discovery there was silence for a moment or two before the man spoke. 'Your mate, quite a fan of hard cash, then? Wealthy, then?'

'Not really,' Sean said, 'just your average millionaire who likes to keep a low profile.'

'Driving this heap of junk,' the man gestured to the dashboard, 'old model, done over a hundred thousand. I'm not impressed.'

'Better to be patient, then,' Sean said.

'How'd he make his money, then?'

'Property investments here and there.'

'That's my line, too,' the man said. 'Investments. Some in property, some in others, all risks.'

'That's what my boss does, too,' Sean said. 'I'll be damned. You could learn a lot from my boss,' he said. The man's phone rang, a fanfare ringtone as for an important announcement. Sean heard a woman's voice asking questions. The man answered, 'Sorry love. Can't make it. Why? Some bloody idiot pranged me.' Realising Sean was behind him did not stop him. 'Yes, a pair of idiots who've been drinking. No damage? You mean to me... thanks for your concern.' He laughed. 'Yeah, I'm fine but the car's practically a write-off. We're sorting it now. Later.' He put the phone back in his jacket pocket. Hash was approaching the car.

'So what's your mate's name, then?' he asked.

'Didn't he tell you?' Sean said.

'No.'

'Well, then.'

'Well, what?'

'Maybe he wants to keep names out of it,' Sean said.

'My neck hurts,' the man said, reaching up to rub his fleshy neck.

'Do you want the cash or not?'

Something in Sean's tone jarred and the man craned round to look at Sean's face. 'Are you taking the piss?'

Hash was climbing into the driver's seat. He passed an envelope over to the bald man and switched on the ignition. 'We're a bit short. Been round four of those 'hole in the wall' machines.' The man opened the envelope to see fifty-pound notes and was soon too busy checking them to feel the Discovery moving.

As the vehicle exited the car park, bumping over the potholes, he seemed jolted to his senses, holding up a note, 'Five hundred short?' he said. Hash looked over, reassuring. 'I just said that, my friend. We're going to get it, right now.'

'What about my car?'

'We'll be back in ten minutes.'

The man was silent for a few seconds more until he saw Hash was driving south, out of town on the Bath Road towards Leckhampton Hill. 'There's no bank out here,' he said, 'you're going the wrong way.'

'Relax, my friend, it's a different bank.' Hash waved a free hand at him. 'Soon be there.' The man went doubtfully silent again, looking down at the wad of notes. 'Unless you want to give me a discount?' Hash said.

'No way,' the man sniffed. 'But seriously, there's no bank out here…is this a con?'

'When do I get to beat the shit out of this arsehole?' Sean growled.

As the man turned, incredulous, Sean slapped him hard in the face with an open hand. The sound of the impact filled the cabin and the bald man's face showed fear and shock. Sean looped a leather belt over the headrest and the man's head and pulled tight. As his head jerked back the man's hands instinctively rose to his neck and the belt, but Sean's weight was against him and he found his head jammed against the headrest. His fingers pulled at the belt and his voice came in choking gasps. The envelope of cash slid off his lap.

'I want complete silence, shithead. Otherwise' – he dug his fingers into the man's crimson neck, fingers probing for his throat – 'whiplash will be the least of your worries.' He slapped the man's face again. Hash kept silent, staring ahead as they drove up Leckhampton Hill.

Sean said, 'I'm going to let you go as long as you promise to stay fucking silent, completely silent. Got me?' The man nodded and held his hands up in submission. Sean let the man's face go, leaving white weals on the reddened skin. The man began to breathe, but his head remained wrapped to the headrest and his body frozen, shoulders hunched in case another blow came from behind.

'The bad news, my friend,' Hash said, distracted by traffic at the Air Balloon roundabout, 'is the last five hundred may take some time after all.'

'But you said…' he started then his voice was choked off by Sean pulling the belt tight.

'Completely silent, shithead,' Sean said. 'Didn't you hear me the first fucking time?'

The Discovery parked at the far end of the Air Balloon car park. Anyone nearby would see three men sitting comfortably, having a chat.

'But there's good news.' Hash turned and looked at the crimson face fighting for breath, head rammed against the headrest. 'The good news is if you and I can do a deal, come to an agreement where everyone is happy.' He signalled to Sean to release the pressure and they watched the man lean forward, gagging for air. Hash clicked his fingers and Sean hauled back, slamming the man's head against the headrest. Hash looked at the second hand of his watch and then at the man's bulging eyes.

'We can go on all day.' Hash held up his hands, palms open. 'It's up to you, my friend, but time is precious.'

'Let me kill him,' Sean said.

'Not if our friend is prepared to help. Give him air, please.' The belt slackened and the man's throat sucked in air. When he had recovered, Sean took the belt away. The man rubbed his neck, staring wildly at Hash and flinching as Sean moved behind him.

'Shall we take a quick look at the video of your car?' Hash let Sean reach forward between them, holding up his phone. The video began to run, showing the silver Audi parked on Birdlip Hill and the conman getting out, smiling as his girlfriend came around for a long embrace.

'Your girlfriend?' Hash took out a sheaf of printed images. 'She is probably a secret you want to keep.' He placed the images on the man's lap one by one. The man looked down at them then across as Hash continued. 'The video…too embarrassing if your wife saw it. Embarrassing if your girlfriend saw it on YouTube,'

Hash emphasised.

'Who are you...what do you want?' the man said in a small, frightened voice.

'You're a fucking thief,' Sean said.

'I don't know what you're talking about.'

'Silence,' Sean growled, pulling the belt tight again. Hash leaned over and tapped the man on the knee. 'My friend behind you is not patient, I am, but he's not and' – he made a show of looking at his watch – 'as time runs his temper gets worse.' On cue, Sean punched the man again, the butt of his hand making a 'slap' sound as it hit the pink scalp. The man's head flicked sideways.

'Thieving money from pensioners is what he does,' Sean said, then jabbed him with a full fist. 'Thieving,' another punch, 'bastard,' and a third punch. The man was sobbing in pain.

'Stop, please,' Hash remonstrated. 'I think we can do a deal, as friends, can't we?' Hash asked, patting the man's knee.

'What are you talking about? My car?' The right side of his face was reddening. He was breathing hard.

'Are you a thieving bastard?' Sean's fist hung poised in front of the man's face. 'Did you take money from pensioners?' He punched the man's crutch. 'Spend it on cars and whores?' The man jerked against the seat. 'Old people's life savings.' Sean's hand rammed into the man's crutch, groping for his genitals. He screamed. Sean slapped him in the mouth. 'Stop crying, you fat, fucking shite.'

'Yes, your car,' Hash said.

'Take it,' the man said.

Sean punched him again. 'We've already got it, you stupid, fat fucker.'

'Then what do you want? Just leave me alone.'

'We want to give it back, my friend.' Hash spoke in slow confidential tones. 'Just borrow it for a few days, then give it back to you.'

'I don't understand,' the man began and was immediately choked by Sean hauling back on the belt. The man's hands went to the garrotte and Sean pulled at the man's scrabbling fingers, catching one and wrenching it back on itself. The man gagged in pain.

'I want to borrow your car,' Hash said. 'It's that simple.' He put his face close to the man's and signalled Sean to ease off the pressure. 'When I've finished with your car I'll leave it, with some more money under the seat.' The man nodded, eyes still bulging, sweat pouring off his forehead.

'Do you understand, now?' Sean said. When the man nodded again, Sean released the belt.

'We take your car, we use it, we leave it with some money in it,' Hash said. 'Car hire…simple.'

'What will you tell your wife?' Sean hissed. The man hesitated. Sean slapped him again. 'You'll tell her it's in the garage, being fixed.' The man struggled to get away from the next blow. 'Sit still! What'll you tell your girlfriend when she gets horny and calls you for a shag?' Sean said, his fist poised.

'I'll tell her it's in the garage…' The man's voice came in gulps.

'How long's it in the garage for?' Sean asked. The man did

not see Sean's fist as it came around from the left of the headrest. 'Until we fucking say so,' Sean answered. The man rocked away from the blow and his head began to droop. Hash shook him to get his concentration. 'We're going to let you go home now.'

'You're not going to the police, are you?' Sean coached. 'Please don't involve the police,' Hash added. 'It would be awkward because...'

'Because you're thieving scum,' Sean spat into his ear, 'and I'll find you.'

'Because we're in a business agreement that you are lending us the car. And...' Hash retrieved the fallen envelope and dropped it together with the sheaf of photographs into the man's lap. 'Keep these safe,' he said. He patted the man's knee again. 'Not for long, just a short while. We'll let you know when and where to pick up your car and,' he tapped the envelope, 'some more of this.'

'Where are the keys?' Sean asked.

'Yes, your keys, please and remember.' Hash held up a restraining hand as Sean was about to punch again. 'Where shall we drop you?'

Hash said goodbye to Sean at midnight.

'You should get to London in a couple of hours,' he said. Sean looked up from the dashboard. 'All these dials,' he said. 'All I need is the cigarette lighter.'

'Where will you rest up?'

'Maybe doss in the car tonight. Then it'll be any place that takes cash. I'll get out to Ascot tomorrow and look it over.'

'Got everything you need? Cash, weapons, plates?'

Sean patted the little suitcase beside him on the passenger's seat. 'All in here, ready to go.'

CHAPTER 27

THURSDAY JUNE 11TH

'The problem is the dog,' Eva said, looking down at the blanket
Hash had spread on the grass. She sat down cross-legged and
held the hamper as Hash lowered it. 'The problem is your boss,'
Hash said.

'He's going away again, and he wants me to come with him.'
She unbuckled the straps and lifted the wicker lid, gazing at
the contents. 'Champagne, strawberries, cream! Hash, you're
amazing.' Hash called Bruno who trotted in, tongue lolling, to
lap at a water bowl. The three sat on the blanket until the pup's
gaze fixed on another dog not far away in the meadow and he
dashed off.

'So beautiful here,' Eva said. 'Thanks to Mister Hash.'

'England in the summer,' Hash agreed, 'the most beautiful
place on earth.' He popped the cork and they both watched as
he poured. Hash and Eva clinked glasses and sipped.

'The problem is your boss,' Hash repeated. 'It sounds as
though he doesn't even want the dog.'

'I have other trouble with my boss,' she said. 'Bloody horses.

We go to Ascot next weekend,' she sighed, 'Every day. Can you believe it?'

'Ascot…horse racing, that's not this weekend, it's next weekend,' Hash corrected.

'Whatever,' Eva shrugged. 'Too soon anyway.'

'Champagne and strawberries every day, then.' Hash lifted a piece of fruit to his mouth. 'Good work if you can get it,' he said.

'Bullshit. A ticket.'

'A ticket?' Hash said, puzzled.

'Yes, a ticket. What the English have to do to each other, how you dress, walk, say hello to The Queen.'

'You mean etiquette.'

'It's what I just said.'

'Don't go,' Hash said.

'Why not? It's my job.'

'It's not safe,' Hash blurted. 'Please don't go. Make an excuse.'

'It's Ascot, England…not Ascot, Gaza Strip.'

'I'd prefer it if you didn't go.'

'You mean get the sack, no etiquette, no job?'

'Say you're sick,' Hash said. 'Please don't go.'

'I can't be sick all week. He needs me to show off to his business friends.'

'Who are these people?'

'Arabs.' She snorted then raised a hand to her mouth. 'Not nice Arabs like you.' She pinched his arm. a

'Where are they from?'

'Here and there,' she said airily. 'Dubai, Saudi, Kuwait. All those places.' She waved her hand. 'My boss wants oil business. They don't look at the horses, though. They look at the girls.' She clucked her tongue at him. 'This is my job. Big hat, short skirt.' She held a strawberry to his lips, teasing him. 'But' – she nipped a piece of the fruit and chewed it – 'He says, some of the English ladies, they look like horses. This is why I am needed.'

Hash watched Bruno in pursuit of somebody else's whippet. There was a play-fight and a frantic chase across the meadow, with the whippet showing Bruno what speed was about. Eva called but he was too far away to hear or care, waiting to catch his playmate as he swooped past. Eva sighed and held out her glass for Hash to fill.

'Your son, did you tell him?'

'Tell him what?'

'You miss him?'

'Of course. But he's with his grandparents and they're good for him. I hope I'll see him soon, maybe I'll visit him in Jordan or bring him back here for some of the holidays.'

'Does he call you?'

'Not very often. He's a teenager.'

'I know,' she trilled, 'he only calls when he needs money. Do you think he would like me?'

'I'm sure he would.' Her phone buzzed and she wriggled to get it from her hip pocket. She looked at an SMS, her lips moving as she concentrated on the text. 'Bloody boss.' She dismissed the phone and dropped it on the blanket. 'He can wait.' She rolled onto her front and looked up at the green bulk of Cleeve Hill.

'Time to go home. Bring the bloody dog back.'

'So soon? We've only just arrived.'

Her phone buzzed again and she turned around to find it. Picking it up, she studied it then suddenly pitched forward as Bruno rammed into her shoulder. The phone fell and the champagne glass knocked over.

'Fucking dog,' Eva hissed, lashing out with her foot, catching the pup in the ribs. Bruno squealed in pain and scurried away with Eva screaming, 'Fuck off, dog!' Hash knelt up to help her, but she shook him off. He picked up her phone and waited until she was ready. He looked at the screen to check if there was any damage. A list of calls with numbers alongside stared back at him. A familiar dialling code held his attention. Bruno was yelping, turning on himself, limping, needing reassurance but too frightened to approach. Eva snatched the phone back. 'Maybe my boss heard that.' She groaned. 'I just don't like dogs.' Hash picked up a piece of food and walked slowly towards Bruno who retreated, keeping his distance, panting. Eventually, Hash tempted him to take the morsel and comforted the pup.

'I have to go. Sorry, Hash,' she said, standing, picking grass off her jeans.

'When am I going to see you?' he asked.

'Maybe we do lunch again tomorrow,' she said, 'seeing as you never take me home.' Hash looked at the 'little girl' pout.

'I'm in court, again,' he said. 'You know it's not that I don't want to,' Hash tried to apologise but she stopped him. 'Yes, yes, the language student, the photos of your wife. It's too early.' She opened and closed her fingers at him. 'Blah blah, too soon for Jim!'

'You know I want you to come home, meet Jim, like him. But it's got to be perfect.'

'Sorry, Hash.' She leaned her head on his shoulder after they had walked in silence for a minute. 'Pressure from my boss and this Ascot thing. Arabs looking at me...you know?'

'Some Arabs are gentlemen. I've heard Libyans are the nicest.' They were standing at her car and she ducked down to check her appearance in the wing mirror. 'My boss doesn't have any Libyan clients, so I don't know about that.'

Hakim was waiting at the small mosque. This time there was concern on his face.

'I have the address. Three men, your son, but so far the woman, we don't know where she is.' He tugged at his beard, thinking. 'She comes and leaves, sometimes with one of the men. Always with the burqa.'

'Can you give me the address?' Hash asked. 'Then I can go as soon as possible.'

'Too risky,' Hakim said quietly, 'Too risky.'

'But you promised.'

'I know exactly what I promised.'

'Sayyid Hakim, I am running out of time. They may move. They are going to Ascot Racecourse. Maybe they will change their accommodation again.'

'How do you know?'

'Not one hundred percent sure, but probably.'

'Why Ascot?'

'Ascot Racecourse,' Hash corrected. 'That's the logical place,' Hash said, 'they've been training for a racecourse and they're looking for The Queen as a target.'

'Are you sure?'

'It's a pattern they set and they're following it...remember Cheltenham Races in March...? Well, this is bigger, more chance of The Queen being present.'

'You have someone helping you, I assume?'

'Just two of us,' Hash said.

'But are you carrying weapons?'

'We will only use them if we've no choice. You know who these people are.'

Hakim sat back on the chair to look up at the calendar. 'Why would they be in London almost a week before Ascot? Why leave the safety of their networks in Birmingham?'

Hash followed his gaze. 'Maybe they want to set up and prepare, give themselves more time. Who knows what else they have planned for that day?'

Hakim looked back to Hash. 'I am not confident about your predictions,' he said.

'Just give me the address, we'll hit the target as soon as possible, maybe tonight, tomorrow morning.'

'This friend of yours.' Hakim switched tack. 'Does he come from that same dark room you were in all those years ago?'

'Yes.'

'So, he's a terrorist, too?'

'Were you a terrorist in Afghanistan, or a freedom fighter?'

Hakim did not answer for a while. 'Maybe I let you have the information and maybe you win.' He canted his head left, then right. 'Maybe it's a disaster.' He looked at the calendar again. 'Or I keep my team on the task and bring you in at the last moment.'

'You will not get much time,' Hakim said. 'So be ready when I call.' He patted his pocket, pulling out a notebook. 'Take down these numbers and give me yours. From now on we can work together.'

'Sayyid Hakim, I don't know how to thank you,' Hash began. 'I can make a donation to the mosque, this one or yours, or both...'

Hakim stopped him. 'We prayed for your son in our mosque and in this one, too.' His eyes swept the squalid kitchen. 'Strangers but true Muslims prayed for his deliverance. So, please those strangers. Bring your son to pray beside them.'

'I've been thinking about it, too,' Sean said. 'I'm not convinced yet. Yes, it's early for Ascot, but they could just be making double sure of their ground before the security steps up. That way they can come in and go to their exact positions.'

'I'm with you,' Hash said. 'Hopefully you'll pick them up or when Hakim's boys give the tip-off.' Hash heard Sean's coughing at the other end of the phone. 'They know about you and they know what we're carrying.'

'Fuck me,' Sean exclaimed. 'Did they have a pair of pliers on your Crown Jewels? So, we're working with them, now?'

'They'll hand over to us as soon as they have the location and can get clear.'

'How do you know they won't ambush us or rat us out?'

'I don't. But I'm trusting them…we have don't have too many choices.'

LATER

Unable to sleep and bidden by an instinct that the endgame was approaching, Hash left his bedroom and went downstairs. As he walked past the kitchen he flicked on the light, waking Bruno who yawned but stayed put. He retrieved the Jameson whiskey tube with the two grenades. Emptying the contents carefully, he took a pair of kitchen scissors and, stacking the grenades one on top of the other, he matched the cardboard tube against them. Measuring where the safety rings on the pins would touch the tubing cardboard, he cut two coin-sized holes in the flank then wrapped the grenades in bubblewrap and eased them back into the tube, so they sat, one on top of the other, rings exposed to view. He tied two inches of wire to each ring so he could ease the pins out and arm the bombs. He contemplated his final statement to the Mukhabarat. When the time came, as Hash knew it would, the person emptying the letterbox, the human link between him and the rest of the cell, would be blown to bits.

CHAPTER 28

Moments earlier, Bousaif and Bruno had watched the ritual polishing of his brogues. 'Old shoes, well-kept are a sign of good breeding,' Hash explained.

'We throw old shoes away because they're a sign that you can't afford new ones,' Bousaif responded. Closing the front door gently, he caught a last glimpse of the pup putting both paws on Bousaif's knees, cadging scraps off his breakfast plate.

The court assembled at nine in the morning and Hash found himself sitting with an elderly magistrate he did not know, also disappointed at getting a tedious morning of traffic offences. There had been no update from Sean since last night and reluctantly he switched the phone off. They made it through three cases before coffee break. Hash read two messages on his phone. The first had come from Sean at nine-thirty and simply reported that there was so far nothing doing in the Ascot area. The second, sent at ten o'clock, from one of Hakim's numbers, relayed the address of a building in London's Philbeach Gardens, in SW5. Hash just had time to pass this to Sean before he had to shut the phone down. Taking his seat in court, heart thumping, he knew that at least Sean was on his way to the target. He became dimly aware of his colleague mentioning something about the next case being more lively as the defendant was there in person to contest the charge. Hash saw the clerk escorting a young woman to the dock where she stood, looking unsure of herself.

Instantly, Hash knew there was something familiar about this young woman and he began to feel uneasy. The charge was, driving without due care and attention and the woman pleaded guilty. His colleague asked the woman what she had to say in her defence.

'I am a carer and cannot do my job without a car,' the woman started. Hash was studying her, a feeling of unease stirring. 'I need my car for the job I do,' she said. 'I look after my mother and father. They both need regular medical help,' she stated then added, 'round the clock.'

'And this care cannot be provided by anyone else but you?'

The young woman shook her head, her confidence cued by the question. 'We live out in the country and I'm the breadwinner, too.' Hash was staring at her, his suspicion becoming acute. She started to work her script, presenting herself as the lifeline. As she was talking the magistrate beside him scribbled 'any questions?' on a scrap of paper and passed it to Hash. Hash shook his head.

'You knew the importance of the car,' his companion began. 'Your licence is your lifeline, as you so eloquently put it. So why would you risk it by speeding excessively?' Hash was barely listening, aware of someone new entering the court. The woman's face looked across and broke into a smile of relief. 'My partner,' she explained. 'In case I lose my licence.'

'Maybe your partner can help with the driving?'

'He doesn't live with me and he hasn't got a car,' the woman explained.

Hash was not looking at the woman or concentrating on his colleague. He was looking at the bald conman. The moment of mutual recognition dragged in agony. The man sat down barely glancing at his girlfriend, his mouth an 'o' of surprise as he recognised Hash. Then his head went down, texting. Hash knew he had to sit it out as the excruciating process dragged on with his colleague asking the ritual questions of who else was available to care for the parents, whether there was a neighbour, bus service or alternative form of transport so that prescriptions could be delivered, should a ban be imposed. As the colleague turned to Hash for his final decision, the public door opened for a second time and the legal aid counsel slipped in, taking a seat beside the conman.

'We find you guilty of the offence,' the colleague announced. 'You are to be banned from driving for two weeks and you will now hand your licence to the clerk.' As they left the court Hash saw the conman and the legal aid counsel watching him.

Hash did not manage to get away until midday and opening up on the phone saw he had missed calls from Sean and Hakim.

'Where the fuck have you been?' Sean said. 'I've been ringing like crazy.'

'Change the plates on the car,' Hash said.

'What the fuck are you talking about? I'm nowhere near the car, I'm on foot. I left the car in Philbeach Gardens.'

'On the street?'

'In a hotel car park. What's the sudden panic? Want me to do it in broad daylight?'

'Change the plates as soon as possible, or your car's done... long story...just do it.'

'I'm on foot, following them out of Green Park tube station.'

'As soon as you can.'

'Thanks to your new friend, we've got our eyes on the whole group...'

'The woman, too?'

'All except the woman,' Sean said. 'You need to get here.' Hash was walking fast, passing the front entrance of the Ladies' College, beginning to feel out of breath, his shoes too tight for running. 'They're going into this big park beside the tube station,' Sean continued. 'Three men, Jim and the bloody drone thing.'

'Sure the woman isn't with them?'

'No sign of her.'

'What's the place look like?'

'One of those typical town house places, big porch, pillars, railings. I haven't been inside.'

'Be careful,' Hash said. 'Don't get too close.'

'They were outside, piling Jim into the building, then they

walked out half an hour later, as if they were going for a stroll.'

'I'm on my way.'

'What'll you do with the new candidate?'

'I have to bring him, I've got no option.'

Hash was outside the Rotunda, thinking a taxi could get him home faster. By now, the conman would have had plenty of time to discover who he was and if he had blown the whistle it was 'game over'. Sitting in Cheltenham waiting for a miracle was out of the question. The realisation struck him hard that Cheltenham was probably over, for good. He prayed Sean's threats of violence were still vivid enough to stall the man for a bit longer.

The taxi dropped him at junction on Thirlestaine Road and Naunton Lane, leaving him the short burst of walking to get him home. Rounding the corner into Naunton Crescent he saw blue flashing lights. As he closed the distance he saw it was an ambulance, not a police car, parked close to his house with a paramedic hauling a wheelchair from the back. As he arrived he saw another paramedic supporting Mrs Hamilton. The old girl's face was deathly pale, her eyes trying to focus on someone she knew. As the medics settled her into the chair she raised a fragile, withered arm to Hash. 'Is that you?' she croaked.

'Mrs Hamilton, how can I help?' Hash asked.

'Fell off a ladder trying to reach something...silly me.' She beckoned him forward, 'Do me a favour...'

'Anything.'

She smiled, her old self surfacing through the pain. 'They

might keep me in,' she said in a conspiratorial voice. 'Bloody hope so. I could do with the rest and the free food. How's Jim? One of the medics started to turn the wheelchair so they could wheel her to the ambulance. She looked uncertain at the prospect of the vehicle, with its flashing lights and the gallery of interested neighbours. 'How can I help?' Hash repeated. 'Tell me what to do?' Mrs Hamilton's eyes closed and her head tipped forward then jerked back. She looked blankly over her shoulder at Hash as the chair was wheeled past him. 'She'll be fine with us,' the medic whispered to Hash.

Bousaif had been watching from the hallway, staying back from the door. He looked past Hash to where the ambulance crew was closing the door. 'What was the problem?' he asked.

'Never mind her. Get your things ready. We're leaving.'

'The dog,' Bousaif said. Hash saw blood on his arms as he pointed to Bruno, lying on his bed, his flank heaving as he struggled for breath. 'We were playing. Now he's sick.' Hash went to Bruno and the pup's tail started to thump. Gently he lifted the dog and saw a deep gash on the flank. Blood had flowed over the dog's coat but was drying.

'We were playing,' Bousaif said, 'in the garden, playing with the ball in the garden.' Bruno was reaching out a paw, trying to get from Bousaif to Hash and Hash took the dog. They went into the kitchen and looked at the tear in the dog's soft skin. 'Maybe a nail sticking through the fence,' Bousaif offered.

'Pack your stuff, we're leaving,' Hash repeated.

Bousaif started in surprise. 'Why?'

'If we stay there is no mission. So, we're leaving.'

'Bruno?'

'We leave the dog with food and water.'

'It is sick, in pain, maybe it will die?'

'Better you kill it and we dump it. Stop wasting time.'

Bousaif bent down and stroked the pup. 'I will not do this.'

'You're going to kill humans in a few days, lots of them. Why should one dog be a problem?'

'Please,' Bousaif said. 'Take care of the dog first and...' His words stopped.

'And what?' Hash snapped. 'You help me with my son?'

While Bousaif was upstairs, Hash settled Bruno and called the vet to set up an emergency appointment. He heard Bousaif moving upstairs and went to the stair cupboard to drag out the sports bag with his share of the weapons. He unzipped the bag for a quick visual check and made sure the Jameson cylinder was set on top of the rest. Then he dashed to the garage for the suicide vest. Bousaif came downstairs holding his bag, looking down the hall to the front door, as though the police were already waiting. Hash contemplated the Arab BlackBerry and the choice between cutting off messages or taking it and giving away his next locations. He put it in his pocket, told Bousaif to pick up Bruno and follow on.

The receptionist at the vet surgery took the pup away for an assessment. The clock on the waiting room wall read one-fifteen and the people he had queue-jumped were looking on with some disapproval. To avoid them he went outside and returned Hakim's call.

'You got the place?' Hakim's calm voice gave Hash a surge of confidence. He made him repeat the address. 'And you've got the numbers of my men? Are you on the way?'

'Just leaving.' Hash looked at his watch. 'I could be there in two hours.'

'Don't rush it,' Hakim said. 'No Hollywood stuff.'

Hash saw the receptionist waving at him through the window. 'Call my team when you get there,' Hakim said, 'Check with them before doing anything.'

As he walked back up the stone steps and into the surgery the girl facing him over the counter wore an expression of embarrassment and anxiety. 'So...Just have to ask this,' she hesitated. 'Is the dog yours?'

'No, he belongs to my girlfriend and I'm dog-sitting.' The girl's anxiety remained, 'Umm...that's OK, then,' she said. 'The vet says the tear is minor and we can glue it, the dog will need one of those cones.' She smiled at Hash, 'but there might be an X-ray needed.'

'Why?'

'The vet says there's a good chance one, maybe two ribs are broken. We must have the owner's consent before we go any further. Is there any chance we can speak to her?' Hash looked at his watch then pulled out his phone and dialled Eva. Waiting for her to answer, he gave the receptionist a reassuring smile. 'Actually, it's a more complicated,' he told her. 'The dog belongs to her boss and she delegated the dog-sitting to me.' He could hear her phone still ringing. 'Not answering,' he said to the receptionist. 'Is the treatment urgent?'

'Well, in an emergency we'll just go ahead, if you're willing to pay the costs...'

'Whatever it takes,' he soothed her, 'I'll pay.' They were interrupted by the phone on her the desk. Apologising, she picked up and he watched her expression flit from concentration, through bewilderment to surprise, with her eyes checking him. She covered the receiver with her hand and looked at Hash. 'We've actually got the owner, from the microchip database. One of my colleagues is trying to call on her landline.'

Poleaxed, wanting to sit down, Hash fought the significance of the words. As he stood there waiting, his brain spun like the wheels on a one-armed bandit, jacked into action, then one by one stopping to ring up three heaps of dog shit. Of course the dog had a past, but Eva had never mentioned the owner was a woman. She had always talked about her boss in the male sense. While he was standing at the counter faking a patient smile, he felt as though he was far out on a frozen lake, too far out, with the ice was cracking underneath his feet. The weight of a microchip in Bruno's neck was going to sink him.

Before he could do anything, the girl said brightly, 'This happens all the time. Sometimes the old owners don't pass on the news so the system doesn't get updated. But she's a breeder and she shouldn't have missed that.' The internal phone rang and again she picked up. Hash saw her colleague had done the maths and had come up with a different answer to her, but essentially the same as Hash's fruit machine. 'So...We've got a bit of a problem,' she said, covering the receiver and lowering her voice. Hash leaned forward. 'The owner says the dog was stolen some months ago. In this case, the procedure is we have keep the animal until...'

'The real owner can come and collect it,' Hash finished her sentence, feeling the eyes of the waiting room boring into his back. 'What a mess.' He held up his phone, trying to stay relaxed. 'Really embarrassing. Nothing from my girlfriend, wait till she finds out. Will Bruno get treated, now? I'm happy to pay, if that helps.'

'That's good of you, but the owner has authorised the treatment. Can we ask you for a few details? Won't take a minute of your time.'

'Where's Bruno?' Bousaif asked as Hash climbed in. Hash ignored the question, strapping in and switching on, watching carefully as he reversed out onto the road. 'Where is Bruno?'

'No more Bruno. Bruno is safe and we won't see him again. You ready to go?' He looked at Bousaif and repeated, 'You ready?'

'Insh'Allah.'

Hash's mind was churning. The immediate conclusion to get away from the vet surgery was the right one, not be too rude, just a show confusion and get away from the place while they were still wondering what to do. They would put it down to embarrassment rather than shady guilt. The jolt of Bruno's theft had set other details clicking into place. The bald conman held a key card and it was better to expect the worst. The police could follow up, now Bruno was remanded in the vet's custody. He kept steering his concentration to Sean. He needed to talk to him, find out what he had seen.

'Where are we going?' Bousaif asked.

'As far away from Cheltenham as possible, West London. The police are getting interested in me...which is bad for you.' Hash drove to the racecourse, parking down by the copse, nosing the Discovery close to the bramble hedge.

'What are we doing?' Bousaif asked.

'You're changing these plates,' Hash said, handing over a set and a screwdriver, adding, 'You'll have covered that at Ben Gashir.'

Bousaif shrugged and took the equipment. Hash lifted the Jameson whiskey tube out of his bag and walked down to the footbridge. While he waited to see who was around, he fished out the Arab BlackBerry. He had made his decision, no longer worried it might be betraying his location. He tapped an SMS telling Tripoli he was on the move with Bousaif, then added they needed to clear the letter box. He opened the tube, took out the tape and replaced it with the BlackBerry. Glancing around to confirm he was alone and Bousaif was still working on the plates he ducked under the wire, heading for the culvert. Pausing to catch his breath, ignoring his soaked feet he looked at the protruding wires for a few seconds. Gently he drew both pins from the grenades, knowing the levers would be held by the side of the tube. Then he pushed the whole tube into the aperture and shoved it in by a few inches. He stepped away, checked around him, dropped the pins into the stream and edged back to the footbridge. He tied three rings of green electricians' tape to one of the uprights. As he smudged the green freshness with muddy water he was struck by the irony of the savage justice he was preparing. It was right here, at this very spot where his tormentors had chosen to wreck his life. And it was here, with their own method, they would be repaid.

'Where am I...?' Hash answered Sean's question. 'I'm watching the guest change a set of plates. Have you done yours, yet?'

Sean ignored the question. 'The group's in Green Park,' he said, 'And it's full of Arabs, kids playing football, women in burqas, picnics, you name it, half of Dubai's here. But they're here and I'm watching them. Jim's been playing with that quadcopter all afternoon.'

'Where am I taking my guest tonight?' Hash asked. 'We'll be in London around six, latest seven.'

'Got to keep him with us,' Sean said. 'He's a trigger and if we lose him God knows what could happen.'

'Where are you staying?'

'Little hotel right here in Philbeach Gardens: perfect for what we need. Cash deal. I'll text you the address. You can park at the back.'

'Can you get rooms for me and my friend?'

'Will do. The place is only 300 yards from their B and B, my window overlooks the street.'

'If we get this right we can take the bastards down tonight and be away, leave the bugger to his own devices,' Hash said.

Hash briefed Bousaif, as they left the racecourse. 'Unless you've got any better ideas. Cheltenham is over, finished, never coming back.' He drew a finger across his throat. 'The police will be looking for us here so we'll hide amongst Arab tourists in London.' Hash looked at Bousaif for a reaction but got none. 'We need to be close to your target in Ascot but not on top of it,' Hash looked at him again, emphasising the point, 'West London is best.'

'What about the mission?' Bousaif said as they drove out onto the Evesham Road.

'What about my son? You promised.'

'He will be OK, insh'Allah.'

'I will kill anyone who harms him,' Hash said, 'even you, Bousaif.'

'I know. You told me.'

'Your mission is close, next weekend at Ascot. When will you tell me about my son?'

Bousaif did not respond and Hash pressed him, 'So I have seven days to hide you and then I find my son.'

Bousaif looked at him. 'Seven days? Where's the vest?'

'I've got it in the back.' He jerked a thumb behind him.

They reached West London as the evening rush hour was subsiding but still strong enough to slow Hash to a stop-start crawl as they worked their way across from White City to the small hotel. After checking in, he left Bousaif in his room and immediately dived back into the flood of heavy traffic on Warwick Road. He made it across Cromwell Road and up to the calm of Holland Park where Sean was waiting, smoking as usual.

'What have you done with him?'

'I left him in his room with plenty of food, watching football on the telly.'

'From what I saw,' Sean said, losing interest in Bousaif, 'they were practising. The men were putting Jim through some drills with the quadcopter zipping up, hovering then dropping.' His nicotine-stained finger described the swooping and hovering, the cigarette leaving a thin trail of smoke in the car.

'And the woman,' Hash said. 'Did you see her?'

'Not at first,' Sean said. 'She came by later, gave them a bollocking and left. When I followed them, it was only the two men and Jim, then in the park a third man turned up with the quadcopter. That's roughly when you phoned.' He looked at his watch, frowned and made a dismissive gesture. 'Roughly but I don't remember exactly. They were down by The Mall then and that's when she got out of a taxi.'

'What did she look like?' Hash said.

'I was hanging back, but from that distance it could well have been your Anna, by the sound of her.' He looked quizzically at Hash for a reaction, then added, 'No burqa or black gown but she was fit and blond and she was the boss…no mistake about that.'

'Slim, athletic…?' Hash prompted and Sean dipped his head. 'Tidy figure but she was bossy.' He shook his head. 'I thought I'd get closer, but…it was one of those weird moments when you know someone's onto you.' Hash watched Sean concentrate. 'I was about two hundred yards away, just about to swing up the phone to get a shot of the group, when her eyes locked onto me, pinned me to the bloody tree.'

'What did you do?'

'You get someone looking at you like that and it sends a steel blade through you. The animal that senses a threat before it actually sees it.' He examined a stained fingernail, 'I've been there, mate.' He flipped an imaginary coin in the air. Heads, they come straight at you, guns, knives, sticks. Tails, if you're lucky, they fuck off, hoping you'll forget them. Sound like your Anna?'

Hash dodged the question. 'The place they've got Jim. Is it an easy place?'

'What are you planning?'

'Whatever you suggest, mate.' Sean winced in pain. 'We'll wait for them to come out in the open. We can watch from my window and then run like hell to our vehicle because they can only drive out one way and they'll probably get slowed turning onto Warwick Road.'

'OK. Hang on a minute. Got to SMS Siddiq.' Hash took a few seconds to type the message.

'It gets worse,' Hash said. 'The dog.'

'What about the bloody dog?'

'It wasn't hers, it was stolen all along.' Hash knuckled his forehead. 'I was taken for a complete ride, all the way, like an idiot. I never saw it coming. She was the one, all the time.'

'Anna?'

'There's something I've been keeping from you, mate.'

'a girlfriend, she's been around for a bit.'

'It was awkward, if you know what I mean.'

'Susan? I know,' Sean said. 'It's your life.'

'No. The exact opposite,' Hash said. 'Nowhere near as good as Susan. Someone else.' He leaned back in the seat and groaned. 'What an idiot, what a complete idiot...' He thumped his chest. 'Eva, she calls herself. She appeared, after Cheltenham when you had gone. So I didn't have to hide her from you.' Sean said nothing, lighting another cigarette, watching his friend.

Hash said, 'From the start, in the car park with the pup. She must have planned it. She reeled me in and I went for it. She got me falling for her, let me into her knickers. Then pretended to get jealous, even came to the house.' He snapped his fingers. 'That was most likely to brief our friend upstairs. He must have known who she was, all along, the bastard.' Hash was aware he was talking to himself, working back through Eva's trail of deception. Sean smoked, watched him rubbing his forehead. 'She was the one beating Jim, then sweet-talking me about the message I would send my son. All the time she had a gun at his head.'

'This is the woman in the burqa,' Sean attempted. 'The one I saw today, I mean.'

'She's Al Qaeda, or ISIS, it doesn't matter anymore.' His phone chirped an incoming message. 'What matters is...' He broke off and looked at his phone, then held it to Sean. 'Tell me what you see.'

'I see your mate, Siddiq, and his bit of stuff.'

'Anna. What time was it sent?'

'A minute ago.'

'From Cheltenham? Probably,' Hash answered his own question. 'Siddiq does Gloucester or Birmingham but never

London, and she would have had to drive like hell to have made it from the West End all the way back to the Bath Road in time for this.' He held the screen up and looked at the image of two smiling people sitting in a booth in a restaurant. 'So it wasn't Anna at The Mall, getting out of the taxi.'

Hash closed his eyes. 'Miles off target. She is good,' he said, 'really, dangerously good. But...' Hash held up a finger. '...She's not the one who stole the dog. She just collected something to get my attention. Whoever stole the dog knew about the breed but not about the microchip system in the country.' He turned to Sean, 'Little Bruno gets a kicking and it blows their game apart.'

'So, can we assume she doesn't know you've sussed her? She came to the house, briefed the bomber and they're carrying on, as planned?'

'I suppose so.'

'Then let's play this cool,' Sean said. 'Don't let on to your man. Let them think they're ahead of us.'

Hash opened his eyes. 'Give me one of those.'

'They'll kill you,' Sean said, offering the open pack. Hash took a cigarette, turning it end to end, examining it before he put it to his lips. He flicked his thumb at Sean for a light. 'Have one yourself,' he said to Sean. 'You're going to need it. This is a complicated one. It's about an idiot with his dick where his brain should have been.' Sean held the lighter and watched Hash draw in the tobacco.

'Like a pro,' Sean said.

'I'm a bloody amateur,' Hash said, his eyes remaining closed. 'From the beginning?'

'Tell me back at the hotel,' Sean said. 'We need to check your friend and we need to set up.

Taking it in turns, they watched through the night. The view from the side of the bay window allowed them to look down the curving street to the stucco-fronted, pillared entrance where Sean had seen the group enter and leave during the day. Now, in the small hours, the whole street was still. An occasional car passed slowly by the front of the hotel, then curved out of sight towards Warwick Road. When a night owl pedestrian made their way past, the movement pepped up Hash's weary senses. As Sean slept Hash was aware of his friend's breath coming in rapid, sawing gasps, his diseased lungs working like ancient bellows in some old, smoky forge. When a man was young, he reflected, sleep had been, an inexhaustible reservoir of vigour. Watching his friend, restless on the bed, ravaged by illness, mumbling occasional incoherent words, he saw how sleep had become precious, the reservoir infinite. He decided to spare Sean his next watch and take the vigil through to the morning.

He looked at the weapons Sean had stripped, cleaned and reassembled earlier.

They had talked about Jim, then Flora and the subject of Eva soon surfaced, as though Sean had something on his mind. 'That's why you never told me about Eva,' Sean had said. 'In case you felt bad about Flora?'

'Because I knew you'd be upset and angry. As though I was moving on, leaving her behind, putting her and the memories with the photos into a drawer and closing it.'

'Were you?' Sean had asked quietly. Hash had taken a moment before answering and the silence made Sean look up from wiping the pistol in his hand.

'You don't move on, ever,' Hash had said.

'Did you love my sister?'

'I still do,' Hash said. 'She'll always be there.' He had tapped his heart.

'That's all I needed to know,' Sean had said.

Hash tried to push Eva out of his mind. He locked his brain onto the frighteningly simple rescue plan, looking for improvements. Just thinking it through made his palms go clammy. At the first sight of Jim leaving the porch onto the street they would react. They were guessing movement could happen after a late breakfast and the weather forecast offering them an opportunity to practise. They would probably call up their driver and head for Ascot, or maybe the London park. It made sense to Hash that they were hiding in plain sight amongst other Arab tourists rather than alone in a racecourse car park where someone would notice the group. When the move from the porch to the car was building, he or Sean, with their police tabards over their jackets would burst from the hotel, one taking the silver Audi and the other running down towards the Bed and Breakfast. They would block them there, and then on the street the police vests would buy them a few seconds and the weapons would do the rest.

No matter how hard he tried, the events in Cheltenham kept intruding and Hash felt crimson embarrassment flooding him at the thought of how easily Eva had insinuated herself into his life. First, Anna had been easy to suspect, she had been in the wrong places at the right time. Good-looking, interested in Jim, flirting to make Siddiq jealous, she had been guilty of no more than being human. Mrs Hamilton's watchfulness and. ablonde visitor knocking on his door when the first bomber was lying dead in the front room; this pattern repeating itself when Eva had come around and met Bousaif. Even then, the finger of suspicion had been easy to hold on Anna, right up to Epsom, when she had been seen two-timing Siddiq.

The body slam had been the microchip, the catalyst that unlocked it all. The sheer coincidences he had wanted to believe now seemed so embarrassingly ridiculous. The gorgeous woman with the unruly puppy, appearing in his life yards from the letter box, allowing herself to be scooped up by a sad widower. She was sugary sweet, had led him to bed, and even coaxed a sad message for Jim. Her temper had been easy to ignore. Kicking Bruno would normally have ended any of Hash's relationships, but she had sailed through. Even with the Libyan numbers on her phone he had almost found in her favour: like one of the soft magistrates he despised, he had not pressed her. The horror of knowing all along that Eva had harmed Jim around placed her on the pinnacle of evil.

Groaning from the bed drew his attention away from the poisonous thoughts as Sean started coughing. A rumble in his congested lungs built up to a series of hacking coughs. Hash walked over and switched on the mini-kettle as Sean sat up, swallowing phlegm and grabbing for the glass by his bed. He stared blearily at Hash, then looked around the room. 'So, it's not a dream, then…what time is it?'

'Just on six, been light for a bit.'

'Shit, Sean lay back, rubbing his face. 'You were supposed to wake me.'

'You were sleeping so soundly, I didn't have the heart.'

'Bollocks. You probably fell asleep yourself.'

He made Sean a cup of sweet tea and watched him grimace at the taste. 'I'll get dressed in a minute and take over.'

'Take your time.'

'Anything going on out there?' Sean nodded to the bay window.

'Quiet all night, the occasional car, someone on foot now and then. Nothing in or out of the place itself.' Sean swung his legs off the bed and sat up.

'Are you ready for this?' He held the mug to the glistening black metal of the Kalashnikovs. 'We're getting close and it's going to get rough. We've been there before, Darky, you and I.'

'We shouldn't rush it.'

'Maybe you should just let me do it all. That's what I'm here for. You bring the car and let me do the shooting?'

'I'm fine,' Hash held up a hand. 'I'm ready.'

'What's this bollocks about not rushing, then?' Sean snapped. 'We're here…it's happening. Is this you talking or is it Hakim?' Before he could answer Sean stood up and went towards the bathroom door. Turning to Hash, he stopped, tapped his temple with an index finger. 'You've got to be ready up here, mate, up here,' he tapped, 'if you're going to back me up out there,' and he pointed down the street towards the stuccoed porch. Hash listened to the sound of running water then looked back down the road. When Sean emerged, he said, 'Our friend upstairs,' he began. 'He's not as keen as he ought to be? No praying the whole time, you know…psyching himself up. He almost went to pieces at Epsom. Has he talked about Ascot…shown any interest?'

'Not really,' Hash considered. 'But he was the same before Epsom, cool and indifferent on the surface. Ascot's still some time away.'

'And the first bomber, wasn't interested in GCHQ, right?'

'Right.'

'Something's not right.' Sean picked up the mug and looked at the dregs. 'I'm going out the back for a smoke.'

At eight-thirty they flipped a coin for who would go down to breakfast. Hash won and left to collect Bousaif and head down to the basement restaurant. He found Bousaif strangely on edge and sensed he wanted to talk. He had started in Arabic but Hash told him to switch to English. He barely touched his food, sipping coffee, darting glances at the other guests. 'What's the problem?' Hash asked quietly.

'Dreaming about Paradise?'

'No sleep, no dreams.' Bousaif shrugged.

'Go back and rest. I'll call for you in an hour and we can go out, if you want.' Bousaif sucked his teeth and flicked his head irritably. 'Think of my son, then,' Hash said. 'Maybe he hasn't slept, or eaten.'

Silenced, Bousaif sat staring at his uneaten breakfast. Finally, he asked if he could take a coffee to his room. They walked back up the stairs, and as he entered his room Bousaif said, 'I am sorry for your son.' Hash heard the snib on the lock click when the door had finally closed. He went back to Sean and took over the watch.

By now the road in front had come alive and the rush hour traffic hummed and throbbed out on Warwick Road. Hash toyed with the TV remote and found a news channel, switching the volume low, hoping he could listen rather than watch and wondering if Sean would approve of anything less than total vigilance. The announcer's voice faded out on a report about increased numbers of tourists expected and the traffic diversions for for The Queen's Birthday Parade. At that moment, the phone in the room rang. His hand hovered over the receiver, his mind filled with apprehension. It might be the police closing in, maybe the plates had not done the job well enough. Maybe it was the bald conman out for revenge. The phone's insistence got the better of him and he picked up. Sean's voice was muted but urgent.

'Am I going mad?'

'Tell me,' Hash said.

'Your car alarm's going. Get the fuck down there and deal with it.'

Hash was met in the courtyard by the receptionist who had come out to see the fuss. They looked at the broken side window. She held her hands to her ears, even after Hash had switched the alarm off. 'Oh dear, sir, I'm so sorry. Has anything been taken?'

Hash moved cautiously around the Discovery. 'I don't think so,' he lied.

'Shall I call the police?' the girl asked.

'Not just yet,' Hash hedged. 'I don't think they've taken anything.' He moved to the rear, crouched and looked through window. The suitcase with the suicide vest was missing. He straightened up, looked at the receptionist with a puzzled look. 'I don't get it,' he said. 'They must have seen something but then run off without it. This car's so old there's nothing worth pinching.'

'Shall I call the police?'

'No need, thanks. Waste of their time. This is an insurance job.'

'Yes, but don't you need a crime number for a claim?'

'I'll take care of it, thanks.' With that, she returned to her office leaving Hash looking up at the windows in case anyone was observing. He took the stairs two at a time and found Sean, grim-faced.

'Fucking good job,' he hissed. 'Smart bastard...' He punched a hand into his fist then pointed at Hash's chest.

'What?' Hash said.

'Your man, the candidate? What's he look like...? Five feet five, broad shoulders, fit-looking guy wearing jeans and trainers?'

'That's right,' Hash nodded.

'Brown jacket?'

'Yes.'

'Carrying a roll-on suitcase,' Sean stabbed a finger at the bay window, pointing to the stucco porch. 'He's just run down there and they've gone.' Hash felt the strength go from his legs and he sat heavily on the bed. 'Gone?'

'Good work, the little bastard,' Sean spat. 'Picked his moment, set the distraction and nicked his vest back, all in one hit. Now they've all fucked off...God knows where.'

'It's happening,' Hash said, squeezing his eyes shut. 'It's happening, now! Not Ascot, it's now.'

'Where the fuck is it happening?' Sean said. 'We're stranded here, all dressed up and we don't know where to go. I saw Jim get pushed into a car and then your friend runs up and away they went.'

'I know where it's happening.' Hash dug in his pocket for his mobile. He hushed Sean's swearing, putting a finger to his lips, whispering, 'Hakim.'

Hakim answered on the third ring, offering a cautious 'Hello'.

'Sayyid Hakim. Are your boys still on the ground?'

'They should be. Why?'

'We've lost them. They are definitely doing the attack today, this morning and it's in the Green Park area of London. If your boys are in our area, then they're looking for two vehicles... wait...' He looked at Sean who began to whisper the details. Hash relayed, 'A blue BMW and a black Mercedes. My son is in the blue BMW with the blonde woman and one man. Three men in the follow-up black Mercedes.'

'Where are they going?'

'The target is The Queen's Birthday Parade. The Trooping the Colour.' Hash saw Sean's head go back as the penny dropped. 'It starts at Buckingham Palace in,' he looked at his watch, 'half an hour, at ten-thirty.'

With Sean at the wheel of the silver Audi, they left the car park and the Discovery behind, halting at the junction to avoid an oncoming car. Sean hissed at Hash to stay back in his seat as he saw the car was a police car waiting to turn into the hotel car park. 'There goes the Discovery,' Hash said. He looked at his watch. 'Five past ten.'

Fifteen minutes later, Hakim rang.

'They are on Cromwell Road heading for Knightsbridge. Two cars as you describe.' Hash could hear him talking to one of his drivers. Hakim updated, 'Hyde Park Corner, wait…wait, Piccadilly Underpass.' The phone went dead.

'This could be the mother of all set-ups, Sean said.'

'Got no option now. Step on it, Sean,' Hash said. 'We can catch them. Green Park was where they were practising. That's where they'll do it. When The Queen's leaving the Palace or when she comes back down the same route.'

Hakim's call came through three minutes later. 'They've stopped in Mayfair. All getting out, two groups, one boy with the woman, and one man crossing the road. Green Park Tube station…' His voice carried on a staccato interrogation of his driver. 'Second group, three men also crossing at the same place.'

'Can any of your men follow on foot?' Hash pleaded. 'We are two minutes behind.'

'Insh'Allah,' Hakim said, continuing a rapid series of orders. Hash waited for him to finish. 'We're parking up now and we'll be at Green Park tube in two minutes?'

CHAPTER 29

Dumping the Audi in Half Moon Street, Hash and Sean crossed Piccadilly at a trot, dodging traffic as they went. Sean dropped back to let Hash take the lead as they approached the tube station. The crowd on the pavement was a mix of people. Some waiting for a tour bus, others entering and leaving the station. As Hash wondered how he was going to recognise his contact, he felt a hand on his elbow and spun round to see Hakim.

'Follow me.'

He guided Hash until they were halfway between the tube station and The Mall. The huge trees in full leaf and the meadow-like atmosphere seemed incongruous to Hash. Hakim suddenly stopped without a word and pointed towards The Mall. A distant crowd fringed the big avenue. Knots of sightseers drifted towards Buckingham Palace. Drumbeats, insistent and rhythmic, carried across, drawing people towards them. Hash watched, his eyes scouring for the telltale signs Jim and, of the group. A couple of Japanese tourists, map spread and held outstretched, paused beside them, orientating themselves for a few seconds. Hakim kept pointing. 'There…look!' until Hash dipped his head to look along the man's arm, over his pointing finger. He saw a group that was static, not drawn along by the lure of the music. A slim, blonde woman in jeans and black leather bomber jacket stood close to Jim who was unslinging a bulky daysack. There were two men beside them, both looking around, hands clamping phones to their ears.

Hash tore his eyes off them and turned, urgently beckoning Sean in. 'Got them, think there's one bloke missing.' Sean advanced as bidden and nodded to Hakim. The two looked at each other without curiosity or animosity, but neither spoke nor wanted an introduction. Hakim's eyes took in the bulkiness of Sean's parka then flickered over Hash's jacket. Hash was sweating in his Barbour and the pistol seemed to bulge in his pockets.

'Is that them?' Sean squinted, following Hash's gaze. Hash pulled out his phone and dialled. 'Watch,' he said. For a few seconds, the drumbeats took over as the wind blew their thudding cadence across the park. Hash's phone began its call over the speaker. 'Watch her, now!'

The blonde woman in the distance felt her phone vibrate or heard it, and her hand shot to the back of her jeans. She jerked the phone out of her pocket with her left hand and examined it. Her right hand went straight to Jim's shoulder and Hash killed the call. They saw her whirl round, first left then right, glaring, searching, instinct telling her she was being watched.

'Christ,' Sean said, 'That's her.' She said something to the two men, whose agitation increased immediately, then she pushed Jim to his knees.

'And that's him,' Hash said. 'About a hundred yards to their left, brown jacket, all on his own, very bulky.'

'Remember your promise,' Hakim interrupted, 'remember what I asked from you.'

'About bringing Jim to the mosque,' Hash said.

'About guns,' Hakim answered. 'I meant what I said. I am handing over to you now.' Sean froze, caught between the urgency of getting at the group but stalled by the intensity of Hakim's words.

Hash said, 'I have to do this my way. Let your conscience as a father direct you. Whatever happens, there will be a package, addressed to you, waiting at the mosque in Cheltenham. It comes with my deepest gratitude.'

'May Allah go with you, my friend,' Hakim said.

Hash could see Bousaif clearly, isolated and hanging back. He felt a pang of pity for this young man, dressed for his death, with the plunger threaded down his right sleeve. He would be sweating with heat and fear, just like at Epsom.

'Let's do it,' Sean urged. 'I'll take the guy with the vest. You go for Jim.'

A trumpet fanfare signalled movement from the area of the Palace and the sound of hooves and drums mixed with a ripple of cheering applause from the crowds. Hash guessed the first of the carriages carrying royalty was passing through the huge metal gates and turning into The Mall.

'The quadcopter's running but not hovering.'

'Do you see any police around?'

'Only on the edge of the crowd. There's no sign of anyone back in the trees.'

Hash detected Bousaif's change of direction. 'He's walking to the left, trying to get some lead on the first carriages.'

'For fuck's sake,' Sean groaned. 'Now or never.'

'Can you do it without shooting?'

'I'll batter him to death with this.' He slapped the bulge under his shoulder. 'Anything...Just say the word.' Hash's mouth had gone dry. He struggled to breathe out the words, 'Good luck.'

He saw Sean break into a trot and then he himself found the strength to run. Caution abandoned, he sped towards Jim and Eva. All he had to do was call Jim, yell at him to lie down. He cut the distance to one hundred and fifty yards. Eva had her back to him, her phone to her ear. She watched Bousaif's progress and her free hand held Jim's shoulder. The lad was back on his feet, hands on the controls, eyes following the quadcopter. It rose and hovered above the pair. Hash knew she could be triggering the vest from her phone in case Bousaif lost his nerve.

Cheering had started in the crowd nearest the Palace gates, swelling in volume as the sightseers realised The Queen's coach was on its way out of the entrance. A rising rattle of drumbeats, jingling harnesses and the clopping of hooves filled the trees. Hash noticed workmen from the Parks Service, spilling from one of their vans, rear doors opening, bulky men, paying little attention to the spectacle...one of them had brought his pet Alsatian. Then the whistling revs of the quadcopter drew his attention away and upwards. The machine screamed as it gained height, floating slowly in the direction of The Mall. It had already reached treetop level and was going to soar above the tree canopy, carrying its camera to a hover above the royal procession. Hash stopped and drew his pistol, trying to steady himself for the moment. To his left, he saw Sean crashing into Bousaif, kicking, raining punches onto his head and face. Few in the crowd were looking backwards, all eyes were forward on the procession. Eva's phone hand dropped in shock as she saw Bousaif go down. Looking around for her backup, she saw Hash, yards away, stalking forward, his pistol held in front of him.

'Leave him or I'll shoot you dead!' he shouted. 'Jim...run away...run!

Eva's face showed recognition but no surprise and she hauled Jim round in front of her for protection. Her hand went for her pocket and came out with a black object. Hash saw a small pistol. Jim's face was white, his mouth open in shock.

He felt a kicking blow from behind and he staggered forward, falling. All breath left him as he bounced off the baked earth. Someone was on his back scrabbling for his hands, the missing minder. He fought the man, kicking and trying to work his pistol from under his body. He glimpsed Eva still holding Jim tightly to her, retreating, her pistol pointing at Jim's head. In his breath-starved fog Hash saw her forearm rising in protection as a blur of brown hit her. Then he felt crushing, blinding pain surge through his whole body.

CHAPTER 30

Sitting at the end of his bed in an unfamiliar room was a boy with long hair. The pursed lip and sardonic grin started cogs of recognition clunking painfully in his mind. Hash closed his eyes for relief but his memory now started to work on its own. When he reopened them, the apparition was still perched, like a bird of prey waiting to strike.

'Jim,' he said.

'Mrs Hamilton said she had just one quick job…the ones that normally take five hours. I only got out of it because grandfather asked her to leave us…'

'Grandfather?' Hash croaked.

'Grandfather,' the boy repeated. Hash tried to sit up but someone restrained him and he felt a plastic straw touch his lips. He sucked sweet fruit juice. 'You mean Grandad and Granny?' he questioned, reaching out to the boy who gently took his hand.

'Dad…' Jim said gently, 'You need to keep up. I told you all this already. Not Bella and the Old Boy. Grandad. The other grandfather...the one from...somewhere, Jordan, I think. Anyway, before he went back there he took me home to get me new clothes. He told me to give you this.'

Hash sat up, helped by a young woman who he decided must be a nurse. 'Where am I?' he asked her.

'Somewhere nice and safe. You're getting better every day,' the girl replied.

Jim smiled. 'Well done, Dad. He left you a present. Not much of one, as he stole it from our kitchen.' Faces swam into focus, staring from an old black and white family snap.

'He's written all the names on the back,' Jim said. Hash looked at the back and saw neat handwriting in Arabic listing names he already knew, his mother, father, sisters. His nephew's name was written, crossed out and the name "Bousaif" was there beside it, in inverted commas.

'Grandfather...' Hash croaked, raising his hand, feeling weakness at the effort. 'Tell your grandfather...'

'Which one?' The boy's face came down to his. 'The new one?' Hash crooked a finger. 'Tell your grandfather,' he whispered, finger still crooking until Jim leaned in to hear him better. 'Tell him...' He paused to draw moisture from his throat and the nurse held the straw to his lips.

'You'll have to speak up, Dad. No one can hear you.'

Hash dipped his head repeatedly, forcing Jim to bend until his ear was by Hash's lips. 'Tell your grandfather...it's urgent,' he whispered. 'I rigged the letter box...green tape...racecourse.'

'Dad, what letter box? What are you on about?' Hash shook his head vigorously then gasped at the pain, his head lolling back on the pillow. The nurse stepped forward. 'He's done enough. He needs to rest now.'

TRIPOLI

The older man looked at a sheaf of air photographs, as one by one the aide slid them in front of his boss. 'It's probably on Google Earth, too,' he said.

'Thanks for that but I've seen the live footage which our new friends were happy to share with us.' The aide nodded. 'How many are you hearing?' the old man asked.

'The last count, according to the Manager, was one hundred and fifty dead and quite a few wounded. '

'What a wonderful result,' the old man said. 'A job lot. And that ghastly Director, hopefully also blown to pieces with all of his horrific protégés.'

'Impossible for him to have survived, sir,' the aide said. 'Again, the Manager timed it to perfection. They were all assembled for some address when the strike took place.'

'My son, how is he coming on…and my grandson, the little Lord?'

'Still recovering. Our liaison officer says it's going to work along the lines of house arrest with privileges. Sort of a weekly check-in…like being released on bail with strict reporting conditions. There's a memorandum of understanding which freezes legal action indefinitely until all parties take the circumstances into consideration…'

'Stop, enough! The flight to UK…when is it?

'Take off in two hours. Arrive Northolt midday local time.'

'Absolutely blinding, old boy,' the old man mimicked in English, continuing, 'I need you to find my old tailor in Savile Row.' He tapped his brow, 'Welsh & Jefferies. Find out if they're still in business and book me in for a fitting. Then find out if anyone's playing at Lord's or the Oval.'

'…Who's playing football at Lord's or Oval,' the aide prompted himself, scribbling on his notepad.

ALDERGROVE AIRPORT. NORTHERN IRELAND.

On his way out of Arrivals at Aldergrove and because he was in no hurry, Sean's attention was easily hijacked by a news monitor and a strapline showing Royal Ascot. The Queen in a pastel outfit, binoculars raised, eyes twinkling with excitement, watched as one of her four-legged hopefuls powered across the Ascot turf. The camera panned to the horses strung out with the leader clear of the other runners, pushing hard for the line. A tap on the shoulder and a whispered 'Excuse me, sir' brought him spinning round to face two policemen. 'Would you mind coming with us?' The words came as a command. He looked back at the screen to see a jubilant jockey standing up in the stirrups, waving to an ecstatic crowd. 'Did you have money on that one?' one of the policemen asked. Sean said nothing, just holding his fists, one over the other, in public submission, and the trio moved off.

Minutes later, inside the warren of corridors, a door opened and a stout, middle-aged man in a suit intercepted them, waving the two uniformed men away with a cautionary 'Leave us, lads. We'll need a wee minute or two.'

Except for the basic furniture of a desk and two chairs, the office was bare and the man in the suit pointed to one of the chairs. Sean sat. The suit stayed standing, looking down at Sean, then held up two fingers. 'Two, isn't it?' he said. Without waiting for Sean's response, he stepped back and tugged the door open, yelling into thin air. 'Dying of thirst! Bring us two mugs of decent tea with two sugars!' Winking at Sean, smug that he had called it correctly, he peeled off his jacket and draped it over the spare chair.

'We expected you earlier. What happened...you get lost?' The suit loosened his tie and began rolling up his sleeves.

'Mind if I smoke?' Sean said.

'Just you set yourself on fire, Sean, old mate.' The suit finished rolling up his sleeves then went to the door again, opened it and yelled, 'Ashtray!' Somewhere, a female voice responded and with a cheery smile the suit pulled over his chair and sat. Sean lit his cigarette and inhaled, his eyes rolling with pleasure.

'Good to be back...is it?' the suit asked. 'Miss the rain, did you?' The door opened and a young lady brought in a tray, offloading two steaming mugs, the ashtray and a plate of biscuits. The suit pushed the ashtray over then lifted a mug and placed it in front of his guest. Sean blew on the surface before savouring the brew. 'Essence,' he judged. 'So much better at home.'

'It's the water,' the suit said easing back, contemplating Sean. 'You alright, Sean? I've seen you looking better.'

'You'd be looking a bit rough if you'd had a police baton up your arse for the last few days.'

'Bollocks…we told them to take care of you. Stop moaning.' He raised his own mug to Sean and held it in salute. 'You did great. Everyone's chuffed with the way you handled it.' He jutted his chin out of the window to green hills in the distance. 'Those wankers up at Castlereagh almost shit themselves at how close it got. We had more plain-clothes people than tourists, by the way. That Japanese couple,' he flapped his hand, 'don't ask how we got them. She Tasered your mate then Kato took him out.' Sean raised a weak smile, reaching for one of the biscuits.

'You hungry? Want something brought in from the restaurant?'

Sean waved his cigarette. 'Tea and a smoke'll do just right.'

'You did a number on the lad with that vest on him.'

'He fought like hell. Must be losing my touch.'

'We've got him locked up. Tough bastard. Not talking so far.'

'One of the police dogs caught the psycho woman. They were hiding up in that old Parks van, waiting for you. Should have seen the old dog take her out. They found all sorts on her… drugs, a pistol, a stack of cash. She's Bosnian, from Sarajevo, only survivor when she was a kid, whole family slaughtered by Serb killers. She was gang-raped by them. Found her way into ISIS…fully qualified psycho. He shuddered at the thought, adding, 'Your mate Darky is a poor judge of women…wee Jim wouldn't have stood a chance.' He smiled at Sean. 'You know there's a pardon in this for you,' the suit said, 'full and final, slate wiped, all-singing all-dancing, tea with The Queen sort of pardon.' He waited for Sean's response. 'Are you listening,

Sean? You're a free man.'

Sean said, 'Free from what?'

'You're free to retire, slip away, get a new start. We'll fix you a pension, enough to…you know…' The suit held his arms apart. 'Keep you in silk stockings and suspenders…in the style you've always wanted. Or' – he balanced one uplifted palm beside the other – 'if you're bored, we'll get you a job. We can fix anything you want. You can be a barman in Majorca next week…just say the word.'

'Thanks, but…' Sean started to say something but fell silent.

'Tell me then?' the suit said. 'We'll get you a medal, the press'll love it. How about' – he raised fingers in inverted commas – 'IRA hero saves Queen from ISIS fanatics, collects top gong…Liam Neeson considering the part?'

Sean looked up from his cup, put it down, then held his fingers up as the suit had just done. 'Or how about…IRA supergrass gets in the way of ISIS, accidentally saves the British Queen, given Brit gong as a death sentence…gets gunned down at Aldergrove…Neeson too frightened, turns role down?' He managed a gravelly chuckle as he picked up the mug, nodding at the suit opposite. 'Fucking smack on, you got that right enough.' He took a sip.

Looking dejected, the suit folded his hands and rested them on the table. 'OK, then…so maybe Daniel Day-Lewis will take the part.'

'I'm fucking dying,' Sean said, tapping his watch. 'Matter of time. That's not my problem…I had that coming.'

'I'm sorry about that, we're all dying, my turn next.'

'It's my mind,' Sean said. He put both hands to his head, thumbs kneading his temples. 'It's playing hell with me. I keep seeing that wee lad's face.' He stubbed his cigarette out and immediately lit another.

'Look,' the suit said, 'you did the crimes and you did your time. You of all people paid…you paid your debt a hundred times over. Not many can say they've saved The Queen. And, my friend, you're not the only one wrecked by the Troubles. Thirty years of waste and people's lives ruined…for what?'

Sean's head was down, his shoulders heaving, tears hitting the table. 'I think about it every fucking day and night,' he gasped, choking back sobs. The suit remained silent, watching. 'The kid,' Sean whispered, catching his breath. 'That poor kid.'

'Darky's kid?' the suit said softly. 'You saved his backside. He's back with his dad where he belongs. You…Sean Barr, his uncle, you saved him, got him back to his dad in one piece…cue standing ovation…beers all round…Liam Neeson reconsiders the part.'

'No…the kid,' Sean whispered urgently, glancing up. 'My neighbour's kid, the tout's wee lad.' Sean's breath came in gasps and he started coughing. The suit reached behind into his jacket pocket. Sean got his coughing under control and wiped his eyes with the heel of his hand, then convulsed in sobs again. 'He knew me, thought I'd come to save him. Then…his eyes when he realised what I was going to do. Those eyes begging me not to do it…but I took that innocent kid's little life.' The suit reached over and held his shoulder as the crying took over again. He slipped a hip flask in front of Sean and flipped off the cap. 'Take a shot of this. Poteen.' He watched Sean take a pull from the flask then took one himself.

'It's the latest treatment for PTSD in Ulster.' Sean stayed silent for a bit then managed a weak smile.

The suit leaned in. 'We were in a war,' he said. 'You did what you thought was your duty: innocent people get hurt on all sides. That boy was caught in the crossfire...he was going to die...you put him out of his misery.' Sean sobbed harder than before. 'Darky couldn't pull the trigger...you told me that... and the wee lad would have been in pain. You've paid for it, Sean. Over the years you saved hundreds of lives...at the end of the day, when the scores are counted up, you're a hero.'

'At the end of the day,' Sean sniffed, recovering a little and looking up at the man opposite, 'I'm just another fucking tout, is all.' He reached for the flask. 'I've lived in Hell here since that day, and I'll go down to Hell when my time comes. The only thing I've dreamed of ever since...,'

'...Is just to see that kid alive and smiling.'

THE GOOD MUSLIM